Dear Oliver,

GEORGE BAILEY
GETS SAVED
IN THE END
KEN O'NEILL

My best,

XO

GEORGE BAILEY GETS SAVED IN THE END

A NOVEL

KEN O'NEILL

Cover and Interior Design by
Inkspiral Design

Author photo:
Joseph Bleu

Editor:
Jerry L. Wheeler

Library of Congress
Control Number: 2016914193
CreateSpace Independent
Publishing Platform, North
Charleston, SC

In memory of my grandmother:
ANNE CREHAN O'NEILL

ONE

ALL THE USUAL INVITATIONS HAD been extended. Yet oddly, not a single friend—*The Strays*, they always called them—joined the Baileys for dinner this year. The lack of guests in no way altered the quantity of food the family prepared. It mattered not whether thirty people attended, or just the eight of them. As far as George's mother, Claire, and his wife, Tara, were concerned, you could not call the day Thanksgiving unless the turkey weighed more than twenty-five pounds. Theirs weighed in at a record-breaking twenty-nine point four. Add the stuffing, all the pan drippings, and the cast iron Le Creuset roasting pan to that number, and George was hoisting a weight just shy of forty pounds when his back went out.

Considering George's relative level of fitness, which was extremely high by American standards, though only average when compared to other Manhattanites, he did not believe it was the weight per se that precipitated his injury. Rather he suspected his troubles were brought on because he had been forced to crouch down when removing the turkey because his wife, for reasons still unknown to him, insisted that the bird go in the lower oven. Not that George blamed her for his mishap. Just at the moment George was taking the pan out of the oven, he remembered being told something about bending with his knees. But by then it was too late. Something deep within his core seized up. As his knees buckled, he lurched forward to the sound of Tara shouting, "Don't you dare drop that bird, George!"

He didn't.

George spent most of the day alternating between ice packs and a heating pad, because his wife said cold but his mother said hot, and he figured it was easier just to keep them both happy.

ᄋᢣ

GEORGE BOLTED UP IN BED, wincing in response to both the nightmare he'd just had and his spasming back. He was frightened and in agony, which somehow seemed an appropriate way to begin Black Friday. Thankfully, the dream's plot, having something to do with both the turkey and his father slipping from his arms and crashing to the floor, was already vanishing from his memory. The stabs of pain, however, had taken up residence in his buttocks and were on a path of southern migration down his right leg. He glanced at the clock on his side table and saw that it was just after four in the morning. Except for George and all the lunatic shoppers at Walmart and Target willing to risk being trampled to death if it meant saving an extra twenty percent on a Cuisinart, the world was asleep.

Tara slumbered beside him. Her breath whispered to him deep and slow. George seriously considered waking her up so he wouldn't be the only one of them miserable. Then he remembered how little she had slept in the last three days preparing their Thanksgiving feast and thought better of rousing her. He did let out a great, loud yelp every time he felt any pain, but apparently he did not yelp loud enough to get her to wake up and help him.

Unlike most of the people Mr. and Mrs. Bailey knew who had wholeheartedly embraced the slogan "Better Living Through Chemistry," George and Tara avoided pharmaceuticals. Actually, George would have quite enjoyed taking the occasional drug in severe situations like this one, but he abstained at his homeopathic wife's insistence. Tara believed if an ailment couldn't be cured by an herb or a root, you might as well give up because the condition was untreatable. George felt this was an extreme point of view, but over the years, he had learned to keep his opinions to himself.

Alas, this meant George wouldn't be taking prescription drugs, but at least he could pop some more aspirin. He'd have to walk to the bathroom, though. It was en suite. However, since he was not even confident he could stand, the ten steps to the john seemed transatlantic. Through gritted teeth, he managed to get first one and then the other foot to the floor. He was shocked when he caught sight of his pathetic form in the mirror above the dresser.

George *had* managed to stand, though he was unfortunately far from erect. The way his upper torso was veering east, he looked like a bisected half of the capital letter Y. The sheer will it took for him to stand in this contorted position caused sweat to pour from his dank and thinning hairline. It pooled atop his buttressing brows before dripping down, stinging his worn out blue eyes, temporarily rendering him both blind and maimed.

Naked and crooked, George stood in front of the medicine chest pushing aside the St. John's wort, the bromelain, the fenugreek pills, and the arnica gel in search of some actual medication. He could not find any. Tara had given him two aspirin yesterday. It seemed highly doubtful they were the last two, but he couldn't find anything remotely resembling Bayer, or even St. Joseph, in the cabinet. Then George pulled out the bottle of bromelain, struggled with the cap until he was victorious, and closely examined its contents. The pills bore a striking resemblance to the so-called aspirin Tara had palmed off on him yesterday.

He needed to get his hands on some genuine pain reliever. Only two things stood in the way of getting to the twenty-four hour drugstore: the inconvenient fact that he wasn't wearing any clothing, and his uncertainty about walking the five entire blocks from the apartment to Duane Reade.

First things first. Getting dressed.

He hobbled back out to the bedroom. George, at least as he compared himself to the other husbands in their set, was a neat and considerate spouse. He was not a slob. His wife was of a differing opinion, however. She complained about George's continuous use of the chaise longue in their room as an extension of the closet. George did so because it was practical, and also because ninety percent of their closet was stuffed with his wife's clothing. This morning, he was grateful to Tara for forcing him out of the crowded wardrobe, because he found his favorite loose pair of drawstring sweats conveniently draped at an easy-to-reach height over the back of the chaise. Since bending was virtually impossible, he hadn't considered putting on underwear but he hoped he could manage the sweats. The process of getting into the pants was grueling and ugly. However, he accomplished the chore with only minimal screaming.

Then he had a brainwave.

George limped to the front hall closet and got an overcoat, which would keep him warm and eliminate the challenging extra step of putting on a shirt. Being a decorous fellow, George felt self-conscious about not wearing any underwear, which the coat would hide as it hung to his knees—the coat that is—eliminating any concerns for his modesty. That just left his feet. He slid fairly easily into the pair of flip-flops he always kept in the closet for trips to the laundry room, or for when he carried the trash down the hall to the incinerator. Despite it being late November, the weather had been unseasonably warm for weeks, so he had no need to fret about frostbitten feet. Like an addict desperate for his fix, George grabbed his set of keys from the hall table and set off on his journey.

Walking actually helped to loosen him up slightly. He was still limping, but he no longer gasped with every tortured step. By five a.m., George approached the entrance to Duane Reade and thought, *Pants? Check. Coat? Check. Phone? Check. Flip-flops? Check. Keys? Check. Wallet? The opposite of check.*

George seriously considered begging the drugstore cashier to give him a bottle of Aleve *now* with the promise that he would return with the money *later*, but he opted not to grovel because he doubted she would take the word of a stooped and desperate man who wasn't wearing a shirt.

George had another idea. He was only six blocks from his family's wholesale business, Bailey and Sons, where he'd surely find some pain reliever. He decided to continue walking north until he made it to the showroom. Stepping from the curb to cross the street, he experienced a twinge so debilitating, he feared he might faint. His intestines rolled with a nausea borne of a crippling muscle contraction and the excesses of Thanksgiving dinner. George squinted his eyes shut involuntarily as he gasped. He instantly pressed one hand against his mouth, while he clasped the other palm to his sacrum. When the spasm finally abated, he let his arms fall to his sides and opened his eyes. For a second, he thought he saw his father and grandmother crossing to the other side of the street. The shock of the vision sent another excruciating jolt shooting right back through him.

His head dropped, and the second piece of pumpkin pie, which he absolutely could not resist last night, rose into his throat. He swallowed hard, forcing the dessert back from whence it came. When he looked again across the street, he saw a girl and boy of no more than eighteen, staggering from what was undoubtedly a long night spent consuming something a lot stronger than turkey and pie. He wondered how he could possibly have ever mistaken those two drunk kids for either his father or for Nan.

Must have been the pain.

And maybe because he was in so much physical distress, he began wishing he really did have his grandmother with him right then. She would take care of him, and he would get better. Nan had always been able to take whatever seemed terrible and make it disappear. Her treatments began with homemade Tollhouse cookies, hot and gooey from the oven. Then, when he was full, she would continue with the administration of a story. Nan began her magical tales with "once upon a time," and ended them with "happily ever after," but the wondrous words she spoke between those two familiar phrases were always original. After a story about kings and queens and virtue and goodness, came the final step. She'd bundle him into a coat and off they'd go for a grand long walk. Even living in the grimy city, Nan was a great believer in the healing powers of fresh air, and so they'd go for a stroll. That is what they always did. It always worked.

∾

WHEN GEORGE WAS TEN, HIS brother Conor underwent an emergency appendectomy. And for five glorious days while his parents cared for Conor, George stayed at his grandparents' apartment. He gorged on Nan's chocolate chip cookies, while he listened to her enchanting tales. One day, as he lay curled on the couch, his head in Nan's lap, she told him that angels spoke to her. Even as young as he was, he doubted that really happened. He assumed it was another one of her stories, or that she was recalling a lovely dream. But Nan said it was true; she believed she was actually communing with heaven. And more importantly, she believed anyone could hear them talking if they were quiet enough, and if they listened closely. Because Nan said the angels often whispered.

George's grandmother must have modeled her own behavior on the angels' because she was a soft-spoken woman. But when Nan did say something, she had no trouble being heard. Silence fell over the room whenever she opened her mouth. Nan showed no interest in being the center of attention, but that's what she always was. People were naturally drawn to her because in his grandmother's presence, everyone became a kinder person. It seemed like all the love and faith she possessed poured out of her, and you couldn't help but catch some of it.

As far as Nan was concerned, nothing came before God. But George's father always joked that, for Nan, fitness came a close second. She did her Jack LaLanne in the living room, and only a blizzard or pouring rain kept her from taking a great, long walk every day of her life.

George took many walks with his grandmother, but while most of the memories of those outings had blurred, he recalled one stroll vividly. And now, immobilized by the throbbing ache in his back, he thought of that day once again. George had stopped by his grandmother's apartment for tea and cookies, and then at Nan's suggestion had joined her for one of her afternoon constitutionals.

This might have been the last time he ever went for a walk with her, though he wasn't certain of that. It was mid-April because the daffodils had mostly finished blooming, but the tulips were just starting to put on their show. It was one of those warm-in-the-sun, cool-in-the-shade glorious spring days. He wore a pair of baggy sweats, a college-era pea coat he still hadn't parted with, and an old pair of Nikes. Nan, though, didn't believe in dressing casually. She wore a dress, a spring coat with a brooch fastened to the lapel, and a pair of sensible heels. Her hair, as always, was perfect. Done up and rinsed a shade a bit more blue than gray.

They were walking through Union Square, and a couple of tough-looking kids came marching in their direction. The kids were shouting and swearing, waving their arms around. Others in the park were giving them a wide berth. George still remembered how frightened he felt as he watched them approach. He assumed these boys were not much more than fourteen. But the way they were strutting around, acting as if they owned the whole park, they were clearly out looking for trouble. George had no doubt about that.

You live in New York your entire life, and you develop a sense about such things. So George was cautious. He linked his left arm tighter through Nan's, and with his right hand, he tapped at his thigh to confirm his wallet was shoved deep inside the pocket of his sweatpants so they couldn't snatch it. Which, on reflection, was a move about as subtle as if he'd been wearing a big sandwich board that read: *Hey muggers, the loot's buried right here.* He looked at Nan, saw her lips moving. She rustled in the pocket of her coat with her free hand. George knew from a lifetime of witnessing such behavior that she had clasped her rosaries and was muttering prayers. His grandmother was never without her rosaries. She always had a pair of beads in her pocket or purse.

The boys were still a good fifteen feet away, but their music was so loud, George could hear it screaming through their headphones. As they got a little closer, he noticed the taller of the two boys eyeing them like maybe he had something to say. George braced himself for what it was going to be, but the tall kid wasn't looking at both of them. He was looking at Nan.

As the kid gazed at Nan, George watched all the meanness drain from his face. Suddenly, he seemed less like a little man and a lot more like a little boy. George was staring straight ahead at him, not at his grandmother, so he couldn't say for sure, but he imagined she was smiling at the kid, because his grandmother had a smile for everyone. George was no longer afraid of this boy.

The boy lowered the volume on his Walkman and elbowed his friend, motioning to him to do the same. It got quiet, and the tall kid yanked the headphones off his ears, leaving them hanging around his neck. He removed his Yankees cap and tilted his head toward Nan, offering a tender smile of his own before he said, "Afternoon ma'am," just as sweet as he could be, a proper little gentleman. The other boy seemed surprised by his friend's behavior, but he smiled politely, if a bit perplexedly.

Nan nodded back. "Thank you, dear. It's a lovely day, isn't it?"

Nan and the boy exchanged pleasantries for a moment more and then, as quickly as the boys had approached, they departed. Off they went, heading towards 14th Street, their music blaring once again.

If this had been 1902 and not 2002, perhaps George wouldn't

have been surprised by their genteel behavior. Or if they were in Savannah or Charleston instead of Manhattan, the scene also might have made some sense to him. But these were loud *menacing* teenage boys. Puzzled, George asked his grandmother how she knew those kids, figuring maybe she'd seen them in church or the neighborhood. George remembered the big grin on her face, and how erect her carriage was, even at ninety-two. Her shoulders were back, her neck long, and her chin was held high, so her eyes were always nearer to heaven than to earth.

"I've never seen those boys before, George. But aren't they grand young lads?" she said, with the hint of a brogue that sixty-five years in New York had not managed to erase.

George, with spine stooped and spasming, stood in front of Duane Reade staring at his flip-flopped feet. He thought about that walk and that boy. Of course, now he realized he must have misjudged those boys when he first saw them approaching. He supposed they had always been, as his grandmother said, "grand young lads," raised to be respectful, as certainly some kids still were. But back then, he was sure they were tough, bad kids. And the only way he could explain the abrupt change in their behavior was they'd been transformed by his grandmother's unwavering grace. He thought perhaps he had witnessed a miracle.

He did not think that anymore and hadn't for a long time, because there were no miracles. Miracles were invented by a shyster looking to take advantage of a desperate man's delusions.

He forced himself to move. He mustn't just stand here all day, so he walked. As he shuffled along, George talked himself into believing his pain was lessening a little. With each step he took, he thought about Nan, who he hadn't thought about in a long time.

Nan, if any angels are out there trying to send me a message, they need to stop whispering, because I can't hear a thing.

Of course, there weren't any angels. George knew that. He wasn't completely free of superstition, though, and wondered what Nan would say if she could see what had become of him. It was probably for the best she could not, he thought as he limped along.

And he limped and limped. Some steps were almost tolerable, others left him nearly incapacitated. He finally arrived at Bailey and Sons, one of the leading distributors of all things related to the holidays except for wrapping paper, which they had never carried in the line. The smell of pine knocked him in the face the instant he opened the door.

Bailey and Sons did not sell real Christmas trees. They did, however, sell a lot of potpourri and scented candles, which created the illusion of a forest—at least as far as George, a lifelong city kid, was concerned. Working here meant every single day was like Christmas, which was a shame since George's disdain for the holiday was immeasurable.

It was the never-ending sameness of it all that made him grow to hate both the season and the business. His grandfather had founded the company, and every day, for nearly four generations, the Baileys managed to have new conversations about the same old things—ornaments, lights, and tabletop. How could one family talk about glass balls for over fifty years without going a little bit mad? It was the constant barrage of Santas and snowmen, glitter and garland, mangers and mistletoe, bells and bows, and reindeer and ribbons that had crushed poor George under the weight of their mass-produced cheer. Twelve months a year carols boomed from the showroom's sound system. He had listened to Brenda Lee sing *Rockin' Around the Christmas Tree* nearly every day of his adult life. Not surprisingly, it had beleaguered him.

He made a mistake coming here on one of the few days that Bailey and Sons was closed. George knew this. Yet here he was, standing on the threshold of this winter wonderland abyss, staring at thirty-five hundred square feet of useless junk. He made his way past rows of artificial trees, their branches heavy with lights and ornaments of endless variety, from traditional and classic to kitsch. He barely glanced at decorations made out of glass, wood, clay, fabric, resin, plastic, lacquer, and even feathers. A dusting of gold glitter coated nearly every surface like holiday soot.

In his office, hidden behind a grove of faux balsams, he unearthed a bottle of aspirin. He swallowed three dry. Then, sitting at his desk, he logged onto his computer. George needed to kill some time while he gathered the strength to face the walk back home. He hoped the aspirin would kick in and dull his pain as he rested.

Being a holiday weekend, George didn't have many work emails to deal with. As a Christmas wholesaler, the actual holiday season was his slowest period of the year. Merchants were crossing their fingers and selling what they had instead of ordering anything else at this late date. Still, even without much work to do, he knew he'd find a way to keep himself occupied. He always did.

If George were a man given to introspection, he would have understood his aimless searching was a way to avoid thinking about all the things that really mattered. But he seemed incapable of self-reflection, so he continued to mindlessly surf, click, and read without ever asking the important question: *What is it you're looking for, George?*

Whatever it was, his brain had numbed trying to find it. His pale, watery eyes had grown increasingly tired. He had stumbled down a bottomless Google Hole and been trapped in it for close to three hours, gorging on useless, trivial information.

George's fall down The Hole began for reasons still inexplicable to him, especially since it was related to *that movie*. When he was a child, he thought his parents had selected his name as a special punishment because he was a bad little boy who didn't love Christmas. In reality, they were merely following tradition, making him the third George Bailey after his father and grandfather. George was teased mercilessly about his name, especially in December, when that awful movie seemed to run nonstop. Undoubtedly the endless badgering by his classmates added to his contempt for the holidays. Always one student or another would be running in circles around him ringing bells and yanking up his shirttails in search of newly sprouted wings. In spite of all his bleak associations with the film, when he crumbled into his desk chair and stared at the Google homepage, a question got stuck in George's brain, and he could not shake it. He typed: Who played Violet in *It's a Wonderful life?*

Up popped pages of information about Oscar-winner, Gloria Grahame.

His quest quickly led to the unearthing of some rather lurid gossip about Ms. Grahame's personal life, which kept him tumbling deeper and deeper as he searched for more salacious details. For example, one of her four husbands was Nicolas Ray, the director of *Rebel Without a Cause*. After discovering that fact, George burned up another forty-five minutes of his life reading about the tragic, untimely deaths of that film's three young stars—Natalie Wood, James Dean and Sal Mineo—before realizing he had, as is so often the case when googling, lost sight of what he had originally been looking for.

Eventually he remembered he was on the hunt for information pertaining to Gloria Grahame, and he immediately returned to her IMDB and Wikipedia pages. Allegedly, Nicolas Ray divorced Gloria when he caught her in bed with his thirteen-year-old son from a previous marriage. She later married said son. Not only that, she had children with both men. It took George about fifteen minutes to grasp that Ray the Son was both the stepfather and half-brother of the kid his dad had with Gloria.

George had no idea why he kept reading this stuff. He reasoned some men had mistresses and some drank too much. He surfed the web, which, in his opinion, was a harmless vice. True, in George's case, he didn't just surf. He surfed and surfed and surfed. He remained trapped in the Google Hole for hours. There was always one more factoid, one more juicy detail to glean. He might still be leapfrogging from one Internet search to the next, were it not for a phone call from his mother informing him that his father had died.

TWO

CLAIRE WAS RELAYING THE INFORMATION about her husband's passing as if she were a reporter or the doctor-on-call. She was calm, clear, and factual. George found her detachment maddening. He assumed her flattened affect was a sign of shock; still, he would have been more comforted by screams and hysteria. Not that the dry-eyed George was behaving any differently. The Baileys were not known for emotional outbursts. They prided themselves on being stoic in the face of adversity. No matter George's propensity towards angst, he always flashed a half-full smile to the world. He sat quietly, the phone pressed to his ear, while his mother continued her impassive description of the scene. She went on and on, but George wasn't listening. He heard nothing after "it was a massive heart attack."

A heart attack? That made no sense.

Over the course of the last fifteen years, George's father had run ten New York City marathons, coming in second in his age category three years ago with a time of 3:21:03. In addition to the marathons, he'd competed in at least a half dozen triathlons. He relished the challenge, though he never had the same passion for biking and swimming he had for running. Yet, George's Iron Man father was dead at sixty-nine.

George had only been aware of his father's death for about five minutes, but already he felt guilty about the selfish thoughts he was having. For starters, he did not want to become the new president of Bailey and Sons. He didn't even want to work there. He had been meaning to give his notice for over a decade, but never found the right moment to broach the subject with his father. Now it was too late. His father wasn't even in the ground, and George was trying to figure a way out of taking over the job.

Also, he wondered about the matter of the heart attack. Not that it was all about him, but how did the addition of heart disease to the family's medical history impact his own lifespan? George managed to appear to be quite fit, his current hunchbacked state notwithstanding, without actually *being* fit. As for exercise, his normal workouts were generally limited to the twenty minutes he walked back and forth to the showroom each day. Like most New Yorkers, George belonged to a gym, but he generally only went there when he was craving a smoothie.

In every arena of life, George's father had been a healthier person than he was. He ate better, drank less, and slept more than George did. He was in every way a happier and more satisfied person, too. He loved his job, which is not something George could say, even though he did say it whenever anyone asked him. George was mortified to report, though honestly not as mortified as he was *to know*, based on one excruciatingly embarrassing conversation with his mother, which began with Claire uncharacteristically saying— "Oh, Honey. We're all adults here,"—that his father (and mother) also had a more satisfying and active sex life than he did. George the Second should have lived for at least another twenty years.

If the robust father died of a heart attack while living an exemplary life, what would be the fragile son's fate? George could see his own funeral taking place in the next seven or eight weeks. Maybe he could eke out another six months if he went to the gym this very moment, but that was not likely to happen since he couldn't even walk. And in a short time, when he was gone, what would be the headline of his obituary?

> *George Bailey III, Extraordinarily Proficient*
> *at Googling, Dead at 43:*
> *At the end he was doing what he loved most.*
> *Body found; head in laptop.*

George had been with his perfectly healthy father yesterday. He saw him in the showroom most days, but yesterday was his father's favorite day. Unlike the son, the father loved Thanksgiving. George II sat at the head of the table, where he'd sat since the passing of his own father, the stag-handled carving set poised to slice into the turkey that had left his son maimed. Like every year, he delivered a toast that ran closer to speech length until Claire finally snapped, "George, stop talking. The food is getting cold!"

The topic of the annual Thanksgiving speech rarely varied from the story of Pop's leaving Ireland and arriving in America with faith and dreams, but little else. One of Pop's first jobs was in a Lower

East Side linens shop. He worked long hours for little pay, but he noticed the store's owners, Mr. and Mrs. Schwartz, worked the same grueling schedule and earned a seemingly modest living for all their hard labors. George's grandfather loved selling, and he had a knack for it, but he quickly soured on the idea of retail as the way to make his fortune. He dreamed of a lifestyle grander than one small shop could provide.

Then came his first Christmas in America. As he decorated his little tree alone in his West 54th Street studio apartment, he had an idea. Or as George's father intoned in his retellings of the story, "An angel came to Pop and told him to open Bailey and Sons."

Setting aside for a moment the fact that George did not believe angels existed, he refused to accept "angels" found the time to visit both Nan *and* Pop. Furthermore, what kind of angel would encourage his grandfather to go into wholesale? The Peace Corps, maybe.

An actual angel might also have told his grandfather to rethink the name of his business, which he started before he'd married Nan. His grandfather, a then childless man, saw no tempting of fate with the inclusion of the word "Sons" in the business's moniker. Supposedly, he chose the name because he had a clear vision of his family's destiny. But Pop, who had left the hardship of Ireland only to land in New York during the height of the Great Depression, had a more practical reason in mind when he came up with Bailey and Sons. Changing the name of the business once he had sons would have meant buying a new awning and stationary.

As it happened, Nan and Pop bore only one son. They also had two daughters. George's Aunt Finn was the first-born. Nan and Pop's second child was the precious baby Tea, who died in infancy. She was literally swept from Nan's arms during the great Hurricane of 1938. Nan would later say, "Tea was carried home by God because she was so perfect."

The birth of George's father took place six years after Tea died. Even though Nan would have no more children, Pop never once thought of changing the company name. Nor did he consider bringing his surviving daughter into the business. In fact, Pop banished Finn from the family when she was seventeen, for reasons that he never discussed. She did not reappear in the life of the Bailey family until the day she stood holding Nan's arm at Pop's wake.

Even if Pop hadn't banished Finn, she never would have been allowed to work in the business. As far as Pop was concerned, it was the man's place to go out and work. Apparently, spending one's days surrounded by garland, glitter and snow globes was too rough-and-tumble an environment for a lady.

"I still believe it was a sign, Georgie," Pop told his son the day he joined him in the business. "Our name will be true soon enough when you have sons."

And so it was.

George could not recall any of his family members ever asking him or Conor when they were kids what they wanted to be when they grew up. There was no need to ask. That question had been answered for both the brothers thirty years before they were born.

"Honey?" Claire asked concernedly. Silence followed. George remembered he was in mid-conversation with his mother. He wasn't certain, but he assumed he had missed a lot of what she had been telling him on the phone.

Instead of being honest with her and saying, "Sorry, Mom. I'm a little in shock. I got distracted thinking about Daddy. What did you say?," he went with the line he had used throughout his teenage years when she was talking and he wasn't listening. "Okay, Mom. Sure."

"Really? Thank you," his mother sighed with relief. "You will? You really don't mind? I don't know what I would do without you, honey." Her voice cracked, but she quickly regained her composure.

Shit, George thought. *What did I just agree to do?*

"Call me back. If I'm not here, it's because I'm out looking for a dress. I don't look good in black. You get to a certain age, black makes you look drawn. It's a mistake. But what am I going to do, wear yellow?" Claire hung up.

George should have called her right back before she ventured to Saks on the kick-off of the Christmas shopping season. He should have asked her to repeat the whole thing again, preferably while he had a pen in his hand. But he did not.

Instead, he typed the following into his Google search engine:

What do you do when your mother has asked you to do something pertaining to the recent death of your father, but you weren't listening to her, you were in shock, naturally—because how is it possible that your unbelievably healthy father is even dead in the first place—so you have no idea what you're supposed to be doing? Help!

Perhaps not surprisingly, while George did find a lot of interesting information about hospice care and euthanasia, he did not find a useful answer for his specific problem.

Then, George did the first rational thing he'd done all day. He shut down his computer. He stood, and to his surprise, his back didn't feel so bad anymore. He thought perhaps the shock of learning his father was dead caused an adrenaline rush, like when mothers snap into Herculean action to lift trucks off the children they'd neglected until they heard the cries from underneath the vehicle. George had vanquished his pain because he had no time for it. He had things to do! True, he did not know what these things were, but nevertheless they needed to be done.

First, he needed to tell Tara. He couldn't bring himself to do it over the phone. Unlike his father and brother, George was not a runner. Or even a jogger. But he dashed home with no twinges or tingles or spasms impairing his speed. Tara would know what to do. She always did. George was the anxious half of the couple, and she was the steady one. She would know how to tell the kids, not that May and Brian were children anymore.

George called out her name as he opened the door to their apartment, but she did not respond. He had been up for hours, but he realized it was only eight-thirty in the morning. He wondered if she was still sleeping. But as he walked into the austerely decorated living room, one sofa dwarfed by empty space around it, he heard the muffled sound of her hairdryer coming from the bedroom.

He found her standing with her back to the door. She was facing the window, even though the blinds were drawn. Strange, George thought. She often dried her hair in the bedroom, not willing to wait for the steam to clear from the bathroom after her long, hot shower. But she generally stood in front of the mirror above the dresser to be sure she was achieving perfect results. Being a balding man, George never fully comprehended Tara's daily twenty-minute blow-drying and comb out ritual.

Tara had a towel wrapped around her hips but was otherwise naked. The hair dryer continued its drone, and would for quite some time. George knew his wife had no idea he was in the room with her, and he couldn't possibly avoid startling her when she became aware of his presence. Tara had the most overactive startle response of anyone he'd ever met. So it was merely a question of *when* she was going to receive the start, not *if*. Since he was in no rush to break his horrible news, he decided to stand quietly, watching and waiting for her to finish drying her hair, no matter how long it took.

While he postponed the inevitability of Tara's surprised gasps, he studied her back, marveling at the raised outline of her shoulder blades, strong and graceful. And her spine, the vertebrae just barely visible, rippling beneath her taut skin. Looking at his wife from this vantage point, the years had scarcely changed her. Her back was almost exactly as it had been that first day he saw it emerging from the pool on Clarkson Street when they were both teenagers. Aside from an additional mole or two, it was the same back he'd spent so many hours kissing, his lips trailing a path from her waist to the nape of her neck.

When they married at age nineteen, their friends thought they were crazy, especially when George told them Tara wasn't pregnant. Many of their friends drifted away, not because they disapproved of the marriage—though most did disapprove—but because the lives of the young newlyweds almost immediately became so vastly different from their own single and newly independent lives. The Baileys were settled, while their friends were all still two or three major relationships away from finding the person they would marry. Several never did find that special person to marry. A few never wanted to.

George felt sorry for the men his age pushing strollers down the street, looking haggard and stressed. At forty-three he would never want to be a new father. But how he remembered himself at twenty-five, chasing May and Brian around the park, feeling lucky his kids provided such an awesome excuse to be able to play all day long. Luckily, just about the time George began tiring of Hide and Seek, May and Brian began to tire of having their dad hanging around every minute.

Now May was twenty-three and Brian had turned twenty-one. George loved them. And every word he could think of to describe this love felt shallow and small, and did absolutely no justice to his true emotions. He could not understand how, even with him as their father, they turned out fearless, independent, and brave. He loved being with them. But he was also relieved they were adults and on their own. He was glad he did not have to run and chase and teach them anymore.

Tara and I could travel now. Go on a real adventure.

They could do so many things. He was thinking they should start planning something, though he wasn't sure what, when the hairdryer went silent.

"Honey," he said, hoping she wouldn't jump but knowing that she would.

Jolted, she turned around instantly. "God, George! You scared the…" She stopped and yanked her towel up, clutching it in front of her breasts like George was a Peeping Tom she'd discovered leering through the window. When he looked at her face, he saw she was sobbing.

George guessed his mother must have called Tara. He thought Claire was leaving that job to him, but he wasn't sure of anything now. George sat on the foot of the bed. He wasn't crying—hadn't yet—but he felt a weight of sadness pressing down on him. The pressure on his chest seemed so intense, he was afraid he might stop breathing. For some reason, Tara expressing this show of emotion about his father made the tragic news real for him in a way his mother's quiet reporting of the events had not.

Tara and his dad had a special bond. They were pals from the first minute they met. Perhaps that is why George's parents didn't object to two teenagers announcing their marriage plans. Instead of raising any concerns, they raised glasses. They popped the cork on a bottle of champagne, which Tara and George were not legally old enough to consume, and celebrated with the newly engaged couple.

George glanced over at Tara. He must have looked terrible, because she immediately sat down next to him, and placed a hand on top of his. "George, I'm sorry. But—"

George interrupted her. "I know you are, doll. I just don't understand how this happened."

She was taken aback. "I didn't think," her voice faltered, "that you knew."

"Yeah," was all he managed. He nodded his head and sat quietly. Tara remained beside him, staring silently ahead. Later, when George would replay this scene, he would realize that they sat like this in silence for a very long time.

Finally he spoke. "Should we call the kids?" She stared at him. Tara looked sadder than he had ever seen her. Her expression of sorrow, which was a reflection of his own, moved him and made him feel a tenderness toward her that he had not felt in a long while.

"No, George. They don't need to know this minute. And besides, we can't tell them over the phone. We need to talk to them in person," she said quietly.

"Right. Of course."

She continued to stare at him, and her expression changed. She looked hurt and angry.

"I don't have any idea what I'm supposed to be doing," he confessed.

At that she exploded with rage. "Jesus, George! How about scream? Get angry for once. Do something!"

George understood grief caused people to behave in weird ways, but he didn't appreciate her outburst. This was not the Tara he knew. Despite how close they were, it was *his* father who died, not hers. He was confused and hurt, and he didn't know what to say to her.

"George! Aren't you even going to ask me why I'm leaving you?"

"You're leaving me?" he asked blankly. He honestly did not understand what she meant.

"What do you think we've been talking about? You know this has been a long time coming."

Then, of course, George did understand. In spite of what Tara claimed, he had no idea it had been a long time coming. Of course he knew they'd hit a rough patch in their marriage. That's how it goes, isn't it? In twenty-four years of marriage, not every day is going to be a good one.

She stood up, walked over to the dresser and started pulling on clothes. "George, I'm suffocating here. I have to go. Please give me a little time, and then we can talk." She headed into the closet and walked out with the biggest suitcase they owned. Furiously, she began tossing clothes into the bag. Spring clothes, too, even though it was November.

"Wait," he shouted. Tara turned and stared at him. For a second, he thought she was going to come running into his arms, but she didn't. She smiled wistfully for a moment and then returned to her packing.

"Please," he begged. She shook her head, but before Tara could say anything George cut her off. "Listen. My father died last night. So, you just really need to stay with me until after the funeral. Okay?"

His chin hit his chest. Soon he felt her wrapping her arms around him. They both wept. George was weeping for his father, for his failed marriage, and because he was terrified about what tomorrow would bring, and how he would ever be able to face the world alone. He imagined Tara was crying for all these reasons, too.

THREE

AFTER HE AND TARA FINALLY stopped sobbing, George tried to stand up. Unfortunately, his back stubbornly remained seated. He gasped like he had been stabbed. So much for that brief, pain-sedating adrenaline rush George experienced earlier when he ran home from the showroom.

"Are you all right?" Tara asked.

Seriously? Is she kidding me?

"I'm fine," George said, his voice remarkably devoid of sarcasm. They continued speaking to each other as if they were foreign dignitaries struggling to negotiate detente. She would call the kids. He would figure out what he was supposed to do for his mother. Then he would contact the funeral home. She would plan for the post-funeral reception. And so on. All very civilized. The way

Parisians must break up, George imagined. Tara brought him more aspirin. George knew it was really bromelain. He took it anyway.

With Tara's help, he changed into suitable clothes. She crouched on the floor before him, putting shoes on his feet because he was incapable of managing the task. George, acknowledging how debilitating his injury was, decided he'd better call Todd if he had a chance of making it through the next few days without using a wheelchair or walker. Todd was George's best friend. He never called Todd that, because "best friend" seemed so thirteen-year-old-girl. Nevertheless that's what Todd was. He was also George's doctor. And while George wanted to get right on the phone to tell his friend about his dad, he wanted his physician to hook him up with some Vicodin even more.

At the front door, Tara finished buttoning George's coat. Being eight inches taller than Tara, he always needed to bend down when kissing his wife. He couldn't do that with his back the way it was, which was probably for the best, as it spared him the awkwardness of having his kiss rebuffed if he attempted one. Instead of a kiss he nodded, since, for the moment, he still had full range of motion in his neck.

"I'll keep you posted," he said. "I'm going to call Todd."

"Why?"

George gazed at her quizzically. She should have figured it out. "Because the bromelain isn't cutting it," he barked.

∾

THE ELEVATORS IN THEIR BUILDING were being replaced, so the tenants had been reduced to one working lift for the last several weeks. This meant waiting a minimum of five minutes for the blasted thing to arrive, and then stopping on at least a half dozen floors before reaching the lobby. Something was always out of service in the building. One day no hot water; the next, no heat. Last month, ten out of fourteen washing machines skipped their spin cycles. Though Tara and George complained about the state of the building constantly to each other, they were aware enough of how privileged they were to refrain from sharing their "woes" with others.

They lived on lower Fifth Avenue in the heart of Greenwich Village, one of Manhattan's most prime neighborhoods. The building they called home was elegant and grand on its most broken down day. The Baileys' apartment was an extremely spacious three-bedroom, steps from Washington Square Park. Not only did they live in a great location, they lived there for free.

The place had been a wedding present from George's parents. If they had wanted to, they could have sold the apartment and moved someplace more affordable than New York, and lived the rest of their lives quite comfortably off the proceeds from the sale. At least that's what they always said. They both knew they'd never leave New York. It was home. Though they might not be leaving the city, at least one of them would be leaving the spectacular apartment.

George's parents purchased the place in 1990 when there had been a real estate crash and dramatic drop in prices in Manhattan. Five years later, after the market had recovered, they bought his brother Conor a one-bedroom in the same building for nearly as much money as they'd paid for George and Tara's three-bedroom. Even after the 2007 crash and sluggish recovery, both apartments had proved to be excellent investments.

By the time the elevator finally arrived, George had decided he was going to let Tara keep the place. Aside from his clothing and a few books, it was all hers anyway—the white furniture he was afraid to soil, the minimalist look, the complete lack of clutter, even the lack of cable, because Tara didn't want a television numbing their brains.

After a brief flirtation with a career on the stage, Tara had become an interior decorator. She had a loyal following of clients who, like her, favored rooms that featured a few pieces of clean-lined furniture surrounded by a tremendous amount of empty space. She had once been hired to redecorate a five thousand square foot loft in Tribeca. After she'd stripped everything out, all that remained were a king-sized bed, a long pine table, two impossibly hard benches, and one white mural with a single beige dot in the center. Tara was a hoarder's worst nightmare.

Their apartment, displayed prominently on her website as one of her greatest achievements, was only slightly less sparsely furnished than the Tribeca loft. With George's departure, the place was about to become even less cluttered. Since he had never lived alone before, he couldn't imagine doing so. Nonetheless, he would go.

He would not point out that his parents paid for their home, while hers paid for their blender. (A blender that she would not, for esthetic reasons, allow to be kept on the counter. It was concealed in a cabinet.) "You can keep the apartment," he would announce upon departing, leaving the word *bitch* unspoken. Then, as he nobly vacated his home with nothing but one little bag containing his meager possessions, he would take some perverse, passive-aggressive delight in being magnanimous while Tara was trampling on his grieving heart.

In the lobby, Vito the doorman greeted him. Thick and graying, with a constant, if unconvincing, smile, Vito seemed to have remained sixty years old for the entire time George had known him.

In truth, Vito had been a very old-looking forty when George moved in and was now a youngish-looking sixty-three. George was about to tell him about his father when Conor darted in the front door, panting. His workout clothes were drenched with sweat. Noticing George, Conor made the traffic cop hand and stood in front of him gasping as he caught his breath.

With his lithe body and creaseless brow, Conor was a very boyish thirty-nine. Unlike his brother, Conor also had the good fortune of inheriting the amazing hair gene. Conor had taken after their father in every way, while George much more favored Claire's family. George had always been struck by the resemblance between his brother and father—envious, if he were to be honest with himself. The pair was almost more beautiful than handsome. His mother had once described them as arresting.

Conor was disarming even spent from his run. He turned his face toward George. When he did so, George became a little boy again. For a second he did not see his brother standing before him, rather he saw his very young, very beautiful, father.

Daddy!

Thankfully the greeting remained unspoken, for just then George figured out his mother's urgent telephone request.

Several years ago, Conor had given up his landline. To him it seemed redundant having one, since everyone he knew called him on his cell. The only problem with his abandonment of the home phone was that he always turned his cell off when he went to bed and quite often forgot to turn it back on in the morning. This morning had been one of those days. And though she had tried several times, Claire had failed in her attempts to contact her youngest son. Claire's directive was for George to knock on Conor's door and deliver the news in person.

Conor did a couple of quick calf stretches and was on the move again. "Tell Tara thanks for yesterday. The turkey was great. Everything was great, as always." He stretched and touched his toes. "You look terrible, George. Back worse?" Since the answer to that question was obvious, Conor didn't wait for it to be delivered. "See you Monday," he said, walking briskly toward the elevator bank.

"Wait," George shouted, stopping him. "Mom called. Daddy died."

"Oh my God! I'm so sorry," said Vito, approaching them with outstretched hands.

Before the brothers could accept Vito's condolences, Conor grabbed George's arm and yanked him toward the elevators. Conor jabbed the button, but of course, with only one working, they were in for a wait. "Are you kidding me?" Conor hissed through clenched teeth.

"Of course not. How could you think I'd joke about something like that?"

"I mean, are you kidding me? That's how you tell me Daddy died? In the lobby, in front of strangers?" Vito was hardly a stranger, but George didn't see the point in mentioning that.

Conor's anger was quickly replaced by grief; he started shaking.

Every movement was a challenge for George. His physical pain, his emotional pain, and the general discomfiture he always felt in moments of intimacy stymied him. Still, he was about to try and give Conor a hug, and apologize for how blunt he had been when he experienced a flash of joy remembering a lame joke that Pop used to tell.

"George," Nan would say through giggles, "That's awful!"

While they did have a sense of humor, as a rule the Baileys had not gone in for joke telling. If Pop was going to have one joke in his repertoire, why he chose this barely funny one, George did not know. But he told it often.

"There were two brothers," Pop would begin, "named Pat and Mike. Well, Mike worked hard and very long hours and never did a thing for himself. But finally after much persuasion, he decided it was time to take a holiday. It was his first vacation in twenty years, and he was going to Miami Beach, for he could surely use a bit of color. Unfortunately, Mike was nervous about the trip because he had a darling cat named Petunia who he'd never been separated from. But Pat promised to take good care of the cat, so off Mike went to Florida.

"The second Mike checked into his hotel room he called Pat to see how he was getting on with the cat. Pat said, 'Hey, I'm very sorry but the cat died.'

"Well," said Pop, pausing for effect. "Mike screamed at his brother. 'That's how you tell me my cat died?'

"'What should I have said?' asked Pat.

"'Today, when I called, you should have said the cat's on the roof, and I can't get her down. But I'm sure she will be fine. Then the next time I called you'd say, 'The cat is still up there, I'm getting worried.' That way I would have been prepared. Then, the third time, you could have said, 'I'm so very sorry; I tried everything. The cat fell and died.'

"'Okay,' Pat said. 'Now I know. I'm sorry.'

"Mike sighed. He was about to hang up, but then said, 'So, how's Mom?'

"Pat sighed, too. 'Mom's on the roof and we can't get her down.'"

George squelched his ill-timed urge to giggle. He hugged Conor warmly, not in the quick and awkward way they typically embraced on those rare occasions they showed each other physical affection. Even though Conor smelled like he'd been on a ten-mile run in clothes that were dirty before he'd started, George held him as if he might not ever let him go. And Conor clasped George back just as tightly, pulling him into a bear hug. Then George whispered in his brother's ear, "Daddy's on the roof and I can't get him down."

Conor laughed but not before letting George know how seriously disturbed he thought he was.

"Go take a shower, sweaty man. Then will you please come to the funeral home with me?"

Conor nodded but didn't loosen his grip.

"Conor? My back. You really need to let go of me. Your embrace is killing me."

They separated. George winced from the pain, but he refrained from actually howling, lest he make his brother feel worse than he already did.

FOUR

The wake was on Monday.

As it happened, Conor and George didn't have much to do to prepare for the funeral since their father had prearranged the service several months earlier.

"We both did," Claire explained. "One day your father said, 'Claire get your purse. Let's go see Tommy Dillon's daughter and pay for the funerals.'"

"Why didn't you tell me? Was he sick?" George asked.

"He was fine, love." Claire took George's hand. The wake was still an hour away from being opened to friends and acquaintances. Jenny Dillon, the fourth generation funeral director at Dillon's, showed George and his mother into the lily-filled room, and then gave them privacy.

They were alone, though George assumed the rest of the family would be arriving soon. His mother was dressed in a simple black dress that wrapped around her and tied at the waist. Claire was right, black made her look even more drawn and tired than she actually was, which was a nearly impossible feat since she had slept a total of five hours since her husband died. She wore a strand of pearls George hadn't seen around her neck in years. She'd stopped wearing them after the Easter he'd referred to them as her Barbara Bush pearls.

George and Claire peered into the casket thoughtfully, as if the man lying in repose before them was a sculpture they were admiring at a gallery opening. All they were missing was the pretentious chatter about "the work's subtext" and glasses of cheap white wine. Neither of them said, "He looks good." Though, in fact, he did. At least, for a dead person. Jenny had done a terrific job creating the illusion of life. With just a little suspension of disbelief, he appeared to be napping, something George's go-go-go father rarely did.

"When we'd finished making all the plans," Claire said, "I won't even tell you what we paid, but this funeral cost more than our cruise to Alaska, and I'm including all the hotels and restaurants while we were in port. Anyway, we got in a cab to go home, and your father looked at me. I could see how relieved he was that we had gotten things all squared away. He said, 'Claire, I spoke to Nan last night.' He said it calmly, like they talked all the time. Like he picked up the phone and dialed Heaven. I really thought maybe his mind had started to go."

For the first time since her husband's death, Claire wept in front of her son. When he tried to hug her, she pressed her hand against his shoulder to halt the embrace. She was not intending to be cold; neither was this an example of her Irish stoicism. For all of Claire's fortitude, she was an affectionate woman, especially with her boys.

George understood his mother could not accept a hug at that moment, because she was sure to breakdown and lose control if she did. And what she needed to tell George was important. She did not want her news sidetracked by grief and tears. So there was no hug.

Claire pulled a tissue from one of the myriad boxes Dillon's had placed around the room, and she hastily dried her eyes. She took George's hand again. They walked back to the first row of chairs and sat. Then she began explaining to George why a perfectly healthy man woke up one morning and insisted he plan his funeral that very day.

"Daddy had been sleeping. You know how he was, a whirling dervish until he hit the pillow and then dead to the world in two seconds. He could sleep through anything. But he *said* he woke up. Of course, I assumed he must have really been dreaming the whole time, but he swore that he woke up. He was sure that he woke up. He told me that he sat up and there was Nan, sitting at the foot of the bed, smiling at him."

George saw that scene so clearly. The bittersweet joy of remembrance washed over him. He recalled Nan babysitting for him and Conor, and the sleepovers, how she sat on the foot of the bed, and with a smile told them grand stories of kings and princes and a magic faraway land called Ireland.

"Daddy told Nan that he missed her. And according to your father, she said, 'I miss you too, my darling boy. But don't you cry, Georgie. I promise we'll be together soon. You and I, and Pop and Tea, too.' Then she walked up to him and bent over and kissed the top of his head. And just like that, she was gone.

"George," his mother stammered, her eyes rheumy and voice

thick. "I thought it was just a dream. I didn't believe him."

"It *was* just a dream, Mom." George suddenly recalled the moment in front of Duane Reade when, for a second, he thought he had seen Nan and his father crossing the street. He didn't mention the vision to his mother. It had been unnerving, more so now in light of his mother's story, but he dismissed that mirage as a strange coincidence.

George hadn't eaten much in the last couple of days and that, paired with thoughts of the ghosts of Baileys past, left him feeling lightheaded and dizzy. Sprays and wreaths and baskets of white lilies were everywhere. The overpowering smell of the maudlin flowers intensified his wooziness, making him feel queasy, too.

"Daddy picked these flowers? They don't seem like him at all. White lilies? They're a bit on-the-nose, aren't they?"

His mother smiled for the first time in days. "Your father chose lilies because he knew how much I detest them."

George looked at her curiously.

"They're terrible, aren't they?" his mother chuckled. "Aside from the obvious funereal connotations, I never liked the looks of them, and the stamens make such an awful mess. I've ruined more tablecloths. Daddy said, 'Claire, whatever flowers they lay across my casket you'll never allow into the house again. They'll only depress you. And you, my dear, should never feel sad when you look at flowers.' That's how sweet your father was, George. That's how much he loved me."

They were silent a while. George gazed at the flowers, while his mother gazed at her husband.

"George," Claire finally said. "I hope I go in late spring."

Panicked, George's eyes widened.

"Relax, sweetheart. I don't mean *this* spring. I just mean *some* spring. Not in May, of course. I wouldn't want to spoil May's birthday or your anniversary. You won't mind if I have pretty flowers, will you, George?"

George assured her he wouldn't.

"How I'd love peonies. Did you know that well-tended peony bushes have been known to live for a hundred years?"

George was about to ask his mother where her facts came from—as a savvy Googler, he knew you couldn't believe everything you read online—when the rest of the family arrived.

Claire didn't want the family sitting during the four hours of the wake. "If people took the time to come and pay their respects," she instructed them, "we should stand up and shake each mourner's hand." She didn't seem to grasp that they were the mourners.

George desperately wanted to sit because his back was still in a tremendous amount of pain. He had been counting on Todd to be his friend and provide him with medication. Unfortunately, Todd decided to be George's doctor, instead. And since George's body had virtually no experience with drugs, Todd thought he should start with Extra Strength Tylenol and see if that helped him before jumping right into addictive narcotics. Also, Todd told George the drugs would make him drowsy, and he thought George would probably want to be awake for his own father's funeral. George did not know where Todd came up with that idea.

Claire asked George to be the first in the receiving line, with Conor to her left, so both her sons would flank her. Conor, however, would have been the better choice for the first position. He had excellent recall of names, whereas George had almost none.

Still, standing in this place meant he was as far as he could possibly be from Tara, which was for the best since he had moved out of the please-stay-with-me phase and was now residing in the

I'm-going-to-figure-out-a-way-to-make-you-suffer phase. This was tricky, since he still needed her to tie his shoes. In addition to Claire and Conor, Finn, May, and Brian stood between the future ex-Mr.-and-Mrs.-Bailey.

At three on the dot, a couple of elderly ladies, friends of George's grandparents, arrived. They must have been nearly a hundred. Though he had not seen them since Nan's wake more than a decade earlier, George remembered them instantly—Mrs. Shea and Mrs. O'Brien. Along with Nan, these two women took turns washing and ironing the priest's vestments and the altar linens. The three had been great friends and walked to church each morning. Afterwards, they would go for a cup of tea to catch up on news. George wondered what they found to talk about morning after morning over all those decades.

Mrs. Shea looked visibly shaken when she took George's hand in hers, as if she couldn't fathom how she could be attending the funeral of her friend's little boy. By contrast, Mrs. O'Brien clasped both his arms in hers with a vigor that surprised George. She looked up at him, revealing a conspiratorial smile that suggested she was about to let him in on a secret. She had always been a small woman. Now shrunken, she looked like an ancient sprite. He wanted to bend down and kiss her, but his back prevented it. He considered explaining his predicament, but didn't. He stood there unbending, like a sentry on duty, as she peered up at him.

"Your dad is home now. Maureen's been waiting for him." Very few people called his grandmother by her Christian name. When George was three, he started calling his grandmother Nan. The rest of the family and even many of her friends soon followed.

She raised George's hand to her lips and kissed it gently. "Really now, don't you worry. I *know* he's with Maureen." She meant to comfort him, but he was unnerved by her prophecy.

The two women moved to the back of the room and joined the circle of old timers who were beginning to congregate.

Bailey and Sons was closed for the day, and the four non-family members of the sales team came in together. George thought their en masse arrival was not likely to be a coincidence and wondered if they'd gone out for lunch first. Probably they had, as they were all quite close with one another. That was notable, considering they worked on commission. They often socialized together, and George always felt unwelcome at their get-togethers. He was a little hurt he had not been invited to dine with them today, which was just plain ridiculous since he had obviously been unavailable. The fact was that George, aside from his duties as VP and head buyer, which he generally shirked, was technically a salesperson, too. Everyone at Bailey and Sons waited on customers. Yet he was usually excluded from their extracurricular events.

Theo Laskaris was the first member of the team to pay his respects to George. Fitting, as he was Bailey and Sons' most senior employee. Theo had just turned sixty the month prior, a milestone for which George's father had hosted a surprise party at Le Cirque in Theo's honor. He'd begun working for the firm while still in high school. He was dressed in black, which was unusual for Theo, who favored primary colors; and he was in tears, which was not unusual, as Theo was a man easily moved.

Like George's father, Theo never seemed to tire of the constant carols and merriment, which was a requisite part of the job. It was not uncommon to hear Theo, without a hint of irony, *Ho Ho Hoing* in the middle of August, even as sweat beaded at his temples. As Theo regaled George with stories about the "old days" with Pop and his father, George could not help but stare at Theo's forehead.

In contrast to his dark suit and the even darker circles framing his black eyes, Theo's brows sparkled a shimmering gold. One of the curses of a life devoted to Christmas is glitter. Sixty percent of the merchandise in the line was dusted with it. Of that sixty percent, at least ten percent managed to rub off and tenaciously affix itself to the hair, faces, limbs, and clothing of anyone who spent any amount of time in the confines of the showroom.

In the shower that morning, George had spent the better part of an hour attempting to rid himself of the stuff, because he imagined it would be hard to look appropriately grief-stricken with glitter stuck to his face.

Theo clasped George's hand and pulled him into a tight hug. George pretended it didn't hurt his back. "What are we going to do? What are we going to do?" Theo wailed, shaking his head wildly. George hoped he wasn't actually expected to respond to Theo's question because he had no idea what the correct answer might be.

The three other salespeople—Alison, Lizzie and Regina (everyone called her Reg)—followed Theo paying their respects. They rather impressively managed to match Theo's level of anguish keen for keen. Like the senior salesman, they too sparkled from head to toe with shiny flecks of gold and silver. Between the crying and the glittering, the employees of Bailey and Sons looked like they were planning to leave the wake and party at the most depressing discothèque in the world.

With each heartwarming anecdote about his wonderful father, the staff kept raising the bar so high George felt he would never be able to live up to their expectations when, or if, he took over the job of president. They made his father seem like their altruistic benefactor or patron saint rather than their boss. George knew he could never be that kind of employer. He was not a bad man, just a dissatisfied one. And his dissatisfaction made it difficult for him to even contemplate being selfless with others.

As he watched them now, moving like a pack, crying, shaking, sparkling, and telling stories about how wonderful Daddy was, George wondered if his father used to look at his employees and think to himself: *Any one of you would be better suited to take the business from me than my pathetic son, George, is.* His father probably worried about his gumptionless son all the time, but he never brought up his concerns to George. On the contrary, he was always encouraging and supportive to his son, in his quiet way.

Right on the heels of the Bailey and Sons contingent, a pudgy man in a shiny suit marched up to George and extended his hand. He was in his mid-fifties, George guessed. Though he spoke of the deceased with a stilted, generic fondness that suggested propriety rather than any genuine relationship, he peppered his speech with enough verifiable details to confirm he had an actual, if somewhat distant, connection to the family, and was not merely crashing the event, which, according to Jenny Dillon, people did. Still, George had no idea who this man was for most of their conversation. Then the man said, "I guess that leaves you and me as the kings of Christmas." At which point, George knew exactly to whom he was talking.

This was Clark Adelman of Adelman Inc. Adelman was Bailey and Sons' chief competitor. Clark's grandfather started Adelman about a decade before Pop started Bailey and Sons. Though late to the Christmas party, Bailey and Sons was very quickly just as successful as Adelman Inc., which apparently irked the senior Adelman to no end. Pop, who was not one to speak ill of others, never liked Clark Sr. According to Pop, Clark referred to him as a "scrappy mick." It was not the word "scrappy" with which George's grandfather took umbrage. There was always a Macy's vs. Gimbels aspect in the relationship of the two families, with both the Baileys and the Adelmans claiming to be Macy's.

George thought it odd that Clark Adelman would come to the wake. They had no old family grudges but aside from their paths occasionally crossing at trade shows, they hardly knew one another. It would never occur to George to go to Clark's father's wake. But since the two of them were now the kings of Christmas, that wake must have already taken place. He thanked Clark for coming and shook his hand a second time before passing him off to Claire. George wondered if Clark enjoyed being the king of Christmas or if he longed to abdicate the throne the way George did.

By 5:30, the funeral home was packed. The number of old college friends who showed up stunned George. He wasn't even sure how they found out about the wake, though he guessed it must have been from Tara. Surely people in their forties had not already acquired the depressing habit of reading obituaries every day to find out which of their friends hadn't made it through the night.

George's college friends were also Tara's, as they went to NYU together. Unlike George, she had also been accepted at Columbia. She swore she picked NYU because of their exemplary theater program. Perhaps that was true, but George always suspected it was so she could be with him. Back then, the one hundred-block separation of the two universities was a divide too vast for the young lovebirds to bridge.

Though they were one of very few couples going steady among first-year students, they did not allow themselves to become insular and cocooned. They were social with their classmates thanks to Tara's insistence that they mingle, and they formed a tightknit new family with a dozen or so of their fellow freshman. Most of their gang was in the I-have-no-idea-what-I-want-to-do-with-my-life

Arts department. Todd was the exception; he always wanted to be a doctor. While the rest of them complained about having to compare and contrast Ibsen and Chekhov, or whined about how tedious the drawing class was, Todd was happily juggling calculus and biology in the same semester.

Todd must have cancelled his afternoon patients, because he had shown up soon after Nan's friends, offering hugs and a silent presence more comforting to George than words could ever be. With Claire, Todd cried. Todd spent most of the wake standing and talking with Tara, which George appreciated. He hadn't yet told Todd that Tara and he were splitting up. George hadn't told anyone. But George hoped Todd's close communication with Tara would make it seem less obvious and awkward to those paying attention that he had not spoken a word to his wife the entire day. George was determined not to become the subject of gossip.

"Dude!"

In George and Tara's NYU gang, there was one guy no one really liked very much—Dennis Day. They all felt a little guilty about disliking him, because he meant well. But he had a juvenile sense of humor none of them really appreciated. He was always quoting some random Monty Python line and holding for laughter. Then, when the laugh didn't come, he'd deliver another line and another until eventually everyone finally laughed, partly to get him to be quiet, and partly because at some point the whole spectacle became funny in a pathetic sort of way.

They also disdained Dennis because he looked like he was twelve, which George realized Dennis couldn't help. But it was not a plus. The worst thing about him was that he was an actor, and not a good one. He was constantly cast as the small child in productions, because no one could play prepubescence like Dennis could, and so they all had to suffer through his shows. George had not seen or thought of Dennis Day in years.

"Dude," Dennis said again, this time bringing a melancholic inflection to the word. "So sorry, man." Dennis was almost unrecognizable, so changed was he from the little boy/man George knew at NYU. He had to be six-three', because he was at least two inches taller than George. When had Dennis finally had his growth spurt? Clearly, it had happened after graduation. He looked like a movie star with his muscular frame, hazel eyes, and annoyingly thick black hair. "I really am terribly sorry," he said clutching George's hand.

George was beginning to wonder why everyone had disliked Dennis so much during their school days. He seemed like a nice enough fellow now. Then Dennis glanced at his father in his casket. He looked back at George with a puzzled expression, and then did a vaudevillian's double take. "I'm so sorry you didn't inherit your dad's head of hair." He laughed. "*His* mane is crazy. What happened to *yours?*" He continued staring at George's towering forehead, a shocked glaze spreading across his stupid, handsome face.

As far as George was concerned, the correct question was: Why had any of them wasted a moment feeling guilty for not liking this oaf? Aside from the undeniably positive effects from the Human Growth Hormone he must have ingested, he was the same annoying boor.

He shook Claire's hand. "I'm Dennis Day, one of your son's oldest and best friends. I'm very sorry about your husband."

George's mother thanked him, but her son could tell she was trying to figure out how it was that he had a best friend she'd never heard of.

Dennis glanced toward Tara and whispered to George, "Who's

the babe?"

Considering his hair issues, which Dennis had been so quick to point out, George was confident the years had changed Tara less than they'd changed him. He was surprised Dennis didn't recognize her. Dennis grinned in Tara's direction, apparently mistaking the wake for a Speed Dating event.

Then, to George's great dismay, he noticed his daughter grinning back. She walked toward them.

"Dude," Dennis said excitedly. "She's coming over. Introduce us!"

When she arrived, George said, "May, I would like you to meet December. I mean, Dennis. Dennis, this is *my daughter*, May. She just turned twenty-three," he added pointedly.

George assumed they would have a moment of polite but awkward conversation before parting hastily. But quite the opposite occurred. Almost immediately, May was laughing at some asinine story Dennis was telling about his years working in LA.

Guess what, **Dude?** *We'd already figured out that you live in LA.* George refrained from comment, smiling dully instead.

At the end of Dennis's Hollywood tale came a disquieting piece of news. He was not just in Manhattan on vacation. "I needed to get away from that West Coast environment. For me it was toxic. It was so superficial. I'm back here full-time. I'm producing a reality show that I'm really proud of."

May and Dennis walked away together, while George consoled himself by taking some small pleasure in thinking of ways he could blame Tara for letting that moron know about his father's wake, and therefore being solely responsible for his successfully hitting on their precious little girl.

Apparently, time flies whether or not you're having fun. In forty-five minutes, the Bailey family would be able to wrap this wake up. George's feet hurt, his back was killing him, and his daughter was copying down Dennis's phone number.

There was a lull in the crowd, and after May abandoned the receiving line, the rest of the Baileys also began to move around a bit. Less out of defiance to her sister-in-law and more out of deference to her bunions, Finn sat down. She had been in a state all day long, arriving with a Bible in hand. Thankfully, she had not yet started quoting from it, which was always a risk because she sometimes did.

George hated to think badly of a relative, but she was an odd, dour old woman. George tried to be kind. He, too, would be strange if he had been shunned by his father. Still, the Bible as prop was a little extreme, especially for a Catholic. George had gone to eight years of Catholic school and never even knew Catholics believed in the Bible. (Later, he learned they did.) But so much attention had been paid to learning the rules and teachings of the church in a thing called The Catechism, he hadn't imagined they cared about the Bible, too. It seemed excessive. But wherever Finn had been all those years when she returned to the fold, she had become a Holy Roller.

Nan tolerated this behavior, but she was nothing like that herself. She was as close to a saint as any person George had ever met, but she was not sanctimonious. Nan saw goodness in all people. He supposed she was not above praying for someone's salvation, but she did it quietly. She never thumped a book in her life, certainly not one by King James.

Finn was seventy-nine, and despite her prim and hard exterior, George always thought of her as looking years younger than she actually was. Today, however, she looked exhausted and every second of her age. For all her attempts at Irish stoicism, and her repeated assurance that "he was in a better place," she seemed lost.

George remembered her telling him once that when she was a girl, her favorite toy was his father. She didn't really want a brother. She was afraid she'd lose him like she lost Tea, but she delighted in having a life-like baby doll to dress up and push around in a carriage. Finn had never married or had children, so in some ways, her little Georgie was always her baby. She mothered and loved him and when she rejoined the family, she seemed to pick up where she'd left off, doting on and protecting him. Occasionally, her resentments flared. But mostly she contained them, saving her public disapproval for the litany of subjects she deemed sinful.

Feeling obligated, George was about to go sit with Aunt Finn when Brian came over to him. Though he tried not to be obvious, George could not avoid staring at his son's mutilated ears. Brian had had *both* his ears pierced several years ago. While George did not really approve of men wearing earrings, he thought a guy who pierced one ear was probably thinking, *I'm rakish. At a different point in history, I'd be a pirate.* It was not true, of course, but there was no real harm in wanting a little *Aye Matey* adventure in your life.

But, to George's mind, two pierced ears screamed, *I desperately wanted to be a rock star, but since I can't play the guitar or sing, I just got my ears pierced instead.*

Last Christmas, Tara and George gave their son diamond studs, and George didn't balk when she bought them. The reason he didn't make a stink was because he knew she wanted him to do just that, so they could quarrel about it. She believed George didn't want their son to wear earrings because it was feminine, and somehow that meant George could not accept the fact he had a gay son.

George insisted this was not true. Refusing to take Tara's bait, he feigned enthusiasm as the jewelry was unwrapped on Christmas morning. Anyway, while he didn't love the piercings, George had gotten used to them. He certainly never brought up his failed rock star theory to Brian.

On Thanksgiving, however, Brian showed up at the house with—George didn't even know what you called them. Big holes, like missing dime-sized pieces of flesh where formerly there had been an earlobe. George thought he was going to throw up when he saw the wreckage of his son's lobes. Oddly, George thought the holes made Brian look less gay, because he generally thought of gay men as being well groomed. He did not imagine a gay person would deliberately do something that would make him look repulsive. In spite of the fact that George thought Brian looked terrible, he made no mention of the new change on Thursday. And shortly after Brian's arrival, George had his ill-fated encounter with the turkey, so he trusted he could be forgiven for his sullen silence.

Brian pointed at his lobes now. He was wearing solid metal studs so at least George could not see the amputated portion of his son's ears.

"What do you think?" Brian asked. George knew he was being tested.

What do I think? I think I'm going to be supporting you for the rest of my life.

Wisely, George did not express that opinion in words. His countenance, disapproving and disappointed, was another matter. Still, he couldn't see the point in starting something. The damage had already been done, literally.

"Brian," he finally said, "I just want you to be happy." Which was of course a lie. What he wanted was for his son to have two intact earlobes.

Brian mumbled something as he moved on to talk to his Uncle Conor.

Soon after, George heard his mother sweetly saying, "Oh, Luke. I did not expect you to come. I hope you didn't cancel a client, dear. This is so kind of you." She was standing with Conor and Brian, and she introduced them to a young man whom George had never before seen or heard of. George guessed this stranger was little more than thirty-three. He might have been Middle Eastern or of some swarthy European background. His black hair was almost completely shaved off. But unlike George, he clearly had a very full head of hair. Apparently, bald was a fashion statement for him. His eyes were wide and green and even from a distance George could see them shining brightly. The man hugged Conor and Brian before walking over to him arm in arm with Claire.

"Luke," his mother introduced. "This is my oldest, George."

George sensed Luke was about to move in for an embrace. Even if his back had not been in spasm, George was not interested in being hugged by a stranger. He extended his hand, and they shook. Luke was not a big man, but his shake was surprisingly firm. His hand felt hot but not clammy. "You must be in a great deal of pain," he said, not letting go of George's hand.

George looked at him askance, and with some effort finally wriggled his fingers free.

"Your back," Luke added quickly. "I can tell from the way you're standing that it's giving you trouble."

Somehow George didn't think Luke had been referring to his back when he made his initial observation, but he was relieved to keep their conversation in the realm of the physical.

"Luke is an amazing healer," Claire said. "I see him all the time." This was the first George was hearing about it. "Daddy discovered him. And I first went because your father recommended Luke so highly."

George might have put more faith in his father's ringing endorsement of this healer's abilities were he not standing three feet away from his open casket. Maybe "The Healer" missed something that say, "A Doctor," for example, might have found.

"I'm so sorry about your father," Luke said. "If I can be of any help..." His voice trailed off, and George assumed he was going to step away, but instead he placed his furnace of a hand on George's shoulder. George felt its warmth penetrating his suit jacket. The sensation was strange, but not unpleasant. "If nothing else, I can probably help you with your back. Claire knows how to get hold of me. Your dad talked about you all the time. I'll be praying for you, George."

When Luke removed his hand, George became aware of how cold the rest of his body felt in comparison. He also became aware of the fact that he was in desperate need of a bathroom. He had been drinking water every time Jenny Dillon had come by with a tiny paper cup in hand. But he had not once left his spot. George caught Conor's eye, letting him know he'd be right back.

The bathrooms were downstairs at Dillon's, and George remembered Jenny saying something about a little lounge down there with coffee and Danish. George was starving. No doubt sugar would make him happy, at least in the short run. After his long delayed pee, he headed for the lounge, hoping the Danish would have a lot of thick white icing on top. A cherry Danish was almost too much to hope for. George hadn't eaten one in years because Tara was against refined sugar.

"But," George said aloud, "She is no longer the boss of me." He didn't care that it was practically the dinner hour. As an essentially single man, he could eat breakfast for supper anytime he wanted. And, since he saw it as one of the few perks of the life that lay ahead, he planned on doing it often.

George flung open the lounge door. To his dismay, he did not see any Danish. He did, however, see Tara, who startled and jumped when he entered the room. So did his best friend, Todd, as he yanked his lipstick-smeared face out of Tara's cleavage. She quickly pulled at her skirt, which had ridden up to her waist, and Todd spun around, his deer-in-the-headlight-eyes glued to George's. The two men stood looking at each other for several seconds before breaking eye contact. Todd made a grab for his pants and underwear, which were bunched around his ankles. He pulled them up in one deft move.

Despite abundant evidence to the contrary, Tara and Todd began performing the *this is not what it looks like* pantomime. They would have actually spoken words to that effect were it not for the booming voice crying out from behind George.

"Dude!" Dennis shouted. He sounded truly outraged, which George found both touching and humiliating. "This is seriously f'd up."

Regrettably, what was even more f'd up was that beside Dennis stood May, in tears, witnessing the sight of her adulterous mother and cuckolded father. Oh, and it likely did not improve matters that Uncle Todd, as May had always referred to him, was also her godfather.

FIVE

Tara and George had agreed to tell no one about their splitting up until after the funeral, and she'd held up her end of the bargain. Technically. Unfortunately, George had neglected to also get Tara's agreement not to have sex with her new boyfriend while she was at his father's wake. Had George done so, he could have really saved his family some heartache.

George was in complete shock. Yet to the casual observer, he seemed, if not fine, at least in control, presenting a facade of composure. He was not about to make a scene at the funeral home. He was not really the type of person to make a scene anywhere. But were he suddenly to start acting out, his father's wake would certainly not be the venue he'd choose for his ignoble debut.

So, as a way of coping with the sordid events he had just

witnessed, he fell almost instantly into complete denial. By wearing a mask of tranquility, he would certainly be able to keep his mother and the rest of the family in the dark for a few days longer. There was, however, the matter of May, who, though only ten minutes into her relationship with a reality show producer, had already adopted the vernacular of his trade. She was cursing vociferously and sobbing bitterly.

And so, born of a survivalist's desperation, George aligned himself with Tara in the goal of subduing their distraught daughter. Wisely ruling out both charm and bribery, George and Tara opted for begging—coming just shy of actually falling to their knees. Once they had managed to calm May down, George and Tara pleaded with her not to say anything about what she'd witnessed for the sake of her brother and grandmother. After her parents put May in this terrible, compromising position, Dennis swooped in to comfort her, grabbing the opportunity to act as May's knight and protector. This gave George yet another reason to blame Tara for being the cupid behind this unsuitable romance.

The group then returned upstairs, with an essentially catatonic George bringing up the rear. They found the rest of the family with coats in hand, eagerly awaiting them so they could leave. As a way of postponing the moment when Claire would be alone in her apartment, they had all agreed to go back to her place after the wake for takeout, and a few glasses of wine. As withdrawn as he was, even George could see from everyone's impatient expressions that they were all more than ready for the alcohol, if not the food.

"Of course we want you to come back for dinner," May told Dennis.

George raised an eyebrow and shook his head at his daughter. He was not subtle, barely containing a censorious sigh.

His sweet little baby girl glared back at him with an expression that communicated, *Dennis and I are keeping your filthy secret. So back off if you know what's good for you.*

He backed off.

At this point things still might have been fine —well, at least for another twenty-four hours or so —were it not for the conversation George had with his mother.

"Can I talk to you for a second?" Claire whispered urgently. He forced himself out of his inertia and prepared for a lecture, assuming Claire wanted to give him parenting advice with regard to May's new forty-three year old boyfriend. She walked away from the group and back towards Daddy in the casket, as George lagged behind. George knew his father wouldn't be able to actually hear them or chime in, but he still did not relish the idea of having *both* his parents present while he was being harangued about his shortcomings as a father.

But he was mistaken. When his mother spoke, it was not of May. "I'm very worried about Tara. She seems almost despondent," Claire said. "You know how she and my George always got on. He was more a father to her than her own was."

This was not a conversation George was in the mood for. He didn't care in the least how Tara was doing, and he felt his mask begin to slip. "Don't worry about Tara. He was *my* father," he snapped.

George looked over at the rest of the family. They were obviously restless but seemed oblivious to what he and Claire were discussing. Jenny Dillon was hovering around, doing everything but switching the lights off and dangling her keys in front of them to get the Baileys to take the hint and go home. Considering Jenny's constant exposure to grief, formaldehyde, and carnations, maybe George didn't have the worst job in the world.

"George Bailey." His mother's voice was quietly ferocious.

"I have loved that girl since she was seventeen years old. As far as your father was concerned, she was his daughter. And I'm sure Tara thought of him as her father. Is this news to you?"

George said nothing, feebly managing a rattled shrug.

"She seems extremely upset to me. And I am asking you—*her husband*—do you think she's all right?"

This is when a rational son would have said *She is very upset about Daddy, but she'll be okay, Mom. Don't worry.*

Instead, this was when her irrational son, tossing aside all cares about impropriety or scandal, screamed at the top of his lungs, loud enough that George had no doubt even his father heard, "I'm sure Tara is fine, Mom. I just saw her downstairs fucking Todd. She seemed quite content!"

Finn, who had shown amazing restraint all day, began quoting chapter and verse on the topic of adultery. But something of much greater significance than Finn's Savant-like grasp of the Old Testament also took place—with the completion of George's tirade, the Bailey family had one less secret.

The time may come, many, many, many years from now when Tara thanks George for his outburst. His family was so outraged by his boorish behavior, that their sympathies shifted in favor of the besmirched Tara. Claire, who never once spanked him and rarely even yelled at him, hauled off and slapped him hard across the face. Every Bailey but May circled around Tara to protect her. He had been newly crowned George the Cad. He made a move toward his only ally, May. But he jumped back when he saw her venomous glare.

Jenny Dillon seemed much less eager to get home now. Presumably, things were going to be less interesting for her there then they were here at ringside. Dennis was typing something into his smartphone, which was most likely the pitch for a new reality show starring the Battling Baileys. And Todd...Todd was nowhere to be found, having slipped out at some point when George was recovering from the sting of his mother's right hook. George found the doctor's escape rather interestingly timed. Considering the force of his mother's blow, he might have been in need of medical attention.

∽

IN MOST WAYS, THE BAILEYS would never be thought of as a stereotypical Irish family. Nan was a lifelong member of the Pioneer Total Abstinence Association of the Sacred Heart, choosing at age eleven to never touch even a drop of alcohol. While none of the other members of the family decided to "take the pledge" against drinking, they were all moderate in their consumption. They loathed the shenanigans associated with St. Patrick's Day. They never watched the parade, and certainly never wore or ate or drank anything green. George clearly recalled his mother's look of consternation when as a boy he asked her to buy him a box of Lucky Charms. His claim that the cereal was magically delicious did nothing to persuade her.

In one way, however, the Baileys were unmistakably Irish. In response to disagreeable or uncomfortable situations, they either pretended they were not happening and ignored them entirely *or*, much less frequently, they flared up quickly and dramatically, and then almost immediately acted as if the sordid event had never taken place.

And so the Baileys arrived the next morning at the Church of St. Francis Xavier, all of them quietly solicitous of each other's welfare. They limited their conversations to fond remembrances of Daddy and talk of the food the caterers would be serving at the post-funeral luncheon. No one mentioned last evening.

Why should they? Nothing happened last evening.

Each member of the clan moved gingerly around George in particular, like he'd just returned from war, and they were all afraid of what might happen if he heard a car backfiring. The events of the previous evening were not discussed, but neither were they forgotten. George's outburst at the funeral home was a bad dream, brought on by grief and stress.

Shrewdly, Claire had taken precautions to avoid any similar disruptions today. His mother informed George that he could stop working on his speech. Conor would be delivering the eulogy. Claire felt it was best to keep him off the altar and away from a live microphone, lest he had the misguided urge to speak the truth again. Luke was a last minute substitute as pallbearer, replacing Todd who Claire had asked to stay at home. And finally, she insisted George have a brief counseling session with Fr. Sal De Luca before mass.

When a forty-year-old Indian man, skinny, bespectacled and dressed in a Columbia University sweatshirt and a pair of worn Levis opened the rectory door, George asked him if he could speak with Fr. Sal. The man smiled warmly, extended his hand and said, "Hey. George? I'm Sal. Claire said you'd be over." When he spoke, he sounded the way *New Yawkers* sound on television, though rarely do in real life. He ushered George into the vestibule. The ceiling was fourteen feet high, and one wall was entirely taken over by an imposing Renaissance-looking painting of Jesus, cross over shoulder, on the road to Calvary. "I'm not in charge of the décor," said the priest, his eyes on the crown of thorns. "That's a bit much to face before coffee, which I haven't had yet. So, if you don't mind, let's sit in the kitchen."

Fr. Sal came to the table with a pot of espresso he'd perked up on the stove and a plate of hazelnut biscotti. After the cups had been poured and the sugar passed, he told George how much he'd cared for his father and how sorry he was for his loss. Then he asked George what had brought him to the rectory this morning.

"My mother made me come."

The priest laughed. "I can relate. I have an Italian mama. I was adopted," he added, ending the mystery of how an Indian man seemed to have stepped off the set of a Scorsese film. "What can I do for you, George?"

"My mother didn't already tell you?"

"Claire mentioned something about some marital difficulties. I would be happy to talk to the both-a-yous."

"I don't think so."

The priest nodded and topped off their demitasse cups.

George picked up his cup, inhaling the coffee's bittersweet aroma. "I know it's only been a few days. I'm obviously still figuring this all out. But I know we're not going to stay together. I just never would have been the one…" George trailed off, letting his attention drift to the cup in his hand.

"A lot of couples—"

"I know the church doesn't allow for divorce, but I'm not a Catholic anymore. I don't believe in that." George did not go as far as saying he didn't believe in anything religious, though he did not any more. He wasn't sure if the good father was shocked by his declaration, but George was. It was one thing to lose your faith, but it was quite another to announce it at a priest's kitchen table. George's admission both saddened and relieved him. He felt relieved he didn't have to pretend anymore, but he was sad to let something go that had once really mattered to him. So many things that used to bring solace now felt empty or, worse, felt impossible to accept.

"Father," he said, "one day years ago, I lost my keys, so I started praying to St. Anthony to find them. Mind you, I did this instead of actually looking for the keys. It didn't occur to me to look for them. I was sitting on the couch, staring off into space, praying, and my wife walked in. She asked me what was wrong, and I told her that I couldn't find my keys. Before I could tell her I was praying to the saint, she shouted, '*Christ, George…*' Oh sorry, Father."

He waved his hand like he'd heard plenty worse than that in his time.

"Anyway, she asked me why I was just sitting there doing nothing. 'Check your coat pockets,' she snapped."

"Were they there?" He asked.

"Of course."

"So, your prayer was answered," said the priest, grinning with satisfaction.

"No. That's not the—"

"George, I don't really care whether or not you believe, though I think you'd probably enjoy life more if you believed something. But it doesn't matter. Truly. You are welcome here at my table, and, if you ever want to go there, you are welcome inside the church." He smiled wryly before adding, "At least as long as I'm still the pastor here. I can't guarantee every priest is going to be as embracing of a self-proclaimed ex-Catholic as I am." He chuckled good-naturedly.

George sipped his espresso slowly and in silence. He didn't have anything else to say, but he wasn't ready to leave the safety of this sanctuary or the presence of this kindhearted man.

"You know, George, there is the official doctrine of the church, and there are other things—matters of the human heart, for example. These things are more complicated. I follow the teachings of the church. But I realize not everyone does. At the end of the day,

I personally think only two things really matter," he paused, giving George a long look. "You gonna write this down?" he asked grimly.

Panicked, George patted at his suit jacket even though he knew he wasn't carrying a pen.

"Relax. I'm just teasing you. What I'm about to tell you is difficult to do, but it's not complicated to understand. Okay, the first thing is to truly be able to forgive others and yourself. And the second is to cultivate kindness. Being kind at all times," Fr. Sal squinted and his forehead scrunched. "That might be even harder than forgiving. But kindness is a great goal. Anyway, these two things together, forgiveness and kindness, they equal goodness. At least that's what I think. You know who taught me that?"

"Your Italian mama?"

"No. Your grandmother."

George looked at him with interest.

"I came to this parish in late 2001, a challenging time to be ministering in lower Manhattan. Nan and I were great friends from the day we met. Did you not know that?"

George was unaware, but not surprised his grandmother had befriended the young priest.

"Almost from my first week at the church, she had me over for dinner every Friday night. You see, when the church ladies learned a newly ordained priest named Fr. Sal was arriving—let's just say, I don't think they were expecting somebody like me. When I showed up, the ladies were waiting at the rectory with a cake. They'd even hung a banner that read *Welcome Fr. De Luca!*

"When I walked in, several ladies gasped. I think they thought I was a terrorist. I'm pretty sure they did. Even though I was almost thirty, I barely looked like I was twenty. I wasn't wearing my collar. And of course my skin was brown," he added matter-of-factly.

"When they figured out I was the priest, they were still horrified. I imagine they were thinking I was going to pull down all the crucifixes and replace them with statues of the Hindu God Ganesh," he laughed easily.

"And then your grandmother marched up to me, took me by the hands and kissed my cheeks. 'Oh father,' she said, 'how good God is. He has answered our prayers and sent us a grand young priest. Aren't we blessed now, ladies?' She sat me down, put the kettle on, and made me a cup of tea. I'm sure she was aware of how the other women felt, but she paid it no mind."

George had to head to Dillon's for the procession to the church, so he thanked the priest for the coffee and the talk. "One more thing before you go," the priest said. "You might want to just mouth all the responses during mass this morning. Don't actually say anything out loud."

"Why?"

"Well, the church in its wisdom rewrote the language of the mass a while back. It's not major, but it's enough to draw attention to anyone who hasn't set foot in a church in a few years. We might as well save your mom and your aunt some embarrassment. You know what I mean? Especially Finn. She knows the mass better than I do."

Fr. Sal walked him out, and they stopped on his stoop to shake hands. "I really enjoyed meeting you, George."

"I enjoyed meeting you, too…" George hesitated. He couldn't get himself to say his first name. The priest had told him repeatedly to call him Sal, but the name wouldn't come out of George's mouth. Technically, George had only been an ex-Catholic for about twenty minutes, and a lifetime of being told it was disrespectful to call a priest anything but Father couldn't be erased so quickly.

"Hey," Father said. "I make a mean *pasta e fagioli*. Are you ever free for lunch?"

He was never free for lunch. He always had appointments with important buyers or meetings with designers or something going on during the day. "Lunch would be great," he said. "Name the day."

The moment George said those words, he decided that very soon he was going to be free for lunch every day of the week—not for the rest of his life, but at least for a while. He left Sal with a smile on his face, which he forced himself to squelch out of respect for the memory of his father.

SIX

ASIDE FROM GETTING A FREE pass on shaving, one of the advantages of grief is that people tend to excuse a lot of egregious behavior. So if people noticed the Baileys' prickly coolness toward one another, no one made mention of it. Nor did anyone mention that George and Tara and the kids had said no more than three words to each other during the funeral or the luncheon that followed. May said nothing to her father at lunch, but she did utter two words to him during the funeral mass. This was at the moment during the service when Fr. Sal had instructed everyone to offer their neighbor a sign of peace. George moved to hug his daughter, at which point she glowered, "Don't *even...*"

In his daughter's defense, George thought it important to point out that the two words she hissed at him trumped what she said to Tara, which was absolutely nothing. He interpreted this as an extremely positive sign. Though it would take awhile, he was certain he could restore his relationship with May. As far as mother and daughter were concerned, their reconciliation seemed less likely. He was surprised to discover that thought only depressed him.

It didn't depress George enough, however, to prevent him from rethinking his strategy with regard to Dennis. Tara, he now decided, was not going to get credit for their meeting. He planned to start pointing out at every opportunity that *he* was the one who brought the lovebirds together, and that *he* couldn't be happier about it. That would ensure the return of the true May, who seemed to have been abducted and replaced by one of the more colorful stars of Dennis's "reality" show.

The silence during lunch gave him the chance to ponder his next steps. He would have liked to take the opportunity to think about his father, but he didn't have time for that. He needed to do two things. He had to find a place to live. If Tara didn't want to stay in the apartment, they could always sell it. George was not going to stay there; he wanted a fresh start. And he wanted out of Bailey and Sons. Selling the business seemed the obvious solution. He was pretty sure Conor also hated his job and would be thrilled to have the chance to do something else. George hadn't exactly talked to his brother about this, but he sensed in Conor a dissatisfaction with life quite similar to his own.

Most importantly though, he had May and Brian to consider. He had heard Brian make ridiculous comments like, "What could be more fun than having every day be Christmas?" when asked (though never by George) about his interest in joining the family business.

To George's great disappointment, May was already working there. She had been on the payroll since graduation. Her time in the business seemed, at least as far as George was concerned, like a way for her to avoid starting her real life. Since he had employed the same tactic twenty-two years ago with painful success, he should know. He didn't want her looking back, realizing life was almost over, and regretting she'd never found and followed a passion. May would be grateful for the push out the door, though probably not immediately.

The family had been taking turns spending time with Claire. Finn had volunteered to go home with her after the luncheon, but George said he wanted to spend time with his mother. He implied he was going to apologize and beg forgiveness for his behavior at the wake, but really he wanted to tell her he was selling Bailey and Sons.

George found it terribly unsettling walking into his parent's apartment and not seeing his father there. Daddy was gone. Yet George saw signs of him everywhere he looked, as if he had just stepped out of the room for a second to grab an apple or some air-popped popcorn and would be back in a jiff. On a side table in the living room, next to his favorite chair—overstuffed, and oversized, it was the only seat in the house purchased more for comfort than appearance—a copy of the *New Yorker* was folded open to a short story he must have been reading. A pair of his glasses rested on top of the magazine.

At least twenty-five dog-eared copies of *Runner's World*, all too precious to be parted with, were stacked in a basket on the other side of the chair. And pictures of the Baileys were everywhere. To look at the photos, you'd think they had only ever been in Manhattan and the Caribbean, which was not far from the truth.

Considering they had the means, they were not a very well traveled group. His parents endlessly discussed their Alaskan cruise before finally taking it. After that, they vowed to go someplace new and exotic every year, but somehow it didn't happen. George's father trained hard for his marathons, and he worked just as hard. He travelled several times a year to Chicago, Atlanta, Las Vegas and San Francisco, attending trade shows for the business. Even though he saw very little of those cities aside from their convention centers, he didn't feel impelled to add more trips to his schedule.

Christmas really was one of the few slow periods of the year. When he took a break, all he wanted was some rest and a warm spot so he could go running without needing to wear gloves. Luckily, it never seemed to matter much to Claire where they went, as long as they went somewhere. As long as they were together. On the plus side, going to the same destination had its perks. After all, it was nice knowing what to expect once you got there. Claire never cared much for surprises.

For as many years as George could recall, the spot his parents returned to over and over again was Martinique. His parents went there the second week of December and returned home around the seventh of January. Sometimes George and his family would go down and join his parents for the holiday week, but Tara and the kids never really felt like it was Christmas if you needed to put on sunscreen. Mostly they stayed behind, celebrating in New York.

They did spend Christmas with his folks three years ago, and there was a photo of his parents and children framed on the mantel from that holiday. The picture must have been taken near the end of their stay, because in addition to looking rested, everyone had a tan. Tara and George didn't keep pictures out at their place. Tara could be quite sentimental, but this was tempered by an intense need for order. She didn't like the cluttered look of mementos lying about. The apartment was clean and spare. All photos had been scanned and could be viewed on an iPad kept solely for that purpose. The iPad was kept tucked away in a drawer.

His mother sat him on the couch facing the mantel. He tried to keep his eyes focused on her, but mostly he looked at Daddy and the kids, framed and smiling.

Claire followed his gaze, and they looked at the pictures together. "I'm thinking I might take the trip," his mother said.

He didn't understand what she meant, but she clarified. "Martinique."

"Oh? Would you like me to come with you?" he asked, even though he could not imagine a worse fate. A newly single middle-aged man escorting his widowed mother on vacation. He flashed to them drowning their sorrows, morosely drinking champagne at a table for two on New Year's Eve.

"No George," she replied without hesitation. "If I go, and I'm not sure I will, I want to be there alone."

He nodded. He wasn't sure what would be harder for her, going on the trip or staying at home. Probably they would be equally difficult in different ways.

"If I do go, would you like to stay here? Do you need a place to stay?"

He needed to get his own apartment as soon as possible. George didn't want to be hopping from guest room to guest room with no real home of his own. "No. I don't need a place."

"Oh, thank God!" Claire exclaimed, misunderstanding what her son had said. She exhaled like she had been holding her breath for a week, and sobbed more freely than she had at the wake. "Your father and I got through it, and you and Tara will too. I promise you that."

What? Your father and I got through it?

George tried desperately to come up with a meaning for the

phrase, 'Your father and I got through it' that did not involve one of his parents having an affair. He failed to come up with one. This was not information he needed or wanted. Too much had happened to him in the last five days, and all of it had been bad. He let his mind drift away from this room and his mother, so as to mentally review the wretched highlights of recent events:

1) Bad back causes crippling pain.
2) Father dies.
3) Wife leaves because...
4) Wife is having an affair with former best friend.
5) Time to embark on the challenging task of finding a new doctor.
6) Gay son is one step away from pulling a Van Gogh on his ears.
7) Evidently daughter has a daddy complex.
8) Faith disavowed while drinking coffee with a well-intentioned priest.
9) Deduce that one (or both!) parents engaged in adulterous relationships.

That pretty much summed things up.

George decided for both of their benefits, he should behave like a good Irish son and ignore item nine for the time being or forever for that matter. "No. I don't think Tara and I are going to work it out. But I do think I should get my own place and not be living in my childhood home."

He knew no good could come from stepping back in time twenty-five years and moving back home, but he did wonder what would happen if he walked down the hall to his old bedroom. It no longer bore any resemblance to the room he had grown up in. His mother, not sharing his taste in Heather Locklear posters, had redecorated years ago. Still, it was his room. On the rare occasion when his parents had guests, or when the kids were little and they babysat, the visitors were always put in "George's room."

"I need to tell you something," he said. His mother clenched her jaw, and he wondered if she was worried he was going to bring up item number nine. "I want to sell the business. I think it's a good idea," he blurted before losing his nerve.

His mother stared, nonplussed.

"I just think—"

"I didn't know you owned a business," Claire said icily. "Are you referring to your father's business?"

He sighed. "Well I assume that it's about to become Conor's and mine. And—"

"Have you spoken to your brother about this plan of yours?"

George admitted that he had not.

"Why do you assume that you are about to inherit the business?"

He considered screaming, and not just because the pain in his back was suddenly so unbearable.

"George, the business is mine. And now I understand why your father drew up his will that way," she said, as if she'd just unraveled a great mystery. "I'm not sure what I'm going to do, but I'm not selling. George, we just buried your father. Really, you're talking to me about this *now*?" She seemed far more disappointed than angry. "I think this conversation has given me a pretty good idea what I should do. When the time comes, I will leave the business to my grandchildren."

"Don't do that. If you love them, don't do that."

His mother shook her head bitterly. "You're acting like I just told you I was going to sell them into slavery."

"I want my children to be happy and to follow their dreams. I don't want them to be trapped."

Claire's eyes filled with tears, and George felt badly causing her upset. But he was not going to sacrifice his children to satisfy his mother and her notion of the family's legacy. He was sure that in the weeks that followed, when some time had passed and everything that had any link to his father became a little less sacred, his mother would come to understand that burdening May and Brian with Bailey and Sons was selfish and unfair.

Finally Claire dried her eyes. She forced a thin smile, but it only managed to make her look sadder. "George, I want your children to be happy and to follow their dreams. Please tell me why you are so certain that they have no interest in being a part of something begun by their great-grandfather. Have you ever asked them what they wanted?"

Since he hadn't, he remained silent.

"I'm a parent, too. And like you I want my children to be happy and to follow their dreams. I know you're not..." She rested her chin against her palm and sighed. "George, probably you should just quit, right? It's not like you are going to starve without a job."

His eyes widened. Even though he'd been dreaming about this moment since before his first day on the job, he was terrified to just walk away.

Then what?

His plan was not to quit. His plan—such as it was—was to sell, make himself and the rest of the family a fortune, thus securing his position as a hero in the eyes of all the Baileys. And then, after being immortalized, he would figure out the rest of his life.

"George, the family's hope in having you accompany me home

today was to keep me cheered up, correct?" His mother managed a laugh. "Honey, I'm afraid I can't handle any more cheering up today," she said not unkindly. "So will you go home or to a hotel or wherever you're living now?"

When he went to stand, he moved about an inch before the shock of pain pushed him back into the chair. He groaned.

"What? Your back? *Still?*"

Still? Despite the plethora of activity in the Bailey household, Thanksgiving was only five days ago.

"That's it! I don't want to hear any arguments. I'm calling Luke."

George wondered how she expected him to get to The Healer's office when he couldn't even get out of a chair.

∾

WHEN LUKE SHOWED UP AT HIS parents' place less than ninety minutes later, George was still very skeptical that this guy's magic touch could help him. Frankly, it seemed impossible. On the other hand, George was pretty much willing to try anything short of amputation if it offered the slightest hope of relief. Luke assured Claire that he didn't need her assistance and shooed her away. She seemed happy to have been excused from the room. Drained from the long and emotional day, Claire retired to her bedroom.

Luke moved the coffee table away from the sofa, pushed an ottoman aside, and moved a floor lamp against the wall. Then, in the space he'd cleared, he set up the portable massage table that he'd brought along with him.

"I'm not going to be able to climb up on that," George informed him.

"No. I didn't imagine you would be," he said softly. Luke

brushed his fingers across the top of his head as if he were running them through his hair, and George wondered if Luke had only recently shaved his head.

Luke took a seat in the chair Claire had previously occupied. "The table is for later, anyway. I thought we'd begin by talking to each other. Usually I begin by asking 'What is it that brings you here to see me?' But, of course, in this case I have been brought here to see you." Luke smiled.

George didn't go for that. It sounded a little too much like shrink-talk to him, and whatever George's problems were, they certainly were not psychological. "My back," he said. "Low back," he elaborated so The Healer would have a better idea why he was incapable of getting out of a fucking chair. At no time did George actually swear aloud. He hoped he was successfully masking the hostility he was feeling, because this was an emergency. Luke had made a house call after all, which was extremely generous, so it wasn't really right to be rude.

Luke kept smiling and nodding. "Yes, your back. And, of course, your dad."

"No. No, not my dad," George insisted, masking his hostility less successfully now. "Just my back. My back went out on Thanksgiving. My father didn't die until the next day, Black Friday. So, as you can see, there is no connection between the two events."

"Really? Thanksgiving. Were you with your whole family when it happened?"

George didn't see how this conversation was going to make his back feel any better, so he decided to thank Luke for his time, compensate him, and send him on his way.

"You know," George started. But Luke was looking at him with an expression so gentle and guileless, George felt he could not dismiss him without at least an explanation. He instantly started stammering. "Here's the thing…I…I mean I definitely appreciate…The thing is…I don't…I'm just more of a western medicine kind of guy."

"That's fair enough," Luke said, seeming to take no offense. "Have you seen your doctor?"

"That's kind of complicated."

"How so?"

"My wife's having an affair with him."

"With your doctor?"

"He's also my best friend. *Was*."

Luke laughed nervously. George couldn't really blame him since the situation was nearly as comic as it was tragic. When Luke saw George had not joined in the merriment, he contained himself. "You're not making this up?"

George shook his head. "I'm afraid not."

"I'm so sorry. How long have you known?"

"I found out about the affair at my father's wake."

"Your wife told you she was having an affair at your father's wake?"

"No. I walked in on them screwing."

Luke gasped, "That's so…" He didn't finish his thought.

"F'd up, right?" George said, repeating Dennis's apt description of the scene.

"Totally."

"But Tara told me she was leaving me on Black Friday."

"Isn't that the day your father died?"

"Yes. It is. But to be fair to Tara, she didn't know my father was dead when she made her big announcement. *But I did.*"

Luke seemed not to know what to say next. He stared at George as if he expected him at any moment to shout *Gotcha*. "Perhaps we've talked enough for right now. Let me do some hands-on work."

No longer in such a rush to get rid of this guy, George said, "Okay."

"Can you take your shoes and socks off, please?"

"I don't think so."

"You really won't take your shoes and socks off?"

"No. I really don't think I can." Perhaps Luke had forgotten George had a reason for not moving out of his chair the entire time they had been talking to each other.

Luke sank to his knees in front of George's feet and instructed him to shout if he felt any pain whatsoever.

George assured him that he would.

It must be true what they say about once a Catholic always a Catholic because seeing Luke crouched down, gently removing his shoes and socks, George couldn't help but think of Mary Magdalene washing the feet of Jesus. Not that he was comparing himself to Jesus. They were nothing alike. For starters, Jesus had an incredible head of hair.

Luke asked George if he could remove his belt and watch, which left him barefoot, beltless, watchless, and stuck in a chair. Then before he really even knew what was happening, Luke was lifting him. He draped one of George's arms around his shoulder, shimmied an arm under George's thighs and—wisely remembering to bend with his knees—lifted him into the air.

Maybe because George was in his childhood home, he recalled his father effortlessly carrying him out of the living room and down the hall to bed. He'd been a little boy then. The task of lifting his four-foot frame was not a challenge for his father. But Luke was shorter than George by several inches. George marveled at his strength, and the ease with which he carried him. George thought

Luke was like King Kong to his Fay Wray. Not that he had any desire to compare himself to Fay Wray. Obviously they were nothing alike. For starters, she had an incredible head of hair.

Luke carefully laid George on the table. He was on his left side in a modified fetal position. "Normally," Luke said, "I'd have the client on his back, but I don't think that's possible for you right now. I'd like you to breathe deeply and let go of negative thoughts."

George took that to mean he was supposed to let go of *all* thoughts, because he certainly didn't have any positive ones swimming around in his brain that he could latch on to.

Luke seemed to sense his confusion. "Just clear your mind, and when thoughts come in, try and let go of them. Oh, and keep your eyes closed."

The first thing Luke did was place his hands over George's heart, even though, as George had repeatedly pointed out, the issue was in his low back. Luke must have been pressing really hard, because George struggled for air. It was like a heavy weight had been dropped on his chest. George thought he might suffocate. Whatever Luke was doing to him felt like the opposite of healing. George tried to look on the bright side. If Luke ended up killing him, that would certainly eliminate his back pain.

Then George felt that flame again. The heat was as intense as when Luke had touched his shoulder at the wake, only now it was his heart feeling the warmth. The sensation frightened him, and he gasped but his breathing returned to normal. He started seeing a lot of colors, and the heat spread throughout his body. George would have said the sensation was like being on an acid trip, but acid could be added to the lengthy list of trips he had never taken. Travel was just one more thing he had only read about, undoubtedly during some marathon Google session.

Most of the rest of his time on the table was a blur of flashing lights behind his eyes and random thoughts of himself as a fool and a super hero and a failure and a king. Then he felt Luke massaging the soles of his feet. Luke had George's heels firmly clasped in each of his palms. As he surrendered to the feelings of pleasure and comfort, George felt one of Luke's hands on his left hip and the other just behind on his low back. As the heat warmed George's pelvis, his pain started to drift away. He experienced it as a kind of floating, with the pain rising out, hovering above him, and dispersing.

The only way George could describe what took place next was that his brain sort of exploded, because something impossible happened. He could feel Luke's two hands on his feet while simultaneously feeling two hands on his hip and back. George counted as his baffled brain cells, incapable of making sense of it all, flew up into the sky. One, two, three and then a fourth hand. One man. Four hands. George could not fathom this. And his body convulsed in response to a sensation both pleasurable and terrifying. He opened his eyes and Luke stood at the end of the table gazing compassionately at him, sweat soaked through his shirt.

After a pause, Luke had George try and sit up. Much to George's surprise, he could. He was stiff, but he was mobile.

"I couldn't help noticing the way your body started shaking. I thought you might jump off the table," Luke said. "I hope that wasn't frightening."

George shrugged. "Not exactly."

"It's a fairly common occurrence. Sometimes when energy has been blocked for a while, when it finally starts flowing again the body jolts in response to the sudden movement."

"Can I tell you something?"

"George, you can tell me anything." He spoke so earnestly and with such tenderness that George believed him. Even though they were essentially strangers, George was confident he could tell Luke anything without fear of being judged.

"When you had your hands on my feet at the end," he paused, puzzling over the impossibility of what he was about to say next. "Somebody else was in here with their hands on my back. It was like there was you, and somebody else who was holding me, too."

Luke didn't roll his eyes or explain to him that was not possible. He nodded and he smiled. "Wow. Cool. How wonderful. That's a lot for a first session. Who was holding you, George?"

George had no idea who it was. He was about to say so when he stuttered, "Maybe my grandmother."

"Would that be Nan?"

Astonished, George nodded his head.

"I'm not a psychic," Luke said. "That was just a guess. But your father often told me that she showed up during our sessions. I think maybe that's why he came to see me so often."

George stood up from the table, feeling a need to backpedal away from all this spiritual mumbo-jumbo. "I'm not sure it was my grandmother. I don't really know why I said that." Just then, George thought he smelled a hint of rosewater. He remembered her tilting the bottle against her index finger and dotting the damp finger behind each ear.

Luke was folding up the table and preparing to leave. George watched the way he effortlessly flipped the massage table on its side, folded up the legs and placed it into its travel case.

As Luke zipped up the bag he smiled warmly. "You're going to be fine, I promise. But why don't you see me again? You don't need to wait until you're in agony." He picked up the table with the same ease he'd picked up George and walked to the door. "You know,

George, you are right. It might not have been your grandmother or anyone. It could have been a dream, or it might just have been the way the energy was moving through you that created that sensation. Or, well, it might have been any number of things."

They said their goodnights, and Luke took his leave.

Luke was right, and George was glad for what the healer had said at the end. It could have been anything, most likely some sort of dream or a nerve impulse that broke the spasm in his back, leaving him pain free.

But George thought back to the eeriness of the moment when he'd counted up four hands on his body. And George knew, even though he did not want to know, that what happened to him was not a response of the nervous system.

Someone, in addition to Luke, had been touching him.

SEVEN

THE NEXT MORNING, STILL DRESSED in his funeral suit, George walked back to his apartment pain free. His movement could not be described as lithe, but it was not far off from his usual way of walking. In the past couple of years, he had become increasingly aware of the rigidity of his gait. He was stiffer than he usually was, but not much.

As had been the trend in recent winters, early December was unseasonably warm. George's clothes felt clammy against his skin. Last evening, Claire had placed a pair of his father's pajamas on the bed, but George had been unable to bring himself to put them on.

He sat on the edge of the bed in his t-shirt and underwear and clutched the pajamas in his arms, breathing in the smell of flannel and the clean scent of his mother's supposedly unscented laundry detergent. Somewhere deep within the fibers of the fabric, he believed he could smell his father. George was tired, and he let his head fall back onto the pillow, still clutching his daddy's pajamas. In spite of his fatigue, he felt unable to sleep. But eventually he succumbed. He awoke the next morning to find one arm of his father's PJs stretched protectively across his chest.

George hadn't bothered showering before leaving his mother's, so he'd been wearing the same grungy clothing against unwashed skin for twenty-three hours. As he had been with Tara since they were seventeen, and since they had lived with their parents until the day they married, George had never had occasion to take the so-called "walk of shame." If being greasy and smelly was what it was all about, he hadn't missed anything.

Vito was on duty when George entered the building. He looked at George askance as he passed by in his day-old funeral garb, and George wondered if Vito thought he was coming in from some illicit assignation. He could have easily mentioned staying with his poor, grieving mother. But he decided it was about time he stopped worrying so much what everyone else thought. What did it really matter if he became the subject of gossip?

His lack of concern for scandal was short lived, because George was struck by a disturbing thought. Todd only saw patients until three on Wednesdays and Fridays, both days when George never got home before six. Perhaps the neighbors were already whispering about him. With Vito's watchful eyes trained on the lobby, he must have known a great deal about the private lives of all building residents. Last Christmas, Tara had insisted they give the building staff huge increases in the amount of their holiday tips. George wondered if those lavish year-end bonuses were really hush money.

George's interminable wait for the elevator would have ended when the doors opened had Conor not come bounding off dressed for a run. George let the elevator go, and they stood in the lobby talking. Or rather, struggling to talk but not having much success at it. Finally, Conor managed, "Stay at Mom's?"

George confirmed—loud enough for Vito to hear—that he had indeed slept at their mother's. Then conversation came to a dead halt again until Conor seemed to remember he should probably ask his brother how he was doing.

George told Conor he was "hangin' in there," which in the Bailey family was as close as anyone ever came to saying, "my entire world is falling apart. I doubt I'll survive this."

Conor nodded. "You aren't crooked anymore. Feeling better?"

"Luke. The healer. Mom insisted."

Conor nodded again. "Maybe I'll call him."

George wondered if something was wrong with Conor but didn't ask. They fumbled a few more minutes with a few more half-finished conversations before giving up and saying goodbye.

When Conor was nearly at the front door, George remembered his really big news. He was terrified at the prospect, since he had no idea what he was going to do next. Still, after the shock and trepidation of last evening wore off, he realized he was a little bit excited. "Oh, hey. I forgot to tell you, I'm quitting," he shouted.

Both Conor and Vito turned. In unison, their eyes widened. Conor bounded back over to him and yanked his brother's arm. Having only been pain free for nine hours, George did not appreciate the assault.

"This is how you tell me?" Conor raged when they were back at the bank of elevators.

Two brothers who never fussed or made waves or really even talked, had now managed to have not one but two tense outbursts

in the lobby of their building in front of the doorman. This
accomplished, they rode up to Conor's sixteenth floor apartment in
silence, which was not unusual for them, but this silence was fraught
with tension. When they were through his door, Conor pointed at
the couch and George sat.

George hadn't been in his brother's apartment in a long time.
When they were together outside of the office, it was at George's place,
or his parents'. As a single man, Conor was never expected to host or
even ever cook anything. Showing up with a bottle of wine was as
much as was ever required of Conor. But as George looked around, he
realized his brother was quite capable of hosting a family party.

George had forgotten what a nice apartment his brother had.
It was much smaller than his, still, it was huge for the city. It was a
corner apartment with a large wraparound terrace and views right
onto Washington Square. Conor had great taste, too. The place was
modern and masculine, with its tailored sofa and glass and chrome
coffee table, but it also had colorful, fun touches. Tara might have
gone so far as to use the word whimsical to describe the room.

Whimsical was not a word George used. Were he to start using
the word, it would not be in reference to his restrained brother. Still,
there it was. The whimsical room. As George looked at the polka dot
pillow on the side chair, the bright, Pop Art print above the mantle,
and the yellow art glass vase, he thought for maybe the thousandth
time, *I don't know my brother at all, and I doubt that will ever change.*

"You quit?"

George explained what he really wanted was to sell the business,
but since Mommy wouldn't let him, he was quitting instead.

Consternated, Conor scratched his forehead. His expression,
stern yet loving, reminded George of his own countenance when
the kids were little, and he was doing his best to remain tough while

reprimanding them for some wrongdoing. "Let me see if I've got this straight," he sighed. "On the day we buried our father, you told our mother that you planned to destroy everything he spent his entire life building. Is that it?"

"If you're going to put it that way," George said.

"George, even if Mom would let you sell, I wouldn't. I don't want to let it go."

This was Conor being contrary. If it was George's idea, of course it had to be a bad one. But George was convinced his brother secretly wanted to sell. Conor had grown irritable, sharp, and as moody as George. The problem was obvious. He, too, felt stuck hawking Christmas ornaments twelve months of the year.

"Let's forget about this," Conor said. "This is not the day for you to be making this kind of major decision. Because you are in shock and not yourself."

George couldn't argue about being in shock. He was. But whether or not he was being "himself" was a more complicated question. He was fairly certain he'd never let anyone see the real George before, not even Tara. George wasn't even sure who the real George was anymore. But today he felt like he was getting closer to figuring out not only who he was, but also who he wanted to be. He was taking baby steps, but it still felt empowering. George thought maybe he should read a self-help book. Or maybe he should write one. Maybe that would be his next career. *Maybe...* Maybe he was getting ahead of himself.

"I'm sorry about you and Tara."

George nodded self-consciously. He never talked with Conor about really personal things. They never shared their *feelings*. While George wanted to change many things, he wasn't sure he wanted to change that. George blamed too many of his problems on the business, but in the case of his increasingly impersonal relationship with Conor, he did think some of that could rightly be blamed on the strain of their time spent at Bailey and Sons.

The brothers were together at work fifty hours a week. During that time, they talked about orders and designs and manufacturing, and which clients were coming in that day, or week, or month. After talking to him for fifty hours, George didn't want to talk to him anymore. George didn't want to see him outside of work. They shared holidays and birthdays, but when they were not in the showroom, they had very little contact. They were great coworkers. Great business partners. But as brothers and friends, they were failures.

"I have to ask you something, George. It's kind of important." His brother's voice was shaking. "You won't be angry if I'm still friendly with Tara, right? You don't expect me to pick a side, do you?"

That was exactly what George expected Conor to do, but before he could make that point clear, his brother continued. "I hardly have any clear memories of my life before meeting her. I was twelve when the two of you started dating. I've always known her. She's always been my..." He ran out of steam and sank down beside George on the sofa.

They glanced at each other, and George saw pain and regret in Conor's eyes. At that moment, he felt like he knew Conor's darkest secret. Maybe, if George were to be honest, he'd always suspected this about his brother. He just never wanted to acknowledge it.

George didn't know what to make of this. He wasn't exactly angry. He found the situation too tragic to be annoyed by it. And really, what did it matter now? He recalled all the times when Conor stayed late after parties, supposedly helping Tara clean up, but really because he wanted to be alone with her. He always sent her notes and gifts on her birthday. George's birthdays, on the other hand, usually passed without much fanfare. George had always dismissed his suspicions as foolishness and never discussed them with anyone, not even Tara. But seeing Conor looking so dejected as he spoke of her, it seemed what George had always suspected was true.

Conor was obviously in love with Tara and had been for a long time. She was probably his first crush, and he'd never let go of the dream of a life with her. This explained why he so infrequently dated, and why the women he *did* date were never quite right, and the relationships never lasted. Conor was thirty-nine. He was handsome and smart and successful and straight, and he was still a bachelor.

Not wanting to embarrass Conor or make him feel any more miserable than he clearly already felt, George ignored his hunch. He didn't see any point in asking Conor if he loved Tara. It wouldn't change anything. He tried to smile, but he didn't quite manage it. George's lips curled upward slightly into what he hoped was not a sneer. Finally, George shook his head. "I'd never ask you to choose between us."

The ridges in Conor's forehead smoothed in relief, and the brothers sat in companionable silence, which was only broken when George finally worked up the nerve to ask his brother if he'd ever had an otherworldly experience like the one he'd had last evening.

"Conor, do you ever see Nan?"

"What do you mean, like in my dreams?"

George regretted asking the question. He was hoping to avoid discussing embarrassing, personal things, but it was too late now. He stammered, "No. Not in your dreams, in real life. Last night I think maybe she was cradling me in her arms."

"You saw her?" Conor asked warily. When George admitted

he had not seen her, that it was just a feeling he'd had, Conor said, "George, you were dreaming."

"I'm not so sure."

"Yes. You were," he said firmly.

And even though George knew Conor had to be right, he continued to stubbornly insist he had been wide awake for the entire session and could not possibly have been dreaming. He did not, however, mention that he'd smelled rosewater.

"I'm a little worried about you. This is too much stress for you to deal with alone. It would be for anyone. Maybe you should see a doctor."

"I would, but I no longer have one. Remember?"

Conor stared down at his feet and mumbled, "Not that kind of doctor. A therapist."

"I don't need a therapist. Just because the ghost of our dead grandmother cradled me in her arms last night, it doesn't make me crazy!"

"Yeah, George. It kind of does."

He laughed nervously. And George joined him, but neither of them found the moment the least bit amusing.

EIGHT

As much as George was loath to admit it, Dennis Day was instrumental in making his transition into a new life, or at least a new home, as painless as it possibly could be.

George was still at Conor's defending his sanity when his cell rang. Since George didn't have Dennis's contact information programmed into his phone and couldn't tell who it was, he answered.

"Dude, I rented you an apartment. Pack some clothes. You don't need anything else."

Who would do such a thing, even if they were friends—and as far as George was concerned, they were not. "You did what?" he shouted.

"Please. No need to thank me. My neighbor is going back

to LA for six months. She is leaving today, and her subletter just backed out of the lease. The place is huge, it's furnished, and the rent is way under market. It will give you six months to figure out your next step."

George agreed to take the place because the apartment was near Columbia, which to his there-is-no-world-above-14ᵗʰ-Street way of thinking was almost as far away as Europe. Therefore, he was confident he'd never run into Tara. Also, his children lived uptown. Assuming they ever talked to him again, he wouldn't be lonely. Aside from the whole being-alone-for-the-first-time-in-his-life thing, the only negative was that the new home came with Dennis as his next-door neighbor.

George made a quick pit stop at his apartment. Tara was out, which both relieved and frustrated him. He left her a note telling her he was moving out so she could stay put, and he hastily packed a few things. Walking out of the building with two suitcases and one MetroCard, it crossed his mind that Conor must be right. He was crazy. He had lived his entire life in two different Manhattan apartments which were a mere six blocks away from each other. Why hadn't he lived in a dorm in college? At least then he could claim three domiciles spread over a less measly fifteen-block radius.

People who are not from New York think of it as one of the biggest cities in the world—the Big Apple, the Center of the Universe! And while, of course, it is densely populated, in some ways, few places have more of a small town feel than Manhattan does. Where else could you happily live your whole life without travelling more than ten blocks away from home?

Certainly you can go farther afield and really experience all that the city has to offer. You could even catch a baseball game if you were willing to travel to another borough. But why not watch it on TV in the comfort of your home, or at the local bar? Within five blocks of most every Manhattan apartment, there are at least a dozen decent restaurants and a deli and a dry cleaner and a post office and a library and a nail place and a hair salon and a gym. So there's no need to go visit any other neighborhood if you don't want to.

At least George never thought there was.

And so, as he ventured uptown, George found himself—a native New Yorker—in serious need of a *Fodor's Guide*. He had been to the Upper West Side before, of course. May graduated from Columbia and still lived in the neighborhood. Brian was in his last year at the university, and had a room in the dorms. Tara and George had visited occasionally and helped move them both, but when he saw his children, it was generally because they'd come downtown to visit.

It was noon when he got on the 1 train. Despite the off-peak hour, the subway car was inexplicably packed. He stood next to an elderly woman who was barely tall enough to clasp her hand around the metal rod overhead. Even though George was also standing, he felt ashamed on behalf of all the young, stalwart passengers with seats who were avoiding the woman's glare. She was pressed into him and was complaining that she'd waited seventeen minutes for the train because of a "police investigation" at Canal Street.

"You know," said a man invisible to George, though he suspected they were standing back to back, "Police investigation is usually code for somebody jumped onto the tracks."

"Or was pushed," suggested a young Asian woman, who sat directly in front of George. She had an infant strapped to her chest, so he had given her a pass on not standing for the old lady. "It happens all the time," she insisted.

"No, it really doesn't. It's just that anytime someone is pushed onto the tracks there is a huge amount of press coverage," explained the invisible man. "But the jumpers—*the suicides.*" His voice ratcheted up precipitously, and he suddenly sounded much less rational than he had seconds earlier. "People are killing themselves out here every day, but *They* don't want us to know about it!" George felt certain if he could see this man, he'd have tinfoil wrapped around his head so *They* would be unable to read his thoughts.

George's heart raced not only because he had a lunatic standing right behind him, but also because he was pressed so close to the woman with the baby, he feared both he and her newborn would be in her arms with one ill-timed jolt.

He had one suitcase between his legs and the other pulled tightly against his chest, yet still he was aware of animosity from his fellow riders. He was hogging space. On all sides, flesh was pressed against him. He could barely breathe. There was not going to be a fire—at least that's what George kept telling himself. But if there were one, he'd never escape. Surely he'd be trampled to death, his meager belongings trodden upon in the resulting melee.

Just then, the baby started to howl. George felt terrible for the trapped little boy, who, like him, had clearly developed claustrophobia at an early age, and who, also like George, was probably hungry and in serious need of a nap. But then it occurred to George that this baby had it awfully good. No responsibilities. No mistakes or regrets to incessantly ponder. He was still a clean slate. This child's father was likely still alive, which was more than George could say. George was also fairly confident the baby did not yet have a cheating wife, which was also more than George could say. Really, what did this brat have to cry about?

"Cheer up, kid. Trust me, it only gets worse!"

Had George believed in God, he would have happily sworn on

a stack of Bibles that he only *thought* those words. However, based on the ensuing jeers he received from his fellow travelers, he must have actually given voice to his rant. The old lady, to whom he would have instantly given his seat if he'd had one to give, stepped on his foot.

"What kind of sicko are you?" asked the invisible man in the tinfoil hat. "He's just a little baby. Are you crazy?"

This was the second person today to question his mental health. In contrast to Conor, however, something told George this guy had more experience with psychiatric treatment, so he was probably an authority on the subject.

Takes one to know one, buddy!

George waited for an angry response, but luckily this time he had kept his thoughts to himself.

By the time he arrived at the 110th Street stop, the crowds had thinned and his claustrophobia had abated. The woman with the baby was still on the train, so he was keeping his distance and staring out the doors to avoid eye contact. The invisible man had exited without George ever laying eyes on him, and the old lady had disembarked at 96th Street, shaking her head in disgust as she walked along the platform.

His new home was located on Riverside Drive at the corner of 114th Street. George was awed when he walked through the main door of the building and glimpsed the lobby. The ceilings were at least twenty feet high, and the floor and walls were made out of a marble unlike any he had ever seen before—white with emerald and maroon veins running through it.

But his initial positive impression quickly dimmed. On closer inspection, the marble had been sorely neglected, dusty and marred with chips and cracks. The massive bronze chandelier that dominated the center of the space was missing more than half its bulbs. The few remaining were harsh yellow fluorescents, which might explain why George initially thought the doorman was suffering from jaundice.

He attempted to introduce himself to the sickly-looking man behind the reception desk and let him know he was a new tenant, but the doorman just pointed at the elevator and said, "Fourteen. You better get up there now."

George didn't think it was possible to have dodgier elevators than the ones in his former building, but this one wheezed asthmatically as it slowly made its ascent. The building skipped from floor twelve straight to fourteen, as if those who believed in bad omens would somehow be tricked by this ruse.

George was generally not a superstitious man, but he did think that in light of his recent string of luck, it might be unwise moving to the thirteenth floor of a building, whether or not they were attempting to pass it off as the fourteenth. Only two apartments were on the alleged fourteenth floor. The door to 14B was open, and five unmatched suitcases were strewn across the landing, as if they had been jettisoned from a burning building.

"Finally. Thank God!" George heard the words but could not see the woman who'd exclaimed them. "Do you play?"

He had always wanted to play an instrument but had neither the patience nor the talent to learn. He was still on the threshold of the apartment. While she had spoken, she had not actually presented herself or offered any sort of a proper greeting, so he merely stuck his head in for a peek while keeping his feet firmly planted outside. He didn't see her, but based on what he did see, Dennis had not been exaggerating. The place was huge. The apartment had the largest entrance hallway he had ever seen in his life. In the center of the vestibule, a Ping-Pong table was set up with plenty of room to spare on all sides.

Just then she appeared with a bag over each shoulder and Ping-Pong paddles in her hands. Her brown hair, streaked through with gray, hung almost to her waist. She wore a bomber jacket, jeans, and black boots that gleamed from a recent polishing.

"Well? Come in!" She seemed surprised a stranger had not just barged in uninvited. "I'm Susie," she smiled. "Susan on the checks. You have first and last for me, right? I hate to be abrupt." She may have hated to be abrupt, but based on this brief exchange, she was quite skilled at it.

George placed the checks on the Ping-Pong table and Susie handed him the keys. "You're saving me," Susie said. "Oh, do you play? Because here are the paddles."

"You want to play right now?"

"I'm leaving in two minutes. I meant you should feel free to use the table. Or just fold it up if it's in your way. Or... Hey, I'm not the type to be coy. Dennis told me about your wife." Knowing Dennis, George assumed he hadn't skipped any of the details. "I guess we're saving each other. Believe me, I get it. *I so get it!* I took this LA gig because of my ex." She sighed and dropped the paddles on the table. "That reminds me, she calls sometimes."

"She?"

"My ex. But not often. Not more than once a week. And only when she's drunk. Basically if the phone rings at three in the morning, don't answer it. You have the keys. Dennis knows all the quirks about this building and my apartment. He loves Ping-Pong, so you're in luck. I have to dash. George, let's wish each other luck on our new starts."

"Good luck, Susie."

She nodded warmly. He dropped his two small bags in the giant foyer and began closing the door.

"George. I could get all my shit into this elevator in three trips, or you could help me and we could do it in one."

He offered to go down to the curb with Susie, but what with her and all the luggage, George couldn't get in the elevator. He was relieved, as all that weight seemed like more than the dying elevator could carry. He stayed behind, watching the doors close before going back into his new home to explore.

The hallway was not the only large area. He thought he had lived in a big apartment before, but this place was massive. It was also falling apart. The kitchen must have undergone a major renovation sometime in the 70s, because the appliances were all harvest gold. There was a formal dining room with a very warped parquet floor, a living room, four bedrooms and three and a half baths.

Based on the abundance of turquoise and peace signs, and the fact that not a single piece of furniture matched another, George decided Susie's decorating scheme had been Yard Sale, meets New Mexico meets The Grateful Dead. A Woodstock poster hung over the mantle in the living room, and something told him she'd actually attended the event. Susie had apparently never heard of the invention of the coaster, because rings dotted every single surface in the house, excluding the Ping-Pong table. Above each of the four toilets were tiny handwritten signs stating: *If it's yellow let it mellow; if it's brown flush it down.* Those would have to go.

Susie had completely emptied the contents from the closet and dressers in one of the bedrooms, so George took that room for his own. From it, George could see Riverside Park and the Hudson and New Jersey in the distance. He unpacked his clothing and toiletries, which took less than ten minutes. Susie had stacked clean sheets and towels on the bed. The gesture was thoughtful, but the linens were old and worn, and the sight of them made him sad, though he could not explain why.

Actually everything about this place made him sad. For starters, the apartment was too big, something no true New Yorker ever says about real estate. But the size of this place accentuated the fact that he was alone. He would have been happier in a studio. Okay, that's a lie, but a one bedroom would have been perfect. This place was meant to house a family. A couple should have lived here. A couple with children, and a dog, maybe even a cat. At the very least, some fish.

George would have gone to bed right then, but he didn't want to use those sheets. And even if he would have used them, he felt like the task of making the bed was beyond him. Also, it was only two-thirty in the afternoon, and going to bed then seemed pathetic even in his current state. He sat on the naked mattress, staring out the window, taking in the view of a darkening sky as black storm clouds began rolling in.

What is the point of living in New York, he wondered, *if all you see when you look out your window is New Jersey?*

NINE

It was still afternoon, but the day's brief period of sun had already begun to wane. George challenged himself to get up, go out, explore the neighborhood, and come home with new bedding.

Eventually he did get up. He did go out. He made it as far as Broadway, and walked into a bar. This was not his typical sort of behavior, but neither was staring off at the distant shores of Jersey for hours at a stretch. He could not recall the last time he had been in a bar. He was more of a glass-or-two-of-a-really-exceptional-red-with-dinner kind of guy.

Still, he went into the bar because it was raining, and Christmas trees were for sale everywhere, and up ahead stood two impossibly cheery guys from the Salvation Army, ringing their bells and shamelessly guilting passersby into generosity. Besides, he was never going to find sheets to his liking in this neighborhood anyway.

So he ducked inside to get away from all the holiday spirit. But even ponied up to the bar, George could not escape Christmas. Cheap silver garland festooned with tiny red bows hung limply around the perimeter of the ancient mahogany bar. George could live with this nod to the holidays, but *It's a Wonderful Life* was playing on the flat screen suspended above the bartender's head. It was his first encounter with his nemesis this year, though undoubtedly there would be others. And as more and more people enjoyed their hundredth viewing of the movie and made the connection between George the character from the film and George the real guy who sold Christmas ornaments for a living, the jokes at his expense would begin again. Fittingly, George had entered the bar just at the moment Jimmy Stewart, frantically stuttering, walked into Martini's.

Curiously, this bar and its antique ringing cash register looked a lot like Martini's. But unlike his namesake on screen, who was desperately trying to be recognized by his fellow patrons, George was glad to be treated like a stranger. The place was dead at four in the afternoon. There was only one other customer, a young blonde woman—or rather a woman around George's age, which he realized was no longer young. She was sitting at the other end of the bar.

He didn't have the obsession with blondes some guys had. Tara had more Mediterranean looks, so he'd always considered that to be his type. But the blonde hair was striking, and it more than suited her. It hung to her shoulders and partially obscured her profile. She was wearing a dress too fashionable for this seedy joint. Her bare legs were long, crossed, and pointed toward him. The pose was sultry if a little studied.

She was perched on one quarter of one butt cheek, and he couldn't imagine how she managed to sit like that without falling off the stool. It was truly a marvel of engineering. Just then she flicked her hair back behind her ear, offering him a better look at her face. She was beautiful, though he tried not to notice. He glanced at her again, two more times, actually. Aside from those surreptitious looks, he kept his eyes on his Manhattan, swirling the cherry in his glass.

Though George's father imbibed infrequently, if he did have a cocktail in the winter, it was a Manhattan—*never more than one, son.* On a special occasion in the summer, he might have a gimlet instead. George always had a bottle of gin at home for his father, but Daddy usually stuck to seltzer because he was always in training.

About ten years ago, George started buying expensive wines because Tara enjoyed it. She enjoyed the collecting more than the drinking. Her only caveat was they could never own more than twenty-four bottles at a given time, which was the maximum number of bottles their wine rack held.

George didn't recall how it began, but at some point he realized they had bonded over the snobbishness of acquiring rare vintages they learned about in *Wine Spectator*. Aside from their shared love of their children, they seemed to have little else in common. But Tara took delight in the fact that he could keep a straight face while opining on the grassiness of an Oregon sauvignon blanc. She was heartened by his uncanny knack for detecting faint hints of chocolate in a Napa Valley cab.

What she never knew was that before George took his first sip, he did Google searches to find out what people who actually possessed discerning palates had to say about the vintages. Only then did he offer his own opinions, or theirs rather.

"Don't you love this movie? A classic."

The woman was no longer at the end of the bar, though she was not next to George, either. She had left two stools between them. Though she had moved, she was still perched in the same, remarkable glamour-girl pose. Perhaps she was hoping he would think she'd always been sitting there and had not made this bold, yet furtive move in his direction if she maintained her exact posture.

He looked at the woman and she smiled. She *was* beautiful, no question about that. But now that she was closer, she seemed a little lost, or maybe she was just tired, or maybe he was projecting his own feelings onto her.

She'd spoken, but he hadn't registered what she'd said. He wasn't accustomed to women he didn't know talking to him, and he was thrown. Raising her wine glass, she gestured toward the TV.

Oh, right. The movie. "You ever wonder *why* it's a classic?" he asked.

"It just is," she declared, confident of this irrefutable truth.

"I don't deny that it is. *But how did that happen? Seriously.* Why would Americans embrace this movie and turn it into a holiday *classic*, as you say?"

"It's so heartwarming."

"If attempted suicide is your idea of heartwarming, then indeed it is."

She looked at him as if he had said the most shocking thing imaginable, but then she unleashed an utterly unexpected sounding laugh. It was as far from a titter as it possibly could be, residing right on the border of snort. Her laugh was throaty, unselfconscious, and it charmed him. To his delight, her laugh was not ladylike. It didn't at all match her posture. He found the contrast between the sound and the picture beguiling, because a howl like that was not meant to come out of the mouth of a woman who sat like a starlet. And something amazing happened to George that very moment. Something deep inside him, long in hibernation, woke up.

George leaned in closer to her, aiming to bridge the gap between their stools. He gazed at her and as he did so, he stunned himself, because he realized he was being flirtatious, which was not a way he ever behaved. As a married man, he avoided that sort of thing to keep himself out of trouble. Not that it was difficult for him to refrain from playing the lothario; he was about as far from being a playboy as was possible. It had been ages since he had even flirted with his wife. "You know what I think?" he asked, his voice deepening noticeably.

"Well, I think you're going to tell me what you think," she said, lightly mocking him as she smiled. Even George, as clueless as he was about such things, could tell she was interested in him and what he had to say, so he smiled right back at her.

"I think ninety-nine percent of people have either jumped off a bridge or have thought about doing it."

She blanched and frowned slightly. "You have any statistics to back up that bold statement, mister?"

"What are you, a scientist?"

"Just an educated consumer."

"It's only a theory, as yet to be tested or proven. If you think this is too personal, you don't have to answer me." He leaned in even closer. He was trying to appear dashing, but he nearly tumbled from his stool, so he straightened back up again. "Have *you* ever thought about it? I don't necessarily mean seriously, and there need not be an actual bridge involved. I'm talking about the passing thought. You know one of those *They'll be sorry when I'm gone* kind of moments."

"I'm alone in a bar at four o'clock on a Tuesday. What do you think?"

It did occur to George that talking about wanting to kill yourself was perhaps not the smartest way to go about wooing a woman, but there was no turning back now. "Excellent! Not that you have suicidal tendencies," he added quickly. "But, I, too, have had these thoughts. Fleeting, thankfully. But nonetheless I've had them. So we are two for two in our research. Should I ask the bartender?"

They both looked at the hunched man, his hand clenched around the handle of a paring knife, cutting lemons into perfect triangles. His brow was furrowed and his eyes had glazed and crossed from his intense focus on the mundane task.

She smiled at George again, this time more wistfully. "I think we can safely say that you're three for three. I accept the theory. At some point, everyone has thought about ending it all. Please continue."

"Thank you. We are all desperate. We all want to be rescued. But most of us don't dive off the bridge because we know there won't really be an angel there to catch us."

She interrupted. "Technically it's the other way around. George rescues Clarence."

"Are you going to be difficult? Because nobody likes a stickler," he teased. Amazed at how easy he found bantering with this woman, George considered the possibility that his body had been taken over by an alien from a planet where the males were born confident, and well versed in reparteé. He downed the last of his drink. Popped the cherry in his mouth. Meanwhile, she assured him she wanted him to continue. "George is as miserable as you and I are. He's more miserable, probably. *Hopefully*. But unlike the rest of us, George Baily gets saved in the end. That's why the movie became a classic. It's a fantasy."

Her eyes filled with tears he did not understand, and she blinked them away. "You don't believe in salvation?"

He thought talking about redemption and his spiritual doubts might be an even worse strategy for seduction than talking about suicide. Instead of answering her, he motioned to the bartender, making a circle with his finger large enough to include his new female friend. "May we have another round, please?"

She graciously refused his offer a couple of times before ultimately accepting. The bartender delivered the drinks without saying a word. Returning to his chores, he picked his knife back up and moved onto the limes. George's new friend was drinking white wine. Considering the jug the bartender poured it from, he assumed he'd never read about this particular vintage in *Wine Spectator*. With her chardonnay in hand, she moved to the stool beside him for the obligatory toast and clinking of glasses.

"I'm Carolyn."

"George."

She glanced at the man on screen who was at that moment clutching Zuzu's petals. "Like Bailey?"

"Exactly."

"So what's your last name? George what?"

"Bailey."

"Very funny." She waited. "Are you really not going to tell me?"

This had happened to him before—the doubters. Like anyone would ever pretend they were named George Bailey. Over the years, he had learned it was best not to argue. He pulled out his wallet and handed her his driver's license. "What do you have to say for yourself?"

She looked at his face. She looked at the information on his license, back and forth several times. "Wow. You look older than that." He would have scowled, but she followed up the insult with her laugh. And so he laughed too, even though he knew she wasn't kidding. George did look older than he was. Discontented men with receding hairlines rarely look youthful.

He looked into her eyes, holding her gaze longer than... It's not correct to say longer than he should have, because he had every right to stare. But he certainly never imagined he would be doing such a thing so soon after separating from Tara. This had to be an enormous mistake which could only lead to more heartbreak.

There were rules about such things, weren't there? He should be waiting a year, or was it six months? Whatever it was, it was longer than five days. But maybe those rules only applied if you were a widower. Was there a different protocol when you got dumped? Certainly there had to be.

Still, only five days later, and when the bulk of those days had been taken up burying your father? He seriously considered pulling out his smart phone and conferring with Google. He might have had he been able to take his eyes off her for even a second. And so he looked and looked at Carolyn until he felt his cheeks heat up, and then he self-consciously averted his glance. He hoped if she noticed the ruddiness in his complexion, she'd think it was the booze flushing him.

"Do you often meet women in bars?"

He shook his head diffidently. He tried finding the confident alien who'd possessed him only moments earlier, but he'd returned to his home planet. "And you?" he mumbled. "Men?"

"Never," she insisted.

He wasn't sure he believed her, but then he doubted she believed him.

"Do you think this is going to end up with us sleeping together?" she asked. George was relieved he had not been taking a sip of his Manhattan at that moment, because sweet vermouth and bitters would now be spraying in her direction. He couldn't tell from her tone whether she had any interest in sleeping with him or not. Either way, he was flustered.

This was all happening too fast for George. He was happily married last week. His wife wasn't, but he was. He thought he was. He pretended he was. He held up his left hand, displaying the wedding band he was still wearing on his ring finger. "I'm married."

"Yes. I had already seen the ring. That doesn't really answer my question."

Obviously he liked this forward stranger, so he decided to backpedal a bit with his answer. "Actually I'm only *technically* married. We're getting a divorce."

"How long have you been separated?"

George glanced at his watch.

Again, he was rewarded with her big, earthy laugh. "Wow. That long, huh?"

He could make her laugh. He was funny when he spoke to her, or she thought so at any rate. Being funny and engaging was so much more enjoyable than the way he usually presented himself to the world. *Hi I'm George, dour guy with a chip on my shoulder. What's your name?*

But despite the fact that he had managed to find some inner effervescence in this woman's company, it was still only five days. "You know, you are so beautiful," he said, leaving the *but* unspoken.

"We're heading for a no."

"I'm still married. I have two children. I am, as you already know, forty-three—"

"I'm forty-four," she said. "Too old for you?"

"Of course not. No. This has nothing to do with you. You're gorgeous. And I like the way you laugh. And a part of me thinks we should get out of here right now. But there are no sheets on my bed, and I'm profoundly unhappy."

"About the sheets?"

He felt a smile coming on, but he squashed it. "Well, yes, as a matter of fact. Unfortunately the state of my linens is not the only thing distressing me. My father just died."

She offered condolences, which he appreciated receiving, but he'd shared the news of his dad's passing for another reason. "It's not that I thought I was immortal before, but now I hear the clock ticking so loudly, it's deafening. There's so little time. Even before he died, I wasn't exactly..." Letting the maudlin thought go, he raised his glass and took a sip of his drink before making a different confession. "Recently I went shopping for a sports car."

"Okay," she said bemused, yet amused, by the non sequitur.

"A Jag."

"Really?" She was either impressed or appalled; he wasn't sure which.

"You know why I didn't buy one?"

"Because they cost like a million dollars?"

"No. Because I wasn't sure how to pronounce it. Are there two syllables because I'm an American, or three, because it's a British car? I didn't think it was crazy to spend a hundred grand on a toy I don't need; I never go anywhere. But I couldn't wrap my head around the fact that I didn't know how to say the word, and I was too embarrassed to ask anyone if it was Jaguar or, you know, Jag— You—Are," he said, affecting a passable English accent. "So I didn't buy it. I hung around for a while hoping someone would say the name, but the salesman kept saying Jag, so I left. Maybe he didn't know how to pronounce it either."

"I can see how that must have been a horrible ordeal for you," she quipped.

"Believe it or not, I'm not as spoiled as that makes me sound. But that's not the only disturbing thing I've done recently. I've taken to wearing expensive suits with sneakers but no tie, like I'm—"

"Ellen DeGeneres?"

He nodded. "I was going to say a player, but sure." He did not dare tell her the worst of it. The day before Thanksgiving, just before his entire world fell apart, he downloaded a brochure from The Hair Club for Men.

"And now I find myself sitting in a bar, of all places, with a strange woman. You're lovely, but you're a stranger."

He thought she was going to say something, so he held up his hand. He really needed to end this craziness. He didn't want to end things with her. But…five days was too fast, and obviously a mistake. "You're so beautiful. I keep saying it, but that's only because it's true. But we're strangers." He took another sip of his Manhattan. "Sleeping with a stranger right now, bad idea for me. I mean I ask you, what could possibly make my mid-life crisis more clichéd?"

"I could be nineteen."

George laughed. He liked that she could make him laugh.

"Yes. You could be nineteen. And I'm so glad you're not. Because if you were, you'd be younger than my children. I started early. Anyway for all these reasons, and so many more, this man walked into a bar today. This is something I don't do. I don't know the man you are talking to, but it's not really me. I suppose the one great thing about you being a total stranger is that I feel free to tell you the truth. If I actually knew you, I would never be this honest."

He was quiet for a minute, taking in this lovely and mysterious woman. She looked weary and lonely despite her beauty. He knew why he was in a bar in the afternoon, but he wondered why she was. He worried that she might sit alone in a bar in the afternoon on a regular basis. "Why do you find yourself here having a drink with me when instead you could be Christmas shopping?"

Carolyn wrapped her long fingers around the stem of her glass. "My husband," she said.

He waited a second for her to elaborate, but she remained silent. He had already noticed she wasn't wearing a wedding band. "He left you?"

"You could say that. He killed himself. Today is the second anniversary of his death."

And for one brief, shining moment, George realized what a complete narcissistic asshole he was capable of being. "Oh shit. I am so sorry. I'm such a jerk. And..." he stammered and flushed and wished he could disappear. "I can't believe I said all that stuff about everyone wanting to kill themselves. It was—Jesus. I'm sorry."

"Don't be. It actually kind of cheered me up."

He looked at her incredulously. "How is that even remotely possible?"

She shrugged. "Maybe my husband was thinking he'd end up like George Bailey and someone would save him."

And then George Bailey, the one who was sitting at the bar talking to this magnificent woman, not the fictional character stuttering away on the TV, thought,

She's an optimist.

Oh no. I have been quasi-single for only five days. And the last time I was single, Ronald Reagan was president. So, okay, I have never been single. This is my chance to find out what it's like to be on my own, and I should grab it. I should. But, I think I might already love this woman.

This could be a problem.

Her glass of chardonnay was still half full. His drink, by contrast, was nearly empty.

TEN

BEFORE GEORGE HAD LEFT HIS new apartment, he hadn't noticed where the light switches were located. He stumbled around the vestibule in the dark, one hand straight out in front of him and the other shielding his balls, as he tried in vain to find the switch while endeavoring to avoid castration on the edge of the Ping-Pong table. Even though he felt some regret about leaving Carolyn in the bar without inviting her home, George was relieved she was not witnessing his blind fumbling.

After a few minutes of unsuccessful searching, he gave up and felt along the wall, hand over hand, until he found the entrance to the living room. He remembered seeing a floor lamp in there. The lights of New Jersey were casting a soft glow, and he easily found the lamp and turned it on. When the room was fully illuminated he walked back into the entry to locate the light switch. Oddly, it was on the wrong side of the door, so that when the front door was opened, it blocked access to the switches. Yet another of the apartment's fine design features.

He noticed a sheet of paper on top of the Ping-Pong table, picked it up and read.

> *Dude, (I actually don't even say dude that much but it's better than George, don't you think?)*
>
> *In case you ever get locked out, I have a spare set of keys to Susie's (your!) apartment— hence my ability to leave you this note.*
>
> *Where are you? I'm taking you out drinking tonight. No buts. I'm knocking on your door at 9:00. Will come in and drag you out if necessary.*
>
> *By the way, the place I'm taking you has great margaritas, but their food, with the exception of the guacamole, not so much. So unless you want your whole dinner to consist of chips and guac, eat something first.*
>
> *Dennis*
>
> *PS: FYI Hallway light switch inexplicably located on wrong side of door.*

George rarely went out drinking, and never twice in one day. He had no doubt Dennis would break in and drag him out if he objected. He could have run away and checked into a hotel, but that seemed excessive. He brushed his teeth, gargled, and went back out to grab some food before round two started. Even though he knew where the switch was now, he kept the light on in the foyer.

It was still raining. Broadway was clogged with hunched pedestrians wielding umbrellas like sabers. All of them struggled to maneuver around the Christmas trees and the poinsettias and the fruit stands as they made their way to apartments or restaurants or gyms. The Salvation Army men were now off duty and had been replaced by two new ones. The extreme level of their cheerfulness managed to eclipse that of their predecessors. They clanged their bells loudly and caroled in full voice. George hoped this location wasn't going to be their permanent post until Christmas, but he had a feeling it would be.

A small crowd was gathered around them. Several passersby joined them in singing a jazzy version of *God Rest Ye Merry Gentleman*. People threw money into the bucket at such a fast clip, George wondered if everyone had forgotten the nation was still in the midst of a never-ending recession. As he slunk by, his money still safely in his wallet, somebody shouted "Happy Holidays," which is what everyone says in New York instead of Merry Christmas because, being the original melting pot city, New Yorkers understand the whole world is not made up of Christians.

Though George did not respond in kind, he did smile. Notwithstanding his personal feelings about the season, he didn't want to be taken for a Scrooge. Besides, he had not yet lost all of his humanity. If the Salvation Army men had hoisted Tiny Tim onto their shoulders, he certainly would have coughed up something for the new crutches, even as he berated them for exploiting a minor.

George never should have had two Manhattans on an empty stomach—actually, he might have had a third. He thought about blurting out *I love you!* but he was pretty sure he hadn't done that. Instead of making a declaration of his feelings—and an ass out of himself—he might have ordered a third drink, but it was all a tad fuzzy now. His head hurt, and his mouth was dry. He was hungry and a little woozy.

Pizza was definitely in order. He remembered a spot he had been to once with Brian. It was farther downtown and on the east side of Broadway, so he crossed the street and continued walking. He couldn't remember the restaurant's name, but he knew he would find it. In addition to the kind of pizza a normal person would eat, they also made "healthy" pies with whole-wheat crust and soy cheese. He had no intention of ordering that kind. He was going to have two slices with sausage and maybe some mushrooms, that way at least he would have one vegetable today. Take that, Tara.

He stopped at the crosswalk waiting for the light, and in the next block, he recognized the awning for the pizza parlor. *Café Viva*, the sign read. His phone vibrated in his pants. It was a text from Dennis Day filled with smiley faces and LOLs, and the prediction that they would be having fun tonight!

George put his phone back into his pocket, so for a moment he was looking down at himself. When he looked back up, he was not alone. A young man stood not more than two inches in front of him. George gasped and jumped back. His response to the young man's sudden appearance was every bit as exaggerated as Tara's would have been.

"I'm sorry, sir. I didn't mean to startle you." The young man smiled sheepishly. His thick dark hair was parted on the side. His eyes were deep brown and unless his blinking was somehow synchronized with George's, he wasn't. He gazed intently at George, who found this comforting instead of creepy for some inexplicable reason. George could not say how he knew him or from where, but the young man looked dimly familiar to him. Maybe he just had one of those faces.

The rain had stopped, and George closed his umbrella, still trying to figure out whether or not he knew this young man. Looking at him more closely, George decided they had never met. He also noticed that the young man was totally dry in spite of the recent rain. He must have stepped out from a doorframe seconds earlier, George supposed.

"May I ask you a favor," the young man began.

Here we go.

Generally, this is when New Yorkers braced themselves for the scam. *My wallet was stolen and I need $26.75 to buy a bus ticket to get back to Maryland.* It's always an odd amount to provide the ring of authenticity. This is when the jaded urbanite always looked for the telltale signs of subterfuge.

There were only three possibilities: The person about to speak was either homeless or a grifter or a junkie. The grifters—the good ones anyway—were the hardest to spot. The junkies were often trembling, missing teeth, and smelled like they had recently pissed themselves. If this guy had been an addict, George wouldn't have even stopped for a second. He was not talking to a junkie.

This young man was wearing freshly laundered clothes. His fingernails were trimmed, and his sneakers were new. If he was a homeless guy, today was his first day on the street, because he was far too clean and healthy looking. He must have been about to lead up to a grift, but he didn't seem like a con man to George. Against his better judgment, George decided to hear him out.

"I thought maybe you were going to that pizza place," the young man said.

They were still half a block from Café Viva. It surprised George that he guessed his destination. Somewhat bewildered, George confirmed, that yes, Café Viva was where he was heading.

"I hate to ask, but would you buy me a slice of pizza? I'm kind of hungry."

Several times a day, every single day, homeless people asked him for a quarter, and George almost always said no. Actually, he did not even say no. He just ignored them, walking by as if he'd never seen or heard them.

He looked at the young man's kind, unblinking eyes and, surprising himself, said, "Sure, okay."

If this was a scam, the stakes were certainly not very high. He was willing to be fleeced out of the cost of a single slice of pizza if it meant he could prove to himself he still was compassionate enough to help someone in need. Besides, if his next question turned out to be *What's your pin number?* George would tell him to go screw himself.

There was another Christmas tree vendor right in front of the restaurant. The sidewalk, narrow to begin with, was now barely passable due to the rows of blue spruces and Douglas firs. They walked single file, and when they entered Viva, George marched alone to the counter, leaving the young man standing three feet behind him. He ordered two slices with sausage and mushrooms for himself, and one plain slice for the young man. He also ordered himself a seltzer to counter the dehydration from the afternoon booze. After paying, he went back to the young man, and waited for the slices to come out of the oven.

George felt awkward. All the questions he could think to ask this guy were rude or didn't really matter. For a second, he thought maybe the young man was a prostitute but quickly he ruled that theory out. Even George knew a hooker asks you to buy things other than pizza. And though his energy was disarmingly loving, it didn't seem particularly sexual. But George didn't consider himself a very good judge of that sort of thing. They stood side by side in silence. When they caught each other's glance, they would smile or nod. Once, the young man nodded and smiled simultaneously.

It was a very long four minutes.

When George saw their slices coming out of the oven, he dashed up to the counter to remind the pizza guy to bag the plain slice up separately. They weren't going to be dining together.

George came back to the young man and handed him his slice. The young man, who was extremely grateful, was smiling even wider now. George, discovering that he was also grateful, smiled too. This had not been a set up. This was just a hungry kid who was probably temporarily low on funds.

"Thank you," the young man said as George handed him the pizza. They both held the bag with the slice for a moment, and in that instant, the young man's unblinking, penetrating eyes made George feel he would strive to become a more caring and compassionate person in the future. *Hadn't Fr. Sal said something about the importance of kindness?*

"What's your name?" the young man asked.

"I'm George."

"George," he said, drawing out the word like it was something to be savored. "Thank you, George. I mean it. I will never forget you or your generosity."

A chill raced along George's spine. The young man turned and headed for the exit.

"Hey," George called back to him. He turned back around and George saw his glowing smile again.

"What's your name?"

"I'm Jesus," he said. And then he opened the door and walked out to the sidewalk.

George was fairly certain he was frozen for no more than three seconds. He dropped his order onto a table and ran out after the young man. He looked right and left, but he couldn't find him. Unless he really was Jesus, he couldn't have jaywalked over the barricade of Christmas trees in front, but he was gone. Vanished.

George walked back into Café Viva and sat down. He was shaking. He tried sipping his seltzer, but his hand trembled so that he couldn't raise the glass. The pizza looked good, and he knew he should eat. He stared at the slice, at the sausage and mushrooms, and felt profoundly uneasy. His thoughts raced.

If I had it to do over again, I definitely would have asked Jesus if he wanted toppings on his slice. And why didn't I offer to buy him a drink?

Hindsight.

ELEVEN

GEORGE WAS STILL STARING AT his uneaten slice, the cheese long since congealed, when Dennis texted again. Due to some behind the scenes drama on his reality show, Dennis was running late at the studio. So they agreed to meet at Margarita Nation, a student hangout where the conversations were loud but the mariachi band was louder.

Meeting the alleged Son of God had completely sobered George up. Also, having failed to eat anything at Café Viva, George was ravenous. Based on the plates of food passing by, the menu was not limited to authentic Mexican recipes. The onion rings looked quite good, but recalling Dennis's warnings with regard to the cuisine, George stuck to basics. A basket of chips and guacamole were in front of him. No matter how clear-headed he felt, he'd already had three cocktails today. Even as he reminded himself to slow down, he slurped his frozen margarita like it was limeade, which, in a way, it was.

Dennis arrived late. As he entered, George heard him chatting with the hostess in what sounded like, at least to George's gringo ears, proficient Spanish. They spoke for several minutes before Dennis kissed her on both cheeks and headed over to join George at the table. Before he even sat down, he managed to simultaneously apologize and insult George. "Stuff at work. Sorry. Some of us still have jobs, you know."

George ignored him. He was thinking about how much he really enjoyed drinks that came with straws. Dennis let him know that his show's first season had wrapped production, so he would have lots of free time to hang out with George over the next few months. And they'd been renewed for a second season, which meant Dennis was going to be living in New York for at least another year. He asked George how his day had been.

Where to begin? Today was action-packed. The highlights would undoubtedly include George telling a defenseless newborn on the subway to get a life, meeting a really awesome woman with a great laugh in a bar, and of course, buying the Son of God a slice. George made a mental note to self: Buy new sheets.

Since he had already been called crazy multiple times throughout the course of the day, he decided to lead with his least controversial story. "I met a girl today."

Dennis had just taken the first sip of his Margarita, and he choked and spit the drink back into his glass. "Get out of here!" He raised his hand for a high-five, but George pretended that he hadn't noticed. "*You* met a girl?"

It wasn't that surprising. Though as he talked about it aloud for the first time, he realized how excited he was by the prospect of a romance with this woman. While he had known love before, he certainly had not experienced courtship and all the nerves and excitement that went along with it for twenty-five years.

"What's her name?"

"Carolyn," he said. George leaned back in his chair, thinking of her and what the future might hold. He didn't say another word.

"Seriously, Dude. Can you paint the picture a little bit for me? Share the deets, please."

The first thing that came to mind was *Her husband killed himself.* But George didn't want to share that news with Dennis. It somehow seemed like betraying a confidence. And that information in no way conveyed what he found so appealing about her, or why he was so attracted to her. Okay, so aside from the fact that her husband killed himself, what else did he know? She had terrific legs, she was blonde and had an infectious laugh, and… what else? Shit. He didn't know anything about this woman. Reluctantly, he confessed that fact.

"When are you seeing her again?"

Never, he suddenly realized. George watched his burgeoning romance founder in front of his eyes. He didn't know her last name or her phone number or her email. And he didn't know these things because he never asked her for them. One minute he was thinking *I might be in love with this woman.* And the next, he was hopping up from his bar stool, shaking her hand and saying, "Nice meeting you." He walked out the door without so much as a kiss on the cheek.

Nice meeting you?

That was not clever, or original. Who says *'Nice meeting you?'* when they meet someone? He shoved a fist full of chips in his mouth and crunched noisily, taking out his frustrations on the defenseless corn as he tried to comprehend how he had managed to leave the bar without obtaining her contact information. He hadn't gotten that because he was too distracted by his fantasy of riding off into the sunset with a woman whose last name he did not know.

Dennis must have sensed his mounting hysteria. "Dude. George. Relax. You have a lot to learn. That's why I'm here. This was your first date of the twenty-first century, and it's not like you had much experience in the twentieth. You have a smartphone, correct?"

George nodded since his mouth was still too full to speak.

"Good. In the future always ask for phone and email. The woman you're interested in may not give her number to you, but you have to ask for it. You don't necessarily have to call her, but you have to get the number. In fact, it might help to start by hitting on women you're not interested in. This will give you practice and lessen the blow when she rejects you." He studied George, still noisily crunching corn chips, before adding, "which is going to happen. Often."

A waitress walked by, and Dennis flagged her down. She looked very much like Frida Kahlo, if Frida Kahlo had had two eyebrows and no limp. Dennis held up his nearly empty glass. "You guys do pitchers of these?"

George objected strongly. He'd already had way too much to drink. But when Dennis started telling the waitress how she needed to be "extra nice to George" because his wife fucked his best friend at his father's wake, he thought it wiser to acquiesce and send her on her way to the bar before she broke down and started crying "*pobrecito!*"

"We are getting you drunk tonight," Dennis insisted. "Have you been drunk in the last week?"

He had not been drunk since New Year's Eve 1999 and the Y2K Millennium madness. And he only got soused then because he got caught up in all the stories about the world coming to an end and computers breaking down, and traffic lights stopping and all that other nonsense.

All he remembered about the festivities was that he and Tara had stockpiled one case of Dom Perignon and twelve cases of Poland Spring. Between them, they drank three bottles of champagne but not a single one of water. In the morning, the electricity worked and the computers were fine. They, however, had suffered serious damage.

The waitress, smiling sympathetically at George, returned with the pitcher and topped off their glasses. George noticed other tables with pitchers, though they were all tables of four or six. As they clinked their glasses Dennis explained why they were going to get drunk. "Believe it or not, you haven't hit rock bottom yet."

That seemed impossible.

"And," Dennis carried on, "you must hit rock bottom. Tonight is the night that you will hit rock bottom."

How many times can he say rock bottom?

"And later, when you are sick and you are vomiting, you will thank me."

That also seemed impossible.

"And that is when you will finally have hit rock bottom."

Apparently, he could say it one more time.

"Besides, you need to get drunk because soon the day will come when you're ready to get laid again and you will be nervous and you will want to have a drink but you will remember how awful you felt tonight and so you won't. That is a good thing, because you have to remember every detail of that first sexual experience."

George had to admit what he said made a kind of sense.

"The sex," he continued, "will be terrible. There are only three possible scenarios," Dennis paused and shook his head. "No. Make that two. Either you will not be able to get an erection, or you will ejaculate within the first fifteen seconds of the encounter. Actually I was right the first time. There are three scenarios. It's also possible that you will not get an erection *and* you will ejaculate within fifteen seconds."

"Remind me again why I need to be sober for that?"

"Aside from the fact that the disastrous experience will teach you an invaluable lesson in humility, you will also learn from your mistakes. But in order to do so, you have to remember making them."

"I appreciate your advice but just because Tara has Todd it doesn't mean I'm—"

"Speaking of Todd, did you get a good look at his junk while he was frantically trying to pull up his pants?"

"Of course not," George said. Though in fact, his "junk" was all he'd seen.

"He's a douche, but I have to give him the grooming props. That hedge was trimmed."

He had noticed that, too. George was troubled by how easily the image of Todd's shorn manhood popped right back into his brain now.

"Let's face it," Dennis noted just as the mariachi band finished their set. Regrettably, Dennis did not modulate his volume. He continued yelling just as if the band was still playing. "Nobody likes flossing pubes out of their teeth," he shouted.

People stared at them. George didn't like being stared at. Despite his traumatizing an infant this morning with his belligerent tirade, he generally did not engage in behavior that warranted stares. But everybody was staring now. And someone, the waitress, George thought, yelled, "Ain't that the truth!" which made everyone laugh. Well, everyone but George.

"Can we change the subject?" he begged.

"No. If you're planning on having sex, you're going to have to work that out. You know, down south." He pointed at his lap in case George wasn't following. "I go to a girl named Kim. Korean. She'll get that forest under control for you."

Whether Dennis liked it or not, George decided it was time to change the subject. "Can you recommend a good doctor?"

"What happened to your old one?"

"It's Todd. Todd was my doctor."

"Todd? You're kidding, right? You went to a *doctor* named Todd? That's just crazy." George was stumped, so Dennis explained. "Todd is a fine name for a ski instructor. You want to learn how to surf, call a guy named Todd. Todd's your IT guy? No problem. *But a doctor?* You do not let a guy named *Todd* examine your prostate."

Clearly there was a joke in there somewhere, but since obviously George was the butt of it, he didn't make it.

"With my insane shooting schedule, I haven't gotten around to finding a physician yet. I've only been back in the city four months. But what an amazing four months with the show and…" Dennis put his glass down, took a deep breath, and looked George squarely in the eyes. "I think I might be falling in love with your daughter," he exclaimed.

Screw these Margaritas. George felt the overwhelming need to be downing shots. "I don't want to hear… I can't talk about—"

"George, I'm a good man."

He considered asking Dennis to define the word good. "You're forty-three!" George shouted, eliciting more stares from the citizens of Margarita Nation.

"No I'm not. I just turned forty-one."

"Dude." *Oh no. I did not just say dude.* "Don't lie to me about your age. We were in the same class at NYU."

"Yeah. But I skipped seventh and tenth grades."

Dennis said skipped, but George heard expelled. He couldn't imagine how Dennis got into college if he'd been kicked out of school twice. Then George remembered how short Dennis was back then and how young he looked. And most disturbingly, as the pieces of the puzzle came together, he understood a child would skip two grades in school for only one reason. "Are you trying to tell me you're a genius?"

"Technically, I'm not a genius. My IQ is high superior/ borderline genius. I don't quite make the cut. Forget it. I wish I hadn't said anything. I don't like talking about it. I'm just a regular guy. So, please don't get all weird on me. Because it's not like I don't think you're smart enough to carry on a conversation with me or anything like that."

How big of him to say so. Because George *had* been concerned he was not up to the intellectual rigor of this discourse, especially since all Dennis had been talking about all evening was getting hammered and the need for George to wax his "junk."

"You seem upset," noticed Einstein. Being a borderline genius, Dennis was apparently equipped with heightened powers of observation.

George slammed his glass down on the table. "I'm not upset. It's just been a long day." He picked up another fistful of chips and was about to shove them in his mouth. Instead he blurted, "I think I saw Jesus."

"On a tortilla chip? Let me see." Dennis got very excited trying to grab the chips out of George's hand. "You know you're going to make a fortune with that chip. The nut jobs are going to think it's a miracle. Why do Jesus and Mary only appear on Mexican food?

Huh? Answer me that? Nobody ever sees the face of God in a California roll."

George must have been getting drunk because he burst out laughing. When he recovered, he explained that he hadn't seen him on a chip.

Dennis either had very little curiosity or a very small bladder, because he asked him to "hold that thought" so he could run to the Gents. While George waited for him, he walked over to a nearby table of college kids who had just finished their pitcher of margaritas. George held up his pitcher, which was still more than half full and asked if they'd be willing to swap their empty one for his full one. They were suspicious at first, but George explained there was no catch. "I'm worried my friend has had too much to drink," he lied.

He shouldn't have approached them because they were already pretty wasted. Aside from their empty pitcher, half a dozen drained shot glasses lay strewn on the table. But George reasoned his liver was twenty years older than theirs, and he figured they'd survive this night of heavy drinking but probably he would not. George didn't have to ask them twice. Not only did they swap pitchers with him, they ordered another round of shots in his honor, though George declined the one they offered him.

When he got back to the table Dennis eyed their empty pitcher. "That was fast. I don't even feel that drunk. So, what's all this about Jesus?"

George told him the story of his encounter.

"Did he look older than thirty-three? Because if he was older than thirty-three, it wasn't Jesus."

He supposed it should have come as no surprise that Dennis wasn't taking him seriously.

Dennis insisted he had been scammed. "He was fucking with

you, that's all."

"I had already bought him the pizza. So what was the angle? He was practically out the door before I found out who he was."

"Dude, you never found out who he was."

Though George hated giving him credit for anything, Dennis was obviously right. Dennis smiled at him kindly. "You're not drunk, and you sucked back that pitcher in ten seconds. We better order another one, or you're never going to hurl tonight."

Dennis darted his head, searching for the waitress. Just then, one of the recipients of the free margaritas came stumbling over to the table carrying the now empty pitcher. This was a disaster. George was certain the sloppily drunk fraternity brother, in his effusive thanks, would reveal his chicanery to Dennis.

The good news is the kid didn't divulge George's deceit. The moment he opened his mouth to speak, he threw up all over George. His aim was extraordinary. Every ounce of puke landed on George. Amazingly, there wasn't a drop of it on the table or floor. For the first time all evening, the noisy restaurant fell into complete silence. For a man who eschewed being stared at, George was becoming quite accustomed to it.

Along with the rest of Margarita Nation, Dennis gawked at him, with mouth agape. "Granted this is not the way I plotted it," he finally said, "but I think it's safe to say that this revolting event can be classified as your rock bottom moment. What do you think?"

George agreed with him.

Or rather, he agreed with him until he remembered he still needed to get home. And in his wretched state, George was subjected to a seemingly endless walk up Broadway from the restaurant at 108th back to his building on Riverside and 114th Street. Naturally, as he passed other pedestrians, they gawked at him with appalled expressions. A few of his fellow travellers even leapt in terror, which George thought an extreme response to the situation.

Rather melodramatically one poor woman screamed and jumped directly into traffic. Thankfully the cabbie hit the brakes instantly and no one was hurt, so maybe things were looking up in George's world. Finally, after the degrading trudge home, Dennis and George arrived at the fourteenth floor of their building, standing at the front doors of their respective domiciles.

As George forced his hand into the sullied pocket of his pants to fish out his keys, Dennis ordered him to stop. He went into his apartment and returned a moment later with a box of black Hefty trash bags. "I don't think you want to let any of that disgusting clothing into your apartment."

Dennis had a point. The smell wafting off George, a mix of bile, tequila and rancid grease, was nauseating. His stomach churned, and he feared if he wore these clothes much longer, Dennis's prediction that he would be throwing up before evening's end would surely come to pass.

Dennis held open the Hefty bag, keeping it at arm's length, and he commanded George to put everything in it. George's coat, which he'd luckily placed on a chair beside him at the restaurant, was unscathed. Dennis had carried the garment home to avoid cross contamination. Fortunately for George, the heat of his shame had kept him warm on the walk home, but now in his dank, feculent attire, his teeth were chattering.

He unbuttoned his shirt and placed it in the garbage bag. He kicked off his shoes. "These can be cleaned," he said. "I'm not throwing away a perfectly good pair of shoes."

"In the bag. Right now," Dennis ordered.

He didn't argue. He undid his pants and tried unsuccessfully to remove them without actually touching them. He tossed them into the bag. "Can I go in now?"

"It's *may I*. And no," Dennis said, shaking his head. "Dude, that stuff is all over your underwear and socks. They have to come off."

The puke had inexplicably saturated his briefs. Still, he protested.

"Seriously?" As far as Dennis was concerned, his stripping was nonnegotiable.

For all George's insecurities, he was not painfully shy about his naked body, but neither was he a nudist. He never went to the gym, but if he decided to, he could undress in a locker room without having to do that awkward underwear change beneath a towel trick, like kids do when they're getting in and out of their bathing suits on the beach.

Still he was loath to take his clothes off in front of Dennis while he watched and waited, with just a Hefty bag between them. For modesty's sake, he wished he'd begun this undressing routine facing away from Dennis, but it seemed silly to turn his back on him now. Besides, the fact was, he had more issues with his ass (George thought it was big) than with his dick (George thought it was big), so he stripped out of his t-shirt, briefs and socks and threw them into the bag. Dennis kindly made no cracks about George's untrimmed hedge. "Can I go in now?" he pleaded.

"*May I*. Almost," Dennis said.

He opened George's door and placed a fresh garbage bag on the floor. Then he laid out a trail of garbage bags leading straight into the bathroom. Once in the john, he ran the shower for George. "There's a lot of it on your head. I didn't want it landing on the floor."

George took the longest shower he had ever taken in his life. When the water going down the drain had long run clear, and the hot water had started to give out, he was confident he was clean. He turned off the taps, stepped out of the shower, dried off, and walked into the bedroom.

The bed was made up with Susie's linens. Dennis must have done that while he was in the bathroom. All the sullied trash bags had been removed, and not a trace of the shameful incident remained. George was forced to acknowledge, not for the first time, that Dennis was a kind and decent man at heart, no matter how annoying he was.

On top of the bed, George found a note he'd left him:

Sleep tight, Dude.
PS: RE: GROOMING. Call Kim tomorrow.
If you tell her it's an emergency (which it is),
she'll definitely fit you in.

He included her number, but since George trusted that Dennis wouldn't actually be making a personal inspection to confirm that he'd gone to see her, he made no plans to call her. George tossed the note into the trashcan. Then, exhausted, he got into bed and had his first uninterrupted night of sleep since the night before Thanksgiving.

TWELVE

HAVING FAILED TO SHUT THE blinds before going to bed, the New Jersey sun streamed in, warming George's face and waking him at seven. Maybe he would leave them open every night. The warmth and the vitamin D were the perfect antidote to a cold December morning. He really did feel that the debacle at Margarita Nation must have been his rock bottom moment. Now, with skin scrubbed clean, he would make a fresh start. Certainly after the wretchedness of last evening, things could only improve.

He brewed a pot of coffee. As he drank it he thought, *More than any day since Thanksgiving, this feels like a new day—a day to continue making big changes.* Today was the first day of the rest of his... well, you know. And as such, he was determined to seize the... well, you know. His thoughts may have been unoriginal, but they were a source of great comfort.

He contemplated what he might do, and all the things he could accomplish. He was well aware the day did indeed demand some kind of action on his part. Regrettably, what the specific action should be eluded him. Maybe he was putting too much effort into coming up with a life-altering plan. Perhaps just accomplishing some chores would be enough for today.

The buying of sheets, so pressing a need yesterday, seemed hardly worth the trouble now. He'd already slept on Suzie's sheets, and the world hadn't come to an end. He could always make a second pot of coffee. That would give him something to do, but now that the family had a history of heart disease, it was probably a bad idea. He stared at New Jersey and began to consider the real possibility that he had been mistaken. Perhaps today was not the first day of the rest of his life. More likely, it was just the first day of him being unmoored and utterly alone.

George had always considered himself to be a loner, a curious self-image for a man who had never lived on his own before. As a member of a family, he always knew someone, as much as he might try and resist, would eventually come along and force him into engagement. He savored having alone time, longed for it constantly when the kids were small, and still he took comfort in knowing that soon enough his solitude would come to an end.

All he had to do was wait. In no time, a door would burst open and Tara, or the children—*someone*—would barge in. The blare of music or the shrieking cries of May and Brian demanding George to play referee had destroyed his silent world a thousand times. And every one of those times, he was more grateful than upset that something had come along to end his isolation.

Unless Dennis burst in with his spare key and his Ping-Pong

paddle, George was going to be staring at New Jersey for the rest of his life.

This should not have been so difficult. He was single, but he was not helpless. He made excellent coffee, and he could cook a little bit. He could not iron, but he was certainly capable of finding a laundromat. He was not nearly as domestically clueless as his dad had been.

Once, after they'd been living in their apartment for years, his father walked into the kitchen and said to Claire, "The coffee smells great. I'd love a cup." Claire smiled at her husband and said, "Sure dear. Help yourself." She went back to her crossword—it was a Saturday puzzle so it was pretty challenging. After a few minutes, Claire realized he was staring at her. When she finally looked at him, he rather sheepishly asked, "Can you give me a clue?"

He was completely lost. He had no idea where she kept the coffee mugs, even though they'd always been kept in the same cupboard.

"That's logical," he said when Claire pointed at the cabinet directly above the coffee maker.

George forced himself to floss and brush. He showered again and put on clean clothes. Ridiculously, these routine tasks felt like major accomplishments. He even put on shoes, meaning he really could go out and do something. George poured himself more coffee, as he thought of his helpless father lost in his own kitchen even though he knew where everything was in his showroom.

A longing to see his father again stung George. He missed him and wanted him back. But his father was never coming back, and knowing that made his ache even worse. Probably he should get undressed and go back to bed. He could certainly use a few more months of sleep. Wasn't there some sort of protocol for grief? Didn't you get to go to bed for six months? Or was it a year?

Whatever it was, George didn't go back to bed, because he had another thought. And though it was in no way a substitute for the loss of his father, at least it was something he could do. Maybe he could find Carolyn. Get her back. He knew the way to do it.

He found his laptop and returned to the safety of his bed. His default screen was Google, which he found to be a terrific timesaver when seconds counted. He typed:

Carolyn.

He looked through fifteen pages of images of Carolyns with no luck.

Carolyn. Widow, he tried.

Nada.

Carolyn. Great laugh. He knew that would result in no matches before even typing it, but he enjoyed typing it nonetheless.

Then George had a brilliant idea. Yesterday was the second anniversary of her husband's death! He knew his excitement was inappropriate with regard to the tragic event, but the exuberance of a man in love cannot be contained.

An exhaustive search of obituaries led nowhere. Out of ideas, he finally gave up. He tried to convince himself it was all for the best. He needed to be single and self-sufficient. He needed to live through this chapter, figure out who he was, what he wanted out of life. Then maybe—in a year, or at minimum, six months—he could think about meeting a woman.

He closed the computer and got up. Noticing the trashcan, he remembered Dennis's note. He retrieved it from the can and read it again.

He did need to do something with his day. But he did not want to call Kim. He recalled that during a former Google session, he learned that people suffering from depression sometimes have difficulty making decisions. Also, maintaining personal hygiene can become problematic. The fact that he had showered and brushed his teeth probably meant he was covered on that score. Still, he did have to do something, and calling Kim would qualify as making a decision of sorts.

In spite of the fact that he lived in one of the greatest cities in the world, George had no idea what else to do with his day. So he called the salon where Kim worked, and he told the receptionist that it was an emergency, even though he knew there was no such thing as a waxing emergency.

∽

THE ONLY WOMEN HE SAW inside the Jeffrey Denniston Salon and Spa were the employees. Their business card described the place as a "men's oasis," but it didn't really conjure oasis. The establishment had been decorated to look like a cross between an English gentlemen's club and a western saloon, with a dash of midcentury Playboy Club thrown in for good measure. The space was filled with dark wood, dark leather, and dark liquor. He couldn't tell if the design team was trying for hyper-masculine or making an arch comment on the sorry state of masculinity in urban society.

He didn't have much time to solve these riddles. A young woman with skin the same dark shade as the leather chairs approached. For a moment, he wondered if she'd been hired because she coordinated so perfectly with the decor. She whisked his coat away and offered him a beverage. He asked for water, but when she found out his appointment was for hair removal, she had an alternative suggestion.

"Trust me, sugar. Let me bring you a scotch. First time? It

hurts a little."

He sat, scotch in hand, in a leather wingback chair and glanced through a stack of books on the mahogany coffee table—a lot of Hemingway and Cormac McCarthy—while he waited for Kim to call his name. He sipped his scotch, but slowly. This was now two days in a row of drinking before five, and he did not wish to continue that pattern. Also he recalled from Google that it took only five days of repetition for something to become a habit. Or maybe it was five weeks, he couldn't remember.

"George?"

He looked up at the woman standing before him. It was not Kim, and his heart managed to simultaneously rise and fall. This was amazing luck. A dream come true but also awkward and terribly embarrassing considering the reason for his visit to the Jeffrey Denniston Salon and Spa. His eyes bugged out and his jaw dropped. "Carolyn?" he stammered.

She too was noticeably shocked. "How did you find me? Are you here for a haircut?"

"Something like that."

"Do you have an appointment with someone specific? Because I'd be happy to take care of you."

"Oh, no. I'm sure you're busy."

"I'm not. I've had a couple of cancellations. Flu going around."

"Right. Well... I just need a minute." And he dashed over to the reception desk just as he noticed an Asian woman, who may or may not have been Kim, emerging from the back of the salon. He immediately pulled out his credit card and tossed it onto the desk, which, he feared, made him seem quite rude, but really he was just, you know, panicked. "This is to pay for the," he leaned in closer to be sure he wouldn't be overheard, "waxing with Kim." Now he smiled widely to compensate for the fact that he'd hurled his credit card at the waif-like blonde girl at reception. "Add a twenty-percent tip, please. I also want to pay for a haircut with Carolyn."

"You want the hair appointment after your *Boyzillian?*" She bellowed this out Wagnerianly. George could not believe such a large sound could emanate from such a small person.

"No," he whispered. "Instead of the hair removal. I am paying Kim, of course, but I'm cancelling our session. I *only* want the haircut."

"Okay. If you want. But it's one hundred and seventy five dollars plus the tip." She punched away on a calculator. "So that's two ten. And the haircut is eighty. Should I add the tip for that now, too?"

Seriously? Including a tip for Carolyn, he was about to spend over three hundred dollars on a haircut. That was ill considered for anyone, but for a man with George's limited supply of hair on his head, it was ludicrous. His best guesstimate was he was about to spend fifty cents per follicle on this styling session.

An antique barber pole, spinning blue and red, stood in the corner of the room functioning solely as *objet d'art*. He sat in a chair facing a mirror, while Carolyn stood behind him, head cocked, staring at his reflection in focused study. She had one hand propped on her hip, the other holding a pair of shears at the ready. Occasionally she'd move the shears in the direction of his head, but she never actually made contact with any hair. She emitted a sigh. Opened her mouth and closed it again. She was flummoxed.

"So," she said at last. "What do you normally do with your hair?"

"I mourn the loss of it."

Carolyn laughed, and her expression softened. She let her arms fall to her sides. "So you're aware of the problem? I don't mean *problem,* but—"

"Of course I am."

"You'd be surprised how many men aren't." She seemed relieved. "The good news is you haven't done anything crazy yet."

"Crazy?"

"Like a comb-over. You haven't pulled a Trump. Or dyed it blonde. I mean obviously if you had done any of those desperate things, I wouldn't have flirted with you yesterday."

So she *had* flirted with him at the bar! George thought she had, but it was nice having confirmation.

"I would never have a comb-over."

"You say that, and I believe you. Or at least I believe that you believe that. But something happens to some men, some kind of awful, tragic break with reality, and the next thing you know, their part is lined up with their chin."

"You do know I'm paying for this abuse, right?"

She laughed again. He decided he should probably never let her know how completely under her spell he fell every time he heard that sound.

"Do you trust me, George?"

He trusted her more than made any rational sense, considering he'd known her for only one day. He nodded.

"This is going to be short," she said, pointing at the top of his head. "Very, very short."

She reached for a spray bottle and wet down his hair. She grabbed a comb, a pair of shears. And she began. There was no chatter. She was focus and concentration, an artist at work. He watched far more hair than he previously believed he possessed fall onto the apron he was wearing and tumble down to the floor. She paused, and he assumed she was finished cutting, but she was just planning her next steps. She leaned in, and he felt her shoulder brush against his. The contact lasted a few seconds at most, but the charge remained, pulsing through him long after they were separated.

At last she stepped back and smiled at him in the mirror. He looked at his reflection. She had not been kidding. His hair was very, very short. Oddly though, it looked thicker and healthier at this length. His hair ceased to remind him of the few remaining boorish stragglers who didn't know when to leave the party.

More impressively, at least to George, for a borderline wimpy guy, he looked pretty virile with his new cut. The transformation was dramatic and reminded George of one of those makeovers he enjoyed looking at in Tara's copies of *Glamour*, which he would no longer be able to read. Probably just as well, as that activity certainly undercut his new rugged image.

Satisfied with her efforts, she smiled at him. And he nodded with gratitude and approval as he smiled back at her. "There's something else I want you to do," she said. "There's a woman who works here named Kim."

His heart sank.

"She's a genius. I want her to fix your eyebrows."

"I didn't realize they were broken."

"They're too big. Are you Russian? Because they remind me a little of Brezhnev's. Anyway, they're casting shadows across your face."

He raised a hand to object, but she stopped him. "George, you're over forty," she said matter-of-factly. "Many men start losing hair where they want it and growing it where they don't, it's no big deal. Which reminds me, as long as she's cleaning up your brows, she can take care of any other areas you may need. Literally, *anyplace*."

Carolyn brushed the hair from his collar and removed the apron, sending even more of his hair cascading to the floor. He stood and thanked her, not wanting their time together to be over.

He smiled awkwardly. Shuffled his feet. Thanked her once again for creating his dramatic transformation, even considered kissing her cheek, but then didn't. Then he turned to go.

"George Bailey," she declared. "Are you really walking away from me a second time without asking for my phone number? Just how often do you expect luck to be on your side?"

He got her phone number and gave Carolyn his. Flynn, he learned. Carolyn Flynn. Her name raced through his brain. Carolyn Flynn, hair magician to the rich and follicly challenged.

He went back to reception to see if Kim was free to "fix" his eyebrows and take care of a few other things as well, since Carolyn seemed to suggest that was a good idea. Kim was available, but of course the two hundred and ten dollars George already paid her for her services could not be applied to this new appointment. He spent an even two-fifty this time, with the additional charges going for, as Kim referred to it, eyebrow reimagining and execution.

"Don't worry," Kim told him as she blew onto the tongue depressor covered in molten wax to cool the temperature down, "I won't make you look like a clown or a drag queen. No one will notice that anything has changed."

For five hundred bucks, he hoped somebody would notice.

"The good news is your eyes won't look droopy and dark anymore," Kim continued. "People won't realize it's the brows. They'll think you're rested and happy."

George reclined on the table and Kim proceeded to press hot wax above the bridge of his nose and around the perimeters of both brows. A moment later, the yanking began. Rip. Rip. Rip. The procedure hurt. A lot. He wondered if making people believe he was happy was worth all this pain.

THIRTEEN

As he stood on the sidewalk in front of the salon, deciding where to go with his newly styled head, an older woman wheeling a laundry cart filled with groceries, passed by and smiled at him. Perhaps she'd done that in response to his happier eyebrows, or because she was one of those kind-hearted individuals who smiled at everyone. Despite rumors to the contrary, such people do live in New York.

Most likely she was grinning because she sensed in George a newly boyish and carefree demeanor. While his experience with Kim was certainly unusual, once he stopped whimpering, he enjoyed it. Or rather, he enjoyed the results.

He felt younger and more attractive than he had in a long while. When he stood up from Kim's table and saw his baby skin, pink and smooth in places that had not been smooth for thirty years, he was more than a little turned on. Excited. He had a spring in his step, though the spring could be a result of the stinging he felt every time his inner thighs rubbed against his pants.

Along with the sting, he also felt the buzzing of his cell, on vibrate in his front pocket. He thought it might be Carolyn already phoning him, and he was disappointed to see that it was only his brother. He answered the call anyway.

In a family of stoics, the taciturn Conor reigned supreme in his unflappability and guardedness. So when George heard rapid fire, desperate sputtering pleas spewing out of his brother's mouth, he was baffled. Conor's anguished speech was so foreign sounding, George didn't even recognize the voice at first. When finally he realized to whom he was speaking, he couldn't understand what Conor was carrying on about.

"Slow down," George shouted, which perversely made his brother pick up the pace. "Slow down," he repeated "Or I'm hanging up."

"Hang. Up. And. I. Will. Slit. Your. Throat. Slow enough?"

Needless to say, George did not hang up. Conor was not usually prone to truculence. Something dramatic must have happened to set him off like this.

With only the slightest prodding from George, Conor vented about the showroom and a design presentation beginning in thirty minutes that their father had scheduled and did not bother to tell him about. (George's assurances that Daddy certainly would have kept Conor in the loop were it not for his ill-timed massive coronary, did little to assuage him.) Conor continued carrying on, accelerating again.

He said something unintelligible, to which George responded, "Have you forgotten that I quit?" He said this far too glibly considering he was conversing with someone who had just moments before threatened to slit his throat.

"If you don't get over here right now…" Conor stopped, letting his silence convey the threat.

George decided to heed his brother's warning and would have told him so had Conor not already hung up on him. Hopping onto a nearly empty subway, George went straight to Bailey and Sons to assist his harried kin.

Conor either just happened to be standing right at the front door when George arrived, or he was deliberately waiting for him. When he saw him, Conor smiled shamefacedly. "Hey," he said by way of apology, "I wouldn't have actually slit your throat."

George was relieved to hear it.

Conor led him through the showroom, subjecting him to a chorus of *welcome backs!* from Theo and the others. George resisted the urge to respond, *Not so fast. Just visiting!* Conor pulled his brother into what their father grandly referred to as the conference room, a hodgepodge space where they kept extra samples and supplies. Since it also happened to have an old dining table and a half dozen mismatched chairs, that's where they held meetings. Upon entering the room, George saw that most of those chairs were filled—by his mother, his children, and a woman he never met.

George had the sinking suspicion he had walked in on an intervention, especially since Brian was here on what was presumably a day he had class. In his opinion, an intervention was uncalled for. Yes, he hastily quit his job, and he had had alcohol in the afternoon for the last two days. Not the behavior of a man truly engaged with the world, but neither could it be called the depths of despair. He exchanged a series of discomfited nods and shrugs with his family and was about to lean in and attempt actual physical contact in the form of hugs when the female interloper asked, "Shall I begin?"

Conor nodded and introduced George as the president of Bailey and Sons, making a crack about his tardiness.

"My brother flatters me," George said with a flourish. "I am not the president. I'm merely a visitor here." He'd been hoping he would come off as debonair, but the impression he created was closer to deranged.

"I'm Bridget Brennan. So nice to meet you," she said, clasping George's hand. Aside from her Minnesota accent, Bridget could have been the spokeswoman for Ireland's board of tourism: She was graced with milky skin, auburn hair, and green eyes. She was wearing a tartan skirt and a Clan Aryan sweater. The heart on her claddagh ring was pointing toward the tip of her finger, indicating she was single.

She nodded at George and, by extension, the rest of the room. "Shall I?" She motioned toward five white Christmas trees ranging in height from four to eight feet, which had been set up around the room. Bridget was not a family counselor; she was not here to arbitrate. She was here to pitch her line: Emerald Isle Christmas.

The trees were merely the props. The ornaments and garlands adorning the trees were what she was endeavoring to persuade the Baileys to buy. The samples were good—very good, actually. And this was the opinion of a jaded, burned-out man who had never been excited by Christmas even before he'd become a complete curmudgeon.

Under the best of circumstances, he found it difficult to muster enthusiasm for a "new" Christmas ornament. The category was open to more interpretations than say, the wheel. Still, how many variations were there on a blown glass ball? In Bridget's hand, it turned out, there were myriad.

The only problem was, that in keeping with the line's name, all her designs were green. They were in a variety of shades of kelly and celadon and chartreuse and lime and, of course, emerald, but nevertheless everything was green.

She finished her presentation, and the family thanked her. When she shook George's hand again, he had the distinct impression she held it a moment or two longer than she had held the hand of any of the other family members. She studied his face and smiled. "What a great haircut."

Conor walked her to the door, enthusiastically informing her that they would be in touch soon. "I don't know what I was so worried about," Conor confessed. "I could have handled this without you."

"Sorry that we dragged you in. I'm sure you're very busy," Claire said, witheringly.

"I guess the only question is how many gross we should buy," said May.

And thus went the effusive chatter, with predictions that Emerald Isle Christmas would lead to record-breaking orders.

Finally they noticed that George was less awestruck. "Since you did drag me here, and I was the head buyer until last week, would you like my opinion?"

Silence. Nobody likes a killjoy. "Sure," Brian muttered begrudgingly.

"I agree that the ornaments are beautiful. Much of the line is very imaginative." He stopped, meeting the gaze of his chagrined family.

"But?" Conor shouted, impatient for George to get to the point.

"Isn't it obvious?"

Apparently, it was not.

"It's green!"

His family, born and raised to sell Christmas ornaments,

seemed not to grasp the fundamental problem. "These ornaments look spectacular," he admitted. "Because they are hanging off white trees. Normal people don't have white Christmas trees in their homes. Normal people have *green* Christmas trees. Right? And on green Christmas trees, these ornaments will be invisible. They will blend in with the green branches and disappear. Merchants who are stupid enough to buy these ornaments from us when they see them displayed in all their glory on our white trees, will hang them in their shops on green trees and they won't sell—not even a little bit. And then these already barely surviving shopkeepers will have another record-setting disastrous holiday season, and either go out of business or never buy from us again because we were the bad guys who shoved *green* ornaments down their throats. Am I making any sense to you people?"

"You don't have to get nasty about it," May shouted, voice quaking. She rose from the table, and George saw her hands were trembling. She raced out of the room.

He called for her to wait, but she was gone. "I'd better—"

"No. You better let me," Brian said, not unkindly, touching his father's arm as he left the room. George turned back to Claire and Conor.

His mother never really worked in the business. Through osmosis and forty-five years of marriage, she'd absorbed a lot, but he could understand why she was so taken by the presentation. Conor's enthusiasm made no sense to George.

"That woman is lovely and obviously talented, and maybe we can work with her at some point. But you absolutely must not order that line. Let's get Lizzie and Alison in here to box this stuff up and return it." George looked enquiringly at his brother. "Green? What were you thinking?"

Conor glared, began breathing heavily. He took a step toward the door, like he might walk out of the room, maybe never come back. But he stopped. Held his ground.

"*What was I thinking?* I was thinking that I can't do this alone. I was thinking that I need some help. I was thinking there's no way my brother would leave me in the lurch on the very day my father died. What were *you* thinking, George?" Conor's words pried their way, scratched and strangled, out of his raw throat. He was desperate to yell out full force. But being utterly unpracticed at such outbursts, he was unable to manage a scream. Still, his words had their intended effect. George stood, shamed and cowed, staring at the floor.

Having said so much—so much more than he'd ever said before—Conor stormed out of the meeting room, leaving George alone with his mother. Frustrated and feeling guilt ridden, George heaved a sigh. He gestured to his mother. "Go ahead," he said, giving Claire permission to berate him.

"What do you mean? I wasn't going to say anything." He could see her struggling to keep the words of chastisement from escaping her lips.

They stood in silence. And he thought how out of place his mother looked here—especially now, wan and still dressed in black. She was often at the office, of course. But her appearances were brief. She was a lightning bolt, running in and out of the showroom on her way to someplace else. She'd dash in to drop something off for his father, or she'd pick up a cake from Magnolia "just because," and run in with it to surprise the sales team.

"How are you doing, Mom?"

She smiled gamely, but opting for candor instead, she abandoned the cheerful pretense and let her smile drop. "I keep thinking about how much butter it takes to make one Thanksgiving dinner. Between the mashed potatoes and all the pies, it must be at least three pounds."

"What?"

"No wonder your father had a..." She chuckled as tears streamed down her cheeks.

He held his mother. Tried to comfort her. He thought maybe he succeeded. He hoped so, anyway. Yet as much as he wanted to cheer her, he found it difficult to offer her solace, because in that moment, in his mother's arms, he was again submerged in his own deep sadness and need. What he really longed for was someone to comfort him.

George did not indulge this sorrow. He fought to keep it at bay, for his mother's sake—to be strong for her, and to not disappoint her again, or let her down again.

His mother pulled back slightly and looked into George's eyes. She had stopped crying. "Whoever did your eyebrows did a wonderful job. They look fantastic."

"Oh, brother. She told me no one would be able tell."

"The esthetician? She was right," his mother concurred. "No one *will* be able to tell."

"What are you talking about? *You* could tell."

"I don't count. I'm your mother. I know everything." Her smile widened, which made her statement slightly more amusing than it might otherwise have been. She pulled completely away from his embrace. All was fine again, because they were jointly pretending now that all their cares were behind them. "Maybe you're right."

"About what?" he asked.

"Maybe we should sell. Based on this afternoon, I don't think we can do this without you. Conor obviously can't."

"I don't know about that," he said, even though he suspected she was right.

"I came in today to get the books, look over things. See where everything stands. You know your father. He never talked to me very much about the business, aside from the fun stuff. He'd ask me which Santas I thought were the cutest, that kind of thing. But the numbers," she shrugged. "I need to get clear about that, because there's interest. I've already been contacted about selling."

That didn't take long.

"Clark Adelman called me. He'd buy us out tomorrow. All I have to do is say when."

"Clark Adelman?" George was eager to unload the business, but it felt somehow disloyal to sell it to "The King of Christmas." It surprised him that his mother would consider such a thing. "Didn't Clark Adelman's grandfather call Pop a scrappy *mick*?"

Claire smirked. "Your grandfather *was* a scrappy mick. How do you think we got all this?" Claire's arms extended outward. The reflection of emerald glass bounced off the diamonds in her wedding band, sending a prism of bright green light sailing across the ceiling.

FOURTEEN

GEORGE DID NOT RECALL CLARK Adelman being over seven feet tall, but apparently he was. Because try as he might, George could not reach the crown atop his head. He jumped, lurched, and grunted, but he never got his hands any higher than Clark's fleshy chin.

He laughed at George. "Bow down before me, for I am king," he proclaimed.

"How could that be?" he asked, completely befuddled. "I'm George the Third."

"George the Third? Wasn't he the mad king?" Between bouts of derisive cackling, Clark bellowed, "You're the mad king, George!"

Then bells began chiming to announce the coronation of Clark, the new king of Christmas. Louder and louder the bells rang, until finally George awoke with a start. He reached for the ringing phone, attempting to sound awake and in control even though he wasn't sure where he was, why Tara wasn't in bed with him, or when he had purchased these tatty sheets.

He hadn't yet said hello, but as he moved the phone to his ear he heard these bitter words: "I finally hate you more than I love you."

"Tara?"

"Tara! I thought my replacement was named Jo?"

He was perplexed. "No. It's always been Tara." Now fully out of dreamland, it occurred to him that this might be a wrong number.

"You're killing me, Susie."

"This is George."

"Oh my God. Is she sleeping with men again?"

"I have no idea. I'm just the subletter." George remembered Susie's warning that her ex sometimes phoned in the middle of the night. "I think there's been a misunderstanding."

"Yes. I think so, too. I believe the misunderstanding was that for eleven years I thought we were being faithful to each other, but evidently Susie did not."

"Oh," he said, empathizing with her. He switched on the bedside lamp. Looked at his watch. It was 3:15. "I understand what you're going through."

"I doubt that very much," she insisted, throwing down the gauntlet.

Accepting her implicit challenge, he explained why he did indeed understand what she was going through.

"Women are such pigs," she said. "Aren't they?"

He had never for a moment in his life thought such a thing, yet swept up in her vitriol, he heard himself saying, "Damn, right."

"So what have you done to that wife of yours?"

"What do you mean?" he asked.

"Revenge wise. Does she have a sister?"

"No," he said warily. "Only child."

"That's too bad. If she had a sister you could have slept with her."

"You know, thanks for the ingenious suggestion, but I'm not that angry with her."

"Oh?" She paused. Her breathing got heavier. If possible, she sounded more agitated than when he'd answered the phone. "Why not?"

He thought about that for a second. *Why not?*

He didn't have an answer to that question. After his outburst at the funeral home he hadn't even been thinking much about Tara's infidelity or their impending divorce. Well, that was not exactly true. He had been thinking a lot about his divorce's effect on May and Brian. He was quite concerned about their welfare.

And he also had been thinking about the divorce in terms of the ways it would impact his future. It might lead to him being alone for the rest of his life, or it might lead to him being with Carolyn. In the moments he allowed himself to think about a life beyond tomorrow, he was alternately thrilled and filled with apprehension. George wished he was less apprehensive, but change always had that effect on him.

Of course he was angry with Tara. He was furious with her. *Why did I say I wasn't?*

She destroyed their marriage. George never would have done such a thing. He would have been content leaving things just as they were. Had it been left to him, they would have limped along for the rest of their lives, each day becoming a little more stuck, a little more distant.

Surely it was never that bad?

He had felt safe with Tara. Perhaps he'd mistaken safety for love. No. That wasn't true. He loved her. He had loved her. He wasn't sure anymore. What he *was* sure of was that with Tara, he acted like he was still seventeen—and not in a good way.

He didn't say any of this. He didn't even know this woman's name.

"TJ," she informed him.

The name struck him as funny. "Do you mind if I ask you a question? Why do lesbians have names like that?" Perhaps he made such an indelicate inquiry because it was the middle of the night, and he was severely sleep deprived. Whatever the reason, he regretted his words the minute they escaped his ignorant, straight-guy lips.

"What do you mean? What kind of names, exactly?" she replied sharply.

Regret or not, he rambled on. "Like your name, for example. You can't tell if it's a man's or a woman's."

"I see. You mean lesbian names like Gertrude, or Alice or Melissa or Cynthia or—Ellen?"

He'd been thinking of k.d. Lang when he posed the question. "Cynthia?"

"Cynthia Nixon."

"I didn't know she was a lesbian," George confessed. He did not confess that he had no idea who she was.

"Have you been living under a rock for the last decade?"

He wisely refused to comment.

"George, if we are going to be friends, you need to not be an idiot."

He told TJ he would try.

"May I call you again?"

Surprising himself, he told her he'd be glad to have her call again. "But maybe a little earlier next time?"

∽

AFTER MORNING COFFEE, WHEN IT seemed late enough to be appropriate but not so late as to seem like he was disinterested, George called Carolyn.

"Hi Cynthia," he began.

"I'm sorry, you have the wrong number."

He realized he still had Cynthia Nixon on his mind, so he explained his error to Carolyn, which probably only made things worse. "Anyway, I really wanted to call you yesterday," he admitted, "but I didn't want you to think I was being too forward."

"Considering you walked away from me twice without ever asking for my phone number, I don't think there was ever any danger of my thinking that." He waited for her infectious laughter, but it failed to materialize.

"So anyway…" He began wondering if calling her had been a bad idea. He was not ready for this, but he couldn't very well just hang up on her.

"Yes?"

"I was thinking maybe you would like to have dinner with me?" He had intended that to be a declarative sentence, but he was incapable of keeping the pleading question from creeping into his voice.

"I'd like that. When?"

"Tomorrow?" He remembered feeling the same nervousness the first time he asked Tara out. The only difference was his voice had changed, so at least it wasn't cracking with each syllable he uttered.

"Where shall we meet?"

Meet? He should have planned a proper date before he called her. "Are you working at the salon tomorrow?"

Fortunately for him, she was.

"Great. I'll pick you up, and we'll go from there."

His impulse was to call Todd and ask for some dating advice. He even punched in the first few digits of his phone number before remembering they weren't friends anymore. He thought about calling his brother, despite the fact that Conor was mad at him. And George would have phoned, but he knew Conor would be no help at all. Conor was essentially a recluse who'd spent his life pining for Tara. He knew nothing about dating. That left…

That left George forced to face the fact that he had very few friends. There was Fr. Sal—not that they were friends, but he seemed like a cool guy. Though if the parish priest had dating tips, George really didn't want to know about it.

And then his phone rang. And the caller ID said Dennis. And beggars can't be choosers.

"Not that it's any of your business," George said in lieu of hello, "but if you're calling to find out whether or not I got my junk waxed, the answer is yes."

"*Dad?*" came the voice of his extremely bewildered daughter.

Had George been focused even a little on what he'd just said to May, he might have been mortified, but he wasn't thinking about his embarrassing confession. Instead, the only thought in his head was that May was calling him from Dennis's apartment at this early hour. Even though George wasn't as smart as Dennis, he was bright enough to deduce that his daughter had spent the night in the middle-aged genius's apartment. "Is everything okay?"

"I think I could ask you the same thing. Can't a girl call her father?" she grumbled. He heard a background voice on her end that sounded like Dennis, and then May's tone lightened considerably, so George figured Dennis had told her to be nice.

"I just talked to Gram. She wants the whole family at her place tomorrow night for dinner. I think she wants to discuss selling the business. I'm sure you're glad to hear that," she said tartly, unable to keep the edge from returning to her voice.

George *was* glad to hear that. The sooner they sold, the sooner they could all begin to move on with their lives. Still, he could not shake the nagging feeling that selling to Adelman was a bad idea. "Of course I will be there."

He hung up. His reservations were foolish. A sale was a sale. George didn't want the business, and thankfully his mother saw the soundness in selling now, before May and Brian became more entrenched. He had no legitimate reason not to sell to Clark. Punishing him for some ancient slur was ludicrous, especially since Clark had not been the one who uttered it.

Besides—and George did feel guilty for this thought—*who cares if selling to the Adelmans would have irked Pop?*

Unlike Nan, George didn't even have many vivid memories of his grandfather. And, though he'd never say it aloud, he knew Pop was not a saint. He was, after all, a man capable of shunning his own daughter. And while the family always downplayed that part of their history, it really happened. As a parent himself, George considered that behavior unpardonable. Pop had no possible justification for it unless Finn had been plotting to kill him, which seemed improbable. That was the possible justification, grown out of George's boyhood obsession with the novels of James M. Cain, which had captured his youthful imagination.

At some point, as he tried to solve The Mystery of Finn for the thousandth time, George had the nagging feeling he had forgotten something. Something important. He checked his email for clues but found none. There was, however, an email from the healer.

George,

You keep popping into my thoughts.
I hope you're well and that your back has
improved. If you think another session would
be of help to you, I would be delighted to see
you again.

Luke

He was about to hit delete, then reconsidered. Maybe it would
be wise to see Luke before the family dinner, which was bound to
be a stressful meal. George called and scheduled an appointment
for right before supper tomorrow. With luck, he would leave Luke's
place feeling surer of himself and a little more in control. Also he
did have things other than the business he wanted to talk to him
about: his wife, his children, his father, the guy named Jesus, and, of
course, Carolyn.

Carolyn!

His heart raced. How did he forget that he had a date with
Carolyn tomorrow? This lapse was rather worrisome, and he feared
he might be suffering from a serious medical condition. He was
young for dementia, wasn't he? He wasn't sure. He forced himself to
name the president and the New York senators, which he did easily.
He drew a blank on the name of his congressperson, but he didn't
think that, in and of itself, was particularly troubling, as they rarely
accomplished anything of note that wasn't scandal related.

After rattling off his children's birthdays and his soon-to-be
former anniversary, he concluded no medical reason could excuse
his lapse. Feeling like an idiot, he picked up the phone and canceled
the first date he'd made in twenty-seven years.

∽

Luke, barefooted, dressed in shorts and wearing a tank top, was rolling up a couple of yoga mats and storing them in the corner of his living room when George entered.

"Take off your coat immediately," Luke advised, before picking up a bottle of water and guzzling thirstily. "Sorry, I also teach yoga privately, so I have the heat cranking in here." He puckered his brow. "Nowadays, yoga as inferno is what people insist upon," he said, as if he himself thought the practice a misguided gimmick.

In deference to the heat, George took off his shirt. His sun-starved arms were just a couple of shades darker than his t-shirt. Then he removed his shoes and socks. From just this little bit of effort, already he was sweating. Though all day he'd been looking forward to talking to Luke, he found himself reluctant to share much of anything, so Luke got him on the table almost immediately and started the hands-on treatment.

Nothing remotely ethereal transpired during George's second session with Luke. As before, he felt heat pouring out of Luke's hands—though considering the sweltering room, if heat hadn't been emanating from his palms, George's belief in miracles might have been restored.

At no time did he ever have more than two hands on him. Neither his grandmother nor his father made a special appearance, and he knew in his heart they never had. He had been in a great deal of physical and emotional distress during his first session. Traumatized was probably not an exaggeration. He had let his imagination run wild, and his mind conjured up that spiritual intervention. That was all that had happened. His rational self knew that.

After this session, he just felt empty and aware of being sad and angry. He felt a little gypped, too. He was a fool for allowing himself to get sucked into this hocus-pocus.

"How do you feel?" Luke asked.

"Fantastic. It was great." George didn't see the point in hurting his feelings.

"Okay," Luke paused, looked at George quizzically. "Are you sure? During the session, I kept tuning into the feeling that you were sad. Angry even."

This guy should work for the CIA.

George stammered. "Maybe. Maybe, yes." he confessed. "That's true. I am."

"That's perfectly understandable. Want to talk about what's going on?"

He did want to talk about it. Yet he did not say anything, or, more correctly, he found it impossible to say anything. He couldn't access whatever he'd long buried down there. And besides they only had ten minutes left to their session. So they ended there and George put his shirt and shoes and socks back on.

"Would you care to see me next week?" inquired Luke without pressure.

George no longer thought this had much of a point, but he said he would like another appointment. Then, hedging, he told Luke he'd call to arrange the session because he'd forgotten his datebook. That much was the truth. He did not have his calendar with him. But George knew full well his schedule was clear.

∽

Both George and Conor arrived at their mother's building at the same moment. It was their first encounter since the blowup in the showroom. As was their way, they acted like nothing had happened and nothing was wrong. But their charade was awkward and unconvincing. Not wanting to share their elevator ride in complete silence, George said, "I'm a bit out of it. I just had a session with Luke."

"He didn't tell me you were going to him."

"You're seeing Luke?"

"What do you mean?" Conor asked defensively.

"What do you mean, what do I mean? You had a session with him, too?"

"Why shouldn't I? You aren't the only one who's suffered a loss, you know."

With that the elevator doors opened, and it was time to face Claire.

"Boys," she said ebulliently. She broke into a grin and George realized his mother must have mistakenly assumed her two sons had come here from someplace together after having a heart to heart talk, a rapprochement, something like that.

"I just, by pure chance, bumped into Conor in the lobby," he said, which vaporized Claire's smile in about a millisecond. "I just had a session with Luke."

His mother raised an eyebrow. "He didn't tell me you were seeing him again?"

George wondered if Luke had any clients whose last name was not Bailey.

As they approached the living room, George caught sight of Dennis, lounging in his father's chair, leafing through a sacred copy of *Runner's World*. "What's he doing here?" he hissed. "I thought tonight was family?"

"May and Dennis were at the door together," Claire whispered through clenched teeth. She looked like a ventriloquist's dummy. "What was I supposed to do, turn him away? Which reminds me, I have to reset the table." Claire scurried off to the dining room to add another place setting.

When he entered the living room, he spotted a second surprise guest. Aunt Finn stood up to greet him, even though George encouraged her to remain seated. She placed a dry kiss on George's cheek and returned to her spot on the sofa next to Brian, who looked trapped. Though she was a member of the family, she did not have a stake in the business. Nan had bequeathed her handsomely, but, per Pop's will, Bailey and Sons had gone solely to George's father when Pop passed away.

George thought it an odd choice on his mother's part to invite Finn here to talk about the future of a business that was not hers. George glanced at Finn. She was rigid and tough, but at the same time it seemed as if she might fall to pieces if subjected to the slightest criticism. Whatever happened between her and Pop had severely marked her. After Pop died, and George began to get to know Finn, all his parents ever said to him about the past was that he needed to be very kind to her because the world had treated Finn harshly. How that harshness had manifested itself remained unknown.

Finn was engaged in a heated conversation with Brian. George could only imagine what Finn, the lone Republican in a family of life-long Democrats, might be proselytizing to his gay son about. He was about to go over and play referee when his mother announced that dinner was served.

"You're not worried about anemia?" Finn asked when both May and Brian passed on eating any beef.

"You're not worried about the cruel, inhumane way that animals are treated?" Brian retorted, snapping sharply at his great-aunt.

"I think once we start treating people humanely, and I don't really see that happening in my lifetime, then we can move onto cows."

Finn excelled at having the last word. Everyone shifted awkwardly in their seats, while she sliced into her beef tenderloin proclaiming it had been cooked to perfection. The rest of the Baileys, carnivores included, jabbed at their food but no forks actually passed lips.

Finally, Claire raised the topic at hand. "Let's talk about Bailey and Sons."

"Speaking of inhumanity," remarked Finn contemptuously.

"I have received an offer from Clark Adelman," Claire said to a chorus of dissent from May, Brian and Conor.

Naively hoping it would nix the idea of selling to Clark, Conor repeated the lore that Adelman Sr. had called Pop a scrappy mick.

"*Scrappy* is not the first word I would choose when describing my father," Finn said before lifting her napkin and wiping blood from the corner of her mouth. She raised another forkful of the filet to her lips. "I think it is an excellent idea, Claire. You're best rid of it."

George looked at his disappointed children, staring at their meals with downcast eyes, their plates two-thirds full because Claire insisted they keep a spot open in case they changed their minds about the meat. Conor had the same dejected expression as May and Brian, but his plate was full.

George felt responsible for letting them down. It suddenly seemed wrong to sell so quickly after his father's death. It was somehow in bad taste. This was not going to help them move on. It would just be one more loss and bring more grief. In their current state, they were bound to do something hasty and make a mistake.

Also, George was certain, as doubtful as it was that his father would have ever sold to *anyone*, that he never would have sold to an Adelman under any circumstances.

"This is all my fault. I'm sorry," George said, trying to make amends. "Look, if you need me to work another six months, a year even, so we have time to come up with a more suitable resolution, I will."

His brother and children breathed deeper, reassured by George's words.

"Just to be clear, this is not a change of heart on my part. I really do want to do something else with my life. But I've been waiting this long. I don't need to make a change today."

George felt noble, heroic even. And knowing he would be free in a year, while not as good as being free at this very moment, was still exciting. He had something to look forward to. He didn't know what he wanted to do with his life anyway. Perhaps in a year he'd figure something new out. He again looked at his brother and children. They smiled back at him with relief. For that he was grateful.

They all looked at Claire in anticipation. Well, not Finn. She was only anticipating her next mouthful of steak.

"So is this settled?" George asked.

"It is," his mother said.

There was a collective sigh. "Thank God," someone exclaimed, though of course, it wasn't George.

"It's settled. I'm selling."

"Mom," George groaned. "Give me one good reason why you're doing this?"

Claire's eyes widened furiously. George knew he was about to be admonished, though for what he was unsure.

"I wasn't there every day," she said. "I really didn't know what was going on. I guess I should have, but I didn't. But you two boys…"

Claire took in her sons, sternly. "You really don't have any idea how bad things are, do you? We don't have any money. If we don't sell, we'll have to declare bankruptcy."

George was dumbfounded, as was everyone at the table. Even Finn put down her knife and fork. Trying to make some sense of his mother's announcement, George looked first to Conor, who was in charge of the sales team; then to May, who had primarily been involved in advertising, and to Brian who, though still in school, was often at the showroom between classes. George had dealt with the designers and did much of the buying. None of them, however, wrote checks or paid bills or in any way concerned themselves with the invoices. Daddy ran the business and oversaw the accountants.

George tried to remember if he'd ever asked his father how things were going. Certainly he had asked, but not in a way that would have suggested he was actually interested in having a meaningful conversation about money. Sales had been down, but he never imagined they were down dramatically. He knew 2008 and 2009 had been terrible. That period of time had been awful for everyone in their industry, among others. But things had greatly improved since those shaky years. Everything had to be fine. They all kept getting paid and getting bonuses. Last year, his father gave everyone a raise. What kind of secret had his father been keeping?

We don't own a successful business? We're headed for Chapter 11?

"What are you saying?" The dire information swirled around in his head, refusing to take hold. "We're poor?" George asked his mother.

Surveying the abundance on the table, Claire slammed down her fork and stood. She scowled at her son, staring at him hotly. "Shame on you," she said reproachfully. Her disappointment in George was palpable. "We are not poor. We're not hungry or homeless. There are poor people in the world. There are poor people in this city, right in our neighborhood. Maybe you've seen them? Sleeping on the sidewalk, in the middle of winter. We own our apartments."

"We don't own our apartments," his children pointed out with unmasked brattiness. "I live in a dorm," Brian added, as if it were a gulag instead of the Ivy League.

George raised both his eyebrows with parental scorn. Thankfully, since George didn't want to get in any more trouble with his own parent, May and Brian apologized. The apology was grumbled, but at least it was made.

Claire softened her tone. "I realize you all must be shocked. Believe me, I am, too. But none of us are going to starve. Pop and Nan really did know hunger. That's why they came to America, and look what they accomplished. We will do the same." Hopes slowly began to rise again around the table, but regrettably, Claire did not quit while she was ahead.

"My goodness," she continued, "we could sell the three apartments and with the profit probably buy a whole town in Mississippi, and live the rest of our lives down there like kings."

Claire waited for smiles but instead got murmurs, gasps, and from her granddaughter, sobs. George was envious of how easily May could access her feelings, but he was concerned for her. In less than two weeks, his daughter had lost her grandfather, witnessed the end of her parents' marriage in graphic detail, and now the fabric of her safety net had been sliced to shreds. Obviously, it was taking an emotional toll on her.

Extended periods of moody silence were interspersed with plaintive questions as they sat at the table doing their best to take in what Claire was explaining. The already astronomical rent on the showroom had gone up more than twenty percent two years ago when George's father renegotiated the lease. The sensible thing would have been to find a more affordable space in a different neighborhood.

But he would not consider moving to another location even though the Flatiron district was no longer the center of the Christmas business. Every other holiday wholesaler had been wise enough to move out of the pricey area years before. But George the Second couldn't let the showroom go. It was the place his father had chosen. They had always made their home at the same address, and he refused to break with tradition.

Years earlier, this very same kind of mulish adherence to tradition had prevented them from buying a building that was available for a song. That building was large. It would have given them an affordable permanent home and provided them with extra space they could have easily rented out for additional income. But it would have meant moving, and Pop had just died, and George's father just couldn't do it.

As it happened, the exorbitant rent increase arrived at the worst possible moment. Bailey and Sons was just beginning to show modest improvement after five years of softening sales. No one on the sales team ever focused on their numbers being down, because what they lost in commissions seemed to be made up in ever-increasing year-end bonuses—big, fat gifts from Santa. Little by little the business went from being in the black to a deeply hemorrhaged red. No one foresaw the impending catastrophe except, of course for George's father and the accountants, who reported only to him.

All the while George's father kept this information to himself, striving to fix things without asking anyone for help. Neither did he make the tough but necessary cuts and layoffs that might have kept the business afloat. Instead, he pretended all was well. And because he allowed his family to believe everything was fine, they acted accordingly, playing their privileged, entitled roles. The Baileys went on buying and spending like the cash flow was endless.

"Assuming we sell to Adelman," said Conor "How much money will we end up with?"

"It would be better if you thought less in terms of us making money and more in terms of us not owing any money," explained Claire.

"So nothing? We get nothing?"

"You certainly could treat yourself to a Broadway show, assuming you bought the ticket at the half price booth." Claire meant this as a joke, but only Finn found it amusing. George stared down at the china dinner plate in front of him. What on earth had Claire been thinking serving filet mignon? Did she not understand they needed to be living on a budget? Things were going to have to change.

Dennis sat pensively, with his hand placed atop May's. George appreciated that he had remained silent during most of the meal. He did not think he could have taken one word of sympathy or advice from him, even though he certainly would need advice from someone if he hoped to find a way out of the mess left behind by his sweet and overly generous father.

And now George understood how it was possible, that in a family with absolutely no history of heart disease, a sixty-nine year old triathlete suddenly dropped dead from a massive coronary.

FIFTEEN

"YOU DID MEAN A.M., RIGHT?"

He did indeed. Which is how George and Carolyn found themselves virtually alone in the lobby of the Museum of Modern Art at eight in the morning, drinking coffee and eating croissants.

"How did you arrange this?" Carolyn asked, sounding duly impressed.

A big check paired with fortuitous timing was the answer. MoMA offered special early access to the museum one morning a month for members who made a significant annual donation. After enjoying the complimentary continental breakfast, one could look at the museum's collection in relative peace for several hours before the doors were opened to the general public.

Though George and Tara had been members for years, he

could not remember the last time he had visited the museum at any hour. He was certain he never attended one of these special member's mornings before. George had decided he better start taking advantage of this perk, as it was unlikely he would ever be able to afford to give MoMA money again.

"How was your family dinner? You know the important one, for which you canceled our first date?"

"Sorry again about that," he said, though he could tell from her grin she had been teasing him. "It was certainly interesting. I found out that most likely the reason my father died was because he lost all of the family's money. He never told us how bad things were. I guess the burden of that secret killed him."

Carolyn's eyes widened. She placed a hand on his knee and gave it a reassuring squeeze. Then, attempting to lighten the mood, she said, "I really know how to pick'em, don't I?" She counted off on her fingers. "You're on the rebound. You have no job. *And* you're a pauper."

"And let's not forget, I have been known to drink in the afternoon."

"Oh believe me, I haven't." She laughed, which made him laugh. He got them each a second cup of coffee and another croissant, scattering specks of flaky pastry to the ground as he stood.

George would have been quite content sitting in the lobby, drinking coffee, eating *pain au chocolat*, and talking to Carolyn, but having breakfast wasn't meant to be the focus of their outing. He finally suggested they take a gander at some art. He almost said, *Even though there is nothing more beautiful than you in this building, shall we…* He was glad he didn't say it. He really felt that way, but he feared it might have come off as a smarmy, embarrassingly corny line. Undoubtedly, she would have groaned and rolled her eyes at him. Instead he thought the words. Extending his arm toward the main wing of the museum, George allowed himself to say just the last two words aloud. "Shall we?"

Though it had been years since he set foot inside MoMA, he'd done a bit of pre-date Googling and learned the exact location of some of his favorite pieces from the permanent collection. He didn't want her to think he was an uncultured boob.

On the way to the things he wanted to show Carolyn, they walked by a massive canvas that was painted red, with a few random vertical stripes on it. As much as he fancied himself a sophisticate, as far as George was concerned this was not art. It was nonsense. It was *The Emperor's New Clothes*. "Really?" he groaned, pointing at the expanse of crimson.

"What?"

He hated being the guy who didn't get it, but he didn't get it. "Am I missing something? It's a canvas with red paint on it. Excellent for a house painter, but the Museum of Modern Art?"

"It certainly is *modern*," Carolyn quipped. "Seriously though, I like it. There is a sort of power in its simplicity."

George saw the simplicity. The power, however, he found to be lacking.

"There is no there, there."

"I disagree." She rose up on her toes and pecked his cheek. "Now, hurry. We mustn't dawdle. In forty minutes, they're going to let the commoners in." She grabbed his hand and broke into a run. He followed, and they dashed through half of a gallery before a scolding security guard ordered them to slow down. They obeyed the order, decelerating to a more civilized stroll until they arrived at Van Gogh's *The Starry Night*. They were the only people in the room, which baffled George. He couldn't imagine being in this building without spending all your time in front of this masterpiece.

"Now *this* is a painting," he said, which caused her to shake her head amusedly. "What? You don't agree?"

"I agree. This is a magnificent work of art. But I disagree that the other is not. You should try to be little more open-minded."

"Maybe I'm just jealous. Now that I'm broke and about to be unemployed, I'd like to figure out how to be the guy who gets paid a million dollars to throw red paint on a canvas."

She began speaking esoterically about modern art, and George flashed back to a hundred lectures he'd sat through at NYU. Fauvism. Cubism. Expressionism. Futurism. So many more -isms, long forgotten. Had the words come from anyone else's mouth, he would have dismissed them as pretentious gobbledygook, yet somehow when Carolyn said, "George, it's not just what is on the canvas. There is so much more to it than that. What is the story the artist is trying to tell us with this piece? What mood does it convey? Why did he choose that vast expanse of red? What's the meaning of the stripes? Why Latin for the title?" George had missed the title, but acted like he'd noticed it. "How does the painting make you feel?"

Successfully fighting the urge to shut down completely in response to her litany of questions, he began thinking about the struggle to create. He didn't know from first hand experience what those challenges entailed, but he knew that making something—anything—was an extremely brave act, which might explain why he'd never tried doing it himself.

It took courage to have an idea and see the vision through until it was tangible, especially considering some yahoo like him was going to take one look at the thing and judge it. Call it worthless. So this guy put red paint on a canvas, and George could easily say *big deal*. The truth was, it *was* a very big deal, and it was more than he had ever done.

Then again, when you compared a red canvas with a few stripes to the work of Van Gogh… "You know that Van Gogh was not recognized as a genius in his lifetime," he told her. "Everyone thought he was crazy."

"George, Van Gogh *was* crazy. A genius, but crazy." She took his hand, squeezed it. "Why do you love this painting?"

He shrugged. Never mind the college art history lectures, at this moment he might as well have been back in seventh grade with the formidable Sr. Helen Christopher calling him up to the board to solve a problem involving an unknown variable. George would quake, chalk dissolving between sweltering fingers because the only thing he understood was the key word, *unknown*.

"Right in this room there is Cezanne, Seurat, Rousseau and Gauguin. I'm sure Picasso and Degas must be around here somewhere. Why did you bring me to this particular painting? Why *The Starry Night?*" she asked again, in response to his reticence.

He studied the canvas and its swirling brushstrokes. Tried to put into words what he was feeling, which was something he could almost never manage to do. "I don't know."

"I think you do," she said tenderly. "Tell me. I'd really like to know."

"The painting makes me…" he paused, searching for the right word, hoping to be profound, failing. "Happy," he settled for. "It makes me happy even as I am aware of deep sadness and the harshness of the world. This painting makes me aware of the possibility of joy, even though there is so much cruelty around us."

She was quiet a moment, analyzing the painting in light of his remarks. "George Bailey," she said at last. "I think you must be an artist." Her eyes twinkled when they connected with his.

"No. I'm not an artist."

"I think you're lying. Though probably just to yourself."

He looked at her curiously. He wasn't sure how to respond. Fortunately he didn't have to. "If you don't mind," she said. "I think this would be an ideal time and a perfect setting for us to have our first kiss."

"I don't mind," he said dumbly.

He paused a moment and his brain flashed on the coffee he'd just been drinking, and he wished he had gum to freshen his breath. But since Carolyn had coffee too, maybe their shared coffee breath would cancel each other out. Besides if he didn't kiss her right now, she might think he didn't want to, or she might kiss him first. He didn't want her to initiate the kiss, because she had already done most of the heavy lifting in their budding relationship and he needed to do something, so he leaned down and put his mouth against hers.

For two or three seconds, the kiss was chaste. The sensation was lovely, magical even. Their lips were just barely touching. Then they pressed more firmly, stayed that way a while. And then there was an opening of mouths, and a movement of hands and tongues. And he thought, *Carolyn was right. This was the perfect setting for our first kiss.* Like the other artists represented in the room, George and Carolyn were creating something. And like the painters of these masterpieces, they were being brave. And maybe they would make something that would last. Their own work of art. Their...

"Excuse me!" blared the security guard, censoriously. "I'm going to have to ask you two to..." His voice trailed off, red-faced with embarrassment. Carolyn and George, discomfited more for the guard than for themselves, separated from each other swiftly.

The guard stood frowning, staring disapprovingly at them until they exited the gallery.

Like all the greats, already they were being judged.

The problem with a morning date was that it was over by ten. Carolyn had to get to the salon and George had to... Well, that was a problem yet to be solved. He had to do something. Something along the lines of saving himself and his entire family from financial ruin. He had no idea how he was going to accomplish that.

His pants made noise, and he pulled out his phone to find a text from Fr. Sal

Just made a pot of soup and remembered I promised you a lunch. Free at noon?

It would be much easier to save his family on a full stomach.

Since George was already in midtown, it didn't make sense to go all the way back uptown to his apartment, as he'd have to turn right around and head back downtown the minute he got there. It was warm for December, overcast but dry and so he decided to walk around and get some exercise. He headed toward Fifth Avenue, but he hit a wall of tourists as he approached. They may not have all been tourists, but at least sixty percent of these people had their faces pointed up to the sky. Either they were taking in the sights or there was a jumper on a ledge. Either way, he didn't want to be there.

Then it dawned on him why Fifth was so packed. It was Christmas time. People were strolling to look at the window displays and assorted decorations. It seemed doubtful they could actually see anything with the sidewalks jammed up like that. He couldn't imagine getting sucked into that vortex, so he walked back to Broadway to take the subway downtown. He could always kill time in the Village.

Train doors closed as he dashed toward them, snapping shut a second before he could get on. He watched the subway car pull out of the station, cursing his bad luck until the glow of its taillight had receded from view. Checking the monitor for the train schedule, he was dismayed to see he was going to have to wait eight minutes. Eight minutes until the next arriving downtown 1. Okay, it wasn't rush hour, but still? Eight minutes? People had things to do. True, *he* didn't, but that was beside the point. What about his fellow travelers? His agitation was irrational, but that didn't prevent it from overtaking him. He grumbled and cussed under his breath.

That's all it took to make him feel rotten, even though he had had one of the greatest mornings of his life. As improbable as it seemed, Carolyn was only the third person he ever kissed. The first was a girl in sixth grade named Charlene, who he kissed only once. Charlene had made it abundantly clear he wouldn't be receiving a second kiss from her. When their lips parted, she informed him that he had a lot to learn. Then she put her gum back in her mouth and stalked off to tell her friends what a chapped-lipped dud George was.

Aside from the abrupt interruption, the results with Carolyn had been infinitely better. Still, he felt rudderless, edgy. He paced the platform. The sign continued to display a seven-minute wait time even though he was certain he had already been waiting for at least three.

And just then, he abruptly stopped pacing. He wasn't anxious or angry. He felt completely at peace. As quickly as his agitation had taken hold, so had it evaporated.

He was calm. He had no reason for anxiety. The train would come. If by some fluke it didn't, he could walk. Going for a walk had been his intention in the first place. Everything would be okay. His was not a horrible life.

As this tranquility infused him, George had the sensation he was being watched. Normally, sensing that he was being stared at would have made him nervous, but now it only made him curious.

He glanced right and left but didn't recognize anyone, and no one appeared to be looking at him. He heard the sound of a train from across the tracks on the uptown side.

He looked toward that platform, at the fortunate folks whose wait was about to come to an end. Standing on that uptown platform, directly opposite the spot where George now stood on the downtown side, was Jesus, who was looking across at George with bright eyes and a beatific smile. The train pulled in, blocking George's view. And then the train departed, revealing an empty platform.

∾

"What's new?" Sal asked as he led George into the kitchen.

"I've seen Jesus."

"Said the atheist to the priest. Ba-da-bump!" Sal laughed, miming a drummer's rim shot. Seeing George mirthless, he toned down the comedy. "I think you had better sit down," he said, nodding thoughtfully.

He served the soup along with warm Italian bread and some kind of incredible cheese with truffles veining through it he said you could only get at Di Palo's on Grand Street. Then George filled him in on his two encounters with Jesus.

"Mostly I've been thinking that I'm probably having a breakdown of some sort, which would be understandable under the circumstances. But this Jesus thing—"

"Buying him a slice of pizza?"

"No. That's when I thought I must be cracking up. But just now at the subway was different. I was agitated. I was pacing back and forth. I might have even been muttering under my breath."

"And this time you did not think you were crazy?" he smirked.

"Are you trying to be funny?"

"Yes," Sal said, ladling a second helping of *pasta e fagioli* into George's bowl.

"Here's the thing," George said. "All of a sudden, I felt totally calm and at peace and like someone was looking at me. And when I glanced up, there was Jesus. So, what do you think?"

Sal smiled indulgently. The priest's expression reminded George of his father's when he gently broke the news to him about Santa. "I don't think it was Jesus. But that's probably the Catholic in me talking."

Having counted on the Catholic priest to be the one person he knew who might accept the possibility of a divine visitation, George didn't understand what Sal meant by his comment.

"I don't think Jesus makes a special appearance for an anxiety attack on a subway platform. I feel like that's a job for a saint. No offense."

None was taken. George could see his point.

"I mean, even to get the Virgin Mary to show up, I think you'd probably have to fall onto the tracks. You know, something life threatening."

"But if it wasn't Jesus, who was it?"

"You have room for dessert?"

He nodded. Sal cleared the soup bowls and cheese plate. He brought over a tray of warm, gooey chocolate chip cookies well over an inch high. The familiar sight of them struck George. With the first taste, he felt like he was ten years old again, just home from school, ready for a snack and a story.

"Good, right? Your grandmother's recipe."

George burst into tears. As mortified as he was by his

exaggerated display, he could not stop sobbing.

What is wrong with me?

It was just a cookie after all, and a common one at that. But somehow, her version of this classic was so different from others. For one thing, the height of the cookie was extraordinary, and they were so moist. Everything about them was perfection. And seeing them reminded him of the great care Nan took of his entire family and especially of him. And just how lost he had become without her.

He sat for a long time before the crying ceased. And even when he had stopped, it was a while still before he could speak. "A couple weeks after Nan's funeral, my mother had everyone over for dinner and we were all talking and we realized none of us had Nan's recipes. My mother was sure Nan just followed the one that was on the bag of chocolate chips. She tried and tried to duplicate them. And never could. Tara and Finn—both better bakers than my mother—tried too, but with the same failed results. Eventually we accepted that the recipe, and the cookies, were gone forever."

"I wish I'd known that. I would have given Claire the recipe."

"I wonder why Nan gave you the recipe and didn't give it to us."

"Well," Sal shrugged, "maybe because I asked her for it."

Sal packed the entire batch of cookies in foil and placed them in a Food Emporium bag for George to take with him. At Sal's front door, George thanked him for everything. "Wait," he said, just as he was leaving. "You never answered my question. If it wasn't Jesus, who was it?"

The priest smiled so warmly that George almost wished he were still a believer. "What difference does it make?" He waited for Sal to say more, but apparently the priest was finished.

"What do you mean?"

"The first time we met, you told me you were an atheist."

"For the record, when we met, I told you I was no longer a Catholic." George supposed to a Catholic priest that was the same thing. Though he never once said he was an atheist, Sal was right. George never said it, but he certainly thought it.

"Now you're asking me if I think the guy from the subway platform and the pizza parlor is our Risen Savior. No. I do not think God was jonesing for a slice so he came down from heaven. Not for nothing, but I think the real Jesus would have been smart enough to pick a joint in Brooklyn and not the Upper West Side, if he wanted a good pie. But I do think for some reason this guy, who is not Jesus, has been sent to you. And for some reason, you are finding spiritual significance in these random encounters with him. Who cares what the reason is? It's all good."

George had really been hoping Sal would give him a simple yes or no. This was just confusing.

"If I found out tomorrow with certainty that there was no God, do you know how I would change my life?" Sal asked.

George shook his head.

"I wouldn't change anything. Well, I'd probably have to find a new job," he chuckled. "But beyond that, nothing would change. Because my commitment to being a loving caring human being isn't linked to whether or not God exists. That makes sense, right?"

George was pretty sure the priest was speaking rhetorically. Still, to be safe he said, "Yes father, it does."

"Look. I try to treat this world and all its creatures with love because it's the right thing to do. I don't act the way I do because I'm afraid that I'll go to hell if I don't. I'm grateful that I have faith—that I believe in God. It's a comfort. If it turns out I'm wrong about the afterlife, I'll be disappointed. But at the end of the day," Sal winked, "you should pardon the pun, it doesn't matter. You understand?"

George did, but he didn't. He remained silent.

"This guy who you think is Jesus is making you wonder if maybe God really exists after all. Great. I see no downside in that. For a minute, let's pretend God exists. Now go make Him happy. In the process you might just make yourself happy, too."

SIXTEEN

If the priesthood doesn't work out for him, Sal should seriously consider a career in sales.

Needless to say, the atheist was struggling to recall how it was that he'd left the rectory committed to making God happy. Even if the Almighty existed, how would George go about bolstering His spirits? And really, wouldn't He already be happy? He's certainly got a great gig. What's to make Him glum? Yes, mortals can be wretched, which must be a drag considering they were made in His image. But on the plus side, there is always the retaliatory smiting to keep folks in line. Having authority for vengeance without accountability would be enough to put a smile on anyone's face.

Abandoning the notion of cheering up God, George set a slightly more attainable goal. He would try to make Conor happy instead. At least he knew where to find him. No doubt, Conor would be sitting in the showroom, pretending he had something to do, which, unless he'd already begun boxing up his stuff, he didn't.

George had the bag of cookies. If Nan's cookies could not put a smile on his brother's face, he was a lost cause. It was brilliant. Happiness achieved through eating was so much simpler than happiness achieved through communication. Maybe George would yell "Surprise" as he handed the bag over. Aside from the money they desperately needed, George could not think of a single thing he could give Conor that he would appreciate more than Nan's Tollhouse cookies.

George raced into the showroom excited and ready to launch his surprise on Conor, which he'd dubbed Operation Tollhouse. But before he could get to his brother's office, he had to make it through the main showroom floor, where he was greeted like the returning Prodigal Son. It being December, the showroom was empty of customers, so the staff had plenty of free time to chat with him and inquire as to his welfare. The more solicitous they were, the worse he felt, and the more he stared at his shoes or at the trees or off into the alcove filled with crèches. These people were so kind and caring and loyal. No wonder his father kept taking cash advances to give them raises and pay them generous Christmas bonuses.

Oh no. Christmas bonuses!

Just as George was about to unravel, Theo wrapped his strong arms around him.

We have to tell these people. They have a right to know.

Of course, it wasn't something that he could just blurt out. Maybe if he gave Conor enough cookies, he could persuade him to deal with telling everyone that there would be no Christmas bonuses and they'd soon have a new boss, who would most likely be cutting back their salaries.

Released from Theo's hug, George found he could barely look at him, so heavy was the burden of this deception. Compounding his feeling of guilt was the certainty that Theo, in loyalty to his recently deceased employer, would never approve of selling to the chief competitor. George forced himself to face Theo and speak to him. He wasn't sure his words made much sense, as the only sound he was really aware of was his own dramatically thumping heartbeat. "Need my brother," George said, motioning his head toward the office as he made a hasty exit. Scurrying away, he heard Theo whispering to Reg, "He's not himself."

"When is the Christmas party this year?" His breathing was approaching hyperventilation as he marched into Conor's office.

"Call you later," Conor murmured before quickly hanging up his phone. "Ever hear of knocking? Also," Conor checked his watch. "You're late. Did you not just last evening lead me to believe that you were going to help me? It's nearly three. I've been alone in here since nine. Hiding from them," he gestured vaguely toward the main floor of the showroom.

Operation Tollhouse was not unrolling according to plan. "Sorry," George said. "But about the office Christmas party?"

"It's on the twenty-third. We can't cancel it. I already looked into that. Besides, Daddy paid for it in advance. So we might as well enjoy it," he added morosely.

"Please tell me it's at McDonald's."

Conor attempted a smile, though the result was closer to a baring of teeth. Their father had hosted this annual party at some of the grandest and costliest restaurants in New York City. Last year the dinner was held at Jean-Georges. "No. Not the golden arches. This year we will be celebrating at Per Se."

"Are you kidding me? That's the most expensive restaurant in the city."

"No it's not. It's the second most expensive. I checked. The most expensive would be Masa. But you know Daddy never cared much for Japanese food." Conor let out one pained burst of laughter, which quickly morphed into a gasp.

"Okay, so it's paid for. It's done. We are having the party. But what happens at the end of the meal when we don't pass out the Christmas bonuses?"

"Oh no. I forgot about the bonuses." Conor put his elbows on his desk and dropped his head into his outstretched hands. "I know this isn't a solution, but will you go away. I can't think about that right now."

George granted Conor's wish, slipping out of the office and down the hall to the lunchroom. He poked around in the jammed fridge until he found what he was looking for. He grabbed a couple of mugs and shoved everything into a bag so Conor would not see what he had when he returned to the office. Operation Tollhouse was back in action.

When he barged in unannounced this time, George expected to find Conor with his head still in his hands. Instead, he found him engrossed in conversation on the phone.

"Let me call you back," he muttered. Conor stared at George, so George stared right back at him.

"If you want privacy," George said, "lock your door."

"The lock's broken, and I can't afford to fix it."

"I see. So who were you talking to?"

"Nobody."

"Well don't forget to call nobody back after I leave," George needled.

Conor blushed. Seeing his crimson-faced brother, George realized he must have been talking to Tara. This would be a smart time to say something about the situation. George knew he should tell him that he understood, that he wasn't angered, or even creeped out by the weird, borderline incestuous crush. He should also tell him that, for his own sake, he'd be wise to pursue an available woman. He wanted to be a good older brother and offer some sage advice. He should have pointed out to him that he was still young. And he was smart. And astonishingly he still had all his hair. Instead, avoiding the subject entirely, George said, "Close your eyes."

"No."

"Two minutes ago you had your head in your hands. Just do it again. Close your eyes!"

They almost got into an argument over this request. Conor insisted on knowing why, and George wouldn't tell him and so he refused to close his eyes because he assumed he was going to be the victim of a prank. After George crossed his heart and promised he was just trying to be nice, Conor reluctantly shut his eyes, but not before being insulted by the admonition of "no peeking!" Then George poured them each a glass of milk, and he took out the chocolate chip cookies Sal had given him, unwrapping the foil and setting them down on the desk.

"Okay. You can open your eyes."

Conor's complexion went ashen. He looked as if he'd seen a ghost, which in a way he had. He bit into one and chewed, and his jaw dropped open, masticated chocolate coating his tongue. "How did you get these?" A spray of cookie crumbs escaped his lips.

"Don't talk with your mouth full."

They ate all the cookies. There were at least twelve, and George had already eaten four at Sal's. He had every intention of saving some for his kids, but Conor was against that idea, reasoning that there would be other batches—and besides she was their grandmother. "They could always eat Grammy Claire's cookies," Conor suggested, eliciting an outsized laugh from George. Their mother was a terrific grandmother to May and Brian and a very good cook, but she had no interest in baking. Her motto was, *why bake when you can go to Magnolia or Balthazar?*

Conor and George talked for at least an hour, but not about things that urgently mattered. They spoke of nothing that was currently going on in their lives. They didn't even talk about the business, though time was of the essence on that subject. But they were communicating, and that was something.

They talked a lot about their childhood. They talked about Nan. George brought up The Mystery of Finn, and Conor said that since only Finn knew the reason she was sent away, and she was too scary to ask, they would never know the truth. Over the years, George had had many Finn theories. When he was a boy, he concocted a story that Pop made her leave because she was pregnant with Sherman Hemsley's baby. He believed this because he noticed Finn scowling one evening while he was watching *The Jeffersons*. George ignored the fact that Finn scowled at most everything.

"It would have been so excellent if Sherman Hemsley was our uncle," Conor cracked.

Finally, the talking stopped. They had barely mentioned their father's destruction of the business—even the word destruction seemed far too harsh to use in reference to Daddy and the thing he loved so dearly. Neither did they mention their own blowup of days earlier. They'd made no action plan. Posited no solutions. Yet, having said so little that really mattered, there was an easy contentment between the two, foreign but welcomed. And now it felt like the time for George to head back uptown to home.

In these miserably short days of December, George knew it would be dark when he left the warmth of his brother's office, which was only one of the reasons he didn't want to leave. He had the urge to hug Conor, but he didn't. No need for dramatics. The talking and the cookies had been enough. He stood and felt slightly queasy from all the sugar he'd ingested. He hated that Tara was probably right about not letting them eat much of it. At the door, he had an overwhelming desire to share something more personal with his brother for once.

"I met somebody," he said.

Conor could not mask his surprise. His eyes widened nearly to popping. "When?" Considering how recent George's separation from Tara was, Conor was trying to calculate the improbable timing.

"Right after Daddy died."

Maybe the sugar had gotten to Conor too, because he looked like he was going to be sick. "Gross. Are you dating Jenny Dillon?"

"She owns her own business," George said, stupidly defending a woman he was not even involved with. "Jenny Dillon is a very nice girl."

"She embalmed our father."

"Relax. It's not Jenny. But seriously, Jenny is hot and smart and probably rich. There is a lot of money in death. Money isn't everything, of course, but considering we don't have it anymore, it wouldn't be such a bad thing if your wife did. Why don't *you* ask her out?"

"Did I not just mention that she embalmed our father? I'm not dating an undertaker."

"They like to be called funeral directors now."

Then they got off track and talked about Daddy and the

funeral and all those awful lilies, which they now knew he could ill afford. And soon George got ready to leave again. This time he gave Conor a hug.

Only when George was standing on the subway platform did it dawn on him that he'd parted from his brother without telling him about Carolyn. He hadn't even told him her name. He considered going back, but it was dark and cold, and he was ready to get home. Besides, today was not the last time he would talk to his brother.

He'd be showing up for work tomorrow, most likely. George couldn't very well let Conor hide out in his office alone. He would hide out with him, or maybe even not hide. Do something. Tomorrow, while they were hiding or doing, he would tell Conor everything he knew about Carolyn, which George realized in that moment was not so very much. He was going to have to change that.

SEVENTEEN

THE NEXT MORNING, HE DID not see Conor at Bailey and Sons.

George went into work extremely early so he could already be in hiding before everyone else arrived. He realized that was incredibly immature, but he did it anyway. After leaving a note on Conor's desk informing him of his whereabouts, George went to his office and locked the door behind him. Fortunately his lock still worked.

Just after nine his phone rang. It was Conor.

"You got my note?" George's voice was hushed, a little cagey. One might have thought he was waiting for his brother to say the secret word before he'd dare continue.

"What note?"

"Aren't you in your office?"

"I'm calling in sick," said Conor, rather robustly.

"You're not even doing the voice." *The voice* was nasal, hoarse, and laced with the occasional mucous-filled cough. George had taught Conor the voice when they were children, and Conor had mastered it effortlessly. Because he used the voice selectively, Claire never caught on to the ruse. The pleasant end result being that Conor always had a few extra days off a year from school. His teacher, George, however, never managed to pull off the *Camille* routine successfully. His cough always sounded false, inspiring Claire to pull out a thermometer for verification. As a result, George had near perfect attendance during his academic career, for whatever that was worth.

"I need a mental health day. Okay?"

George could hardly argue with that. He told Conor he'd hold down the fort, but he didn't mention he was barricaded within it.

This left him with a day to fill, and thoughts of Carolyn.

After the triumph of the museum date, he was finding it impossible to plan a second outing more original or inspired than the first. For all his self-flagellation, he had no idea what to propose for an encore. He couldn't think of another thing that would be special or interesting or different for a second date. Everything he considered for a follow up either seemed like he was trying too hard, or like he wasn't trying hard enough. Movie? That was both pedestrian and overdone.

He had pretty much settled on taking her on a cruise to nowhere along the Hudson until he recalled that while it was unseasonably warm for December, the temperature could not be described as balmy by even the hardiest Siberian. He might have gotten around the weather issue with blankets and hot cider, but he didn't want to reveal his predisposition to seasickness just yet.

At a loss, and looking for inspiration, George did what he did best: a Google search of the Upper West Side. Three hours later, after an unforeseen detour into the history of the Franco-Prussian war, which to the best of his knowledge was not fought anywhere near the west 70s, he stumbled upon a Druze restaurant called Gazala's.

He was not planning on a mere dinner date with Carolyn, but he thought he would earn extra originality points for selecting the fairly obscure Druze cuisine. And after an additional twenty minutes of Googling, he was confident he could explain to Carolyn what exactly Druze cuisine was. He was going to have to describe the food without actually saying the word, however, because for all his searching he was unable to ascertain whether or not the final *e* was silent.

∾

For a weeknight, the restaurant was extremely busy. Its mosaic-tiled walls conjured an image of Israel meets Santa Fe, not that he had ever been to Israel or Santa Fe. They sat at a table in the center of the restaurant. George had hoped for the intimacy of a corner table, but a large group celebrating the holidays, unwrapping gifts from their Secret Santa, had occupied most of the desirable tables. He was grateful that the hostess had been able to accommodate them anywhere.

The superior stuffed grape leaves, hummus, and lamb more than made up for the inferior location. Because it was the truth, and because it was an easy topic of discussion, they spent a good deal of time raving about how sensational the food was.

When they exhausted that topic, there was a moment of silence George felt desperately needed to be filled, lest Carolyn think he was boring and had nothing to say. He smiled inanely, racking his brain for an apt *bon mot*. Though he was now well versed on the subject, it seemed foolish to bring up the Franco-Prussian war. Certainly he could talk about someone a little more germane than Otto von Bismarck.

With the well of witticism dry, he resorted to truth. "I don't have a great deal of dating experience," he confessed, even though Carolyn already knew that. Had she been unaware of this fact, his awkwardness would have made the matter abundantly clear.

"I dated quite a bit before I was married, which feels like a very long time ago. Since my husband died, I had one disastrous date about six months ago, and that's it. I mean until now," she smiled encouragingly as she reached for another stuffed grape leaf.

"What was so disastrous about it?" Probably it was a mistake to talk about former dates, but it was clearly an improvement over a discourse on nineteenth century European history.

"He was not funny. Or rather, he was funny, but not in a good or intentional way."

George began running through the list of times he heard her laugh at something he'd said, and he gained a little confidence.

"Also he used the word 'bourgeois' three times in the course of one coffee date."

"How bourgeois of him. Incidentally, I'm not sure that I have ever used that word before this moment."

"Glad to hear it. Believe it or not, I might have overlooked that. But he also managed to say 'jejune' four times."

Were there ever a moment for a pithy retort, this was it. But alas, George couldn't think of anything funny or clever because he didn't have an inkling what *jejune* meant. He was strongly tempted to pull out his iPhone and surreptitiously look up the word, but he confessed his ignorance instead.

"I didn't know what it meant either, until he came out with, 'Never a jejune moment.' He said this in reference to the frantic week he had."

George was still not completely certain he understood. "So jejune means dull?"

She nodded her head. "Yes, or without interest. It can also mean juvenile. He really was insufferable. The whole date lasted only forty-five minutes, which was fine with me. A mutual friend, obviously lacking in judgment, set the two of us up. And after the date, my friend called me and told me that Roger thought I was extremely jejune. She was super excited when she relayed the news, because she also had no idea what the word meant."

"Believe me. You are jejune's antonym." She smiled at him like he had just delivered the first line of a love poem.

"Carolyn" by George Bailey III
You are jejune's antonym
The riveting image on the artist's scrim
The engaging lyrics of a lover's hymn
The inspired muse of cherubim
Your gripping words make my heart brim.

Working for Hallmark might be a good next career, if his writing improved.

After sharing a plate of baklava and a pot of Turkish coffee, George offered to escort Carolyn home.

"I don't think I'm going to walk all the way to Hamilton Heights."

She noticed his blank stare. "The west 140s," she explained.

"You know, *in Manhattan.* I thought you were born and raised here?"

"I was." His eyes were a bit glazed. He had never heard of a place called Hamilton Heights. "But I don't get out much because I'm a little jejune."

She laughed. "Cheap joke, George Bailey. But amusing, so you get a pass. Hamilton Heights was where Alexander Hamilton had his farm. The house is still there. It's a national memorial."

He shrugged. "Cool," he said, which made him feel like an illiterate, but she smiled, so maybe it wasn't so bad. They agreed to share a cab. He would get off at Broadway and 114th and she'd continue to 141st. A minor miracle took place when they got into the taxi. The driver was not blaring his radio or talking on his cell phone, or interested in chatting with them. He recorded the two addresses and began silently driving, leaving George and Carolyn to their conversation.

"Maybe you would give me a tour of the 140s sometime."

She shifted restlessly in her seat. "I live with my mother," she told him pointedly."

"Okay," he said, seeing neither the connection nor the problem.

"I haven't mentioned you to her."

Aside from his recent use of the word cool, and not knowing the meaning of the word jejune, George considered himself to be a fairly articulate man, but her words left him at a loss. He squinched up his forehead in confusion.

"It's just..." she began.

Perhaps her mother would not approve of Carolyn dating. But since she had already been a widow for two years, that seemed improbable. Could it be Carolyn's mother would not approve of her dating him specifically?

"It's just..." She began again, "well, you don't look great on paper."

He understood what she meant, even if he didn't want to hear it. "Because of my recent separation, you mean?"

"There's that."

Is there more?

"And your father just died, and your business is failing, which doesn't really bother you because you hate your job anyway and," she stopped before enumerating any more of his flaws. "I just don't think you're exactly what a mother wants for a daughter whose first husband killed himself."

This wasn't great news, but he accepted it as a kind of surmountable hurdle. "But what about the daughter? What does she want?"

"I want to take it slow."

"You picked the right guy for that. I'm happy to take it—"

Carolyn kissed him, her hands on the side of his face. She pulled him closer and pressed her tongue fervently into his mouth. Carolyn was not only the antonym of jejune, she was also the antonym of "taking things slowly," which was fine with George, as he had not been entirely truthful when he said those words in the first place.

Obviously he knew they should take things slowly. But he also knew he had no intention of ever stopping this. This kissing and touching her and…

Then it stopped. His head snapped back as the cab came to a screeching halt. It was such a swift ride. He could not believe they had already arrived at his address. And that was because they had not.

With a scream and a raised fist, the cabbie evicted them from his taxi, claiming he was not being paid enough to be subjected to indecent behavior. Considering the seven-minute ride cost nearly fifteen dollars, George begged to differ with him.

In spite of the fact that he was the wronged party, George

apologized profusely. After he paid the fare, they got out and stood at the corner of 109th and Broadway. George was close enough to walk to his apartment. It would have been so easy, if he had the nerve, to suggest that Carolyn go home with him.

Be brave, George. Ask her if she'd care to spend the night with you.

Before he found his courage, she kissed him again. This time they were somewhat more reserved in their display. As their lips parted, she raised her hand and another cab pulled to the curb. She got in and the taxi sped away. Alone on the sidewalk, George watched until he lost sight of the taillights.

He made his way home. He was frustrated he was making the stroll alone, because all he wanted was to be with Carolyn. But he was also a little relieved. He was aware of his history of rushing headlong into things only to quickly lose interest or become overwhelmed, at which point he let things slow down to a deadly halt. He should try breaking that pattern. Maybe, at least for the time being, slow was good.

Turning the corner onto Riverside, he saw Dennis and a beautiful young woman stepping out of a cab. He was seized with ire on his daughter's behalf. The woman had on a black dress that managed to convey both reserved elegance and sex appeal, covering just enough, but not too much, of her curving figure. Her hair was piled high on her head, a nod to sixties glamour.

George hung back for a moment unsure whether he should confront Dennis with his new woman. If he did make a scene, he'd have the unwinnable job of letting May know her boyfriend was a cad, and she probably wouldn't believe him anyway. If he ignored the situation, he'd only make things worse for May by delaying the moment when she would be heartbroken by this bounder. He marched toward the couple.

They had their backs to him, and Dennis had placed his arm around her shoulder while she rested her head against his chest. The pose was easy and loving, which infuriated George. They laughed softly as they walked together into the building. In this unguarded moment, they seemed like a good match. George was livid, imagining May alone in her apartment in her flannel PJs, devouring a carton of Ben and Jerry's and wondering why her "boyfriend" hadn't bothered calling to wish her goodnight.

He followed the couple into the lobby and as they approached the elevators George could contain his anger no longer, "Hey!" He shouted.

They turned in unison. Dennis smiled like he couldn't be happier.

"Hi Daddy," May said giddily. "We were at the wrap party for Dennis's show."

"That must have been fun," George managed through his shock.

The elevator arrived, and the three of them took the ride up to fourteen.

Approximately ten years earlier, George had taken May to see *Thoroughly Modern Millie* on Broadway. He couldn't remember why they went without Brian and Tara, but they had. It was a father-daughter date night. He had waited impatiently in the living room for her to dress, knowing as the time got tighter, they'd have to take the crowded subway when he would have preferred the privacy and space of a cab. He shouted finally that they would be late.

And she walked into the room, his date for the evening. She had done something to her hair. Instead of her familiar ponytail, it was big and bouncy, curling up at her shoulders. She wore makeup, a bit overdone but not terrible considering he was fairly certain she'd never worn any before. Also she was in heels and wearing a dress, which exaggerated her brand-new cleavage.

His impulse was to send her back to her room to wash her face and to change into something age appropriate, but they didn't have time for that. So he took her arm and off they went, making it to the theatre moments before curtain. As they walked through the lobby, George clocked a half a dozen husbands, no doubt forced to the theatre against their will by their wives, checking out his date. He was horrified. But he also assumed these men had no idea they were lusting after a thirteen year old.

George remembered nothing about the musical. All he remembered was sitting in the orchestra fretting about his soon to be grown-up daughter. And the future.

And the future was happening right now in this elevator. He had not gotten a good look at her face when they were on the sidewalk. He had been a fair distance away. Still, how had he not recognized his own child? He grimaced. George thought she was beautiful and womanly and worst of all, sexy. She looked like a suitable match for Dennis.

No one spoke during the short ride. If they did, George was too shocked to hear anything. The elevator doors opened, and they stepped out into the hall—three people with two apartment doors to choose from. There was an awkward moment. It was awkward for George, anyway. Dennis and May seemed unfazed.

"Well, goodnight," Dennis said, fiddling with his keys. "Sleep tight, Dude."

Aside from his constant use of the word *dude*, George was finding it harder and harder to justify his disapproval of May's involvement with this man who was generous, kind, handsome, successful, and a borderline genius.

"Goodnight," George said. As much as he tried stifling them, he felt tears in his eyes. He reached out and took his daughter's hand. "You have never looked more beautiful than you do right now." He pulled her tightly into his arms. "And that's saying a lot," he whispered into her ear. "Because you're always beautiful."

May cried too, which was happening with such consistency these days it was taking on the air of a running gag. Maybe she thought so too, because she laughed self-consciously as she rubbed the back of her hands against her eyes. Even with mascara streaking her face, she looked sensational. George could not deny that for all the recent tragedy and heartbreak, this budding relationship with Dennis was obviously a positive development for her. May seemed peaceful, contented and—with a twinge George acknowledged—completely grown up.

May and Dennis disappeared behind the door marked A, leaving George to enter B alone.

EIGHTEEN

FOR THE FIRST TIME SINCE moving out, George awoke without feeling surprised to find he was in bed alone. As always, he reached his arm across the mattress, but he knew his hand would only graze the unslept upon pillow on the other side of the bed. He pulled his knees to his chest and stared at the ceiling. The healer had encouraged him to stretch, but until today he had failed to take his advice. He lay there, holding, breathing, willing himself to be limber. He wasn't sure it was working, but maybe it took more than a minute to see results. He gave it another go but stopped when he was struck with an idea.

For years, Adelman Inc. and Bailey and Sons were located on the same block—Fifth Avenue between 25th and 26th Streets—along with a handful of other smaller holiday and general gift wholesalers.

As the neighborhood changed and prices soared, several of the smaller places went out of business. Adelman wisely, George had to admit, moved their operation to the more affordable West Thirties. George had never seen their new showroom, even though Clark had relocated eight years ago. It was high time he paid a visit. So George called his brother and said he was doing research, whatever that meant, and that he'd be in late. His brother said George could take the whole day off, if in return he could take off the following day. Agreed.

∾

ADELMAN INC. WAS LOCATED ON the sixth floor of a nondescript building on 35th Street. When George got off the elevator, he saw that they occupied the entire sixth floor. A large sign at their entrance read:

WELCOME TO ADELMAN INC.
Where America Celebrates Christmas.

The sign irked George.

Really? The whole country? That's a bit presumptuous, isn't it?

Clark came out onto the showroom floor. His suspicious stare in response to George's unannounced appearance was quickly replaced with an ersatz salesman's smile. "You should have called. I would have taken you to lunch," he said, in spite of the fact that it was only ten in the morning.

The sales staff all appeared to be quite busy, though not with customers. One man in a crisp, if cheap, suit, was obsessively rearranging Santas while another was shuffling papers. A middle-aged woman with red nails held two red glass spheres, her eyes darting back and forth between the two balls. She studied them as if they held the Universe's secrets. Every single employee, without exception, was pretending to be busy. George was certain of this, since he himself was a master of such behavior.

George thought it odd that they were not taking advantage of the slow period by relaxing. In a month's time, these people would be genuinely busy. Undoubtedly they would be working ten or twelve hours a day from mid-January through the last of the trade shows in August. Why not relax when you could? He pictured the team at Bailey and Sons solving crossword puzzles, playing Angry Birds and shopping online.

"What brings you here to see me? Curious what a successful operation looks like?" As George bristled, he added, "Relax. I'm just playing with you." He laughed aggressively.

Once again George wished another buyer could be found—an ex-warlord, perhaps, a reformed drug kingpin, an assassin looking for a change of pace, really anybody else. But he knew that would never happen, certainly not with all their mounting debt.

It didn't even really make sense that Clark had offered to buy them, and George knew he should be grateful, but he wasn't. Then something struck him he hadn't thought of before. "Why would you want to own two Christmas wholesale businesses?" he asked. He refrained from adding, especially since you *already* own the one where all of America celebrates Christmas.

"Sentimental, I guess. I've been thinking about it for years. I mean the writing was on the wall for you guys for a long time. I talked to your father about selling to me a year ago," he said smugly.

George acted like he was aware of that, even though he wasn't. As with so many aspects of the business, he was clueless about that, too. Sadly this was confirmation of something he already knew. His father would never have sold to Clark Adelman.

"Yeah, I stopped by the showroom to talk to him. I'd heard a couple of rumors that things weren't going so well for you guys. And when I saw all those shelves full of nativity sets right near the front—Christ, they were the first things I saw when I walked through the door—I knew the rumors had to be true."

"What are you talking about?"

Clark looked at George like he was a moron. "I carry two different nativity sets, a cheap one and an expensive one, and I only stock those to keep my mother off my ass. You have thirty-fucking different crèches in your line."

"So," George said uneasily.

"So? Thirty reindeer, fine. Thirty snowmen or Santas, of course." Sensing shirking in the distance, Clark looked over at the salesman who had just stopped rearranging the display of Santa figurines. "Yo, Carlos. You need a project?"

A frenzied-looking Carlos assured him he did not, leaping to his feet to resume miming productivity.

"Boy, you have to stay on top of them every second, don't you? What was I saying? Oh, yeah. Not thirty crèches. You're not making any money off of that. They're just taking up space. Jesus doesn't sell. You should know that. Not that it's information you need any longer." Clark slapped George on the back. They both pretended the gesture was good-natured. "So, you know I've been trying to give your mom all the time she needs, but are we close to bringing in the lawyers?"

George grunted out a noncommittal response. "I do have one question. How long will you expect me to stay on?"

"What do you mean?"

"To run things."

Clark was quiet, which was welcome if unsettling. Then he grinned, like he was a little slow, but he got the joke now. "Hey George Bailey, good one. I've seen the movie. This is not the building and loan. You staying on and running the joint is not a contingency. It's not even an option. Christ, I could do it in my sleep." Clark shuffled restlessly. "So if there's not anything else. I'm kind of busy here."

"No. No. I'm good. I was just in the neighborhood. Thought I'd say hi." George considered hauling off and slapping Clark's shoulder, but it wasn't really his style.

Clark, ever the salesman, smiled again. "That mother of yours is a good negotiator, but we should have it hammered out by the end of the year. You'll be glad when you're rid of the place. Don't worry, I'll take good care of it." He headed back to his office, but not before barking at another one of his employees. "Yo. I'm not paying you to update your Facebook status. You need a project?"

∾

MINUTES AFTER HE LEFT ADELMAN, George felt the urge to go home and take a long hot shower, but Claire called him and asked him to come for lunch. Even though he was on the sidewalk and his datebook was in his apartment, he said he'd look at his calendar, because he didn't want his mother to think he was idle. Claire explained that she meant today.

George went through with the pretense of checking his book anyway, leaving her on hold while he stood aimlessly on 35th Street. A guy in an elf suit walked by. Even for a guy in an elf suit, he looked hopeless. George wondered if he was heading to Macy's or someplace where it would be even more degrading for an adult to be caught in that getup. He watched the man trundle away, green and white striped tights disappearing in the crowd.

What am I going to be doing for a job this time next year?

When a convincing amount of time had passed he spoke. "Looks like I'm free, Mom. Noon?"

George showed up with a pot of paperwhites, which his mother loved. Though they grew at most anytime of the year, Claire filled the apartment with pots of them at Christmas, preferring the delicate daffodils to the more traditional poinsettias or amaryllis.

He didn't see any pots of them now, and no Christmas tree, either. There were no decorations of any kind. Under the circumstances, this didn't surprise him. But the lone pot of paperweights was a sharp contrast to the way this apartment normally looked in December, with its three Christmas trees and garlands and wreaths. Even though George's parents were rarely in New York on December 25th they always had a lavish party earlier in the month, which was part celebration and part launch of the new line.

Claire teared up when she smelled the paperwhites. She looked like she hadn't been sleeping well, but she'd made an effort to do her hair and put on makeup. Even the dress she wore might have been new. It was dark gray, one baby step away from black. The obvious care she had taken to make herself look presentable somehow saddened George, because he always thought of his mother as being effortlessly chic and turned out at all times. Today she seemed frail, breakable.

She led George to the kitchen, setting the flowers in the middle of the small table. "Hungry?" she asked.

Neither of them had much of an appetite, but nevertheless each of them ate for the benefit of the other. She had made grilled cheese and bacon sandwiches and cream of tomato soup. It was a meal she might have served him when he was ten, and it comforted him. The soup was salty but delicious. He wondered if it was Campbell's. His father never would have allowed processed food in the house, but his mother could buy whatever she wanted now.

They spoke little over lunch. George didn't see the point in mentioning his visit to Adelman. The whole encounter had depressed him. His telling Claire about it would only do the same to her.

"What are you doing for Christmas?" Claire asked, carrying the soup bowls to the sink and running the tap so they could soak.

George hadn't given it a thought. He assumed he'd come here, but then he remembered she said she might go to Martinique.

"I'm not up to the trip," she said, which was probably true, but George worried it was because she was afraid to spend the money. "We'll have Christmas in New York. I can't do it, though. Will you?"

George had never hosted anything in his life—at least not without Tara, who did everything but man the bar when they threw a party. George wondered if he should propose dinner in a restaurant, but Claire seemed to read his mind. "I can't be around a lot of strangers. You'll make dinner in your new apartment. May says it's huge."

May had not been in his apartment, but presumably Dennis had the same floor plan.

She suggested they have dessert in the living room. "Would you like cheese cake, flourless chocolate cake, assorted cookies, or pecan pie?" she asked before exiting the kitchen.

George's mother was never the health nut that his father was, but she always ate very well. George found her menu of offerings a little troubling and hoped she wasn't planning her own early checkout via heart disease or diabetic coma.

"Don't look at me like that," Claire said. "People show up. They bring this stuff. It's as if the whole world has decided that sugar is a perfectly acceptable substitute for a dead husband." She shook her head. "Though I must admit, and I'm not usually a fan, the pecan pie is quite comforting." Claire laughed, "You look like you could use a piece."

She carried two plates, each holding a large slice of pecan pie, topped with a scoop of vanilla ice cream. As they settled in on the sofa, she handed George his plate and acknowledged the addition of the a la mode. "Why not? It's the holidays. And we're in mourning."

Claire was right. The pie was comforting. George took several bites of the rich, gooey dessert before looking up and seeing his father. Not his ghost, but rather his image, framed on the shelf in front of him. He was tanned and smiling alongside pictures of Pop and Nan. One picture showed Nan alone, taken no more than a few months before she died. George recognized the coat she wore. She was standing in Union Square. She could have been on her way to church or to a party or just the grocery store. It was impossible to tell with his grandmother because she was always well dressed.

"Can I look at the albums?" asked George. Claire got up without saying a word and walked into her bedroom, returning a minute later with five, oversized leather-bound books stacked in her arms. Her bedroom was not where the albums normally lived. Claire usually kept the photo albums in a closet in what would have been the small maid's room, if they had had a live-in maid. So she must have pulled them out herself recently, not satisfied by the two dozen photos framed and kept on display at all times.

When Claire returned, she sat back down closer to her son.

She curled up her legs and rested her head on George's shoulder, like a child or a sweetheart. And George slowly flipped the pages. There was a photo of his grandmother with Finn, who was all of five or so, peering out from behind Nan's skirt, grinning and bright-eyed. It was hard to believe Finn had ever been joyous, but in this photo there was no denying it. In the same picture, the infant Tea was in his grandmother's arms. The child, according to Nan, so precious that God took her into his mighty arms and quickly brought her home.

"When was this taken?"

"That had to be 1938. Probably not long before the hurricane."

"I don't know how Nan could have lived through such a horrible ordeal and carried on. More than carried on. Still had that unshakeable faith."

Claire shook her head. "I used to think I understood, but I don't anymore."

They turned the pages, though there were no more photos of Tea. Then his father appeared, little baby George in the arms of his ten-year-old sister Finn. And then a few more photos of Finn before she, too, disappeared, though not because God took her home.

"What happened to her?"

"Do you know I dated your father for six months before he told me he had a sister? He was only seven when she left. And all he knew was that he could not mention her in front of Pop."

"You really don't know what happened? Do you think she was pregnant?"

"That seems hard to believe, doesn't it?" Claire said. For a moment they tactfully resisted, before succumbing to laughter.

"When I was pregnant with you, Nan came over one day for lunch. She must have prepared the meal for us, but I know we were in our first apartment, the one on Jane Street." Claire said this as if George would recall, though he was only a year old when they moved out of it.

"And we were sitting together on the couch and she took my hand and held it. You only remember your grandmother as affectionate and loving, and she was always a very sweet and gentle person, but we didn't hold hands, not back then. She even leaned in and kissed my cheek, which surprised me, moved me." Even all these years later the memory misted Claire's eyes. "Then Nan said, 'You must think I'm a terrible mother.'

"Honestly I thought she was talking about the way she'd raised Daddy, which didn't make sense. I wasn't following at all. Then she squeezed my hand a little harder. 'I should have put my foot down with George, but I didn't,' she said. All you Georges, I wasn't even sure if Nan meant her George or mine, but I realize now she meant your grandfather."

"Nan didn't say anything else?"

"Not then. But later I learned she saw Finn once a month or so. She would sneak off to the Upper East Side or another part of town where she didn't know people and visit her, but your grandfather never knew about it. Sometimes she would come to Jane Street to bake a batch of cookies for Finn." Claire picked up her plate, pausing to take a bite.

"Nan didn't want Pop to smell the treats when he came home. And your father didn't know, and I never said anything, but he'd come in, the apartment smelling like a bakery, and he'd start looking for the sweets. I'd lie and tell him it must have been coming from another apartment. I don't recommend deception in a marriage, but it worked for us." She stopped, struck by what she'd just said. In frustration, she slammed her plate down onto the coffee table. "I thought it worked for us," she said in a rage. "I am so pissed at your father."

George held onto his plate, stared at the crumbs. His mother's wound was too hard to look at.

"What was he thinking for the last five years not telling me?"

"He wanted to protect us."

"Well, he didn't." She got up and walked out of the room. George followed with his eyes, but remained seated. He wasn't sure if she was planning on coming back, almost hoped that she wouldn't. He had no idea what he could do or say to help her. He felt she must blame him for not knowing how much trouble they were in. He certainly blamed himself.

She returned with a knife and the rest of the pie. Without asking whether he wanted it or not, she cut two more slices. "What the hell," she said resignedly. "I can't let this become a habit, though. Already everything's a little tight." She sucked in her stomach. "Let's face it, I certainly can't afford to replace my wardrobe." This struck her as hilarious. Gallows humor, George guessed. "Open another album," she ordered, when finally her laughter had quieted.

George knew so little about his family. For someone who could spend hours searching useless trivia on the Web, he had surprisingly limited curiosity about his own relatives. He asked his mother to tell him more about their history.

"I remember once, when you kids were young, Nan and I had packed a picnic and took you boys to the zoo in Central Park. Then later, Nan and I sat on a bench, worn out, while the two of you were still running around. We were watching you boys playing and Nan said 'Georgie is so much like his father.' And I just smiled. Then she said, 'Conor is more like Finn.' But of course I had never met Finn, so I was curious how she meant that. When I asked her to explain, she just changed the subject."

George thought about that for a moment. He didn't think he was like his father at all, not in looks or temperament. It was Conor who favored their father. What an odd thing for Nan to say, though not as odd as comparing Conor to Finn. No wonder Nan's observation had stuck with Claire all these years.

"Conor," George said. "Like Finn?" Then, as he thought about it, he supposed maybe Nan was on to something. They certainly both seemed to him so very enigmatic. "I just remember Finn suddenly appearing at Pop's funeral and being introduced to her. And thinking how weird it was I was meeting my aunt for the first time at my grandfather's wake. I figured she must have flown in from Europe or something."

"I think she just took the crosstown bus."

They'd come to the end of an album, but Claire wanted to look at one more, so George hauled it up onto his lap, and slowly began flipping pages. He was still thinking about the day he met Finn, and the death of his grandfather.

"I remember something else about Pop's funeral. The singers."

Claire looked blankly at her son.

"The three nuns with the guitars."

"Oh yes," Claire said, recalling them. "They were very talented."

"Mom! The closing hymn was *Leaving on a Jet Plane*."

Claire laughed. "Those were the times. Folk masses."

"It was 1984. Those times had been over for more than a decade. And Nan, who I assume would have preferred bagpipers, acted like a Peter, Paul and Mary cover band was absolutely perfect. She was so appreciative."

George turned another page of the album and staring back at him was his nineteen-year-old self. There he was, clueless and naive on his wedding day. Tara stood beside him. In her makeup and styled hair, Tara could have passed for thirty. But, aside from the fact that he was in a very classic black tux, not a powder blue one, George looked like he was on his way to the prom. Faint acne scars were visible on his chin.

"What a nice picture," Claire said. George realized she was looking at the next page, a shot of Claire and her husband dancing at their son's wedding. "I looked good in that dress."

"Mom, why didn't you ever tell me I was too young to get married?"

Claire frowned. She picked up her fork, but seeing that she'd already finished her second piece of pie, set it down again. "You were happy. You seemed happy, anyway."

"But Mom—"

"You were not a happy child. Not really. You were born old. And you were too wise for your age. You understood the difficulties of life."

George found that hard to believe, since he thought himself rather puerile at forty-three. But maybe what she said was true. Manhattan had been a gritty place in the seventies and eighties. His childhood, though privileged, was tougher than his children's. The neighboring East Village, now filled with million dollar apartments, was filled with drugs and crime back then, and the homeless population was not so successfully hidden away. Walking those streets as a boy both terrified George and made him feel incredibly guilty. Avenue A was a border he never dared cross. When he would approach, he saw sorrow in the eyes of the downtrodden, and he felt as if he were personally to blame. And since he had no idea how to go about fixing the problem, he retreated.

"I never seemed to be able to shield you from the truth," Claire continued. "Then you met Tara. And I saw a smile on your face like I had never seen. I liked that you were finally acting like a typical teenager."

She had tears in her eyes again, so George didn't point out that in the late twentieth century, typical teenagers did not marry the first girl they ever dated.

Claire glanced toward her pie plate, but it was still empty. She sighed. "When you announced your engagement, it wasn't a great time for your father and me. Did you know that?"

George had no idea. He wondered if his parents had been good at hiding their problems, or if he'd just been too emotionally checked out to notice.

"We had been having a hard time, and I needed something positive to focus on. I'm sorry, George. I didn't just want you to be happy. I wanted to be happy, too."

Once again, George thought of his mother's previous allusion to infidelity and wondered if that's what she was referring to now. Had his father been the unfaithful one? He decided it wasn't any of his business. Even if it were, it didn't matter. Whatever his parents' troubles had been, they'd come to terms with them. George looked at the photo of his smiling parents, twirling around the dance floor. "Mommy," he said. While he often referred to his father as Daddy, Claire was almost always Mom. "See," he said, pointing at the picture. "You were right. Look at us. We were happy."

Claire smiled. "Don't worry, George. I won't be mad at your father forever. I never could stay mad at him for long." She pushed the pie tin with one sliver remaining to the other side of the coffee table, out of reach. Then she began piling up the albums. "I have copies of everything. Take whatever photos you like."

George took a great stack of pictures of the four generations of Baileys that were represented. He knew almost nothing about his ancestors who came before his grandparents. Once while Googling, he'd been shocked to learn that Bailey wasn't even an Irish name. Its origins were French and English. Like his grandparents who had come to America from County Cork for a better life, some earlier generation of the family had perhaps left France for Ireland. He knew nothing of their journey. That story was lost forever. And someday the story of the Baileys of Manhattan and their life devoted to Christmas, would be forgotten, too.

But for today, he took a small step at keeping their stories alive for another generation or two. Claire gave him a paper bag from Whole Foods and he carefully placed his stack of photos inside. On top of the pile was an image of Nan, smiling as always, her hair just so. She was wearing her elegant spring coat.

NINETEEN

Apparently Kmart had been opened in Manhattan for over fifteen years but George had never noticed the big box giant before despite its prime Astor Place location. He was only aware of its existence now because he'd Googled *Where can you buy cheap picture frames in NYC?*

He arranged his silver-framed photos around the living room and felt hopeful in the company of the Bailey clan, even though he could not explain why. He had taken no steps to rectify their financial troubles aside from buying bargain-priced picture frames instead of actual sterling ones, and he knew that didn't really count. The sale of the business would go forward despite his misgivings, because there was no alternative. The bright side was he'd be free of the job he hated for so long. And if, as it seemed, he was now officially a failure in the career department, maybe he still had a shot at being a success at love. That was the even bigger bright side.

Now that he was dating, George had a whole new point of view about receiving texts. He used to find them intrusive, a disruption of his busy schedule, never mind that his schedule was rarely that busy. In his current situation, texts had become Cupid's arrows. Each ping held the promise of flirtation. After receiving texts from his mother, brother, Dennis and May, all appreciated but still somehow disappointing, it occurred to George he could text Carolyn himself if he was so eager for romance.

"Hi!!!!!! ☺" he said, wishing he had shown a tad more restraint with regard to his use of exclamation points. The emoticon probably should have been left out completely.

After several long minutes, "Hi," came her single word reply.

He took it as an extremely ominous sign she had not included similarly exuberant punctuation in her return text.

"Swamped," she added in a subsequent text. "Only working 'til four today. Meet me at salon then?"

"Will do!!!!!!!!!!!!!!!!"

Once he hit the exclamation point, it was near impossible for him to stop. He needed to bring it down a notch, which —in spite of spending the last twenty years displaying almost no enthusiasm for anything—was proving to be difficult.

Carolyn had her coat on and bag in hand and was ready to leave work exactly at four. He asked if she'd like to go for coffee, but she told him that she had planned their date.

'Shall I hail a cab?" he asked as they approached the curb.

"You can't afford it. We're walking."

He wondered if he should tell her that this afternoon he had shopped at Kmart instead of Tiffany. He thought that was enough of a nod to frugality for one day. He hadn't been reduced to penury yet. "Unless you are dragging me to an outer borough I can afford to pay for a cab. I mean, even then…"

She waved her hand indicating the subject was closed, and they began walking.

"Are you going to tell me where we're going?"

"Of course not. That wouldn't be any fun." She linked her arm through his, which was easy and felt completely natural. He almost made a comment about how easy and completely natural it felt, but he remembered he was trying to bring it down a notch.

"George Bailey." She had a way of announcing his full name that suggested she was launching into the recitation of an official proclamation. "How have you been keeping yourself busy since last we met?"

"I went to visit Clark Adelman, the guy we're selling to. He treats his employees terribly. And he's crass. And I know my father would have never sold to him. And now I don't want to sell to him either, but we have no other choice because, for obvious reasons, no one else is ever going to buy us. We have nothing left but our name and our reputation. That's really all we're selling," George's words came out in one animated rush.

She smiled and pulled her arm through his a bit tighter. "You know for a guy who is supposed to hate his job, you perk up and get energized every time you talk about it."

He had noticed that, too. He supposed he'd better figure out why that was, because his recent behavior was a bit contradictory when it came to the business he supposedly couldn't wait to be rid of.

"The problem," he explained, "is that there is no alternative to this jackass."

"There are always alternatives, but carry on."

"My mother is really upset over the position my father has left us in, but I know at heart she doesn't want to sell. My brother claims he doesn't want to, as do my children. Only I want to sell."

"You do? Because it doesn't seem like it to me." She spoke with such tenderness that he felt supported rather than mocked.

"I don't want to sell to Adelman, but I don't want to keep the business either. And even if I did want to keep it, I can't. I'm broke."

"George, it is probably a bit early in the game for us to be talking about money, but didn't you tell me you and your wife own a three bedroom downtown?"

"Yes, we do."

"Why don't you sell it?"

"How would that help?"

Her expression said she'd begun wondering just how astute George actually was with regard to financial matters.

"I get that it would give me some cash—okay, a lot of cash—but I'd need to buy another apartment. Two actually, since Tara will need to live someplace. I won't be in my cheap sublet forever. So with my half of the proceeds from the sale, and then having to buy another place, how much could I possibly have left over?"

"Well. You could get a place outside of Manhattan, even outside of the five boroughs. I have good friends who bought a house about forty-five minutes up the Hudson for less than the cost of a studio here. They have an easy commute on the train. And, better still, they're living in nature."

George fought the urge to say that was the worst idea he'd ever heard in his life. "Nature. That would be something. I bet they have a lot of deer around."

"As a matter of fact they do," she said enthusiastically.

"Not for me." He shook his head. "I'm not interested in living any place where checking yourself for ticks is the highlight of your day."

She laughed a moment before stopping to study him. "You know, I'm not sure whether you're a little bit insane or just have a delightfully offbeat sense of humor. Which is it?"

He went with offbeat sense of humor, guessing that was the only answer that would guarantee him another date. Yet even after he said it, she looked at him like maybe she had a few lingering doubts about his mental stability. If she did, she shook them off.

Carolyn instructed him to head east on 49th Street. George told her she should probably rethink that plan. "We will never get across Fifth," he said. "I tried to do it the other day, and the tourists were clogging everything up. It was pedestrian gridlock. Do these people really have nothing better to do with their lives? Who needs to see another store window decorated for Christmas? How many versions of the Sugar Plum Fairy can one take? Am I right?"

The instant he saw Carolyn's crestfallen expression, he knew strolling by the Christmas decorations was supposed to be their date. Surprise!

He apologized, sort of, by saying that if he'd known she'd planned to take him to Saks Fifth Avenue, he would have kept his mouth shut. It didn't really help the situation, so he took another stab at gaining her forgiveness. "I'm truly sorry," he said. "The truth is I just don't like crowds very much."

"That's why you should move to the country." She laughed. At him. But still, she laughed. So, he trusted the evening could be salvaged.

"If you promise to hold onto my arm extra tight, I'm sure I can cope with the crowds."

"Has this all been some elaborate ruse on your part just to get me to touch you more?"

"Yes. Now let's go check out the sights."

They tried to get over to Rockefeller Center to look at the tree, but it was unbelievably jammed. Throngs of people were just leaving work, and it was dark outside—perfect for appreciating the lights, yet not too late an hour for families with small children to still be milling about. Between all of the business people making their way home and all of the kids screaming and squirming to catch a glimpse of the tree, there was pandemonium on the streets. Still, George kept his mouth shut and acted like he was glad to be in the middle of this mess. "I'm totally game. Should we just push through?"

She looked at him and smiled. "I like it that you're a terrible liar. These crowds are too much even for me. You aren't going to hyperventilate on me, are you? I couldn't live with the guilt."

Carolyn took his hand and led him away from the crowds. Even exiting was tricky, as so many others, thirsty for some holiday spirit, had pressed in behind them.

"I have an idea," she said, dragging him toward 50th Street. As the mass of pedestrians on the sidewalk came toward them, Carolyn and George were like two lone salmon fighting their way upstream. At 50th, the crowd was much less intense. Carolyn headed west and cut in at the side entrance of Rockefeller Plaza.

"Very clever."

She winked at him "Trust me. It gets better."

They headed toward one of the buildings flanking the plaza. Carolyn opened the door and ushered him inside. They got on the elevator and headed up to the third floor, exiting into the lobby of the Equinox Fitness Center. They approached the front desk, and Carolyn pulled out her ID card. A pleasant looking girl who was probably in her twenties but looked about thirteen smiled at them. Her hair was in pigtails, and she wore a simple black t-shirt with the word "Greet" printed in white across her boyish chest.

"May I bring in a guest?" Carolyn asked, as she pointed at George.

"You don't need to do that," he said.

"Don't be silly, George. It's my treat."

"No. I mean you don't need to do that because I'm a member."

"You are?" In his opinion there was a bit too much incredulity in Carolyn's tone. Did she really find it so strange that he belonged to a gym? Because for a man who rarely broke a sweat, he appeared to be very fit. He looked down at his stomach. It was definitely flat—ish.

After several minutes of failed searching for his membership card, he gave up looking for it. The greeter looked him up in the computer system and let him in.

As they walked away from the desk, the girl yelled out, "Have a great workout. If you hurry, you can still make the 5:30 Zumba class."

"Please tell me that's not our new plan for the evening."

Carolyn shrugged, determined to successfully pull off at least one surprise this evening. She took him by the hand again and led him down a long hall past photos of the herculean-looking trainers, and out on to the gym floor. They stopped right in front of a bench press, stacked with about three hundred pounds of weight and a big heavy bar designed for doing dead lifts. It occurred to George he better start hoping they had just stopped here temporarily before heading off for Zumba.

Thankfully they had just paused, and not to restack weights or locate the classroom. Carolyn told him to close his eyes, which he did not want to do. But then he remembered how much trouble Conor had given him when he made the same request of him just days earlier. In that case, the reward had been cookies, so he acquiesced.

She led him by the hand. With each step he took, he was certain he would trip over a dumbbell and crack his skull open, but he played along gamely not wanting to be seen as a killjoy or an hysteric.

When they came to a halt, and she allowed George to open his eyes, they were in the far corner of the gym floor surrounded by mats and physioballs, standing in front of a large window. There, straight in front of them, was the towering Rockefeller Center Christmas tree, its lights blazing. From inside the gym, they had their own private and warm view, while outside the masses jockeyed for a glimpse in the chilly evening air. He had not seen the tree in at least fifteen years.

He had a vague memory of corralling the kids one December and braving the crowds to make the pilgrimage to Rock Center. The outing had been a disaster. Brian had a meltdown because he thought Santa was going to be there. Despite George's detailed explanation of Santa's busy schedule making toys at the North Pole, his son would not be consoled.

As Brian wept in despair, George swore he would never return to this awful place, when the only thing on view was a huge tree. A stupid *tree*, of all things, when all George did was look at Christmas trees every single day of his wretched life. He became incredibly cranky and miserable and nearly as disconsolate as his son, stopping just shy of actually shouting "Bah Humbug," before heading back to the subway, because there was not a cab in sight.

But George had a dramatically different experience tonight. He was game to stand here as long as Carolyn liked because he wanted to please her. If she wanted him to look at a tree, so be it. It wasn't going to kill him. He'd be a good sport. So he looked. It helped that he was warm and away from the crowds below.

Then something wonderful and unexpected happened, and it

wasn't just because he had ample space around him and didn't have claustrophobia to contend with. Inexplicably, he found the tree to be beautiful. It was vast and grand, and even with the crowds milling about on the plaza, the overall effect of the scene was peaceful. The more George looked at the tree, the more tranquil he became. A calming hush quieted his insides. And so he looked and looked, his eyes delightedly following the fluttering lights.

As glorious as the tree was, something made him stop staring at it. Instead, he looked over at Carolyn. Or, more specifically, he looked at Carolyn looking at the tree. He tried to be surreptitious so she wouldn't be aware of his gaze and become self-conscious. But she was so engrossed in the view in front of her, he probably could have jumped up and down and made funny faces, and she wouldn't have noticed.

Carolyn was in her forties, yet it seemed as if a sorcerer had transformed her into a little girl. Her eyes had widened near to bulging, and her mouth had formed a small O of wonder. Transformed by the power of this towering tree, it seemed she had become a believer in miracles and magic. She saw joy and hope and endless possibilities. Seeing Carolyn in this state of unadulterated bliss, it seemed impossible she had ever known heartbreak, tragedy, and loss.

She squeezed his hand but didn't shift her eyes from the majestic spruce. He squeezed back, still watching her instead of the tree.

And a thought struck him. Obvious really, but he had never considered it before. The effect the tree was having on Carolyn was exactly what had motivated Pop and his father to devote their lives to Christmas. Maybe it wasn't ever about the stuff itself so much as it was about the way all those lights and balls they were selling made people feel.

George began thinking about Bailey and Sons in a new way. Some great and positive shift and the beginning of a sense of pride, took hold of him. George had never seen magic in the merchandise they sold until this moment.

He had only seen monotony and a way to make a buck. He had found the whole enterprise soul crushing. He saw the boring sameness of what he did for a living, as year after year he tried to convince people to buy endless crates of identical, never-changing crap. He spent years wanting to scream, wanting to knock down the trees and smash every ornament.

What he hadn't seen, what he now finally saw because it was visible in Carolyn's eyes, was the experience they created for people. It was never really the ornaments. That's not what the customers were buying from Bailey and Sons. They bought memories.

They bought stories, which connected to their very real lives. Come December, someone would pull an ornament out of a dusty shoebox that they stored on a shelf or in the basement for eleven months. When they looked at the glass ball or star, or felt-covered elf, they would remember where they were when it first came into their lives. And they'd remember why they bought it, or who had given it to them—the first baby, the first anniversary or the first year in the house. So much joy attached to each little decoration.

Of course, George understood not all memories would be happy ones. He imagined a woman pulling out a tree topper from its storage box. He saw her buying it on her last vacation, the one right before her husband's illness. She shed tears at the sight of the object, as did all the members of her family, because they knew its significance. In his mind's eye, George watched her climb the ladder to crown the tree. As she positions the topper, she thinks of her husband, misses him desperately. But then, she recalls the wonderful last trip, and the joy they shared.

George knew that objects and memories could be powerful and healing, but it now dawned on him with the weight of inspired epiphany. Everywhere now as Christmas trees went up, he thought, memories of lives and loves were being formed and recalled. And though no one would ever know it, George's family was a big part of those memories. Nan used to say that you should never give a gift with the expectation of thanks, because the giving was reward enough. Now he saw that Nan was right.

He pulled Carolyn into his arms and kissed her. Her eyes widened in surprise, but she eagerly returned his affections. In his enthusiastic ardor, he lost his footing and they tumbled together against the physioballs, and both the balls and the two of them rolled across the floor.

"Hey. I'm very sorry, but this can't... You can't..."

The personal trainer who was attempting to break them up seemed at a complete loss as to how to disentwine them. Odd, since he must have been at least two hundred pounds of solid muscle. It mattered not. They spared him the task, standing casually, as if everyone rolled in dress clothes across gymnasium floors in the heat of passion.

Carolyn placed her hand to head, discreetly trying to fix her now disheveled hair. Thanks to the super short cut he had received from his girlfriend, George had no such problem. They exited the workout floor. This being the third time someone in a position of authority had chastised them for their public display of affection, they were becoming quite adept at assuming an air of indignation.

"What got into you? Not that I'm complaining."

"I'm not selling."

"This requires a big conversation," she announced, at a loss as to what had precipitated his shift. "But first the ladies room."

Carolyn and George both had need of the restroom, so they headed for the respective locker rooms, agreeing to meet in the lobby when they were finished.

He had never been to this Equinox location before, not that he had really been to any of them, aside from his yearly trip to the Flatiron Equinox to hand them another check. Abuzz with love and determination and, as suspect as it seemed, holiday spirit, he walked through the long aisle of lockers looking to find the bathroom. He found sinks and turned right, but that way led to the showers. He was about to try doubling back left, when a shower door flung open and out stepped Todd, dripping and shorn. Todd was startled, as was George. Todd seemed to recover instantly, which was more than George could say. He frowned, and his newfound holiday spirit quickly made an exit.

Todd reached for his towel and began casually drying the hair on the top of his head, which was essentially the only place he had any, while George looked on in both fury and embarrassment.

He was overcome by a rancorous case of déjà vu, this moment tangling up with their last encounter when he had also been fully dressed while in the presence of a naked Todd. George was grateful for small favors. At least this time Todd was flaccid.

"What brings you here?" Todd asked convivially, like they were a couple of swells who had bumped into each other by chance on the Riviera or at the Kentucky Derby.

"I have to urinate," George said, which was a response both factual and preposterous.

Todd stared at him sadly. He seemed to be in no rush to move that towel from his head to his waist. "How are you?" he asked George, deeply focused now on the drying of his upper extremities.

"You don't get to ask me that anymore. That's the kind of question one friend asks another." George's legs were shaking, and not just because he had to pee so badly.

"I'm sorry, George. We didn't mean for… It just happened."

"At my father's wake?"

"It never occurred to either one of us that you'd just walk away from the receiving line like that," Todd said with an edge of disapproval that suggested it was George's fault for catching Todd and Tara *in flagrante delicto*.

Three more guys, perhaps post-Zumba, walked into the shower area. Either because of the incongruity of George standing there fully dressed, or because they picked up on the tension between the two men, they stared suspiciously at them before finally hanging up their towels and disappearing into their respective stalls. George realized if he'd ever actually worked out at the gym, Dennis's stern lecture about the grooming habits of the twenty-first century urban male would not have come as such a complete shock to him.

Todd finally finished with his painstakingly thorough drying and tossed the wet towel into a hamper. He strode naked and unselfconsciously away from the showers. Why was he parading around like this? George felt like screaming. *Jesus Todd, you used to be my doctor. You've seen my dick. You know I'm bigger. So what exactly are you trying to prove?*

When the three Zumba students' soapy heads popped out of the showers, he realized he hadn't kept that thought to himself.

Todd, refusing to succumb to humiliation, or to display any vestige of decorum, simply smiled. "If you must know," he said, "I'm a grower."

"I know that," George spit. "Have you really already forgotten the way in which you presented yourself to me at the funeral home?"

Todd was silent.

"I'm not going to prove it to you. You're just going to have to take my word for it. Trust me, I've got you beat." George walked away from him, disgusted by both Todd's behavior and his own, for it was not like George to allow things to devolve to such a base and tawdry level.

"I didn't destroy your marriage. You did that yourself. Tara didn't leave you for me, you know. We're not even together. I haven't seen Tara since the wake. And that was only the fourth time we fucked."

George was shocked by the information. But he was less shocked by Todd's words than by Todd's delivery, his tone. How could someone whom George considered his best friend for more than half of his life spew such acid at him? Apparently, Todd was not content merely to kill their friendship. He also needed to bury it deep in an unmarked grave so it could never be found again.

George turned back around to face Todd. He had never been in a fight before, but it seemed like a great time to rectify that situation, especially since his fists were already clenched. He barreled toward Todd, winding up for the ready. As George rushed toward Todd, he saw flecks of lights in front of his eyes that were either images of the magical mighty tree, or the precursor of an aneurysm. When George was right in front of him, the lights stopped flickering and were replaced with an image of Sal.

George could hear Sal's voice. The kindly priest was sharing wisdom. Then Sal too was gone, replaced by Nan sharing the same simple truths. On the strength of Nan's advice, George unfurled his fingers.

"Todd," he said, struggling to make sense out of his hallucination. He stopped. There would be no violence. That much he was certain of. Sal was right: What he was about to do was difficult, but it was not complicated.

George sighed heavily. He would be kind and forgiving, even though that seemed nearly impossible to manage. "Todd, if I have ever done anything to hurt you or make you angry or resentful, I'm sorry. I really am. I promise I didn't mean to. I'm sorry our friendship ended, because it meant a lot to me, and I will miss it. And I'll miss you, too."

George turned around and headed toward the exit. He almost got there. But then he was achingly reminded of the reason he had entered the locker room in the first place, and so he walked back in to search for a urinal, passing a stunned, silent, and still naked Todd frozen in the spot where he'd left him.

TWENTY

"I WAS BEGINNING TO THINK you'd slipped out a back exit."

Carolyn and George were at the steak house, Del Frisco's. Steak was no longer in George's budget, which Carolyn had pointed out when she countered with pizza. George, however, ignored her suggestion because he had an overwhelming need to eat red meat after his run-in with Todd, and, anyway, the restaurant was right across the plaza from Equinox. They were sharing a Porterhouse and struggling to make themselves heard in the acoustically booby-trapped room over the boisterous crowd. Everywhere people were exchanging gifts and wishing season's greetings.

George had told Carolyn about his altercation with Todd, omitting all references to their dicks and to the figurative (and in Todd's case literal), swinging of said members. Carolyn empathized with his urge to use violence but seemed quite relieved that he had not.

"So now you really don't want to sell? What happened?"

"You."

"Don't blame me."

"Do you like chocolate?" George asked.

"Of course. I love it."

"Okay. But imagine how you might feel about it if you ate it every single day."

"I do eat it every single day. Are you suggesting there are people who don't?"

George waited for her to smirk, but as it happened she was being completely earnest.

"So that was a bad example. Wow. Every day?" George wondered what it would be like sharing your life with a woman who ate chocolate every single day—probably pretty awesome. "For me, Christmas every day was not so good. I've never excelled at being merry. But for some reason, tonight watching the tree—"

"You mean watching me, don't you?"

George's cheeks went as red as the center of their steak. "I thought I was being subtle."

She sliced into the beef and took a bite, the chewing preventing her from commenting.

"I don't want to move out of the city, as clever as your idea was, but I'm going to figure out something to keep from having to sell."

"You know," she said after some time had passed. "The truth is I would never move to the country, either."

He looked at her curiously. "Then why did you suggest... Ah," he said, "I get it. So. I'm not the only one with an aversion to ticks."

"Checking for ticks is not so horrible if you have an able and willing assistant helping you find them. It's important that you look very closely," she said. "Because they could be lurking anywhere." She raised her glass and took a sip without letting her gaze break from George's.

George still hated bugs, but never had he been so aroused by the possibility of coming in contact with a disease-carrying insect.

"I would never move out of the city," she repeated seriously, even though he didn't want to be serious. He wanted to continue with their thinly veiled sexual banter. "If you live in the country, it is impossible to be truly aware of the moments when fate intercedes in your life."

He nodded a couple of times knowingly before admitting he didn't have any idea what she was talking about.

"Okay," she explained. "So let's say you live in a really small town. Main Street has a post office, a hardware store, a drugstore, perhaps one diner, and not much else. Can you picture it?"

"In all its dustbowl grimness."

"Good. So one day you're walking down Main Street and you see a handsome man."

"I do?"

"I do. One does. Don't be so literal. Just listen. Anyway the person sees the handsome stranger, and she doesn't speak to him because she is shy. She just goes home and pines for him. And a few days later when she goes back to town, she sees the man again, maybe at the hardware store this time. Maybe she still doesn't say anything. And certainly she doesn't give any thought to the significance of bumping into the stranger a second time, because it would be odd if she *didn't* bump into him. They couldn't avoid each other in such a small town."

George nodded in agreement.

"And there will be a third meeting. They may talk to each other or they may not, but never once will it cross her mind that they are being brought together by fate or some kind of destiny."

"I suppose, but I still think my anti-bug anxiety is the real reason to avoid the country," he laughed. She did not.

"Pretend to be glib if you want, George Bailey, but I've got you pegged as a romantic. Let me say this..." The waitress came by and refilled their wine glasses; they gave her appreciative smiles, and she withdrew from the table. Carolyn sipped before continuing. "If you see a stranger on three separate occasions in Manhattan, when you sometimes go six months without bumping into people who live in your own building, you can not deny that the hand of fate is trying to bring the two of you together."

She had obviously given her theory a great deal of thought. "Well, you and I had our initial meeting at the bar, and then we found each other at your salon. Sadly that's only two meetings," he said. And he was a little sad, because he liked her theory, and he liked the idea that this new George who was hatching might turn out to be a romantic. "I guess at two chance encounters, we are still in the realm of happy coincidences."

Carolyn took another sip of wine. She placed her glass on the table, and reached across to rest her hand on his. She shook her head as her eyes filled with tears. "That's not true. The bar was two. The salon was three."

He stared at her, nonplussed.

"I was feeling really down the day we talked to each other in the bar. I was thinking a lot about Danny." He knew she meant her late husband, but he realized that she had never mentioned him by name before.

"Anyway, my mood did not improve as I tried making my way

uptown. I had to wait twenty-five minutes for a train. And when I finally got on, it was packed. I managed to shove myself in toward the middle of the car, and just out of the corner of my eye I saw your deeply troubled but handsome face in profile. And I thought, well, his hair isn't to my liking, but everything else is great."

He didn't think she would make this story up. Still, the skeptic in him couldn't quite believe her. He sipped some wine and tried to keep the look of doubt off his face.

"You reminded me of my poor husband." Carolyn must have sensed George's unease because she quickly added, "Not Danny toward the end. But when I first met him. In the beginning of our relationship, when he had a bad day, he was easily cheered by my presence. And when I saw you on the subway I thought to myself there's a man who is just temporarily down. If I talked to him, I could make him feel better. But of course I couldn't get close enough to you in the packed train. Even if I could have, I wouldn't have actually done it."

They were quiet for a while, gazing into each other's eyes. "And then you screamed at a poor, defenseless baby, 'Trust me kid, it only gets worse!' And I thought, oh no, this is not a temporary condition—he's actually crazy."

There was an awkward moment of silence, which fortunately ended with Carolyn laughing. And so George, in what was becoming a pleasant habit, laughed along with her, even though it pained him to discover she had been witness to that awful, out of control moment.

"I talked to you in the bar because I figured the bartender would protect me if you snapped. He did have a paring knife in his hand." She spoke these words without the humorous inflection he would have hoped for. "And then you didn't seem at all crazy, which was a relief because, you know, I've already done that. Still I decided to let you leave without offering my number because I knew if it was supposed to be, fate would step in and provide the third chance."

"And so it did," he said in utter astonishment.

"And so it did, George Bailey."

Fate. It was hard to argue with Carolyn's mystical reasoning and logic, and he saw no point in even trying.

∽

SOMETIME AFTER ONE IN THE morning, George grabbed for the ringing phone. In the process, he knocked over a glass of water he'd placed on the bedside table before he had gone to sleep.

"Hello," he answered groggily.

"Hey, It's me."

"Who?"

"How quickly they forget."

"TJ, I asked you not to call so late."

"And for that reason I did not. Last time it was after three. It's not even two yet. Are you all right? You sound as if something terrible has happened to you." Based on her excited tone, he couldn't help but get the feeling she was hoping something had.

"I believe you are picking up on the fact that I have just woken up, also there is water dripping everywhere."

"What a dump. Who said that, George?" TJ howled. He'd never heard her laugh before. "I can't believe I said what a dump to a guy named George. Do you get the reference?"

He didn't.

She refused to tell him. "Google the line." Maybe he would and maybe he wouldn't. He had Googled, but he had not been on a search binge in days.

She started complaining about how the apartment was always leaking. "I'm glad to be out of there." He hadn't quite grasped he was living in TJ's former home. Perhaps the lease had been in Susie's name alone. He explained that he didn't have a leak.

"I knocked over a glass of water."

"You really should be more careful, George."

"I will try to keep that excellent advice in mind the next time I am awakened from a sound sleep by a ringing phone in the middle of the night."

"Somebody's grumpy," TJ sang as if to a three-year-old refusing to eat his peas. "Seriously. Tell me. Of course you're upset, after all you've been through."

He told her that he had bumped into Todd that very evening. She was hungry for lurid details, and while he could have offered a few of those, he decided to tell her he had apologized to Todd on the chance he might have inadvertently done something to upset him.

"*You did what?*" George pictured the cartoon version of TJ. One moment her lid was securely fastened, and the next it was flipping wildly through the air.

"I—"

"I heard what you said. Why did you do that?"

He explained as best he could. He told her he was surprised himself because his original intention was to hit him. TJ strongly asserted that would have been the more sensible course of action, especially in light of the way he'd besmirched George's honor. She actually used the word besmirched, which kind of made George like her more.

"I'm in love," he said. "I met a girl. A woman," he quickly corrected because he suspected TJ would not approve of him referring to a grown-up female as a girl. She probably wouldn't even approve of the alternate word George had selected unless she was confident he'd spelled it womyn.

She was silent for a minute, which is always unsettling when one is on the phone and not face to face with the other person. He might have asked if she was still there, but he could hear her labored breathing. "I'm very happy for you," she said in a pinched voice that suggested she was anything but.

"Thanks," he said, not striving for sarcasm but achieving it nevertheless.

"This whole enlightened, positive attitude routine, Susie set you up to this, didn't she?"

He had no idea where TJ would have gotten that idea. He informed her that aside from his one brief meeting with the *womyn* the day he moved in, he'd had no more contact with her. He had been in the apartment less than a month, so he had not even mailed Susie a rent check yet.

"It's just that you seem to be moving on, and I am not. And I feel like I must be doing something wrong. Why can't I get over her?" George felt badly for his late night phone friend.

"Maybe you're having trouble letting go because you really miss your old life. Whereas I seem to be discovering that…" He paused a moment, running through the thrill and terror and all of the changes he'd undergone since Thanksgiving. "I think I like my new one."

"You figured this out in two weeks?" Her words were laden with incredulity. "That's ridiculous!"

She hung up on him before he could tell her that it had in fact been two and a half weeks.

TWENTY-ONE

AND SO, GEORGE REASONED THAT if he could fall in love with both a woman and a major holiday in less than three weeks, surely he could find a way to save the family business in the week or so before Claire signed the agreement with Adelman. How hard could it be?

He called his mother and asked her if she'd be willing to have the family over for dinner again. Without going into details, he explained to her it was important that they have a meeting. She proposed the following evening.

"Thanks," he said. "Mom, in light of our current financial reality, maybe serving pasta would be a smart choice."

On the subject of the menu, Claire was noncommittal.

CLAIRE'S APARTMENT WAS REDOLENT WITH the smells of garlic, lemon, and rosemary, which meant she was roasting chicken.

"What happened to the pasta plan?" George asked.

"If you think I'm going to have my family over and not serve them meat…" As far as she was concerned, what she was saying was so obvious she didn't have to finish that sentence, so she did not. She kissed his cheeks and returned to her kitchen, apparently having forgotten once again, that both of her grandchildren were vegetarians.

"No chicken?" Claire asked with seeming bafflement when May and Brian passed the platter without taking any poultry.

"Mom, they don't eat meat."

"Even chicken?" She shrugged. "So, next time I'll make fish."

Once again Dennis had accompanied May to dinner, meaning that, with Finn, there were seven people around the table. George stood, which was unnecessary and a bit theatrical, but he felt the magnitude of the declaration he was about to make justified his posturing.

"May I have your attention?" he asked, unnecessarily since everyone had been silently staring at him from the moment he stood up. His mother was wearing her patented sit-down-your-food-is-getting-cold face.

"I have some very big news. You're going to be shocked." George felt a flush of excitement as a grin spread across his face. He was like an idealistic politician, because while he had dreams about carrying on the family's legacy, he had no concrete action plan developed to actually achieve his goal. But he would step up and do whatever needed to be done. With his brother and his children, he'd figure out what to do.

"Oh my God," Conor said, shaking his head. "This is sudden. I don't think you should rush into this."

This, George realized, was what it meant to have a brother. You didn't even have to say what you were thinking, but already he knew. An almost psychic bond, which he never thought he shared with Conor. But he must have. It was just late in revealing itself. Funny, because George had always considered his brother to be a genetically linked stranger, but here Conor was reading George's mind.

"Yes. It seems sudden, I know. Especially in light of, well, everything," shouted George "but I know it's the right thing for me. For us."

"George. This is crazy. You can not propose to a woman you've known for two weeks."

The other Baileys had been watching this exchange with confused stares, and now George was also confused. His eyes widened when he realized what Conor was talking about. He looked at his dumbstruck children, who had no idea he had even been on a date. Had George had his wits about him, he would have said, *What are you talking about? I'm not dating anyone.* Or at least *ixNay ethay alktay aboutyay emay atingday!*

Instead he said, "Conor that was supposed to be private." He quickly added, "and I'm not getting married."

May dropped her fork but did not burst into tears, making this the first time he had seen his daughter in weeks when he had not made her cry. Of course, the night was still young. Brian grabbed a chicken thigh and ate hungrily. George didn't see a connection between his love life and his son's return to the eating of flesh. Oh? Maybe he did see the connection. Anyway, the sight of chicken grease running down Brian's chin certainly pleased Claire.

"I am dating someone. That is true, but—"

"Speaking of dating," said Brian. A thighbone, stripped clean of all signs of meat, lay discarded on his plate. He reached for the platter and snatched a breast. "Why is it," he began indignantly, "that May is always invited to bring *her* boyfriend to these family-only dinners, yet the same invitation is not extended to *my* boyfriend?"

This was the first George was hearing that his son had a boyfriend. He ignored the interjection for the moment. "We *never* invite Dennis. He just keeps showing up! And it's not like I brought my girlfriend." Either because of the reference to Carolyn or because George had insulted Dennis, his daughter wept. And so his score remained perfect with her.

George had not come here to talk about dating. He had come here to talk about their futures. George wanted to get back on point, and maybe he would have were it not for Finn.

"Your boyfriend?" She shook her head disapprovingly at Brian. George didn't know what that was all about. The Baileys were not a family that talked about sexuality or much of anything for that matter. But they had never hidden the fact that Brian was gay. She must have known. He tried to think if she had ever been in the room when the subject had come up. Maybe she hadn't. Certainly George never brought it up.

Then Finn began quoting the Bible, or maybe Shakespeare, George wasn't sure which. She wasn't actually reading from a book, which would have tipped him off. Aside from Adam and Eve and *Romeo and Juliet*, he wasn't really well versed in either subject, so it was a coin toss. He'd narrowed the source of Finn's ravings down to the work of either the Bard or King James because there were a lot of superfluous –ths tacked on the end of words.

"*A man shall not lieth with another man,*" Finn proselytized. George was taken aback by his aunt's stridency. But after hearing the last quote, he assumed she had probably plucked the words from the Bible. He highly doubted Shakespeare would have said that.

He should have jumped to his son's defense, but he stood there shocked and mute, which allowed Finn to continue her spiteful railing.

"I need to talk to you. Get up right now. Follow me," Conor said threateningly to his aunt. Had it been George who'd addressed her, Finn might not have been so startled. George, after all, had very recently displayed his capacity for uncontrolled fury. But quiet, you-could-almost-forget-he-was-in-the-same-room-with-you, Conor? His outburst shocked everyone, especially Finn. She abruptly stopped speaking when she saw his angry face. She did not dare disobey his order. She got up and followed Conor silently into the living room.

George was about to comfort Brian, but May got there first. So George remained standing in his spot, like the idiot and coward he was, waiting to deliver news that probably didn't even matter.

Dennis got up from the table and tiptoed to the doorframe. He made an exaggerated show of putting his hand behind his ear, miming eavesdropping. It was childish, and just exactly the kind of tension-busting stunt the moment called for. They all watched him, hoping his reconnaissance might actually proffer some useful information. He scurried back to the table, indicating Conor and Finn's imminent return. May also rushed back to her seat, leaving George the sole person standing.

When Finn walked back into the room, she was ashen and shaking. She sunk into the chair, barely able to maintain erect posture. George looked at his brother, but Conor's hard expression offered no clues as to what had transpired in the other room.

"I'm sorry," Finn uttered barely above a whisper. And Brian muttered something in reply.

"Would it be okay if I continued?" George asked. Brian said that it would be, and in that moment Brian was the only one George was concerned about. He recapped as succinctly as possible how he'd come to feel differently about Christmas, and he wanted to honor his father and find a way to save the business.

"So what should we do?" George asked, confessing that he didn't really know how to accomplish this.

No one spoke. Heads were shaken and scratched.

"You sell, *of course,*" said Finn, *of course.* "What else can you do? As I understand it, if you sell to Adelman, at least you make a little bit of money. And if you don't sell to him, Bailey and Sons will soon be out of business anyway and you'll get nothing."

"Well," said Conor. "If we don't sell, we go out on our own terms with our pride intact."

"Fitting," Finn said, "since pride goeth before the fall." George was going to insist that she stop quoting the Bible, but then again, he wasn't certain if that came from the Bible. He thought maybe it was just from a t-shirt.

"I say don't sell," Brian said, glaring at Finn.

"Don't sell," said May.

"I'm in. We don't sell," Conor said, also staring pointedly at Finn.

"I don't want to sell. I can't sell," George said, wishing he'd expressed this newfound passion to his father even once.

George looked over at Dennis. He had the tact not to voice a vote, but he grinned and gave George a big thumbs up.

Claire stood and began clearing the table even though George hadn't eaten anything yet. "You are all forgetting that this is not a democracy. Your father left this business, such as it is, to me. It's mine to do with as I see fit. Your father would not want this to end with us in bankruptcy."

She began collecting dishes, her hands trembling. As she rattled the plates together, she looked warningly at Finn. Finn, already reprimanded once tonight, shrank in response. George had never seen his mother respond harshly to his aunt, in spite of the countless occasions when that treatment would have been warranted. But tonight, she was like a mama bear. Finn had made a big mistake attacking one of Claire's cubs.

With the last of the plates scraped and stacked, Claire returned her attention to George. Her cross expression softened. "So I guess we better find a way to avoid bankruptcy. I'm not saying I'm not selling. But I'll give you until after Christmas to come up with an alternative." She smiled at George, and he felt confident his mother believed he really would find a way out of this mess, which almost made him believe that he would, too.

In unison, the usually subdued Baileys cheered—well, everyone but Finn. George hugged his children, and he was especially relieved when they hugged him back.

Soon after, Finn took her leave. George was angry about what she'd done to Brian. And yet as he watched the sad, frustrated old woman go, he wondered what had happened to her to create such bitterness.

Claire pulled out a bottle of champagne, even as she acknowledged that it was premature to do so. They toasted and drank to the memory of Daddy. And George felt grateful to be a part of this family. But as the evening went on, fear crept back in, because nothing had been resolved. He had no plan for saving the business. All he had was the desire to save it. Finn was right. They were letting pride cloud their reason and judgment. Then George saw something he had not seen in a very long time. Everyone in the room had smiles on their faces.

He realized it had been ages since either of his children were particularly joyful around him, and not just since Thanksgiving. For quite some time before, they had begun mirroring his ennui, as they responded in kind to the negativity they saw in their father.

How could they have not been affected?

He hated work. He had a bad marriage, even if he refused to see that he did. He wasn't passionate about anything. In a way, his behavior had been ridiculous, because back then with an intact family and a job and plenty of money, he had every reason to be satisfied, yet he was not.

Having lost so much, he had every reason to be miserable, but here he was, with this totally foreign feeling brewing inside of him. Happiness.

TWENTY-TWO

HE RESISTED THE URGE TO shout *at last!* when Carolyn called and invited him to come to Hamilton Heights. They hadn't seen each other in nearly two days, and in the whirlwind of recent events, that felt like a long time.

He was eager to see where she lived, but he'd never been that far uptown. He wasn't even entirely certain that her address fell within the confines of Manhattan. "I'll take a cab," he said, hoping he was masking the trepidation he felt about venturing to Harlem. "Give me the address."

"You do know that the subway goes there? Hamilton Heights is serviced by mass transit."

Like the privileged, sheltered, former denizen of the Gold Coast of Greenwich Village that he was, George was about to ask if taking the train to that neighborhood was safe. She read his mind.

"Take the train to 145th Street, scaredy-cat. I will be on the corner when you come out of the ground. At no time will your life be in any danger. Text me when you're getting on the train, and I'll be waiting for you."

Again he tried to get her to give him her address so she wouldn't have to stand on the street alone, and, of course, so he could take a cab, but she wouldn't reveal it.

She sighed in a way that let him know she thought he was foolish and out of touch. "Besides," she said, "I have an ulterior motive. I need your brute strength." She laughed at this, though George had no idea what she thought was so funny.

As promised, she was waiting for him at the top of the steps when he came up out of the ground. They hugged but refrained from kissing since their track record with public displays of affection was so abysmal. Taking his hand, Carolyn led him across the street. There was a Rite Aid drug store on the corner, nearly hidden behind a row of Christmas trees which had been set up by one of the many Canadian vendors who annually made the trip down to New York to gouge its hapless citizens.

"You're the expert," Carolyn said. "What kind of tree do you recommend?

"Artificial. We carry them in every height from two to twelve feet. I can even get you one that's pre-lit."

"I can't imagine anything worse." Carolyn stuck her nose into the bough of a tree and took an exaggerated inhalation. "That smell," she exclaimed, and then stopped. Of course, there was no need to say anything else. It was a great smell. George had to admit that the scented candles and potpourri he peddled, as evocative of the real thing as they were, could not compare to the smell of a freshly cut tree.

"Sorry. I know nothing about this. I think we better talk to the Canadian."

Actually, it turned out to be two Canadians. Alain and Isabelle had been married for only three weeks. Isabelle hastened to display this new status by removing her gloves and showing off her ring. They had run the stand at this very location for the last four years, taking over from Alain's father. Sipping tea from a thermos, they commented on the unusually warm weather. It had averaged close to fifty degrees every day since Thanksgiving. Gauging from the layers of down and flannel they both wore, this mild weather was cold enough when you were standing outside for fourteen hours at a stretch.

"The worst part about running a street corner business," Isabelle said, "is that our bathroom is located in that McDonald's across the way. On the plus side, I never have to worry about the toilet seat being left up." She smiled conspiratorially at Carolyn. "You know how men are," she said with a sly smile at George.

Alain gave George a knowing look, as if they were the two Neanderthal husbands good for hunting and procreating but who otherwise needed to be watched closely at all times. Alain pulled out an eight-foot blue spruce from deep within the stack. It was thick and densely branched with no holes. The top branch was long and straight, perfectly sized for an angel. "This is your tree," Alain declared. Of course it was not really going to be *their* tree, just Carolyn's and her mother's, but George liked that Alain thought it was theirs.

The tree cost a hundred and twenty dollars, which seemed a staggering price to George, especially in Harlem where he just assumed things would be cheaper. But he had never been good at negotiating. Besides, Carolyn was paying, so it wasn't his place to say anything.

"We'll take it," said Carolyn, who evidently was not a skilled negotiator either. She rummaged around in her pocket and pulled out cash. She had two twenties on her. "I could have sworn I had more cash on me. I'm so embarrassed. I'll run right home."

"Don't be silly. I've got it." Carolyn began to protest, but George leaned in and whispered to her that she could pay him back later. He could have said the words right out loud, but he was enjoying the Canadians believing they were a married couple. He had no desire to disabuse them of that belief.

He pulled out his wallet and discovered that he too was short on cash. "MasterCard okay?"

He handed Alain his card. "Isabelle, look at this," he said breaking into a wide grin.

She took the card from her husband's hand and soon she too was smiling. It was baffling. They were smiling and looking at the credit card, but they were not running it through the charge machine. Neither of them made a move to complete the transaction.

"Oh my God. You're George Bailey?" Isabelle squealed with delight. "We love that movie. I mean everyone loves that movie, eh?"

Since George's spirits were unusually high, he did not bother to contradict her.

"But for us," she continued, "growing up on Christmas tree farms, the movie has extra special significance." She jogged into their makeshift shelter and ran out with a tiny little bell. "See. I usually have this hanging from one of the trees." She laughed as she rang it. Then she pulled out her phone and pleaded for a picture. George obliged even though he did not understand why Isabelle would want to have her picture taken with a stranger who, while happening to have a famous name, was not famous himself.

Finally Isabelle ran George's credit card while Alain pushed the tree through the netting machine, so they could more easily carry the tree the four blocks to Carolyn's place. As they lifted up the tree, the Canadians thanked them for making their day. It wasn't cold, so the red in Isabelle's cheeks must have been her blushing. "I don't suppose by any chance your name is Mary?"

Carolyn turned to her and smiled warmly. "As a matter of fact, it is. And you know what's even more unbelievable? My maiden name was Hatch."

Both Alain and Isabelle's jaws dropped in amazement. George was amazed too, less by Carolyn's lie than by the fact that she recalled the maiden name of the fictional Mary Bailey. Just how many times had she seen *It's a Wonderful Life?*

Finally, the pair departed. As they walked away, the bound tree between them, Alain and Isabelle called out, *"Joyeux Noel,* Mr. and Mrs. Bailey!"

Carolyn and her mother lived in a brownstone that at first glance seemed very grand. On a block filled with homes fifteen feet wide, at twenty-five feet, theirs dwarfed the others. They had vaulting bay windows on both the parlor and second floors, and ornate panels of stained glass framed the front door. This was a majestic home.

Or it had been in an earlier time. The house had been abandoned in the seventies and taken over by drug dealers and a series of squatters. There had been at least one fire, assorted lootings. In the early nineties, Carolyn's Uncle Claude, always looking for the next adventure or challenge, bought the place from the city for next to no money. For fifteen years, he singlehandedly set about restoring the place. Unfortunately, he was not the handiest of fellows. Everywhere George looked he saw a mismatched tile or an unevenly installed piece of molding. There were lines of visible tape where he had botched up replastering a wall. Uncle Claude deserved an A for effort. And Claude's workmanship was far superior to what George could have accomplished, but, sadly, that was saying almost nothing.

When the project was nearly complete, Claude was diagnosed with cancer. He died within a year. Without a wife or children, Carolyn's mother inherited the townhouse. Since the rapidly gentrifying area was becoming the hot neighborhood of the moment, she moved in. And so did Carolyn and her late husband.

Introductions were put off until Carolyn and George had positioned the tree into its stand. He held the trunk as Carolyn crawled under to tighten the bolts.

"I'm Cora," her mother said, extending a limp hand. She was shorter than her daughter, more hourglass, a bit more handsome than beautiful. Still, he could see the relationship. Cora stared at the tree. Then she took several steps back. She tilted her head. "It's not straight," she remarked sourly before leaving the room.

George wondered if she had left for good, but doubted he would be that lucky. He prided himself on being a likeable fellow, but in his limited dating experience, he failed to win the approval of mothers. Tara's mother hated him. She had never approved of their marriage. George was willing to concede she did have cause for objection with regard to their ages. But by the time he was forty, one would think that would have become a moot point. Tara's mother was probably thrilled her prediction of marital failure had finally come to pass.

"What are you thinking about?" Carolyn asked, snapping him from his trance.

"Nothing."

She smiled. "Your lips were moving. Don't worry. My mother's just in a mood. I'll be right back. I'm going to get some ornaments."

"Do you want some help?" He didn't want to be left alone in case Cora came back.

She insisted she was fine. Alone, he took a seat on the worn, tapestry-covered sofa and literally began twiddling his thumbs. Now that the tree branches were beginning to fall, he realized what an enormous specimen Alain had picked for them. He was about to decorate a tree with a woman he barely knew, and he had almost no memory of doing the same thing with his wife or children. Images flashed before his eyes of ornaments and trees, but they were all scenes from the showroom or gift shows. He didn't remember actually putting up a tree in his apartment. They had a tree, naturally, but it always just seemed to appear fully decorated. Tree trimming was not a family ritual.

Besides, there was an art to decorating a tree, and he didn't have it. You didn't merely hang things on branches. You had to have a design—a theme, an overall concept. He was good at critiquing. He knew when the trees worked, when they'd excite the buyers, and he could also explain what was wrong with them when they were off. But he could not decorate one himself. Though it wasn't really his job, his father, in a pinch, could make a tree look good. But no one was better than Brian. His son was amazingly gifted at creating breathtaking Christmas displays.

"You look like you need a project." Her voice was stern, but at least Cora smiled. "Come help me with the tea."

George followed Cora down a flight of stairs to the kitchen. "These houses were not meant to be lived in by people who don't have servants. The kitchen is down here. The original dining room was two flights up, but we moved it to the parlor floor, so we only have to carry things one flight."

"Is there a dumbwaiter?"

"There was one before the meth lab exploded," she laughed, and in it George heard a trace of Carolyn. "How things have changed since my brother moved up here. The house up the street just sold for close to three million. Can you imagine?"

George tried not to appear shocked, but he failed.

"That house had a more professional renovation than the one my brother did. Irish Breakfast okay, or is it too late for caffeine?"

He assured her that caffeine was just the ticket. Perhaps George had misjudged Cora. This was going very well. The conversation was superficial but at least it was easy and unforced. She seemed to like him. And why not? He could be charming.

"So George, let me just say one thing." Cora was still smiling, but the grin had become strained. "I think you are bad for my daughter. And if you hurt her, I will kill you."

Technically that was two things, but why quibble?

"Also I'm going to be watching you like a hawk."

Three things.

It was disheartening that mothers seemed to dislike him so.

"Let me be clear. I'm not suggesting you're a bad man, but I feel certain you are bad for my daughter."

He stared at the kettle willing it to whistle. "I can assure you I would never do anything to hurt Carolyn."

"I'm sure you believe that. Remind me, how long ago was it that your divorce was finalized?"

"I'm not divorced," he admitted.

"George, I'm a divorced woman. I understand about being on the rebound. Though I managed to remove my wedding ring before I started dating again." She stared pointedly at his left hand. "Do me a favor. Go have your midlife crisis with someone else's daughter."

And then, having spoken her mind, Cora's natural smile returned. "How about some cookies? I have gingerbread."

She assembled the cookies on a china plate and got down three cups and saucers. She placed everything on a large tray. At last, the water boiled and she filled the pot. "Will you?" She gestured to the tray and George carried. "When you live on four stories, it's all about the trays."

He hadn't noticed how crooked the stairs were when he had gone down them. Going back up, with the tray blocking the view of his feet, he was forced to lean into the banister to keep from tumbling. He thought back to Thanksgiving and Tara's frantic yells when she thought he was about to drop the turkey. Cora did not actually speak the words, but George felt her tense energy boring into his back as she followed behind him. *Don't you dare drop the tea, George.*

He didn't.

When he came back into the living room, Carolyn cleared a place on the coffee table and he set down the tea. "I'm sorry," she mouthed when they caught eyes.

"What did you say?" asked Cora even though Carolyn had not actually voiced the words.

They sat. And desperate to gain favor, he praised the tea with such excessive enthusiasm, one might have believed that Cora had just returned from the fields of China where she had grown the plants, done the harvesting, and dried the leaves herself.

"It's Twinings." She looked at George like he was an imbecile.

"But you know just how long to steep it," he said, incapable of abandoning his obsequiousness.

"It's not that hard. The directions are on the box."

He gave up. This old house was drafty and poorly insulated.

The breeze came through the gaps along the window frames, rustling the curtains and creating an even greater chill than Cora did. In spite of this, he was drenched in sweat.

"Carolyn tells me you don't have a job."

"Mother!"

"It's okay." George figured it was best to get it all out there so he could begin damage control. "It's a little more nuanced than that."

Cora stirred her tea, waiting for him to elaborate, which George knew he should do, but since Cora had fairly accurately summed up his employment status with her initial statement, he didn't know what to add. Fortunately, Carolyn interceded. "Thanks for the tea, Mom. Didn't you say you had something you needed to do?"

"Did I?" Cora shook her head. They began to mime a negotiation, which ended with Carolyn and George alone by the tree, and Cora sulkily retreating back down to the kitchen. "I'm so glad you enjoyed the tea," she said as she left the room. "Would you like me to give you the recipe?"

Carolyn apologized for her mother's behavior. "I'm so sorry. She's usually so warm. She's never like that."

"I'm glad it's only me that brings out the hostility in her."

Carolyn tried to laugh but she could not, because what he said was the truth. That stopped all other conversation for a while, but George didn't feel any need to babble just to be talking again. It was fine being with her, even without words.

"Did you always want to have children?" she asked breaking their silence.

"I don't know if I ever wanted to have children. We had them at such a young age, I never even asked myself if I wanted to be a parent. I'm very glad I have them. I love them. They are mysterious. They're much smarter than I am, which makes me both proud and annoyed."

Carolyn glanced toward the still unadorned tree. She seemed melancholy and he wanted to ask why but debated whether or not to do so. It seemed pretty clear what had caused the sudden mood shift. "Did you want to have children?" Her expression, solemn and mournful, was all the answer he needed.

She nodded. "I thought there would be more time. And at some point, I knew I shouldn't have children with Danny, but I couldn't get myself to leave him either, because sometimes he was so… fine. And then it was too late."

"If either of my children take after me, and I hope they don't, you could be a grandmother soon." It just slipped out, in that Freudian way things do, and he stuttered a recovery, "I mean I could be a grandfather."

She stood, and the sorrow of a moment earlier seemed to fade. "George Bailey, will you help me decorate this tree?"

"With pleasure," he said. "Do you realize that you often address me by both my first and last names?"

"Does it bother you?" She opened up a large cardboard box, dank with the mustiness of a leaky basement. She wrinkled her nose. "This house was built directly over a stream. I only keep things down there that I know won't mildew." She proceeded to pull out a collection of worn glass ornaments. Most of them probably dated from the fifties and sixties. The colors had faded to clear in spots and most of the glitter had long ago flecked off.

"I know a guy who has a connection to some new ones of those," he said pointing at the tattered boxes. "You want him to hook you up while he still can?"

"George Bailey. Oh, you don't mind that I call you that, right?"

He shook his head. She could call him anything she liked.

"Thank you for the kind offer, but I will stick with these." She gazed at them like they were family.

Carolyn hadn't put up a tree for three years. George was not so dense as to ask why. Neither was it lost on him that she'd chosen to put one up again so soon after meeting him. They tested the lights, and they still worked. After they had them strung, and the tree was illuminated by their soft white glow, they began to hang the ornaments. As they did, Carolyn told him the story that each ball conjured.

They worked this way for at least an hour. He would hold something up and Carolyn told him where it came from. Most of them were older than she was, passed down from her grandparents.

"Popcorn," she said. "Pro or con?"

"Generally pro, but I'm not really hungry."

"Not to eat. To string on the tree. Should I make some?"

He grimaced. "I've never put popcorn on a tree. The Baileys have never done that," he said staunchly.

"Why not?"

"Because we don't sell it. You buy that at a grocery store. And I guess in some way, our trees always acted like advertisements for the business. I don't think my grandparents or my parents ever had the same tree twice. Every year was totally different, with things from the new line. Tara and I had some keepsakes for the kids, but we still mostly had things that would be used only one or two years before being cast off."

"That is so sad," Carolyn said. "No wonder you hated Christmas for so long."

"I didn't really hate Christmas. I was just disappointed by it."

Carolyn picked up her cell phone and started texting with the single focus of a teenager, as if he had been dismissed. "Lining up another date?"

"Telling my mother to make popcorn."

"Isn't she still here?"

"It's a big house."

They went back to work, hanging ornaments and talking. Carolyn assured him he was going to love poking a needle and thread through the corn. It was going to absolutely make the tree.

"George Bailey? Tell me something that you have never told me before."

"Anything?" That was a wide field. They hardly knew each other, even though he felt like they knew each other very well. There were so many things he had not told her. And then he thought:

I'm going to tell her that I love her.

Because like she said, meeting each other was fate. And what difference did it make that it all happened way too fast. Who made up the rules about what was proper and right? If George said this feels right, and she agreed with him, then it *was* right.

His heart clamored to be freed from the confines of his chest. "Carolyn, I…" He inhaled. There was nothing to be nervous about. Either she will say, *I love you, too.* Or she will say, *Yeah, about that, I don't feel that way. Sorry.*

Maybe this wasn't the right moment, after all. He was not ready for rejection. So instead of talk of love, he said the first thing that popped into his head. "Carolyn, I saw Jesus." Then realizing that wasn't entirely accurate, he added, "twice, actually. But I only talked to him—"

She dropped a frosted glass icicle, which shattered against the wood floor, sending jagged shards in all directions. When he moved to pick up the pieces, he noticed Cora had entered the room carrying an industrial-sized metal bowl brimming with popcorn. She was scowling at him, so he turned his attention back to Carolyn who had not yet made a move to clean up the mess. She seemed so upset. It must have been a favorite ornament. But there was no need for her to worry. George could replace it for her easily.

He was about to tell Carolyn the story of the slice, which was really a nice Christmas story. It was certainly the perfect anecdote to go along with tree trimming, and no doubt it would cheer her up and make her forget the broken glass.

"Oh my God. Why didn't I trust my first instinct? You have to go," Carolyn screamed. "This. I can't. I can't. Please, go!"

There was an abrupt end to the action. It was as if the curtain fell and everything stopped, which was a phenomenon George had not experienced before. Obviously, the planet must still have been revolving. Even in this room, surely time passed. Events continued—but not for George. He ceased to be one of the players. He'd left the stage and was trapped for some immeasurable interval in the darkened wings, unsure of what was going on. When finally the curtain rose again, he was pushed back out, stumbling, to finish his performance.

Shaky and frightened, he had no idea where he was or what his next line might be. The utterly baffled George was only aware of the sting of acid as it crept into his throat. He rasped, bile choking him, "Carolyn, let me explain." It did seem, under the circumstances, like that was the line to be delivered, though he hadn't the foggiest notion what he was supposed to be explaining.

"No," she shouted. "You have to go."

One minute they were having a genuinely intimate experience, sharing confidences and now she was screaming. Thank Goodness he hadn't told her he loved her.

George did not know when Cora had dropped the popcorn,

but it was no longer in her hands. Those were free, and she was using both of them to shove him toward the front door. He pleaded helplessly all the way into the vestibule.

"I knew it," Cora spat. "I knew you were too good to be true."

This confused George even more, since his impression was that Cora had not found him to be good in any way whatsoever.

"I knew you were going to hurt my daughter, but I didn't think you'd manage it in one afternoon."

"I really don't know what happened. I love your daughter. I love her."

She slapped him hard. "Remember I told you I'd kill you? Be grateful that's all I did to you. Get out!"

George tumbled back onto the front stoop as the door slammed in his face. He stood there for a minute, stunned. Stunned and angry. As he stormed down the steps, he noticed another sucker carrying a Christmas tree on his shoulders. He pitied the idiot. George muttered and cursed the whole way back to the subway, pushing through the congested sidewalks. Crowded sidewalks even up here? Who wanted to live up here? Some jackass paid three million dollars to live this far uptown? The world was coming to an end and maybe that was just as well!

"Merry Christmas, Mr. Bailey! Merry Christmas!" The Canadians, Alain and Isabelle, were grinning at him as they shouted, waving their mittened hands over their heads.

They had a lot of nerve. They started all this with their useless, rip-off priced trees. George marched right up to them.

"Merry Christmas," they repeated.

"Merry Christmas? What's so merry about it? I wish we never even had this stupid holiday!"

And with that outburst, George stormed off again. It was hard to hear because of the muffling effects of the mittens, but the sound of applause was unmistakable.

George turned around and saw Alain and Isabelle clapping and laughing. They grinned even wider.

He was puzzled by their behavior until it occurred to him that they thought he had been acting out a scene from that damn movie. They thought he was pretending to be the fake George Bailey, railing away at anyone who'd listen while he was in the midst of his nervous breakdown. Considering his name and his erratic behavior, George understood why the Canadians were confused.

TWENTY-THREE

Alone with his misfortune, George spent half the night staring at the phone and wishing it would ring. All the while, he chastised himself for having insisted TJ stop her middle of the night phone calls. He needed to talk to someone, but it was two in the morning and none of his friends lived on the West Coast. Even if one of them had, it was already eleven out there, which was still pretty late to be making a phone call even if you did feel like your life was coming to an end.

And so, after some debate, he eliminated every name on the very short list of friends he considered calling. But perhaps he could impose upon a relative. Surely he would be forgiven for burdening a family member at this late hour—not his children, or his soon to be ex-wife, or his mother, obviously, but maybe his brother. He had, after all, been thinking quite a bit about making more of an effort to have a deeper relationship with Conor. George had to admit making a frantic, desperate call in the middle of the night might not be a constructive first step in that direction, but he was going to call him anyway until he remembered Conor always turned his phone off before he went to bed.

He tossed. He turned. He tried to figure out what exactly had gone wrong with Carolyn and how he was going to fix it. He was stumped by both these riddles. Finally, some time after the sun had come up, overcome with fatigue, he surrendered to sleep.

Carolyn was standing by the Christmas tree. George stood across the room from her. For some unknown reason, a cowbell hung from his neck, and it rang whenever he moved, which was embarrassing and drew unwanted attention. To silence the clanging, he tried to remain still, which proved impossible because he was agitatedly crossing and uncrossing his legs. He desperately needed to pee because of all the tea he'd been drinking. Tea, George admitted now, that he had not even liked that much, but that he had guzzled because he wanted to make a good impression on Cora. And just then Cora appeared. She was no longer offering tea. Instead, she was carrying a butcher's cleaver and grinning maniacally. "Every time a bell rings, an asshole gets slaughtered," she said to George's horror.

The bell rang again and George jumped up. The phone. He grabbed it, but he failed to speak, still trapped in the memory of his nightmare.

"It's 8:45. You aren't up already?" It was TJ.

"I don't think I got to sleep until after eight this morning."

"What are you telling me, I could have called at three?"

He admitted that is what he had been hoping for.

"You're sending me mixed messages. Believe me, I had enough

of that nonsense with Susie." She settled into lecturing him about the importance of being clear in his communications with her if he expected things to work out between them. He rubbed his bleary eyes to remove the sleep, but since they had only been shut for twenty minutes, there was none to find. "This isn't why I phoned," she said kindly. "I noticed you haven't called me since the night I hung up on you."

"I've *never* called you. I don't know your number."

"You never heard of star 69?"

"You have to pay for that."

"What's our relationship worth to you?" Whatever kindness she'd had in her voice was now gone.

Since they had never met in person, George doubted one should describe what they had as a relationship. He did not, however, point this out to TJ because, strangely, he enjoyed chatting with her. "Actually the real reason I never star 69nd is because I didn't want you to think I was stalking you."

She laughed. "Sweet talker. Okay, we're friends again. I'm really calling to thank you. Because of what you said the other night, I've made big progress with my anger. I called Susie, which wasn't easy."

"I imagine. I'm sure it took a great deal of strength."

"No. That's not the reason. It wasn't easy because she changed her cell so I wouldn't be able to find her."

George wasn't entirely sure he wanted the answer, but nevertheless he asked how she'd managed to get hold of Susie's unlisted number.

"You've heard of six degrees of separation, right? With lesbians, it's never more than three degrees. It's impossible for us to hide from each other. Anyway, I called her. Once I assured her I had no intention of breaking the conditions of the restraining order, we talked. And I acknowledged my part in our breakup. And I wished her well. And that was that. I feel so much better."

"That's great," George said miserably, thinking of his own breakup. He proceeded to tell TJ all about his last date with Carolyn and its abrupt end.

"You want my advice?"

Obviously he did, since he had been awake all night waiting for it.

"That mother sounds like a real piece of work. I'd call her a bitch, but I don't use that word because it was invented by some misogynist for the express purpose of keeping women in our place, and from fully owning our power—as if strength is only a virtue when it comes with a penis attached to it. Am I right? Besides, I'm endeavoring to be more Zen. Anyway, the mother is the problem. You need to see Carolyn when that *bit*— when her mother—isn't around. Talk to Carolyn. Find out what happened. This is fixable."

"I don't know," he hesitated. "Are you sure?"

"George!" She screamed loud enough to make him jump. He heard her softly counting to ten before proceeding more calmly. "Of course, I'm sure. I'm going to give you the same advice that you've probably heard a thousand times before, but it bears repeating. Ready? Here goes. 'Don't give up the fight.' 'Quitters never win.' 'If at first you don't succeed…' In case you hadn't guessed, I'm a big believer in clichés. Do you know why certain sayings are repeated over and over again and become clichés, George?" TJ paused for less than two seconds before she shouted again. "Because they're fucking true. Now. Go. Find. Her!"

George was surprisingly revved up by her hackneyed pep talk. "That won't be hard. I know where she works."

"Then why are you on the phone with me? Put on a nice shirt, one that makes you look thin. And go win that girl back!"

George wondered if at some point he had led TJ to believe he was fat? No matter. Anyway, he did have such a shirt that made him look very thin, even though he was by no means fat. And now he had an action step, too. He was about to thank TJ for her advice, but once again, she'd hung up without saying goodbye.

∾

MOMENTS AFTER THE JEFFREY DENNISTON Salon opened for business, George, confidently clad in vertical stripes, ran through the doors. They had put up a Christmas tree since his last visit. The ornaments were all miniature scissors and razors, which simultaneously conveyed both whimsy and menace. At the top of the tree was a twelve-inch replica of a barber pole, spinning blue and red. George wondered where they had gotten it. Bailey and Sons did not generally carry items with such limited niche appeal.

The same diminutive receptionist with the braying voice whom he'd encountered on his initial visit was again working the desk. He asked her if he could speak to Carolyn.

"Do you have an appointment?"

He told her he didn't, but he would gladly wait for her because he only needed a minute, even though he imagined he'd need a lot more time than that to get everything straightened out. Then, eyeing a copy of *A Farewell to Arms* in the reception area, he headed for the leather sofa.

"She's not in today," came the bray before he ever got the chance to reacquaint himself with Hemingway.

"Then why did you ask me if I had an appointment with her?"

"What are you, CSI? She called in. She's taking a leave of

absence."

"When will she be back?"

"Do you have a warrant or something? Because you're kind of creeping me out. Who are you, anyway?"

"I'm George Bailey." The statement, while true, did nothing to help his cause. The exaggerated eye rolling from the receptionist, told him he'd be earning no points for originality. "I'm a friend. It's really important that I talk to her."

She arched an eyebrow dubiously. "You're a *friend*? Really. Then might I suggest you call your *friend*. Or email your *friend*. Or anything really that doesn't involve you standing in the middle of this salon where, I should point out to you, there are a lot of very fierce women with scissors in their hands."

∾

His frequent calls to Carolyn went unanswered, and so did all his emails. What he learned from his many attempts at getting her back is that it's very hard to aggressively pursue someone without starting to seem creepy and unhinged.

"You've just got to hear me out," began each desperate voicemail. "Why aren't you talking to me?" "Hey! George again. Have you not gotten my fifteen emails?" "Just please contact me so that I know I have the correct phone number?" he left this final plea even though Carolyn clearly identified herself on her outgoing message.

Even George had to concede that if he were Carolyn, he'd never —not in a million years—return the calls of such a clingy suitor.

He needed another strategy. Or rather, he decided to return to his original plan of talking to her in person. Since finding her at work was out of the question, he returned to Harlem. Marching with purpose up her front steps, he allowed himself a moment of jitters before he rang the bell.

He didn't really think she would answer the door, at least not the first time he tried. But the plan was to go once a day at a reasonable hour, perhaps noon. He would ring once, wait five minutes, and then leave. Assuming she didn't call the police, he figured ultimately she would be moved by his fortitude and let him in. He imagined he'd wear her down in ten days or so.

He rang the bell on day one, and, within seconds, he heard an elaborate series of locks being turned. Having assumed he would have another nine days to prepare the speech that would win Carolyn back, he was completely unprepared. He never expected results on the first try.

'Quitters never win and winners never quit!' TJ was right—Clichés are clichés because they are the truth! He made a mental note to be sure and write TJ a thank you note for offering such astute advice, but he realized he did not know her last name or any of her contact information.

The door opened about a foot. He was *met*—since it definitely could not be said that he was *greeted*—by Cora.

"I'm here to see Carolyn," he demanded, undaunted by Cora's laser-like glare.

Cora shook her head. Her arm hung stiffly at her side, hand balled into a fist.

"I don't understand what happened," he finally said when it became apparent Cora wasn't planning on saying anything. "We were having a nice time."

"We *were?*"

"*We* were. Carolyn and I were. And then all of a sudden, she said she never wanted to see me again. And I don't—"

"Don't tell me you don't understand. You can't be that thick. Think about it."

George stared back dumbly.

"You talk to Jesus!"

"Not true. You are misquoting me," said George, taking offence. "I said I *talked* to Jesus. It was just the one time. The second time I only saw him. We didn't speak to each other then."

"Oh. Just the one time? In that case you're right, my daughter had no reason to get upset with you." After that bit of sarcasm she raised her still balled-up fist to the door and rushed to slam it. But since quitters never win, George was not about to be dissuaded so easily. Without weighing the consequences of such a rash act, he thrust his left hand into the frame seconds before the door closed, causing it to bounce back open upon impact with his fingers, most likely fracturing a phalange or two in the process. They were both stunned by his impetuous move, but only George whimpered in response to it.

Cora's expression softened. "You're going to need ice for that hand."

"Thank you."

"You misunderstand me. I'm not giving you any, but you should certainly use some once you get home. George, let me do one thing for you, though. Give me your hand."

He was reluctant, but since she couldn't inflict any more damage than he'd already suffered, he let her take it. She held it tenderly for a moment before yanking at his wedding band.

"That hand is swelling. Another few minutes, and it would have to be cut off," she said, grappling with the stubborn band. George assumed she meant that the ring might need to be sawed in two, but with Cora, he wasn't positive.

Finally the ring came free, and Cora lurched back a step as the wedding band left its home for the first time in twenty-four years. She handed it back. He wasn't sure what he should do with it. Would Brian ever wear the symbol of his parents' failed marriage? Probably not. Still George slipped the ring into his pocket. He would store it in a drawer when he got home, he supposed, and then cart it to the next apartment when his sublet was over.

"For the record, usually the wedding band comes off *before* you start asking women out again."

George nodded his head. His eyes were tearing and not just because he had a broken hand.

"Carolyn deserves better than you. How could you have been so insensitive?"

As seemed to be his constant state, he stared in confusion.

"You know about Danny?" It was more statement than question.

George performed a muddy, hybrid move, part nod of the head, paired with a shake and topped off with a shrug that he hoped suggested *I know he was her late husband and he killed himself, but I know nothing else.*

"He was schizophrenic. He was diagnosed the year they got married. It was soon after they got back from their honeymoon he told her about the voices that he'd been hearing for years. In particular the voice of God, who told him to do things."

"I don't hear voices. And I know I didn't talk to the real Jesus," he said, surprisingly disappointed by that obvious truth.

Cora glanced sympathetically at his hand, swollen and already turning a nasty reddish purple. "Don't forget about that ice," she said concernedly before slamming the door in his face.

TWENTY-FOUR

FINDING A NEW DOCTOR HAD not been high on George's to-do list, especially with so many more pressing things still unaccomplished. Besides, he was months away from his next scheduled physical, and, aside from a predisposition toward hypochondria, he was remarkably healthy. He could not remember when he had last been in Todd's office for anything more serious than his annual checkup. He would have gone in more often were it not for the fact that Todd generally said, "There's nothing wrong with you. You just need to relax." But now an eggplant was attached to his wrist where formerly there had been a hand.

The ice didn't seem to be doing anything, perhaps because George kept removing the ice pack to see if it was doing anything. After failing in his attempt to buy Aleve on Black Friday, he had never gotten around to picking up a bottle, so he had no pain reliever in the apartment. After triple checking to be sure he had his wallet, George went out to buy a bottle, which was a sensible idea he should have stuck with. But when he got to Broadway, he walked two blocks up to the subway instead of heading downtown toward the pharmacy.

Even as he did this, he knew it wasn't well thought out. He didn't have a doctor, but he did still have a mother. He decided to go home and let her take care of him. No recently widowed and bankrupt mother needs the burden of caring for her supposedly grown-up son. George knew this, and yet he swiped his MetroCard anyway, entered the South Ferry bound platform, and waited the three minutes for the train's arrival.

By the time George reached 72nd Street, he knew he could not go to his mother's, but he didn't know where to go, and he couldn't find the will to stand up and get off the train. He could find a drugstore near whichever stop he got off, and he wasn't in a rush. He almost disembarked at 34th Street, but that would have put him right in the thick of Macy's and Penn Station and the Garden, and he certainly didn't need to get tossed into that mess, especially with an eggplant hand that needed protecting.

Finally, at 23rd Street, he figured out what he should do. He made a dash for the exit just before the doors closed. He didn't have a doctor, but he did have a healer. He darted up the subway steps to the sidewalk where he'd have better cell reception. With luck, maybe Luke would see him immediately. It was worth a try.

George shoved his un-engorged hand into his pocket and felt his wallet. The other pocket yielded keys. As for a phone, he could not find it anyplace. Instead of checking for his wallet three times, he would have been better served if he'd checked for his iPhone once, because he wasn't carrying it. He had a clear memory of setting it on the kitchen counter while he had been fumbling with his one good hand to remove ice from its tray.

When George was a boy, there were pay phones in Manhattan that worked. But despite copious evidence to the contrary, his actual childhood was long past. Since this was an emergency, he decided to walk to Luke's apartment and ring his buzzer. He hoped he would find him at home and that he wouldn't be disrupting someone else's session.

Turning the corner onto 22nd Street, George could not believe his good fortune. Halfway down the block, he spotted Luke standing on the sidewalk in front of his building. Picking up his pace, George jogged so as not to miss Luke before he went on his way, for surely he wouldn't just be standing outside on a December day getting some air. Then George saw something so incredibly shocking, he stopped dead in his tracks.

The Healer, in one steady, languorous move, lifted his hand toward his mouth. Nestled between his fingers was a cigarette, which he glanced at for a second before placing it between his lips and inhaling deeply. After a moment's pause, smoke fogged the air around Luke's face.

George didn't know what to do. It was like walking in on his parents having sex, which thankfully he had never done. He wasn't entirely sure why he was so troubled by this sight. They were Luke's lungs, and he had every right to destroy them if he wanted. But the sight left George genuinely dismayed. Luke being a smoker didn't make sense.

George found it hard to wrap his brain around the notion that a man who devoted his life to healing others was incapable of taking care of himself in such a fundamental way. The guy taught yoga and did energy healing and basically had no job that required wearing shoes. This guy smoked?

Yes he did. George stood there, watching Luke do just that. He was very practiced, swallowing the carcinogenic fumes and holding them for ages before reluctantly setting them free. Then the butt fell to the sidewalk and Luke pressed it out with the sole of his shoe—his profession might not have required them, but city streets did. George could leave unnoticed, or run up to him before Luke went back inside. The urge to flee was strong, but it was defeated by the urge to be pain free.

As George pondered what to do he noticed, much to his surprise, that Luke was not returning to his building. He was just standing there, glancing up the block away from George. Was he planning on smoking another cigarette? George could not imagine anything more incongruous than a self-proclaimed healer chain smoking. George continued a few steps before once again stopping in his tracks. Conor was approaching from the other end of the block, heading straight for Luke.

This could be perfect, thought George. *My brother is Luke's next client and undoubtedly he will let me take his appointment when he sees the dire condition of my hand.*

George managed a few more steps before stopping yet again, this time by a sight so truly shocking that he all but forgot that moments earlier he had been shocked to discover Luke was addicted to nicotine. What on earth had made George think seeing someone smoking warranted being shocked? That was not shocking. This was.

George saw Luke and Conor kissing, and not on the cheeks like the French do. The other kind of French kissing.

For so many embarrassing and confusing reasons, this was more than George could handle. He needed to turn around, walk away, and go home, forget about what he'd seen. And he would have done just that if Conor and Luke had not stopped making out at that very moment and spotted George gawking at them.

ര

THE ELEVATOR RIDE UP TO Luke's apartment—Conor, Luke, George and a German woman with Crocs on her feet and a bulldog named Fritz on a leash—provided a momentary distraction from the events of the sidewalk because Fritz was drooling uncontrollably, perhaps explaining the woman's choice in footwear.

Aside from one halfhearted "*Nein!*" the German woman was pretending it wasn't happening. For their part, the three men slid their feet about in an attempt to dodge the mess, making it look as if they'd spontaneously decided to play a game of Twister.

Once inside Luke's place, Luke vanished to make tea, leaving the brothers alone in the clean, modest space. A well-worn love seat, the arms near ready for reupholstery, a pine coffee table strewn with candles, but thankfully no ashtray, and a couple of Shaker-style side chairs decorated the space. Three yoga mats were propped up in the corner along with a large physioball.

The brothers stared at each other. George was profoundly upset. Not because he just discovered he had a gay brother, but because that possibility had never once before even crossed his mind. What did that say about their relationship that he was unable to sense this fundamental truth about his brother? How had he failed to consider a scenario in which Conor might be gay? Instead, he had come up with the preposterous theory that he was desperate to screw Tara.

"I came because I hurt my hand," George said, which he'd

already said on the sidewalk when they caught him staring. A part of him was still hoping he could convince them he hadn't seen the kiss, or that they could at least all come to an agreement to pretend he had not seen that—which, after all, is the Bailey way—so he thought it best to try and maintain focus on his injury.

"Yes. You said. That's got to hurt," Conor added, pointing in the direction of George's swollen fingers.

George nodded sheepishly, feeling vaguely guilty for refusing to be a grown-up and acknowledging what he'd witnessed outside. Ignoring the kiss was unwise. It would only damage his already middling relationship with Conor. This was his moment to do the right thing and say something loving and reassuring to his brother. "How come you never told me?" He really had been aiming for loving and reassuring, but the end result was accusatory.

"Every single thing is not about you, George," Conor snapped.

"I never suggested it was. That's not fair."

"It's not? You planned on selling our business without even discussing it with me because you decided you didn't want it anymore. You just assumed it would be fine with me."

George rolled his eyes. He could not believe his brother was still harping on that. "That's kind of a moot point now, isn't it?"

"I don't want to have a fight with you," Conor said, but his armored stance suggested otherwise.

"Neither do I!" Equally armored. "Who knows about this, anyway?" George was referring to his brother's sexual orientation, though he might as well have been asking him about a newly discovered malignant tumor, or a recently plotted bank heist for all the *gravitas* of his inquiry.

"Just my supportive brother."

"I am supportive," he said wanting to be, even as he was failing miserably at it. "I'm just surprised, that's all. So. What? You've been living on the down-low?"

"Check you out with the lingo! Google has taught you so much." What little patience Conor had for his brother's line of questioning was fast disappearing.

This was going horribly, still George soldiered on. "I'm just curious."

"That makes two of us," said Conor suggestively.

George blushed. "No. *I'm* not curious. I didn't mean it that way. I meant I'm curious about you—"

"I know what you meant. You're such an idiot, George. I'm just joking with you. I'm well past curious."

George had so much more to say, but he could not find words. Somehow everything he'd said made him seem disapproving and homophobic, and he really didn't think he was either of those things. George didn't know how to fix this. He was quiet. He was thirsty, and there was no sign of tea. His hand throbbed like a son of a bitch. Then he stopped thinking about himself and instead thought about Conor for a change.

"I'm very glad you've met someone." Thinking about his brother's decades of loneliness made George's voice crack and his eyes fill with tears, which startled both of them. They glanced away from each other, looking off in the direction of the kitchen, but there was still no sign that Luke would be returning any time soon with tea.

The silence washed over them, but it felt companionable, and George wasn't in a great rush to break it. Finally he decided to make a confession. "I thought you were alone all these years because you were in love with Tara."

Conor shook his head. "And of course you thought this because it's always all about you, right down to me coveting my brother's wife." The words hung there a moment before Conor smiled. "It's okay. It may be all about you, but on the plus side, at least I'm always right."

They sat for the first time since entering the room. The kettle whistled in the distance, and soon after Luke would return with the tray, and they would no longer have this time alone together, which George was not entirely happy about. "I have one question. How can you stand kissing him?" George whispered this since Luke was right in the next room.

Conor's jaw dropped. "You always have to ruin everything," he said flabbergasted. He raised his hands as if he might strike George, and then as if recalling that he was not a violent man let them fall back to his side. "And you wonder why I didn't want you to find out."

"Oh, no. I'm sorry. That came out completely wrong. Forgive me," implored George. "I don't mean because he's a man. He's a smoker." George pulled an exaggeratedly disgusted face.

Conor sighed. "Nobody's perfect, George."

Just then, Luke entered with three steaming mugs on a tray. George noticed the way his brother looked at the healer. Conor's eyes softened, and his face lit up in Luke's presence. Perhaps no one was perfect, but Conor seemed to think Luke came awfully close.

George had so many questions for his brother. He wondered if, like May and Dennis, they'd met at Daddy's wake, or were they already seeing each other then. But for some reason, someone mentioned Fritz the slobbering dog, and they replayed that silly scene. And then it was talk of a French film they'd seen and recommended to George. Finally Luke offered to teach George yoga once he had a functioning hand again. George was polite, but noncommittal in his response.

Conor stood to clear the tea, placing the mugs back onto the tray. "Luke, is there any hope for my brother?" When Luke didn't answer, Conor clarified. "I mean regarding his hand."

"I'll see what I can do. But George you have to promise me if it is not much, much better in the morning, you must go and get an x-ray. I'm not a miracle worker."

With that Conor left them to their session. Luke set up his table while George kicked off his shoes.

"I really appreciate this," George said, climbing onto the table. "It's just that I don't have a doctor, and I didn't know what else to do."

"George, if your hand is broken, you are going to need some Western intervention, in which case I'll send you to my doctor. But let's see."

George closed his eyes. Luke talked him through some diaphragmatic breathing exercises that made him think of coaching Tara through her labors with May and Brian. He became lightheaded and felt like the room was spinning. As the world swirled around him, he let his weight sink deeper into the table. As in past sessions, he was mostly aware of the heat of Luke's hands above his heart. George appreciated this touch but wondered when Luke would start attending to the area that was actually injured.

In the flurry of thoughts that rushed through his head, George saw his parents and Conor decorating a Christmas tree. It was a made up memory. Trees in the Bailey household were usually decorated by the showroom merchandiser. He would leave off four or five ornaments for Conor and George to hang—the photo op. Or maybe what George was seeing now was the truth, and the other memory was something he made up to justify how miserable he was. The scene ended, and he was in his childhood bed. Nan was at the foot smiling at him, ready to tell him a story.

George opened his eyes to look at her, but when he did, he saw

Luke smiling back at him. "You were so out, I didn't have the heart to wake you. But I didn't want to leave you alone." The host of candles on the coffee table illuminated the room, casting a soft golden glow over Luke's complexion. Standing, Luke handed George a glass of water, which he drained in one thirsty gulp.

"You still have a lot of healing to do, but you're so much better than the first time I worked with you."

"My hand?"

"I think maybe I overreacted. It's probably only a bruise, but I'm not a doctor." George wondered if he had a friend who was a lawyer who'd advised him to say 'I'm not a doctor' every time he voiced a medical opinion.

Luke offered to let George stay the night. George was tempted since he was still groggy from the session, but he decided he'd best learn to take care of himself so he declined the invitation. George paid him, though Luke would only take money for the session and not for the extra hour he'd babysat George while he slept.

"You must really love that woman. That was quite the grand, romantic gesture," he said taking another look at George's now noticeably less swollen hand.

George was silent thinking about how futile his love was.

As George was about to leave, Luke touched his index finger gently to George's heart and rose on to his toes to kiss his forehead. The intimacy of the act surprised George. The tender peck was so like the ones Nan gave when she tucked him in. Before George could comment, Luke said goodnight and wished him safe travels home.

∽

GEORGE SLEPT IN THE NEXT morning, drifting in and out of consciousness, occasionally stirring to readjust his hand, which he'd propped on a pillow. He woke up fully when he heard footsteps. An intruder was breaking into the apartment.

As far as George was concerned, the man entering his bedroom was definitely an intruder, but the scene couldn't technically be described as a crime, since he had used his own set of keys to get in. Dennis had arrived with an ice pack and placed it gently on George's hand.

George flinched when he felt the cold.

"You're such a baby," Dennis accurately assessed. "May sent me to check on you."

Luke, worried that George would not seek out medical help should he need it, had apparently called Claire, who in turn called May who in turn handed off the job of checking on George to her boyfriend. George wondered if he should call Brian and Finn so the entire family would be kept abreast of the situation.

"How did you manage this?" Dennis asked.

George considered lying, but he was always so bad at it, and he couldn't think of a lie any less humiliating than the truth.

Dennis was impressed by, as he eloquently put it, the size of George's balls, enthusiastically presenting his palm for George to slap with his good hand. As was his habit, George pretended not to notice.

"Thanks for the ice," George said, wishing Dennis would go away.

"You're welcome," said Dennis, taking a seat on the edge of the bed. "That ice needs to stay on your hand another ten minutes. In the meantime, I'm going to explain to you why it's so great that you're not with Carolyn anymore."

George feared he would be given more advice about the

benefits of alcohol poisoning, but Dennis made no reference to getting wasted or even to getting groomed. "I can see how much you like this woman. You managed to get to middle age dating only one woman. I think it would be sad dying having only dated two."

Which was another way in which George was different from Dennis, because to him the prospect sounded fantastic, especially when the second woman was Carolyn.

"Maybe you will win her back, but for now, let's concentrate on finding you some hot girl to go out with."

George was desperate to change the subject, so when his cell phone rang he grabbed it.

"George?" It was a woman, but not one he knew. "This is Bridget."

George needed more information than that.

"Bridget Brennan."

"Bridget! Hi!" George exclaimed in spite of the fact that he still had no idea who he was speaking to. At George's utterance of the woman's name, Dennis began to dance around the bedroom giddily, mouthing for George to Ask. Her. Out.

"So you remember me?"

George was about to say that he most certainly did, but that would have only led to a tortured round of twenty questions, so he admitted that he didn't.

"We only met once. At your showroom. I presented my Christmas line."

"Bridget, of course," George said, shielding his eyes from Dennis who had added lewd pelvic thrusting to his pantomime. "Funny, I though you had a brogue."

"Just an Irish sweater and a tartan skirt."

George didn't laugh, but he smiled appreciatively. She had a sense of humor, always a plus.

"So I know we aren't going to be working together, and I am sorry about that. But it did make me wonder, since you're not going to be my boss, if you might like to have coffee some time?"

George had his cell pressed tightly to his ear, though clearly Dennis was still managing to pick up Bridget's side of the conversation. "Yes!" Dennis exclaimed.

"Great," Bridget said. "Did you drop your phone? You sounded a little far away."

Whether he wanted it or not, George was planning a coffee date with Bridget. Maybe this was for the best. He had no interest in a romance with this woman, but she was incredibly talented, if somewhat color challenged. Maybe with some luck, they could work together someday, somehow.

He switched the phone to his left hand so he could jot down her number. It was a moment before he realized he had no trouble holding the cell with his injured hand.

When the call was ended, Dennis took a great flourishing bow, like some seventeenth century French fop. "My work here is done." Whether Dennis was referring to George's date with Bridget or his miraculously healed hand, George was unsure. Either way, Dennis departed leaving George wriggling his fingers with ease, as he stared at them in wonder.

TWENTY-FIVE

ON WHAT WAS OFFICIALLY THE first day of winter, the weather decided to align itself with the season, sending an arctic blast roaring up the Hudson, leaving behind temperatures struggling to reach the low twenties. All the climate change doubters took to the blogosphere proclaiming the frigid weather was proof positive global warming was a leftist conspiracy.

George doubted the existence of so many things, but climate change was not one of them. Generally, he was not in the habit of reading the ravings of right-wing wingnuts, but he'd had a bit of a relapse. The second breakup, the failed business, the deceased father, all sent him back to obsessive web surfing. If he'd learned nothing else in the countless hours he'd spent trapped in the Google Hole, he'd discovered that the planet had more than its share of extremists, and most of them had a homepage.

Today at least he had a very good reason for going online. He wanted to know what the temperature was outside.

George had begun that search over two hours ago—long enough for the mercury to drop another three degrees.

Opening up his closet, he looked for something warm even though he already knew he wasn't going to find anything suitable to wear. When he'd hastily moved uptown, he'd crammed an impressive amount of his clothing into two small suitcases.

Even after losing an entire outfit the night of the vomit incident he still had two suits, two pairs of jeans, cords, khakis, three pairs of shoes, seven shirts, socks, t-shirts and underwear. He even had a bathing suit and workout gear, despite the fact that he neither swam or exercised. What he had not packed were any of his sweaters or turtlenecks or long johns. He did not have a scarf a hat or any gloves.

He could either buy new clothing and put himself deeper into debt or go home, get what he needed, and maybe even talk to Tara.

As it turned out, Tara requested he come between one and three when she would be out. She was more than civil when she made her request, and he was equally gracious when he assured her he wouldn't dream of coming a minute earlier. When he arrived at his former residence, he assumed he would go directly up to the apartment, but Vito stepped out from behind the desk, tightly gripping George's hand as he firmly slapped his back with equal parts warmth and aggression.

It was like Clark's greeting had been, though Adelman's handshake had been entirely aggressive. His grandfather had greeted men in that fashion as well, a clasp of the hand paired with a smack to the body. It was how Pop welcomed his most important buyers, the guys from Macy's or Neiman Marcus, into the showroom. For

Pop, acknowledging the men in that fashion was a way of showing he was both completely at their disposal and totally in charge.

When George shook a buyer's hand, he used moderate pressure. Never was it accompanied by a slap. He was certainly completely at their disposal, but he was not totally in charge.

"This is a surprise," Vito asked awkwardly as he returned to his post. "Here to see your brother?" The guest book, opened to a half-filled page, sat on the front desk between them, and Vito was eyeing it, perhaps coincidentally, perhaps not. George wondered if after all the years of living in the building, he would now be expected to sign in like the delivery guys carrying up laundry or Chinese food. The idea galled him.

"I'm going up to my place," George announced, as Vito's eyes widened in alarm. "Tara knows," he added. "She didn't tell you I was coming by?"

Based on the wariness of Vito's gaze, she hadn't. The doorman was clearly torn as to what to do. On the one hand, no one wants to be the guy responsible for letting in the deranged, estranged spouse and on the other, nobody wants to get fired from barring a homeowner entrance to his own domicile. After an awkward moment of deliberation, Vito waved him toward the elevator. To George's relief, none of his former neighbors had witnessed his front desk interrogation.

He entered the apartment and, much in the style of his wife, gasped in alarm. He was not alone. Tara was standing directly on the other side of the door, a coat over her arm and a purse in her hand.

"It's 1:30," he informed her.

"I know. My fault. Running late." Flustered, she looked about suspiciously. Something was plainly amiss.

"All set," boomed a man's voice from out of the bedroom. Tara acted as if she'd heard nothing.

Come on? There's a guy in the bedroom?

Quizzically, George examined Tara for clues. Though surely there had to be a more reasonable explanation, George had the awful premonition the mystery man was a paramour. Consumed by the throes of passion, their assignation had run long, and he'd yet to depart. Yes it was brazen behavior, especially with your husband due to arrive at any moment, but it didn't seem an outlandish scenario when compared to her having a tryst at the funeral home.

All set, the mystery man had said. What had that meant? *All set, I found my cell phone, my wallet, my underwear, my handcuff?* Tara had a patently guilty look on her face. What else would explain it?

George's replacement came sauntering out of the bedroom. He was young, thirty maximum. What he had in youth, he lost in style. He was clad in a boxy, blue uniform, a hand-me-down from Chairman Mao.

"Sorry it took so long. A little harder than expected, but you should be fine for a good long time," he said shamelessly to Tara. As the man passed by, he eyed George and George eyed him right back, reading the insignia on the Maoist's pocket: Time Warner Cable.

Tara was engaged in an activity far more surprising than taking on a new lover. George grinned delightedly, at having caught her in the act. She had installed cable. Cable was present in the home of the woman who had proclaimed television to be the ruin of all civilized society. TV was mind numbing and designed to control the masses, and now it was available on a flat screen in the bedroom. "So. Why was there a cable guy here?" George goaded, barely controlling a chuckle.

"If you don't make a crack, I'll give you a dollar," she frowned.

These days, he'd take a buck anyway he could. George extended his open palms. She smiled, but the grin quickly vanished. She stood there in a daze.

"I'm not kidding. I want the cash, or I'm going to enumerate the ways in which television has destroyed our brain cells."

He thought this might get a smile out of her, but her mind was miles away.

"Hey. I'm just joking around. My apartment has cable, too. You're going to love it," he said even though he'd barely turned his set on since he'd moved. "What's wrong?"

"Nothing," she said. She was staring glumly at George's left hand. For a second, he thought she might be looking at the hint of bruising still visible on his hand. He was going to tell her it was nothing. He was fine. Then he realized it wasn't the hand that she was focused on. It was the sight of his ringless finger that had thrown Tara. She was still wearing her engagement and wedding rings. "Well, I'll leave," she stammered. "So you can—"

"I won't be long. Stay." He wanted to say something more. He wanted to scream in frustration. He wanted to tell her how furious he was with her. He also wanted to apologize. He wanted to say he would never see her again, or talk to her, or have anything to do with her. And he wanted to beg her to come back to him. In the end he did none of those things. "So? Did you sign up for HBO?"

He wasn't long. In Tara's organized home, he had no trouble finding his winter clothes. He shoved a few sweaters and scarves into his bag and put on a heavier coat. He could have taken more, but then he wouldn't have an excuse to return.

Without thinking, he bent to kiss her as he was leaving. Their lips met passionlessly, and he realized sadly that this post-breakup kiss was no different from most of the kisses they'd shared in recent years. This might have been any random day of the week as he trudged off miserably to work. The kiss lasted a second, and when they parted, he almost said, *Have a good day, sweetheart*, just as he always had. But he caught himself and remembered they no longer used endearments when addressing each other.

Here he was kissing his wife goodbye, like he'd done thousands of times before, only they weren't a couple anymore.

Why did I just kiss her?

He was still hurt by her betrayal, yet he leaned in without thinking, pressing his lips against hers. He kissed her because it was a habit, not because any passion was connected to the gesture. So much of their relationship had devolved to thoughtless routine. When he walked through a door, he was conditioned to kiss her, to ask her about her day and to tell her about his own. This way of being wasn't the result of a great marriage. It was merely a Pavlovian response he couldn't break.

What saddened him now was the realization that he had been acting in this thoughtless, careless fashion around Tara for years. All the real and spontaneous emotion had slipped away longer ago than he could recall. What was left was a charade. He had kissed her, and he had his coat on, and he was heading for the door. Beyond the lame premium cable crack, he'd asked her nothing and had told her nothing. She was still clutching her coat and purse.

"Could I persuade you to take a walk with me?" he said.

To his surprise, Tara put on her coat and they were in the elevator within a minute, because miraculously the entire bank of elevators had been in service for nearly ten days. Vito watched the pair leave. George could feel the doorman's eyes trailing him as they passed by.

For a while, their conversation fluctuated between nonexistent and innocuous. They talked about how warm it had been and how cold it had suddenly become. Or was it really cold? Had they just become so used to fifty degrees in December that any dip in temperature now seemed abnormal. Hadn't it always been cold like this when they were children? The weather topic may have spelled danger for the planet, but for George and Tara, it seemed to be the only topic safe enough to discuss.

When they said everything they could think of about the climate, they returned to silence. Representatives of The Salvation Army were clanging away on the corner, and George asked her if it seemed like a lot more of their battalion was out on the sidewalks looking for donations than there used to be. It really did seem like they were stationed every ten blocks. "I'm seeing them everywhere."

"Well we're living in hard times, George." He nodded in agreement, and they continued walking along. "Brian told me about the business. I know it's all so complicated for you, considering how unhappy it's made you. Still, I wish it wasn't going to end like this. It seems wrong."

He had the urge to be closer to her, and it was a real feeling, not just a reflex. He took her arm, and she did not pull away. "You'll never believe this, but I actually want to save the business. Mind you, I don't know how. No rational person would ever invest in this failed enterprise. I have a date with a woman tomorrow." George felt Tara's body tense for an instant, before relaxing again. "I want to talk about the business with her. She's a very good designer. I don't really think she can help. It's a bit late in the day for that."

They continued on for a block. "I'm glad you've spoken to Brian," said George. "What about May?"

She shook her head forlornly. "I don't know how I'm ever going to be able to fix what I've done. What about you? Have you talked to her?"

"Yes. We're fine. But I have managed to make her weep every time I've talked to her. Things were pretty shaky between us at first. I'm not exactly sure why she thought *I* was the bad guy in all this," he said, regretting the comment the second it came out of his mouth, even though the urge to say it had been irresistible. Whatever closeness they'd shared abruptly ended. She let her arm drop away from his, feigning need of a tissue. When she finally unearthed a Kleenex from the bottom of her bag, she didn't use it. Nor did she retake his arm.

With the exception of recent notorious events, Mr. and Mrs. Bailey didn't go in for big drama or scenes. That was not their way. They hurt each other with not-so-innocent barbs and jabs—a comment here, a look there. They both did it. They both wanted to change the behavior, but it had grown into a deep-rooted, insidious pattern.

"Are we just out for a walk, or are you taking me someplace in particular?" She sounded eager to end this excursion and return home.

They were nearing 12th Street and George hesitated, torn between heading east and west. He had not planned on anything more than a walk. But then here they were, practically at the door. "Have a drink with me?"

He was sure she was going to say no, and he wouldn't blame her. "It's not yet five." She looked at him darkly, almost frowning. But then she clasped his arm again and nodded. George led the way, though certainly she knew where he was taking her.

Almost everything about the neighborhood had changed from when they were first married. With the exception of the Strand, almost all the booksellers were gone from these blocks. One or two antique stores had hung on, despite the astronomical rents. Most every restaurant had changed hands at least four times in the last twenty-four years. Retailers were suffering the same fate that was now befalling Bailey and Sons. George couldn't keep up with the turnover. Yet the Gotham Bar and Grill seemed to carry on. Both the room and the menu seemed as fresh and modern as the day it opened in 1984.

Gotham was their favorite restaurant. And though neither Tara nor George actually used the phrase "our place," that was absolutely what the restaurant was to them. Gotham was their go-to spot for all anniversaries and special occasions. The first time they went there was the day they returned from their honeymoon, still eager to celebrate. While they sat at the bar waiting for a table, they ordered a drink and told the bartender they were newlyweds. He congratulated them before he carded them. And then the bartender toasted them with Perrier.

When George finally turned twenty-one, three months after Tara had, they returned to discover the same bartender on duty. The couple presented their Ids, and George ordered them each a single malt scotch, because the drink seemed so incredibly grown-up.

Now, as then, he ordered Glenfiddich. They raised their glasses, and, because it was what they had always done before, they clinked them, stopping short of saying cheers.

The first sip had a slight peppery burn going down the throat, but the second was smooth and sweet like marmalade. George was breathing in the aroma of orange and spice when Tara asked, "Is this when you tell me that I'll be hearing from your lawyers, George?"

He hadn't even thought about contacting a lawyer yet. Of course he would have to eventually, but he didn't see any need to rush.

"Obviously," Tara said, "I'm not in a position to be difficult, but even if I were, I would not be."

They sipped their drinks. The hostess recognized them and stopped at the bar to say hello. Putting on smiles, they chatted with her, acting as if everything in their lives was wonderful. She wished them season's greetings and joked about how much she always enjoyed saying Merry Christmas to Mr. and Mrs. George Bailey. The hostess raised an eyebrow and nodded knowingly to the bartender, and within moments, a cheese plate was in front of them courtesy of the management.

They ate. "You look great, by the way," she said. "You've never had such a good haircut."

And I never will again.

He was bereft at the thought of losing Carolyn, mysterious, and funny, and talented and… He remembered he was sitting with a different woman now.

Tara leaned into him, like she had a secret to share. "Your eyebrows look great, too. They make you look younger," she said, proving once and for all that Kim was a liar.

"Geez. I was told no one would be able to tell I'd had my eyebrows waxed."

"No one will be able to tell." She swirled the scotch in her glass and looked at it instead of him. "The hairstylist. You're seeing her?"

"Did Brian tell you that?"

"Conor."

Of course. His brother, as always, sharing everything with Tara—well, not everything. He shook his head. "That's over."

"Were you seeing each other a long time?"

What a ridiculous question. "How long could it be? You and I have been separated for less than a month."

"I thought maybe you met before—"

"No. Not before. So how is Todd doing?" He asked partly

wanting to see if she would confirm his story about them not being together and partly because he wanted to hurt her.

"I really don't know. George, I am so sorry." Her eyes filled with tears, which she tried without success to hide from him by placing her hand in front of her forehead.

Even as he told himself he had no reason to feel guilty, he felt terribly guilty for upsetting her. He didn't quite understand this emotion. He'd done nothing wrong. If George wanted to hurt Tara, if he chose to spend his life reminding her of her failings, he felt well within his rights to do so.

She cried. He watched. He felt like an ass. He also understood exactly why he felt so guilty for punishing her. Tara's bad behavior had given him the enormous gift of a get-out-of-jail-free card with regard to their marriage. George could torture her for the rest of her life, or he could be grateful to her for setting him free.

"I know you're sorry," he said. He put down his glass and touched her hand. He thought about Sal's advice again, and he realized it wasn't just about forgiving others. He needed to be forgiven, too. "Tara, please look at me. I don't know when I stopped… I'm every bit as much to blame for our problems as you are. I'm so sorry. I hope someday you'll forgive me." From the way she looked at him, he thought maybe she would.

In unison, they raised their glasses and sipped. "How is your new apartment?" she asked after some time had passed.

"You would love it. There's a Ping-Pong table in the hallway. It's exactly your taste," he grinned.

"The other night," said Tara, "I was trying to recall if I'd ever spent a night alone before you moved out. I was pretty sure I hadn't. Then I remembered a weekend when I was about fifteen. My parents had been planning this trip for months, and I was supposed to stay at my aunt's. But the day before, my mother and my aunt got into a big fight, and they weren't talking to each other. So, reluctantly my parents let me stay home alone."

"What did you do with your freedom?"

Tara sighed. "Nothing. I watched videos. And I checked and rechecked to make sure all the doors and windows were locked. I was terrified."

George tried to remember when, if ever, he had been alone. He'd attended trade shows without Tara, but he had either shared a room with Conor or his father. "Pathetic as it may sound, your one weekend on your own has me beat. I was never alone until three weeks ago."

They laughed grimly, both of them middle-aged and taking their first baby steps toward independence. Once again, he wondered why his parents never raised an objection all those years ago when they announced their engagement.

"Was this a mistake?" Tara asked. Because he was afraid, he was about to say yes it was. Let's fix this. Let's get back together. But that's not what she meant. "Do you think we never should have gotten married?"

The bartender returned and poured another round before retreating to the other end of the bar. "Getting married was absolutely not a mistake." George sliced into the runny Camembert. "Though maybe we would have been better served with a longer engagement." On that, they clinked again.

"I'll call the lawyer after the holidays."

"Yes," George said. "I will, too."

"George, this woman you're seeing tomorrow, the designer..." Tara seemed to lose her thought. She stared, first at her glass and then at George. "Why did you never design a line? You'd be so good at that. You'd be drawing."

George didn't have an answer. Studying art was a thousand years ago. And he wasn't talented, not immensely. That's what he thought anyway. That is what he believed.

They talked about May and Brian, taking turns reassuring each other that their children were strong and smart and loved, and they would someday recover from this. Again they said they'd be fair to each other with regard to a settlement. In light of their new economic reality, they would figure something out. Tara had just booked a new client in Connecticut, a country home being entirely redecorated. The job would last for months and pay her handsomely.

"A minimalist country home?"

She took a steadying gulp before answering. "Not exactly. But a girl's got to eat, as they say. I have guaranteed there will be plenty of chintz and bric-a-brac. Perhaps I should go wild and suggest a Ping-Pong table."

They finished their drinks, declining a third. He paid the check, thanking them for sending over the cheese. George wondered what the staff at Gotham would think when they didn't see them again. He didn't think he could come back here again with anyone other than Tara. He hoped she would also want to keep this as their place. Then he forced himself to abandon this melodramatic thinking. Neither of them had died. They were breaking up. Someday, with some luck and care, they might be friends. And maybe, as friends do, they'd meet at Gotham—it would still be their place. They would sit at the bar, order a scotch, catch up, and reminisce.

George offered to walk her back to the apartment, but she had errands to run so they said their goodbyes on the sidewalk in front of the restaurant. Leaning down, he kissed her warm cheeks, which were flushed by emotion and the single malt.

"Tara," he said taking her hand, "what are we going to do without each other?"

She was quiet for a moment, and then sighed, both relieved and terribly sad. "I think we're going to grow up, George."

TWENTY-SIX

THE THING ABOUT LIVING so far uptown is that it's... So. Far. Uptown. It was a considerable trek from his apartment to anyplace George actually wanted to be. When he left his place in the morning, he was pretty much committed to being gone for the day. He couldn't run back home for a minute before setting off for the next appointment. Like the Bedouins, he'd taken to carrying a bag with him wherever he went, lest he find himself away from home without water, a snack, or a book to read on the train.

His social life had pretty much ground to a halt, but today he found himself with two engagements on the calendar. One was formal and one was not, which presented a challenge, and is why he was overdressed for his coffee date with Bridget. He would, however, look just fine when he attended the evening's Last Supper, which is what he'd been calling the Bailey and Sons Christmas party at Per Se.

Removing his tie, he stashed it in his pocket, attempting to affect a more casual appearance. That still left him wearing a pinstripe suit and wingtips when jeans would have been more appropriate. He wasn't wearing just any suit. It was the same suit that he'd worn to his father's funeral. The garment saddened him now. It was a mistake to wear it again, but that's what men did. No guy spends two grand on an item of clothing and then wears the thing once. The suit you put on to commemorate yesterday's tragedy is the same one you'll wear to celebrate tomorrow's triumph. That's just the way it is. If a man wears an outfit only once, it's a safe bet he rented it.

George was milling about the Bouchon Bakery in the Time Warner Center. He'd suggested the spot because it was only one floor below Per Se. Bridget was late. He grabbed a table in the half-walled open space and waited, staring out over the expanse of Central Park, white lights flickering in the distance. He looked back across the restaurant and noticed a woman sitting on the opposite side of the room. George was certain he knew her, but he could not recall from where.

She was wearing a variation on the Independent Urban Career Woman's uniform of black sweater, black slacks, and black shoes. She had on black horn-rimmed glasses. Her hair was pulled back into a very tight ponytail. She was focused on a book she was reading, but he couldn't see the cover. She glanced up from her book in the braced and guarded way beautiful women do when they know they're being watched.

"George? I didn't see you come in," Bridget said.

George joined her at her table. "Oh. Sorry I didn't recognize you without…" He pointed at her black attire as he sat down.

"This is the way I normally dress. The kilt was really just a costume."

"Have you had the chocolate tart here? I noticed it on another table. It looks amazing."

"I don't really eat much sugar, and I already had chocolate once this week. Have you ever had the Bibb lettuce salad?"

He had not, nor would he be having it today.

While they could not agree on food, they were in accord when it came to beverages, both favoring double espresso. Having so much sugar and bitter coffee on an empty stomach was a mistake. He felt sick and high-strung, but he kept eating and drinking because he didn't really have anything to say to this woman.

Why had I thought she could help with the business? She can only help me if she has a trust fund.

As desperate as he was, George knew he couldn't ask her if she was by chance heir to a fortune, at least not on the first date. So he sat shoveling in the chocolate tart instead of chatting. By default, Bridget was forced to keep the conversation going, which she was gamely trying to do. She asked him countless questions, waiting through excruciating silences while he searched for replies that refused to come.

She was perfectly nice, and very attractive in the severe New York kind of way George normally responded to. She was talented, always a plus. But whatever that thing called chemistry was, they did not have it. And George, lovesick, heartbroken, grief-stricken, and finally accepting that the business could not be saved, refused to pretend that they did. Even taking into account his troubles, his sullen behavior was intolerable.

He ate and ate, answering her with monosyllables. He did eventually mention the excellent dessert he'd just devoured, but since she hadn't tasted the tart, this did not launch a lengthy discussion. After the failed tart talk, he couldn't muster the enthusiasm to say much of anything else.

When he'd scraped his plate clean and finished his coffee, the complete lack of banter could no longer be ignored. Bridget looked at him understandingly, a testament to just how incredibly generous a person she was, and broke their awkward silence. "I think maybe this is all too soon for you."

George sighed, his relief palpable. "I think so. I'm sorry. It's only been a few days."

Bridget lifted a puzzled brow. "I thought it had been several weeks, which, granted, is still not much time. But days?"

"I see the confusion. My wife left me three and a half weeks ago. That's true. But my girlfriend only broke up with me the other day."

George was delighted to get that misunderstanding straightened out, though Bridget, in full glower, seemed less delighted. "You broke up with both your wife and your girlfriend in the span of three weeks?"

"No. They both broke up with me, but only my wife had a good reason."

Bridget stood brusquely, leaving George genuinely confused by her action.

"Yes," she said. "I can imagine that finding out your husband is having an affair would be a *good reason* to leave him."

"Please sit down," George said.

Bridget ignored his request. Arching her back and raising her righteous voice, she drew the attention of the surrounding customers, who had all seemed to decide at once this might be an excellent time to take a break from their own conversations and listen in on this one instead. "George, I have dated so many men exactly like you."

George was pretty sure she hadn't.

"Men who disregard us. Treat us without respect. Like we are just one more conquest." She was obviously flashing back to her own personal history.

George had become so accustomed to creating scenes in public places that he was hardly bothered by this one. In fact, George fought hard to keep from smiling. He felt a little guilty at the pleasure he was taking in being mistaken for that kind of man. George Bailey a cad? Not with his bedpost still looking pristine and notch free.

"And to think I felt so sorry for you, losing your father, your wife, and your business."

"You aren't trying to refute the death of my father, are you?"

This comment silenced Bridget, who took a moment to scan the room. She discovered a sea of eyes all focused squarely on her, awaiting her reply. She sat again.

"My father did just die, and my wife did leave me, but I never had an affair. The business I want to save. That was partly why I wanted to meet you today, though I can't explain why. I don't know how you could help me. Obviously, I don't expect you to have a giant trust fund that you want to invest in a Christmas business." He laughed like that was a joke instead of the desperate, wishful plea that it was. She was silent, so probably she wasn't an heiress. "Anyway, I guess I'm going to be selling."

"I'm sorry about that. Even if you were cheating—"

"Which I wasn't."

Bridget waved a dismissive hand before explaining that three of the last four men she'd dated had cheated on her, so she hoped she would be forgiven for her sensitivity on the subject. "This date of ours was a disaster," she declared.

"But the chocolate tart was great." George smiled, glancing at her half-eaten salad.

Bridget got up to leave, and then as if she'd forgotten something important she sat back down. "I love everything about Christmas, and I'm so sorry that Bailey and Sons is going out of business, because your things were always the most beautiful, special. Magical, even. I used to be a buyer for Saks. Your father worked with me personally. He was such a lovely man."

George nodded appreciatively. He stomped down his grief. He had to get rid of this suit, vowed to donate it to Goodwill. "There will still be a Bailey and Sons, just without the Baileys." George felt a little lightheaded, the sugar already causing him to crash. He rested his head in the palm of his hand as a thought occurred to him. "Hey, this deal isn't going to be finalized until after the New Year. How do you even know we're selling?"

She leaned in confidentially. "I also did a presentation for Clark Adelman. He asked me if I had shown my line to anyone else yet. I told him I had shown it to you. And he smiled at me, just like Trip used to. He was the first of my cheating boyfriends. And I instantly knew Clark Adelman was a very slimy man," she said grimacing. "And then he aggressively flirted with me even though, *hello*, it's business, and also I'm pretty sure there is a Mrs. Adelman. He bragged to me he was in the process of buying you out, and that once he had acquired you, he'd be liquidating the company, so I should not expect to get an offer from you."

George was speechless, less stunned by Adelman's actions than by his own naiveté. It had never occurred to him that Adelman wanted to buy the company so he could destroy it. But of course it made perfect sense. Clark certainly didn't need two businesses selling the same stuff. With competition from the Baileys gone, he'd gain all those customers who would be forced to buy from him.

He didn't need Bailey's showroom with its enormous rent and very well paid employees. George thought about all those loyal, truly devoted people who worked for his family. He'd felt bad enough when he thought they were going to be working for Adelman. Now he realized they were just going to be unemployed.

"On top of everything, that bastard didn't even make me an offer. He's probably in China right now knocking off my line." She shook her head.

"You're very talented. Please don't say anything to anyone, but my family has changed its mind. We aren't going to be selling to Clark Adelman. But he doesn't know that yet." George didn't mention his family didn't know that yet, either. George had not figured out a great solution to the problem. He had merely decided that, under the circumstances, declaring bankruptcy was a better ending than being stubbed out by Adelman.

He would have liked to kiss Bridget's cheek, especially considering the information she'd just leaked to him, but he decided a handshake was more appropriate. "Who knows? If I actually find some money at the eleventh hour, perhaps we can speak again about possibly working together. Would you ever consider redoing your line in gold and silver?"

∾

THE ONE HOPE GEORGE HAD clung to during these difficult weeks—that the loyal staff of Bailey and Sons would not lose their jobs—had been dashed. In an hour, he'd be forced to face them. They would soon all be unemployed. And tonight they would not receive bonuses, unless they considered gorging on overpriced duck confit a bonus.

He rode the escalators aimlessly up and down, without entering any stores. Since he needed gifts for his children, actually walking into a shop was going to be a necessary first step. He got off at the ground level and began roaming the halls. It was two days before Christmas, and shoppers were out in force.

For May, he could always buy a piece of jewelry. Brian was the bigger challenge—earrings were out. George walked by The Art of Shaving. *He's a man. He has facial hair, maybe I should go in there.*

As was the case with every store in the mall, this small shop was jammed with people. The five salespeople behind the counters were all busy with customers. A line of people eager for help waited to be assisted.

George queued behind a young woman clad in down, leggings, and Uggs, a fleece headband covering her ears. George was jostled from behind, and he in turn pressed into the woman. In contrast to the rude person behind him, George apologized profusely. She turned to look at him, bundled up and sweating, and accepted his contrition graciously. "Don't worry about it. It goes with the territory. I always vow to shop early, to avoid this madness, and then I never do."

George nodded in agreement.

"I don't know what I was thinking with this outfit," she said, panting as she pointed at her parka. "It was great for my walk through the park. But in here? Not so much. You will catch me if I pass out from the heat?" She smiled. "Don't worry. I'm kidding," she added, which was a relief because George didn't really want to be responsible for saving the girl's life.

"What are you looking for?" she asked.

"Ah. The universal question. If only I knew," George said philosophically.

"In terms of gifts," she said, her eyes sparkling.

"Something for my son."

"You have a son who's old enough to shave?" She pulled off her earmuffs and shook free her hair. George thought maybe she was flirting. And perhaps she was a little bit, not seriously, just to keep in practice. She nibbled her bottom lip. "I'm here for a present for my boyfriend."

Just then a salesperson became available. He asked the young woman if he could help her. "My friend and I are both looking for gifts," she said, pulling George along up to the counter by her side. "I want something for my boyfriend, and he needs a present for his son who has just started shaving," she said. George did not bother to correct her.

The salesman smiled, adjusted his tie. "All our products are wonderful, of course. But if you want something really special, something that will last a lifetime, might I suggest a silvertip badger hair shaving brush? I think it's just the thing." From the case, he pulled a brush with a hammered nickel handle. It reminded George of Pop's shaving brush, and he wondered what had become of it. Probably it had been abandoned years ago in favor of canned shaving cream.

"How much is that?" she asked.

"Two fifty," the salesman said lightly and without apology. In George's opinion, he was a good salesman. Confident but not cocky. George may not have known many things, but he knew sales.

The woman inhaled.

"I do have other brushes," said the salesman taking a pitying glance at the poor-relation shaving paraphernalia in the display case. "But this is by far the finest."

She shrugged. It was hot. It was crowded. She was done. "I'll take it."

"And for you, sir?"

George was not going to spend two hundred and fifty dollars on a thing Brian was probably never going to use. But he might appreciate a nice razor.

"Oh, I'm sorry!" the woman exclaimed. "I need something else. I completely forgot about my father. I want to get him a shaving brush, too." George smiled at her. She was about the same age as May. Her parents had obviously done a fine job raising her. She was a sweet girl.

"So you'd like two of these brushes?" the salesman inquired, doing a nice job of keeping the excitement about his rising commission under wraps.

"No. Definitely not. What's the cheapest one?" she whispered. "I don't want to spend that kind of money on my father."

Maybe it was the crowds. Maybe it was the heat. Maybe it was the suit he was wearing. Maybe it was because at that moment he would have given anything to be able to buy his father one more Christmas present. Whatever the reason, he turned on her, his eyes narrowed to slits. "How long have you been dating your boyfriend?"

"Nine months," she beamed.

"Nine months," George repeated. "My guess is in a few years, you'll barely recall his name. And if you can remember his name, you'll wish you couldn't. But your father?" George sighed regretfully. "You are going to think about your father every day until the day you die. Someday, maybe sooner than you think, you won't be able to buy your father a Christmas present. He'll be gone. And all you'll think about is what you didn't do for him, and the thousand ways you failed him and how much you wish you could go back and fix..."

George didn't say anything else. He couldn't. He'd reduced that poor girl to tears, but he could not see them, so blinded was he by his own.

∾

THEY WERE IN THE HALLWAY in front of the entrance to Per Se because the hostess would not seat them until the entire party had arrived. She had invited Conor and George to wait at the bar, but the brothers were not sure if the bar tab had been prepaid by their father. Neither of them was feeling flush enough for twenty dollar cocktails. The only reason they were so early was that Conor had had excellent luck with the train, and George had been thrown out of The Art of Shaving before he could make a purchase.

"Please tie my tie." George's hands shook as he handed his necktie to Conor. He noticed his brother was also wearing his recycled funeral garb.

"What's wrong?" Conor asked, finishing the knot and sliding it under his brother's collar.

Where to begin?

He told Conor about Adelman's plan to dissolve the business. He didn't tell him that once again, he'd snapped and screamed at a stranger. On the bright side, at least this time his victim had not been an infant.

The brothers decided to get through this night pretending they were enjoying themselves. There would be no bad news tonight. They would come clean with the staff tomorrow. They would then do their best to explain the situation, even though they themselves didn't really understand what was happening.

Only moments after George had plastered on the wide fake grin he had intended to wear throughout the night, Brian arrived, also early. As it turned out, George only managed to maintain that false smile for about two seconds.

Brian wore his funeral suit, though he had paired it with a green and red tie, his nod to Christmas. All this was fine and would have allowed George to keep smiling a few more hours. But Brian was wearing earrings that exposed his gaping holes. And, far more egregiously, said holes were noticeably larger than when George had last seen his son.

Sensing his brother's consternation, Conor quickly moved in for hugs and an excessively cheery greeting, while George growled stiffly.

Brian unsuccessfully attempted to say hello to his father.

"Are you out of your mind?" asked George, by way of greeting.

Like a foreign tourist lost in a land where he does not speak the language, Brian looked helplessly to Conor in hopes of finding an interpreter.

"Your ears!" George screeched.

Eyes rolled. A put upon sigh was released. "Dad it's a process.

The gauge size increases gradually. Relax. I'm only going to let them get a little bigger."

"Oh? Only a little!"

"God. Will you chillax? It's no big deal. Everybody's doing it."

Did children, even adult ones, still think the 'Everybody's doing it' line was a winning strategy in a fight with a parent? Though it was a challenge, George did possess enough self-control to resist asking whether or not his son would jump off a bridge if all his friends were doing that.

"You know what everybody was doing when I was in college? Wearing fanny packs. They were all the rage. I had a magenta one. Wore it every day. Well let me tell you something, kiddo. I'm awfully glad I didn't have the thing surgically implanted onto my ass, because I looked like an idiot." George's eyes shot through with red. He thrust a finger toward Brian's ears. "One day those disgusting things aren't going to be the fashion anymore, and you won't be able to get rid of them. Where will you be then? You'll be left looking like a fucking f—"

He hit the first F of that word with staggering virulence. The remaining letters strained to burst forth to complete the ugly statement. He most certainly would have said the word had he not seen something vanish from his son's eyes. A light left Brian, and something dark moved in to take its place. And George knew that he was responsible for that somber shift. He had just killed a piece of his son's soul. It was that dramatic, and that instantaneous. Maybe someday he would be forgiven for this moment—this betrayal— but that part of his son he had just destroyed was gone. That was never going to return.

"Say it, Dad," whispered Brian, beaten. "You've wanted to for years. Go ahead. Call me a faggot."

George was silent. That word had never crossed his mind. Never. Not with regard to his son or anyone. What had he done? How had he acted around his son that Brian would think him capable of such a thing? He'd done plenty over the years to express disapproval. Why shouldn't Brian have jumped to that conclusion? And what was he supposed to say to rectify the situation now? *Brian, you've got me all wrong. I was only going to call you a freak.*

Brian walked away. George had to do something. He grabbed his son's wrist and pulled him back to him. "Wait. Please. I'm so sorry. I don't mean any of this. I'm just…" George was quiet. Finding whatever scrap of courage he could, he finally admitted, "I'm terrified."

George had been governed by fear for most of his life, but to his credit he'd worked very hard to shield his children from the fragility of his psyche. For the most part, he had been successful. Mostly they thought him brave and strong, even though he could be sentimental and tender. He had been a good father, even if he was screwing it up so badly now.

George loosened his grip on Brian, but he did not storm off. Instead, Brian stood there, staring at his father. George wondered if his son was, for the first time, seeing him for the man he really was—not a hero or protector, but someone in the midst of real crisis, vulnerable and in desperate need of rescue.

Since Brian was frozen in place, George tried reasoning with him. "I shouldn't have said those things. But you have to stop this. Who is going to hire you looking like this?"

"Your obsession with my ears is pathological. This is why you're terrified—with all your problems—because I wear earrings? Besides, I don't need to look for a job. Or have you given up on saving the business, too?"

Brian moved away again, and as before, George yanked him back to him. "There is no business! I was just dreaming. It's all gone."

Conor shook his head urgently, his eyes pleading with his brother to shut up. George ignored Conor. Maybe he couldn't help his son, but he could be honest with him. So he told him, in detail, that all was lost. That he had no plan to save Bailey and Sons, and he never would have a plan, because all roads led to the same dead end. So Brian better start worrying about his future and his prospects, because his family no longer had the means to support him. "And dammit, you look like a freak!"

The last part really did slip out in the heat of the moment, which did not justify the outburst. George regretted his words. But no amount of regret would cancel out what he'd said. This time Brian marched off, and George, figuring he'd botched things up badly enough for one night, let him go. Conor was staring over George's shoulder and shaking his head in more of a nervous twitch than an intentional gesture.

Following Conor's gaze, George turned around. He'd managed to attract a rather large audience. Based on the group's shocked expressions, they'd been there quite awhile. Claire and May and Dennis and Finn and Luke stood propping each other up. The presence of the family was bad enough. But Theo Laskaris and the rest of the sales force from Bailey and Sons had also witnessed the proceedings. They looked like they were about to be sick.

A hostess appeared then, offering to seat them if the entire party was present. George hated to miss the Last Supper, but just like Judas he needed to skip out early. As George made his way to the elevator, he heard Dennis whisper to May: "This is seriously F'd up."

TWENTY-SEVEN

BELIEVE IT OR NOT—*BELIEVER* or not—moments after George escaped from Per Se, when he was alone in the elevator, he started praying. Technically he started muttering, but at some point he heard himself calling upon God. He was so lost. And he felt completely powerless. He needed help. He needed something. He needed a sign.

The doors opened, and George rushed out, but he knocked into a man who was rushing in. "God!" blurted a surprised George. The collision stopped George in his tracks. Apologizing, he checked to make sure the man was uninjured.

"Jesus!" George cried. "Jesus?"

It was, in fact, Jesus. Or at the very least, the man George had come to think of as Jesus. Tonight, George was less confident he was in the company of the Risen Savior. For starters, the young man was wearing a suit, which somehow didn't seem super Christ-like. Although, on second thought, it didn't look like an expensive suit. It desperately needed tailoring, and his shoes were worn and scuffed so who knows?

In the moment of startle, he forgot that he'd just been asking for a sign. But what George did remember was Carolyn's theory regarding fate. In this city of eight million plus, George had seen Jesus for a third time. And while he didn't understand the significance of this encounter, he knew it must be significant.

Damn! He also realized he could prove to Carolyn he wasn't crazy, at least with regard to his talking to Jesus.

"Jesus?" George asked again. "Don't you remember me?"

Jesus squinted, struggling to place him. Also not super Christ-like. The real Jesus must have an awesome memory, though he does have the entire planet to keep track of.

"I bought you a slice."

And Jesus beamed. "George."

"I really need your help. Will you come with me?"

"I can't. I'm sorry. I'm supposed to be—"

"This will only take a minute," George promised, which was a boldfaced lie, because even on the A train, which, as the song rightly states, is the quickest way to Harlem, you can't get there from Columbus Circle in a minute.

"Here's the thing. I told a woman I hardly know but whom, nevertheless, I'm madly in love with, that I bought you a slice of pizza. And now she won't ever talk to me again."

Jesus gave George a befuddled shrug. "I don't understand? Why do you love someone who objects to you committing random acts of kindness?"

"It wasn't so much my generosity she had an issue with."

Another befuddled shrug. Jesus's obtuseness would suggest that he was nothing more than mere mortal.

"I referred to you by name."

The young man was about to shrug again, when finally he had a glimmer of understanding. "You didn't tell her I was the original Jesus, did you?"

Since he hadn't been clear in his communication with Carolyn, George remained silent.

"You're kidding, right? I don't have a beard. I don't part my hair in the middle. I don't have a robe. I don't have sandals."

"Do you have a driver's license?"

Jesus nodded.

"Good. You're coming with me."

He clasped his hand on Jesus's shoulder. George was relieved this was just some guy he was manhandling, and not in fact Christ, because what he was doing might technically be considered kidnapping.

∽

When they were approaching Carolyn's block, George asked Jesus if he was homeless.

"No. I'm not. I should pay you for the pizza."

George dismissed the offer.

"I'm getting my Master's in theology from Columbia. I've been doing a paper on kindness. And I've been running this experiment to see how people respond when I ask them for help. When people do come to my aid, which isn't that often, I usually return right away, give them back their money and explain what I'm up to."

"Why didn't you with me?"

"I should have. But the lost way you were looking at me, something told me you needed to be reminded you were a good person, which I think you are. I was afraid if I came back, I'd spoil whatever comfort and hope you'd found in our encounter."

They walked the rest of the way in silence.

If I'm his idea of a good person, the bar has been set pretty low.

"Probably it will be an older woman who comes to the door," George explained to Jesus as he was ringing Carolyn's doorbell. "Whatever you do, don't stick your fingers in the doorframe, because she is more than capable of slamming it right on your hand."

"I may not be the Son of God, but I'm not an idiot."

The door flew open revealing Cora in the vestibule. "What now?" she barked. Then she noticed Jesus. "You better step back. Watch your feet and hands, I'm about to slam the door."

"Wait!" George pleaded.

George nudged Jesus to show his driver's license. But now, realizing George's advice wasn't so asinine, he was wisely reticent to stick his fingers anywhere near the swinging door. He did not present his ID.

But George was undaunted. "Behold, I bring you Jesus."

"By that, he means a guy named Jesus," Jesus clarified, seeking to minimize confusion.

Unimpressed, Cora rolled her eyes and moved to slam the door, but another hand appeared and stopped her. After assuring Jesus no harm would come to him, Carolyn took the license from his hands, glanced at the information, and handed it back. George recalled the first time they spoke, and how he'd handed her his license on that occasion. She'd made a joke about his age, and he heard her laugh. He wondered what she'd say now, and how soon, if ever, he'd receive the gift of her laughter again.

"Did you put an ad on Craigslist looking for a guy named Jesus?" she asked George skeptically.

"Of course not. This is really the guy. I always thought he was just a guy. I tried to explain that to your mother."

"You should believe him. I'm really the guy. He really bought me a slice. And now I really have to go, because I am an hour late for dinner." He nodded at Carolyn. "By the way, it's been my experience that very few people will pay for a stranger's pizza. You should get back together with him." Then he extended his hand to George. "We're even now, right?" Jesus let go of George's hand, and he darted down the steps. "Hey, Merry Christmas," Jesus shouted back, but he was already out of sight.

Even though she wasn't wearing a coat, Carolyn stepped out onto the porch. She dismissed her mother, who had been unsuccessfully trying to close the door through most of this brief exchange. Cora left, but not before stating her opinion that this was not a movie. This George Bailey was no Jimmy Stewart. He would only ever bring heartache, trouble, and misery.

Misery? George felt that was laying it on a bit thick.

"It's almost Christmas, Mr. Bailey."

"We should make plans."

Eventually they would, but not just then. Instead, they reached for each other and started kissing. Maybe they should have behaved more discreetly. They were out in public, after all, which had never before worked out for them. Finally their luck changed. People did walk by, but no one shouted. No one tried to break them up. Only the weather took a stab at parting them. The wind picked up, howling fiercely, swirling Carolyn's hair and the hem of George's coat. They clung to each other tightly, but they would have done that anyway. They never noticed the chill.

TWENTY-EIGHT

ON THE MORNING OF DECEMBER the twenty-fourth, two hours before the showroom would normally open, Conor came in with a Starbucks in hand and was flummoxed by the sight of his brother. "What are you doing?"

"Looting," said George blithely, his arms filled with boxes of ornaments. I need to put up a Christmas tree and grocery shop and…" George put down his boxes, hugged his brother, and then reached for a strand of white lights. "You and Luke are coming for dinner tomorrow. I'm hosting. I was supposed to invite you weeks ago, but I've been distracted."

"Did I miss something? Why are you happy?"

"Why shouldn't I be?"

"It's an awfully long list. How much time do you have?"

"I'm in love, Brother," George exclaimed, stripping a tree of its German glass.

"Congratulations," said Conor somberly. "Are you planning on sneaking out of here before our staff arrives to clean out their desks?"

George frowned. "I'm sorry about last night. And no, I'm going to stay and face them and apologize," George said resolutely, though it had not occurred to him that they'd be coming in on Christmas Eve.

Conor nodded with grudging respect.

"Where's the ladder?" George asked. "I need to steal a tree topper."

Conor pointed toward the utility closet at the back of the showroom, and George trotted off. A moment later, he found it buried in the corner of the cupboard behind a stack of musty cardboard boxes. He was reaching for the ladder when Conor yanked open the door.

"Do you know when we started storing the ladder in here?"

George shrugged.

"I don't know either," Conor said heatedly. "But I'm going to guess that it's been kept in the exact same place since before we were born."

George yanked carelessly at the boxes, and they came toppling over. Out spilled a pile of their old merchandise catalogues, a visual history of more than fifty years of their wares. "Why do we even still have these?" George asked.

"Since you've found what you need, I'll be in my office having my coffee. You remember where my office is, right?" Conor let the door slam on his way out.

What have I done now? George groaned. He was swimming in catalogues, the ladder was inches out of reach, and his brother was obviously mad at him. George knew he should ignore his brother's pique. Conor was stressed and upset, and he had every right to be. But George had Carolyn, so really what else did he need, aside from this blasted ladder. He reached. No. If only his arms were an inch or two longer.

As he struggled to get his hands on the ladder, he thought about his father. Or more accurately, thoughts of his father completely absorbed him. On some level, he'd been thinking about his father every second since his death. He remembered again his father lost in his own kitchen, searching for a coffee cup. But it occurred to him now that it wasn't entirely his father's fault it took him twenty-five years to discover where the mugs were kept.

Almost every morning of his life he had gotten up earlier than Claire. Gently tucking the covers back around her, he'd quietly pad to the closet to put on his shorts and sneakers before heading out for a long run. When he returned, he would wake his wife with a kiss. Then he'd head to the bathroom. Shower. Shave. Dress. By the time he was ready to face his day, she'd gotten up and had their breakfast prepared. It was a fine arrangement that suited them both.

His father didn't know where things were kept at home because he didn't need to know. George made another grab for the ladder, but he lost his footing and landed on a pile of old catalogues. He'd spent countless afternoons and weekends here when he was a kid. For the last twenty-one years, this had been his place of full-time employ. The only excuse for not knowing where the ladder was stowed was apathy.

He got to his hands and knees, almost sliding again on the glossy paper, before shakily landing on his feet. He walked through the showroom, studying everything that until recently he'd taken for granted. Everything was so beautiful here. Now that he finally realized that, it was time to say goodbye. When he reached his brother's office, he knocked on the closed door. Conor muttered something unintelligibly, which George chose to interpret as 'please come in.'

Neither brother spoke. What else was new?

George sat. Fidgeted. "Has the ladder really always been in the exact same place?"

Conor exhaled tiredly. "Not only that, I've seen you get it a hundred times."

"Really? Do you think I have Alzheimer's?"

"George, you have something, but it's not a disease." He put down his coffee and clasped his hands, wringing them anxiously. "I'm glad you're happy. I really am. And I can't wait to meet her. But she can't fix everything, George. You have to do that for yourself. I'm trying to learn that lesson, too."

George guardedly crossed his arms in front of his chest. He sensed his brother had more to say, and he was bracing himself.

"You haven't asked me anything about how the Christmas party went. You know, the one you stormed out of shortly after calling your son a faggot."

George uncrossed his arms and slammed his hands down on the desk. "You know I didn't say that!"

"But you wanted to," Conor said sorrowfully.

"No I didn't." George said, quietly shaking his head. "No. I've never. Why would you think I'd say that? Is that why you never told me you were gay?"

"I'm actually not gay. But no, that's not why I never told you."

George didn't know what Conor was talking about. He had a boyfriend.

Isn't that the definition of gay?

"I love Luke. I think he's the one for me. But I'm also attracted to women."

George resisted the urge to roll his eyes. Conor had been in the closet until age thirty-nine. He might as well come out fully and forget this unnecessary hedging.

"I wasn't completely truthful the other day when you suggested I was in love with Tara." Conor looked down at his coffee. "I never... Nothing ever. She never even knew," he rattled off. "Fortunately that crush ended a few years ago."

Oh. George felt the joy of being right. He felt the sorrow of it, too.

"Are you bisexual then?" George was working hard to sound accepting and not judgmental, but the truth was he thought only women could be bisexual. "Why didn't you ever tell me?"

"You don't know why Pop banished Finn, do you?"

"No one knows," George insisted.

"Shortly after Pop died, I woke up from a bad dream, and I went to find Mom and Daddy. When I got to their bedroom door, I heard her telling daddy that Pop made Finn leave because he came home and saw her with a girl. I was glued to their door, listening. Apparently, Nan confessed this to Mom in the ladies room in Dillon's."

The family had a history of tawdry revelations at that funeral home. "Why didn't you ever tell me this?"

"I wanted to. I was scared. I literally had had my first crush on a boy like a week earlier, and I believed God punished me for my impure thoughts by killing Pop, and that God had deliberately awakened me to hear this warning message about Finn. I was convinced I was going to be shunned like she was." Even all these years later, Conor seemed frightened by the memory.

"So Finn is a lesbian?"

"I have no idea. She was just a kid. I'm not sure that Pop saw anything more than a kiss between her and the other girl. Maybe she was experimenting, or maybe it was the great love of her life."

"Daddy never would have disowned you," and again a thousand images of their loving, generous, and compassionate father flooded George's brain. If their father had failed at business, he had excelled at everything that really mattered. "Do you remember the peppermint patties from Howard Johnson's?"

Conor shook his head.

"I don't remember where we were going. Some vacation, I guess. Daddy had rented a car. I'm not sure I'd ever seen him drive before. I have this memory of thinking he'd decided to become a cabbie. Anyway, you and I were both cranky and having a meltdown. We were somewhere on I-95, and we stopped at a rest stop for lunch. It was a Howard Johnson's. I remember that you were crying. Or maybe we both were," George admitted. "Mom ushered us through the meal as fast as she could. And when we got up to leave we paid at the counter.

"Next to the cash register was a glass fishbowl filled with individually wrapped peppermint patties. I begged Daddy to buy some. Mom said no. As a parent, I would have done the same thing—kids, car trips and sugar are a bad combination. But I sulked and fumed. I remember feeling, as we sat in the backseat, that life was over. I was distraught, inconsolable. Anyway we drove and drove in miserable silence. And then I felt something land in my lap. It was a peppermint pattie. It was like it had been sent from heaven. Then another came and another."

Conor looked at his brother curiously.

"Somehow, without us noticing, Daddy had purchased a whole bag of them. As he drove, he was tossing them over his shoulder into the backseat. They were raining down on us." George was a child again, romping through a blizzard of candy.

"I loved Pop," George continued, "but Daddy was not like Pop. Even as a boy I saw how hard Pop could be on others, especially Daddy. Of course he was always sweet with us—the sacred, predestined sons."

Conor opened the bottom drawer of his desk and pulled out a canvas sack. He placed it on his desk. "I was at Mom's the other day. I told her. She was not even a little surprised. After all the fear I had about coming out, I almost hoped she'd have reacted badly to justify my decades of silence. Not only was she great and accepting, she told me she suspected as much, and had even talked to Nan about it."

"In her prayers, or actually talked to Nan while she was still alive?"

"The latter. Like fifteen years ago. I didn't even know fifteen years ago. Well, I didn't want to know." Conor pulled a stack of photos from the bag and began leafing through them. "Apparently, Mom was upset at the prospect of having a queer son and raised her suspicions about me. Nan said, 'Claire, has he killed anyone?' And that was it." Their grandmother had a way of getting to the heart of matters.

Conor found the photo he was looking for and plucked it from the stack. "Mom gave me some photos. She said she'd given a bunch to you. I guess she didn't want me to get jealous." They both chuckled, even though their ability to feel slighted over the smallest of perceived oversights was astronomical. Conor grinned at the photo.

"Are you going to let me have a look?"

"I am. I am giving you this photograph in hopes that you will use it to fix things with Brian. You're right. Daddy wasn't like Pop. And neither are you." He handed George the photo. George looked at it and cringed. He was going to have to go back to Kmart for another frame.

When he walked out of Conor's office, George spotted Theo Laskaris on the main floor of the showroom. He was placing a mug, a datebook and a few personal items into a cardboard box. George wondered how a man who'd spent more than forty years at the same job could have amassed so little. Tucking his photo in his coat pocket, George approached Theo with trepidation.

George was prepared to be ignored or shouted at, maybe even shoved. He was not prepared to be pulled into Theo's strong embrace. As the men hugged, George became aware of Theo's tears. "I'm sorry, George," he said.

George stepped back and squeezed Theo's hand. He too was becoming emotional. "You don't have anything to apologize for. You put my family before your own. You have dedicated your whole life to this business. I'm sorry that it's ending this way. I should have told you. I should have told everyone, but I thought I could fix things. I spent so many years hating this place, and now I really don't want to let it go. My father needed my help, and I was too blind and selfish to see that. I've let my father down completely."

Theo peered up at George, shaking his head despairingly. "You didn't let your father down. But I did. Yes, he was my boss, but he was also my great friend."

And again, Theo, the most emotional man George had ever met, was crying. "I don't know why you and your brother were so, I don't know, uncurious about the business? You were here every day, but not really. Okay, that wasn't great, but it is what it is. But I knew the sales were down. And I knew that every other wholesaler left the neighborhood because the rents had gone so out of control. And every year when I got a raise and a bigger bonus, or when I got a check just because my daughter got into Yale, I just said thank you and took it. I never once said how can you afford this? What's going on? Are you okay? Those questions I never asked, because I didn't really want to know the answer. I had mine, that's what mattered." Theo buried his head in his hands, while George, discomfited, stood by in silence.

Before George took his leave, the men hugged again. "Do you pray, George?"

George couldn't get himself to say no, not anymore. He didn't want to lie, either. He was quiet.

"I'm going to pray on this," said Theo. "Who knows? Things could still work out." With Theo's help, George bundled up his pilfered Christmas ornaments and left Bailey and Sons.

∾

PERHAPS BECAUSE HE WAS HEADING to a campus, George thought of his own long ago school days, and the countless all-nighters that he pulled. He couldn't recall why, as a studio art major, he needed to stay up so often, so late, to accomplish his tasks, but he always seemed to be typing a paper on Brach or Brancusi at four in the morning. If he had any hope of hosting his beleaguered family and friends for Christmas tomorrow, he'd be awake straight through. But first, Brian.

He'd forgotten about the security guards, but that was the world we live in now. One could not just stroll into a building on the Columbia campus and waltz by the checkpoint. So he presented his ID to the guard on duty, telling him in his best quavering voice, that Brian's grandfather had died. This, of course, was the truth. If the guard chose to believe poor Brian's grandfather had passed away this very day, George saw no need to disabuse him of this notion.

The guard asked George to sign in, extended his condolences, and sent him up in the elevator.

George was gambling here. He hadn't called his son because he assumed he'd never pick up the phone. Also, while George needed to speak to him, it was imperative he showed him something. George knocked on his son's door. He held the photo, framed and wrapped in front of him.

The door opened, and Brian in worn jeans and a Columbia t-shirt, frowned. "This isn't a good time. The dorm is closing soon for Christmas, and I have to pack up and get to Mom's." Hearing Brian refer to the family home as Mom's was jarring. It stung, even though he knew it shouldn't. He let the feeling go. It was irrelevant.

"Can I help?"

"Dad. Why are you here?"

"I brought you your Christmas present."

Brian took the gift and started to shut the door.

"Wait. Please. I need to say something. Last night," he paused, trembling. "*That word.* I would never call you that."

"Okay. Fine. I believe you," Brian said dismissively.

"No. It's not fine. Listen to me, please, for a second. It doesn't really matter that I wasn't going to say that. That's beside the point. The problem is I obviously have behaved in ways that made you think I was capable of saying that." George's voice choked. "I'm sorry for that. You're brave and talented, and I don't tell you that nearly enough. By contrast, I'm fearful and maybe out of touch."

"*Maybe* out of touch?" His son said kindly. "Okay, Dad." They stood looking at each other, neither sure what to do next. "I really do need to get packed."

"Just open the gift in front of me, and I promise I will leave."

Brian sighed. He was in a rush and every muscle of his face

expressed how put upon he felt. He tore open the paper and let it fall to the floor. Brian stared at the photo for a long moment. For a second, as George watched Brian's lips cracking open, he thought his son might laugh. But then Brian bit his lips, and his eyes bugged in horrified recognition. "This... What is this? Is this photoshopped?"

"I wish it were."

Brian fought as hard as he could, but he was stressed and tired, and he'd somehow survived finals while his whole world was crumbling around him. He desperately needed this release and he burst out laughing. "Dad, you look..."

"Say it," George pleaded. "If you have ever loved me, and think you might ever love me again, please tell me what you think."

"You look like a freak," Brian said, staring at the image of his father circa 1992.

George was dressed in a pair of ballooning harem pants, like MC Hammer wore in the *U Can't Touch This* video. He was wearing MC's gold shirt, too, opened to the waist, and this was not for Halloween. The only difference between George and MC, aside from MC's superior dancing ability, was that George had opted to gild the fashion lily with the addition of his fanny pack. It was propped at a jaunty angle atop his right hip.

"I'm just saying, fashion moves on, as this picture proves."

Brian's eyes were still glued to the snapshot. "This is a very cruel, perhaps unforgiveable, stunt," he said, though he grinned as he said it.

"I was out of control last night, and this picture doesn't make up for that. I'm sorry. It will never happen again, unless, of course, the holes in your ears get any larger."

"Fair enough."

"Please tell me you are coming to my house for Christmas."

Brian nodded. "I'll be with Mom tonight."

"What about May?"

"Believe it or not, she's going to Mom's, too. It seems Dennis brokered that deal."

George was relieved to hear that. "I'll take the photo back," said George extending his hand.

Brian clutched it to his chest. "Not a chance. You never know when I'm going to have to keep you in line, and this should do the trick." He leaned in and kissed his father's cheek.

George had made it nearly to the elevators before remembering something important. He ran back to Brian's door.

"Please," George said, after Brian greeted him again. "I hope you'll bring your boyfriend tomorrow, if he doesn't already have plans for Christmas. I'd very much like to meet him."

Brian said that he would like that very much, too.

∽

"THIS IS NON-NEGOTIABLE." CAROLYN WALKED into George's living room carrying a large bowl of popcorn. George was standing by the lit tree, hanging the last few ornaments.

"I can't. My kids have never had popcorn on the tree. It's already going to be a strange and different Christmas. Popcorn might be the last straw for them."

"This is not to string. It is to eat. What's non-negotiable is that every year on Christmas Eve, I watch *It's a Wonderful Life*."

George protested determinedly, but then Carolyn laughed, which instantly silenced his complaints. And that is how it came to be that George and Carolyn were tucked up on the sofa sharing a bowl of popcorn, watching the Frank Capra classic.

Within ten minutes, Carolyn knew something was peculiar. George was responding to the film with a tremendous amount of surprise. He gasped when Mr. Gower accidentally put the poison in the pills. Granted that is a shocking moment, but surprising? After twenty or thirty viewings?

"George Bailey, do not tell me you've never seen this movie."

"Of course I have. Well, most of the scenes. But never in one sitting from the beginning to the end. You know it was always on television and I'd catch—"

"Silence. There shall be no more talking. Just watch."

Carolyn had brought over the restored, anniversary Blu-ray edition. Even though George had a list of chores to accomplish, he ignored them. Instead, enthralled by the residents of Bedford Falls, he sat in rapt attention.

Carolyn shed tears a dozen times, though George stayed strong until near the end of the movie, when the friends, family and acquaintances of George Bailey rushed in with the money needed to save the day. He wept for the simple message of loving thy fellow man, and for the pure kindness of George's friends. He wept too because he knew there would be no similar last minute salvation for George and his family.

"It's funny," George said. "Since seeing Jesus last night—for a third time," he added pointedly, "I've been thinking about what you said about fate. It was fate that I saw Jesus again last night, because without him we wouldn't be back here together. I would have never watched all of *It's a Wonderful Life.*"

Carolyn furrowed her brow. "I agree he was brought to you by fate. But the reason you met him has nothing to do with him bringing us together. If you had never met him, we never would have parted in the first place. You met him for a reason. I have no doubt about that. But that reason has not yet been revealed." Carolyn moved the empty popcorn bowl to the floor and snuggled in closer to George. "Did you love the movie?"

"It was okay," he said obstinately, and she chucked him lightly on the shoulder. "I liked it. I did—very much. I especially like that he gets saved in the end."

Carolyn moved her lips to George's ear, gave it a tender kiss. "And what about you, Mr. Bailey? Do you get saved in the end?"

"That remains to be seen," he said, turning his head toward her so that their lips met. Then they kissed in a totally private place, with no fear of interruption. How novel.

He stood, took her hand, and then he led her to the bedroom.

No question now that he would need to pull an all-nighter. And that was fine. There was so much to do to get ready for tomorrow, but all of it could wait.

TWENTY-NINE

AT THE STROKE OF MIDNIGHT, the phone rang. George, who was slicing celery for stuffing, put down the knife and picked up the receiver.

"Merry Christmas! I wanted to be the first to say it." The woman was so filled with joy, it took a moment for George to realize it was TJ.

"Merry Christmas to you."

"I won't keep you," she said. "I know you go to sleep early."

"It's fine. I'll be up all night."

"So I can call at three?" He sensed her smirking on the other end of the line.

"Do you have plans tomorrow?" he blurted out. They were strangers, but wasn't the holiday about caring for others? "I know it's last minute but I just—"

"What time?" she asked, before George could make another unnecessary apology.

He began giving her the address, but she reminded him that until recently she lived in the apartment.

George returned to his chopping. He was glad there would be some non-relatives—*The Strays*, as the Baileys called them—in attendance. Everyone was always much better behaved around friends than they were around family. He'd called Sal earlier in the day to wish him a merry Christmas, and to his surprise he was without plans, as his mother was visiting Sal's brother in Cincinnati. Since Sal couldn't very well get off work to join her, he would be arriving with Toll House cookies after he said his last mass.

Carolyn had left before ten to get ready to attend midnight mass with her mother. George and Carolyn had spent several hours in bed, and some of that time they were talking. George was relieved that Dennis's dire prediction about the first time had not come to pass.

Sometime after four, George decided things were under control for the big day. He set his alarm and got three solid hours of sleep. Astonishingly, he awoke refreshed. He showered quickly, shaved and put on a suit—but not the one he wore to his father's funeral.

To his delight and amazement, Carolyn arrived hours early to assist. She hadn't even promised to come at all, as she wasn't sure what she was going to tell her mother, or how she could justify leaving her to spend the day with a man she'd known three weeks. But Cora had surprised her daughter saying, "I still think he's crazy, but he's certainly ardent. And it's so nice to see a smile on your face again. Go. Merry Christmas."

George offered to call and invite her to join them. Carolyn said Cora was going to a cousin's house, and maybe they should take things a bit slower. Easter would be here soon enough.

"I could use some help," he said.

"You sure could. Strip, right now," she insisted.

He didn't have time for this, but that wasn't about to stop him.

"Just to the waist is fine."

"Doesn't that leave out most of the good parts?"

Carolyn smirked, took him by the hand and led him to the bathroom. "You need a trim. That's the thing with short hair. You have to stay on top of it."

She cut. She clipped. She combed. When she was finished, they both admired her work in the mirror.

"I know this didn't work out so well the last time I asked this question, but tell me something you've never told me before."

George frowned. "You're a glutton for punishment. I feel like I should be given some parameters."

She put down her scissors and clippers, brushed a few stray hairs off of George's naked back. "Quit stalling," she said, kissing the top of his head.

He had thousands of things to tell her. If he told her one a day, how many days of new information would they have? A lifetime?

For his first secret revealed—well, the second after the Jesus debacle—he told her, "I wanted to be an artist."

"Me, too," she said empathetically. "So I became one." She took another admiring glance at George's haircut in the mirror, a look of satisfaction spreading across her face. "I brought you a present." She pulled a package out of her bag. When he opened it, he discovered a sketchpad, a box of assorted colored pencils plus four additional red pencils.

"I got extra red in case that painting at MoMA inspired you."

George was dumbfounded, especially since the gift was

presented on the heels of his confession. "How did you—"

"You're fairly transparent. That's one of the things I like about you." She kissed him tenderly, ran her fingers through his short hair. "Get dressed now, Mr. Bailey. We have work to do."

Carolyn set the table. George went into a sturdy squat to protect his back before taking the turkey from the counter and placing it in the oven. For all his frantic preparations to get everything accomplished, all seemed in great shape now. They even had time for more kissing. They were embracing when the bell rang.

"You know what that means," Carolyn said. "Every time a bell rings…"

"I should answer the door?"

"Correct."

Claire and Finn arrived together. George kissed his mother and wished her a merry Christmas. "How are you, Aunt Finn," he asked as he pecked her cheek.

"I can't complain," she said with an edge that suggested given the slightest provocation, she'd do just that.

As soon as he'd introduced his mother and Finn to Carolyn, Dennis and May arrived. "This is my friend, Carolyn," George said to his daughter awkwardly. May shook Carolyn's hand warmly before introducing Dennis. "And this is my *friend*," she said.

George reached for Dennis's hand, clasped it firmly. "He's my friend, too," George said, trying the word out for size as he glanced back at Carolyn and May who'd already begun chatting animatedly. "Merry Christmas, George," said Dennis.

Conor and Luke showed up with the appetizers, which made George happy, because he was always at his best when he could talk about food. Luke offered to help George in the kitchen.

"The last time I took a turkey out of the oven, I threw my back out."

"That won't happen today because you're happier. But, since I haven't gotten you to a yoga class, let me show you something for your back."

Moments later, Finn came into the kitchen and found George in downward facing dog. "What on earth?" she asked.

"Luke is teaching me how to do a sun salutation."

"Of course he is," she moaned. "Leave it to my nephew to begin praying to a pagan god on the birthday of our Lord and Savior."

The bell rang, and George stood again, feeling more limber and grateful that he had an excuse to escape his aunt. He left her with the healer, wishing Luke a silent good luck.

At the door was a woman about Finn's age, but the similarities ended there. She was wearing tight black riding pants tucked into black boots. A black leather jacket covered a white silk blouse with several buttons undone. She had blue eyes, and straight blonde hair pulled back with a band. She was juggling several bottles of red wine. "George," she asked?

"Yes," he responded tentatively.

"TJ."

He had conjured a completely different woman in his mind. She was twenty years older than he thought she would be. But even though she was older than he had imagined, she was much hipper, more youthful in every other way, and more glamorous than he had expected. He ushered her in, made a few introductions and returned to the front door for the next guest. It was Sal, cookies in hand. He was smiling but hoarse.

"Three masses yesterday and four today," he croaked. "I feel fine, but that was two more tales of Bethlehem than my throat could take." Finn rushed to greet the priest, and she whisked him to the kitchen to make him tea.

George looked around the room. Everyone but Brian had arrived, and it was getting late. George worried his son had changed his mind. Maybe George's apology and his cheap trick with the photo had not been enough to make amends with his son. He was heading over to check on Carolyn when at last the doorbell rang again. He dashed back through the foyer banging his thigh on the corner of the Ping-Pong table as he passed.

"Hi!" George shouted with relief, before realizing it was not Brian. "Hi," he said again, this time befuddled and somewhat wary.

Theo Laskaris, along with Alison and Lizzie and Regina, were huddled in the doorframe smiling sheepishly. George smiled back, but he was stunned by the sight of the unemployed Bailey and Sons' sales team and didn't say a word.

"May we come in?" Theo finally asked.

"Of course, how rude of me" sputtered George. He led them into the living room. Conor came over to greet them, followed by the rest of the Baileys. The Baileys pretended this was a normal occurrence, wishing them each a merry Christmas. But this was not a normal occurrence. What the family really wanted to know was why they were here and not home with their own families. Of course, not wanting to be impolite and wanting to avoid conflict, they did not ask that question. The Baileys chattered away like they'd been expecting them all along.

"We're so sorry to intrude," Alison said.

"Can we have a word with you?" asked Theo. "We just didn't think it could wait."

George considered moving this conversation to his bedroom for privacy. However, one thing that had not been accomplished on his long list of chores was straightening his room or making his bed. So he told Theo they had no secrets, and that they could talk right here. TJ, Dennis, Carolyn, Sal, and Luke huddled together in a corner, pretending to be engaged in their own conversation, but it was pretty clear that they were straining to figure out what was going on.

"We have all been talking," Theo began. "Hoping maybe we could come up with another buyer for you."

Good luck with that, thought George.

"If you didn't have to, would you even want to sell?"

"No," said the Baileys in one voice.

"So then don't sell," said Theo, which George thought a sweet sentiment, but impossible and not practical. "Don't sell, but take on a few more partners."

Lizzie, bursting, shouted, "He means us!"

"I'm sure, if you're amenable, we can reach an agreement. Between the four of us, we have a significant amount of capital," explained Regina.

Of course they did. His father's years of extreme generosity were going to end up being their salvation.

"We hope you will give our offer serious consideration," said Alison.

"Of course we will have to immediately move to a more affordable location. Also," said Regina, "though we won't make it a deal breaker, we hope you will consider a new name. Something like Bailey and Associates."

"So we would all be owners?" asked May.

"That's the idea," said Theo, getting choked up, as he was wont to do.

George looked at his mother and Conor. They nodded in assent.

"I think it's a fine idea," said George. "I think Daddy would approve. Let's bring in the lawyers and make it work."

"So what are you saying? Now we're Socialists," grumbled Finn, loud enough for all to hear. TJ laughed, which startled Finn. She glanced at TJ. To everyone's surprise, Finn grinned at her.

The former staff and future partners took their leave, eager to get back to their own families to share the major news that they were about to become business owners.

Luke was right. George removed the turkey from the oven without incident. The bird had been resting on the counter for nearly twenty minutes. The gravy had been made. Everything was ready. Yet, still no sign of his son. George could not stall much longer. Brian or no Brian, they would have to eat soon. Just as George was about to give up, the doorbell rang again.

This time it was Brian. "Sorry I'm late, what did I miss?"

"Aside from the fact that we aren't going out of business, nothing." Brian opened his mouth to speak, but George interjected, "I promise all will be explained over dinner. You're alone?"

"No. He'll be right here. We forgot the wine."

The elevator doors opened, and the boyfriend emerged. George nearly fainted. "Jesus?"

"You two know each other?"

"George! I never put that together. You're George Bailey."

Both Jesus and George were nodding vigorously, like recently struck bobblehead dolls.

"It's a pleasure to meet you, Mr. Bailey. Brian tells me that you hate your name. That you think it's a burden to share a name with a fictional character. Sorry, but I have no sympathy for you," said Jesus sweetly.

"Are you going to explain how you two—"

"Yes, Brian, I will, but please both of you come in."

This city kept getting smaller and smaller. Shrinking, really, into a hamlet. Jesus was here, in his apartment, for Christmas dinner. *How*, George wondered, *did I mistake my son's boyfriend for the Son of God?* Was this why fate kept pulling the two of them together? George didn't understand the lesson, and maybe there wasn't one. Surely his judgment with regard to this fate theory was clouded by his love for Carolyn and his desire to believe everything she said.

Meeting Jesus again and again was a coincidence. He had nothing to learn. Nothing to know. It was time to eat.

George walked through the living room and noticed Jesus standing alone in front of the mantle, admiring one of the Kmart framed photos. George walked up behind him, placed a hand on his shoulder. "I love that photo," George said, staring at Nan in Union Square, dressed to the nines. "She was my grandmother."

Jesus turned to George. He was ashen; his lips trembled. "She was your grandmother? She saved my life."

"You knew Nan?"

"No. No, I didn't. Not really."

George looked at him, at a loss.

"We only met once. Barely even spoke to each other. But even so, I might be dead now if it wasn't for her. I'd be in jail for sure. I didn't have a great childhood. My parents' brief flirtation with spirituality lasted just long enough for them to name me. After that they were mostly absent, drugs and stuff. Anyway I was trying to take care of myself as best I could. Basically I was a pickpocket. I also mugged a couple of people, with a water pistol, though they didn't know the gun was fake. And one day I was walking through Union Square with my friend. We were looking for our next victim. Our music was blasting—"

Right then, George was transported back to that glorious spring day. He was walking through the park with Nan. He was suddenly scared, because there was that tough looking kid.

That was Jesus? Somehow that troubled child had grown into this sweet, spiritual man.

"I saw her," Jesus said. "And there was this aura of light around her. It was like I'd seen an angel. I can't really explain it. It was like I was freed. I was calm. I knew I would be okay. In that moment, my life turned around. For the first time, I had hope."

George always did need to have things spelled out for him. But even he understood why Jesus had been sent to him, and what it was exactly that he was meant to learn from their encounters.

Sal's voice continued to vanish, so he declined George's request to say grace before the meal, leaving the job for the host. George looked at the head of the table and the lone empty chair, which was his now to sit in. Claire had brought the carving set, and George wrapped his hands around the stag handles, placing the knife in his right hand and the fork in his left. He pierced the breast.

He had dim memories of Pop doing this same thing and vivid memories of his father. Now his prints were on the handles, too. And just as his father and grandfather had done, he would now say the prayer, deliver the speech. He would acknowledge the family's sorrows and loss, and he'd celebrate their good fortune and gifts. He caught his mother's glance. With a pang, they both understood this was how life went, moving forward while at the same time honoring the past.

"I miss my father," George began, delivering the opening line from the eulogy he had not been allowed to give. "This, the carving and the talking, this was Daddy's job. I don't know why my brother and I never outgrew calling our father Daddy, but somehow it was the right name for him. It was the perfect match for the sweet man who spent his life coated in glitter, decorating Christmas trees.

"Daddy always used to begin this speech telling us how an angel came from heaven and told Pop to open Bailey and Sons. I had the good manners not to roll my eyes, but I always thought that was the craziest thing I had ever heard." His family laughed and nodded at the memory of former holiday speeches. "Now I wonder, did he really mean an angel like I imagined, with a halo and flapping wings, or was he talking about something else?

"My," he almost said friend again, but this time he was clearer, braver. "My *girlfriend*, Carolyn, has this theory about fate. If you see a stranger three or more times, you're being brought together for a reason. You may not know what that reason is, but there is one. No doubt about it. Maybe an angel is orchestrating those moments of fate. Maybe that's what Pop meant. Or maybe angels are just the people who come along and touch our lives," he said, glancing at Jesus.

"I know Pop wasn't perfect." George looked over at Finn and held her gaze for a moment. She had seated herself next to TJ. He hoped there would be a spark between the two of them. He knew the reason he hoped that was because, as Carolyn had pegged him, he was a romantic. He was also being rather foolish. People didn't change when they were eighty. Did they?

"But Nan was the most perfect person I ever met. She believed in angels, and miracles, and God, and the whole thing. And even with all that faith, and all that devotion to the church, all that mattered to her was that you were kind and good and forgiving. In the years since she's been gone, I somehow lost sight of all her good lessons, but I promise they're coming back to me now. I'm trying."

He looked at each of the guests seated around the table. There was so much love in this room. He felt it. Saw it reflected in the eyes of his children, his brother, his mother, his friends, and even his aunt. When he looked at Carolyn, he felt love coming from her, too. Though from Carolyn, that powerful emotion was also mixed with passion, desire, curiosity and a hundred wonderful things he couldn't name. He would wait no longer. Right here, right now he would tell her he was in love with her.

He opened his mouth to speak, but Claire interrupted:

"George, stop talking. The food is getting cold!"

With his mother's shout, another Bailey tradition continued. Just as his father had always done, he obeyed his mother. He didn't say another word, which was fine. Probably better to save that declaration for when they were alone. Besides, every single day he planned on telling Carolyn something he'd never told her before, so there would be tomorrow.

George sliced the turkey breast. He took a moment to silently give thanks, and then he began serving his family.

ACKNOWLEDGMENTS

I am extremely grateful to Max Rhyser who spent hours listening to me as I pieced together this story. Thanks, also, to Max for inspiring the creation of Luke. Without you, this would be a very different book.

Thank you to everyone who read early drafts of this manuscript, and offered me valuable feedback: Laura Patinkin, Neil Dennehy, Diane Domenici and Helen Rogers. Thank you Alison Russo for your constant encouragement and general cheerleading.

In my first book, I explored my Macedonian/Romanian heritage. George Bailey brought me closer to the Irish side of my family. For their strength, faith, humor and humility, I am beholden to my father (I love you too, Mom!) my aunts, uncle and the entire O'Neill and Crehan clan.

I thank Eric Rayman for his generous advice and counsel. Thanks to Joseph Bleu for the fantastic headshot and Joey Albanese for web design. I'm deeply indebted to Jerry L. Wheeler. His edits made this a much better novel. Even though, at the time, I hated cutting all those extraneous thats (and parenthetical phrases). And thank you Matt Bright of Inkspiral Book and Cover Design. I can't imagine having a more beautiful book.

Finally, I give my thanks and love to Marcus Edward. In the end, everything I do is for you.

ABOUT THE AUTHOR

Ken O'Neill is the author of *The Marrying Kind*, which won the 2012 Rainbow Award for best debut, and the 2013 Independent Publisher Award Silver Medal for LGBT fiction. *The Marrying Kind* was also a finalist for the 2013 International Book Award in the Gay and Lesbian fiction category. The book was included on Smart Bitches Trashy Books list of top three favorite novels of 2012.

Ken lives in NYC with his husband and their two cats who think they're dogs or, perhaps, people. When Ken is not checking his Amazon rating to see if anyone has purchased his books, he enjoys reading, dancing (though usually only when no one is watching) and eating dark chocolate, purely for medicinal reasons. He is at work on his third novel. Visit him at: **kenoneillauthor.com**

35732937R10197

Made in the USA
Middletown, DE
13 October 2016

THE WHITE ARCHER

JAMES HOUSTON
THE WHITE
ARCHER
AN INUIT-ESKIMO LEGEND

HOUGHTON MIFFLIN COMPANY

BOSTON

Atlanta   Dallas   Geneva, Illinois

Palo Alto   Princeton   Toronto

In memory of Pootagook and his son Inukjuakjuk
and for the great family that follows them

KUNGO raised his head and listened carefully. Somewhere out in the vast Arctic silence of the Ungava, he had heard a strange sound. He remained kneeling on the scrap of white bearskin, listening, but the sound did not come to him again.

He bent down so that his face was level with the man-sized hole in the ice. Motionless, he watched and waited, peering into the shadowy blue depths of the frozen lake. A short time passed, and then a big trout drifted silently beneath him. Its tail waved gently in the current as it moved its fins like small wings to steady itself. Then another trout glided under him, and behind it three more big ones floated like green ghosts in the icy water.

Tightening his grip on a double-pronged fish spear, Kungo took careful aim and drove the shaft downward with a lightning thrust. The bone prongs of the spear slipped over the back of the largest fish, and its curved teeth caught and held. Kungo heaved the struggling fish out of the hole, forced open the prongs of the spear, and released it. The big trout flipped twice on the ice and then lay glazed and still, instantly frozen to death in the intense cold.

Kungo's sister, Shulu, who had been silently fishing with a short hand line at another hole, came quickly across the snow-covered ice. Kungo smiled at her as she picked up the huge fish to feel its weight, for it was half as long as she was.

Kungo's short, strong body was clad in the handsome sealskin parka and pants his mother had made for him. His feet were covered with dark close-fitting sealskin boots that reached his knees. Kungo's hair was very black, his eyes were dark and lively, and when he smiled, his strong teeth flashed brightly against his dark brown skin.

The evening air around them was still and sharp like thinnest crystal that might break at any moment in the bitter cold. The low white hills beside the frozen lake cast long shadows across the snow, and the winter sky blazed like frozen fire as the sun cast its rays at the first pale shadow of the moon.

Using a bone ladle, Shulu filled a sealskin bucket with water from the hole in the ice and followed her brother across the snow-covered surface of the small lake to the hill that lay above their camp. There, Kungo put down the heavy trout, and Shulu rested the bucket on the snow. They looked down at the four snowhouses that were the only dwellings in their tiny village. Around the houses many paths curved through the snow. Two long heavy sleds lay upturned, ready for icing, and three delicate skin-covered kayaks rested high on stone racks away from the sharp teeth of the dogs. The igloos seemed deserted except for the dogs scattered around them, and even they lay quietly as though they were carved in stone. Nothing moved. Everything was silent.

"Our family will be glad to taste that fish," said Shulu. "It's the first to be caught during this moon."

Her tawny brown cheeks glowed like the red throat of an Arctic loon, and her long black hair had a blue sheen like the wings of a raven. She was strong and quick, with endless good humor. Her legs were short, but Kungo knew that she could run like the wind.

As they started down the hill, Kungo stopped suddenly and stared into the cold blue distance. He pointed up the wide river that curved in a long frozen path from the inland plain through the low hills until it reached their camp by the sea.

"Do you see it?" he asked.

She did not answer. Her eyes searched the vast expanse.

"There it is. Moving. Far up the river. It must be a dog team, but who would be coming from the inland to visit us?" Knowing that their own dogs and sleds were in camp, he said, "They must be strangers from far away. Listen. Listen," he repeated, and faintly, like the measured sound of dripping water somewhere out in the vast silence, they heard the "harr, harr, harr. . ." of a driver urging his dogs forward.

Eager to be the first with news that visitors were coming to their lonely camp, Kungo and Shulu hurried down the slope to their father's snowhouse.

When it was almost dark, all the men, women, and children of their small village gathered together before the snowhouses in a silent group, ready to meet the strangers. In the half-light they saw a long heavy sled with three men on it swing into view around the river bend. They watched the strange men cross the wind-swept ice and drive their dogs up the steep bank. Two of

9

the men ran beside the sled, working hard to guide it between the boulders that lay exposed on the icy shore. A third man, bigger than the others, remained half sitting, half lying on the sled.

As the strange team rushed into the camp, wild excitement broke loose, and a dog fight started. Everyone helped to kick and pull apart the two powerful teams until finally the dogs settled down, content for the moment to snarl and stiffly circle each other.

Two of the strangers came forward to greet everyone. Rough men they were, with faces burned dark by the wind and cold, eyebrows white with frost. Their fur clothing was worn and torn, which showed they had not had any women's care or mending for a very long time. Their hair was long and black and wildly tangled. With their hoods pushed back and their mitts left carelessly on the sled, they seemed not to notice the cold. One of the men who had run with the sled, a short, strong man, limped a little as though he had lost some toes long ago from freezing.

Kungo heard his father say to the other driver, a lean man, "I knew you when we were young at the River of Two Tongues. Your father's name was Tunu."

The stranger nodded.

The big man who had remained on the sled raised his left hand in greeting. Kungo looked at his right arm. It hung limp by his side. Kungo could see in the fading light that the sleeve of his tattered parka had a long knife slit in it and that his hand was wet with blood.

10

Because Kungo's father had known the lean man from the River of Two Tongues, he was bound by politeness to invite the travelers to sleep in his snowhouse. This he did, and the three men gladly accepted. Kungo's mother hurried into the igloo and took her proper place near the edge of the sleeping platform beside the lamp, ready to welcome the strangers to their house. Others in the camp unharnessed and fed the visitors' dogs.

The three men tugged off their worn parkas and lay back on the wide sleeping platform, while the women pulled off their sealskin boots and placed them on the drying rack above the stone lamp filled with seal oil. The big man plucked some soft down from a white bird skin that lay near the lamp and carefully placed it against the long knife wound to stop the bleeding. A seal was cut open for them and prepared for feasting. They greedily drank quantities of fresh cold water and some hot blood soup. After the feast of delicious seal meat, which they had eaten raw, sliced thin, half thawed and half frozen, they lay back in the welcome warmth of the igloo and talked to Kungo's father. The people from the other igloos gathered to hear the news. Everyone listened.

The lean man from the River of Two Tongues recounted their long sled journey. He told of their travels through the range of coastal hills onto the great wind-swept plain in search of caribou. For weeks they had seen nothing but one half-starved wolf. Fierce blizzards had raged inland, and they had gone hungry. Their only food had come from the few ptarmigan they managed to catch. When this news was told, the listeners nodded, for they also knew those small white furry-footed birds inhabiting the inland plain. Their flesh had saved the lives of many travelers. Finally the three men had been forced to eat one of their own dogs, but some time after that they saw a few caribou tracks on the very edge of the Land of Little Sticks.

There they stopped, for it was tree country, dreaded territory belonging to the Indians. The dwarfed trees that grew there were permanently bent by the icy blasts of the north wind. They were few and scattered, and scarcely any of them was taller than a man. There was little soil, and only tundra moss grew there, clinging tightly to the rocks. The Land of Little Sticks was a terrible land, feared by the birds and beasts of the true forest and shunned by the animals that roved the open plain. It was a starving land. Three stone images built to stand like men marked this place. To the south, on the distant horizon, lay vast forest and lake country, a land that suffered a short hot summer alive with black flies and mosquitoes that could drive a man mad.

The Eskimos feared the Indians and their country. The harnesses of their dog teams became entangled in these little stick trees. Ancient Eskimo stories told of terrifying nights spent there, for the wind made the trees moan and whisper like lost souls. Cruel Indians were said to live and hide in this tree country, and no Eskimo considered himself safe there.

Yet the hunger pangs of these three men were so terrible that they overcame all their fear and traveled on and on up the narrow frozen river between the sharp-pointed shadows of the little stick trees. When they climbed a hill to look out over the country for signs of caribou, the big man pointed to a thin wisp of smoke rising in the cold, still air. Frightened they were, but starving as well, and they drew closer until they smelled boiling meat.

The big man, made bold with hunger, left his two hunting companions and the dogs behind and stalked alone through the dreaded trees until he reached a rise in the ground where he could watch the camp. He was careful to stay downwind so that the Indian dogs could not smell him and warn their masters of his presence. He remained there, hiding and watching, from noon until the evening sky turned red. Then he retraced his steps to tell the other two men that the camp was small, having only one tall man, one very old man, a woman, a girl, and two young children. The camp, he said, had only four dogs, which were so small that they looked like starved black foxes. Besides the dogs, they had only one toboggan and a small skin tent hung on poles. But they also had some frozen caribou meat tied up in the trees, safe from their hungry dogs, and rich otter skins stretched on wooden frames for drying.

"I am going to take some of that meat tonight," he said to his companions, "for I am starving."

Pointing to the southeast, his companions replied, "We saw

the smoke of ten fires rising beyond those hills, and we heard the sounds of countless dogs fighting. We warn you, there are many Indians there."

"I care nothing about them," said the big man. "I must have food or else I will die. Will you come with me tonight?"

The two hunters were frightened, but because there was only one sled, there was no way for them to part, and so they finally agreed to go with him. That night when they had carefully anchored the dogs by turning the heavy sled over, they set out for the small Indian camp. In single file they moved cautiously through the dreaded, unfamiliar country. It was deathly cold, and the stars seemed to wheel and dance overhead. The night sky glowed with eerie green northern lights that magically shifted and faded like underwater weeds waving in a river. The trees in the forest cracked loudly with the frost, and dry powder snow, lying on the branches, showered down on the men without warning. All of these things made them nervous, angry, and afraid.

At last they saw the yellow glow of firelight from within the Indian tent, and the big man, again smelling the rich odor of cooking meat, went forward at once. The other two remained at the edge of the clearing. For some time there was silence. Then a dog barked, and then another, and they could hear a man's voice shouting excitedly in a strange language. There was a woman's high-pitched scream and the sound of fighting and more dogs barking. The big man's voice then called to them, shouting their names again and again, and they both ran forward. Their coming must have frightened the Indians, for they

15

saw no one except the big man, who came stumbling through the soft snow carrying the double haunches of a caribou. They saw his knife glistening in the starlight, and there was blood spattered on his clothing.

They turned and ran hard until they reached their sled, and all that night they drove the dogs along the frozen river until they were safely out of the Land of Little Sticks. In the morning they rested briefly and ate their fill of the stolen caribou meat, giving most of the remainder to their starving dogs. Then they hurried on. They followed the wide flat river course toward the coast and the safety of other Eskimo camps, but they did not return to their own camp at the River of Two Tongues. They knew that the Indians would not venture far from the Land of Little Sticks, for the Indians hated and feared the great treeless, barren land where they could find no wood for their fires nor lodge poles for their tents and became lost traveling in endless circles out on the terrible wind-swept plain.

Kungo's father looked at the three men after he had heard their story and said nothing. In his view they had acted foolishly to be caught starving in the Land of Little Sticks, and certainly they should not have stolen or acted violently. They had broken the laws of the Eskimo people.

The family and the three unwanted guests drifted off into an uneasy sleep only to be awakened twice by the big man who cried out in pain, perhaps because of the knife wound in his arm or because of some terrible dream that had come to haunt him from the Indian camp.

The next day the three men stayed on the sleeping platform

until noon, and although they were not offered food, they made no plans to leave. The big man sat sullen and silent, holding his right arm as he rocked back and forth to ease the pain. His arm and hand had swollen in the night.

The three visitors prepared to spend the second night, and Kungo's father again gave them food. But this time they all ate in silence.

When his father went out of the snowhouse after eating, Kungo followed him, and they stood together in the cold star-filled night. They listened carefully. The father looked up the river from whence the three men had come. He thought of their sled tracks, of their footprints, and even of the drops of blood from the big man's arm that all led straight to the camp. They had left a trail in the snow that even a child could follow. Kungo's father looked at him in a worried way, and Kungo felt the hair stir on the back of his neck, for he knew that the Indian people from the Land of Little Sticks would have good reason to be angry.

Neither Kungo nor his father had ever seen an Indian, although his father had once passed one of their campsites on the edge of the barrens. There he had seen a dead fire and the cleared place where they had pitched their strange tents. Bones and feathers were scattered everywhere, and the smell of smoked skins still lingered in the damp tundra moss.

Kungo followed his father back inside the snowhouse, where the three men were already asleep. Kungo's mother smiled at her husband and son as she trimmed the wick in her seal-oil lamp until it caused a gentle glow to reflect from the glistening

18

snow walls. She then arranged the boots on the rack over the lamp so they would be dry in the morning.

On this night Kungo slept in his clothes with his head toward the foot of the sleeping platform, which is sometimes the custom of young boys when the only bed of the house is crowded with guests. He slowly drifted off to sleep and dreamed of peering through the hole in the lake ice, where he saw a hidden world wrapped in green shadows with fishlike people swimming among strange houses that looked like igloos piled one upon the other.

Suddenly he awoke. What he saw was not a dream. Strange men with dark hats were crowding into the low entrance of the snowhouse, filling the room with their harsh words and violent movements. He saw a knife flash. Then someone kicked over the lamp. In the dark there was angry shouting, screaming, and the sound of stabbing. Kungo jumped up as he felt a sharp cut on his ankle. Clinging to the wall, he crouched down and felt his way around the edge of the house until he came to the entrance. Bending low, he rushed past a tall, gaunt man who smelled of smoke. The man tried to grab him as he ran out into the night, but he was able to break away. Where could he go? The house was full of fear, of shouting, of words and sounds he had never heard before.

Kungo ran past the neighboring igloo and beyond the rack of kayaks until he reached the snowhouse of his uncle and aunt. They were both sitting up in bed, terrified by the sounds they heard. They quickly grabbed him and hid him under the thick pile of caribou skins on the bed, and then they lay on top of him. He heard running footsteps and more strange voices. A

19

man rushed in looking for him, but seeing only two old people in bed, the Indian grunted with disgust and hurried out again.

When the first light of day allowed them to see, Kungo poked a small hole in the wall of his uncle's snowhouse and looked toward his father's igloo. One wall had been broken in, and their household things were scattered everywhere. He saw no movement.

In front of the house he counted eleven Indians. Tall, thin men they were, with faces made terrible by painted black streaks. They were wearing strange pointed hats and long coats with weird markings. Each man carried a bow or club or knife in his hand. They were calling to each other in excited voices. Several of them were shooting arrows into the igloo and into the bearskin and two sealskins that were stretched out to dry. With their knives they had slashed the pelts and cut the sealskin dog lines into pieces. They had pulled the kayaks from their racks, had ripped them open, and had smashed their long, delicate frames. They were gathering all the food they could find, and they were preparing to go.

Suddenly Kungo caught a glimpse of his sister, Shulu. He watched with terror as the Indians led her down toward one of their toboggans on the river.

Then as dawn turned the village gray, they started to search the other igloos again. Kungo's aunt quickly made him put on her long-tailed woman's parka and handed him a skin bucket. Disguised as an old woman, he bent over, his head hidden deep in the hood, and hobbled away from the igloo. He went off toward the side of the village as though he were going to the

lake to get water. Halfway through the camp he saw one of the strangers, the big man, lying face down on the snow with two arrows in his back, his bloody arm flung out stiffly before him.

Out of the corner of his eye, Kungo saw an Indian point at him and another place an arrow in his bow and take aim. The arrow whistled past his face and buried itself in the snow. Fortunately the Indian did not aim again. Kungo hobbled over the hill beyond their sight. Once at the lake, he threw off his aunt's parka and snatched up a broken ivory-bladed snow knife that lay by a hole in the ice. Then he ran.

He ran as far and as fast as he could. He headed northward, following the coastline so he would not lose his way. Far up beyond the River of Giant Men, he knew there were Eskimo people who would help him.

When night came, he struggled to find strength to go on. He lay in the snow, exhausted, and his eyes filled with tears as he thought of the fate of his mother and father, his relatives, and his sister, Shulu. Then slowly a terrible anger started to grow within him. Dark thoughts rushed through his mind. He had only twelve winters of life upon him, but if he could live to reach the next Eskimo camp, he swore inside himself that he would avenge the terrible wrong done his family by the people from the Land of Little Sticks. He pounded the hard snow with his fists and swore this to himself, again and again.

He was afraid to build a snowhouse for fear he might be followed, and when he had rested a little, he went on despite the darkness, because he knew that if he slept without shelter, he would freeze to death. To avoid leaving a trail, he traveled along wind-packed drifts that were so hard his footsteps left no mark.

Worn out and starving and driven by fear, he slowly made his way north. After the first night he would cut blocks out of the frozen snow and pile them in a circle to form a house scarcely big enough for a dog. Some nights it was so cold that he could not sleep, but the little houses protected him against the biting wind that swept in from the frozen sea, and he was able to stay alive. He lost count of the number of snowhouses he built and the days he limped through the killing cold. The knife slash in his ankle pained him.

One evening, a seal hunter called Inukpuk, returning to his camp after hunting out on the sea ice, saw the boy staggering half frozen among the ice hummocks near the shore. He carried Kungo to his sled, wrapped him in a caribou skin, and put his arm around his shoulders to steady him. Inukpuk got the boy safely back to camp, where his wife put him into the center of their warm bed and fed him hot blood soup and little pieces of rich seal meat. She cared for him like a mother until he was well and strong again.

For two long years he stayed with Inukpuk and his wife, watching and waiting as each season advanced across the land. He searched for eggs and fished with the other young people of the camp, but there was a dark and fearful quietness that seemed to brood inside him. He never spoke of the fate of his parents, or of his sister, or of the people of the Little Sticks, but they were always in his mind.

In the late autumn of the second year, after the first big snow had turned everything white so that the dog teams could travel

23

again, a hunter came with his son from a camp farther to the north. One evening he told a long story of a visit he had made to a distant island that could only be reached by sled during the two moons of midwinter. There he had met a strange old man full of mystery, with a knowledge of the ways of men and animals. His eyes and body seemed weak, but he could draw a huge horn bow that the strongest man among them could not even bend, and his old eyes could still see well enough to drive an arrow straight to its mark no matter how far or how small. His wife, it was said, could hand-stitch the seams of a kayak with sinew so that no water could ever enter, and she could so tightly sew a cut in a man's skin that one could never see the stitches. Their only sadness, said the hunter, was that they had no children. The old man had said that he would soon go blind.

During the night, Kungo thought about all that he had heard, and in the morning he said to Inukpuk and his wife, "I give thanks to you for your kindness, for you have saved my life and been a family to me. But now I wish to travel north with that man who visits and his son, if they will take me, for I long to see that old man on the island and talk with him."

Inukpuk said that he would be glad if Kungo would stay in their camp and be a son to them. But Kungo only thanked them again and said once more that he wished to go north.

The visiting seal hunter agreed to take Kungo to his camp, and so they set out one dark and windy morning in early winter when the snow was hard and the sled could move fast. Inukpuk's wife had made Kungo new sealskin boots and mitts. She gave them to him for the journey, and Inukpuk gave him two seals, one to help feed the dogs on the trip north and one as a gift for the people in the new camp.

After saying farewell, they traveled north for five days, following the coast through a frozen empty land. During their journey they crossed only one fox track and saw no other sign of life save two thin ravens that croaked loudly as they chased and tumbled with each other across the evening sky.

On the fifth night Kungo saw the glow of lights from the ice windows of the three snowhouses in the seal hunter's camp, and the dogs raced forward, delighted to be home at last. Everyone came out to welcome the returning travelers, and they showed Kungo every sign of friendship.

The long, hard snowdrifts were driven high against the hills, and Kungo waited patiently for the midwinter moons when the weather would be even colder and the sea hard frozen, and when the sun would not light the river valleys.

The seal hunter knew that to go to the island was very important to Kungo, and for this reason he planned to make the trip. His wife was worried, for she knew the danger of crossing by sled from the mainland to the island because the great tides could at any moment tear out the ice bridge between the two. When they were preparing to make the perilous journey, she begged her husband not to take their son, for she feared that they might both be lost to her, and to this he agreed.

Kungo helped the hunter ice the lightest and fastest sled in the camp, spitting a mouthful of water along the upturned runners and polishing it into icy smoothness with a scrap of bearskin. The other hunters lent the seal hunter their strongest dogs so that the sled would go swiftly, and they loaded it with nothing save two thick fur sleeping skins, a harpoon, a snow knife, and a seal for food.

They traveled north along the coast and slept three nights on the way. Then they turned outward on the frozen sea, and Kungo realized the terrible hazards that lay before them. The barren rock island was hidden from view, wrapped in whirling drifts of snow. Dark patches of open water and frightening black holes showed dangerously against the whiteness of the snow-covered ice. In the bitter cold these open holes threw up gray fog against the darkened sky, and mists froze and fell back like snow into the black water. Many times the hunter had to walk before the dogs, feeling with his harpoon for a safe passage across the treacherous sea ice that was broken by the rising and falling tides.

At last Kungo saw stretching out toward the island a great ice bridge, and they started along this narrow strip. But soon it grew dark and the wind rose, and they were forced to stop for the night. There was no snow there to build an igloo, just naked ice, and the howling wind swept down from the north with increasing fury. The hunter and Kungo turned their sled on its side to give them protection against the wind and rolled themselves up in the sleeping skins. With the dogs huddled around them, they managed to stay alive. Kungo lay shivering, listening in fear and wonder to the great sighing of the new-formed ice. If the ice bridge broke, they would drown in the freezing waters.

As if by magic, in the early morning the wind died, and the hunter sat up and looked around him. The air was still now, and the whirling snow had faded away.

26

There, plainly visible, lay the island, known as Tugjak. It was high and rocky, the point of a hidden mountain thrusting its stone head out of the frozen sea. Only in one place were the sheer rock walls broken by a narrow cleft. Around the island was a huge ice ledge, and beyond this was a rough broken collar of ice chunks that rose and fell with the moving tides. Snow filled every crack in the dark rocks, but the hard, smooth places were all blown clear by the savage winds that roared over the island.

The hunter drove his team along the ice ledge on the south face of the island cliffs toward the narrow opening in the rock wall. The entrance to the steep passage stood before them like a needle's eye. They began the climb, and so hard was the ascent that they often had to help the dogs to find footing. At length they reached a narrow slit in the top of the cliff. It led into a huge round place surrounded by rust-colored granite walls rising higher than a man could throw a stone. It was roofless—and so wide that Kungo thought he could not cross it in a hundred leaps.

27

At the base of this stone room, there were many entrances into dark caves and passages, and higher up among the steep, smooth rocks, there were narrow walks and holes in the stone wall that looked like windows.

Kungo followed the hunter forward across the open, snow-carpeted area until they came to a small house half buried in the ground, with walls that were shoulder high and made of stone. The roof beams of the house were the ribs of whales, covered with large sealskins weighted in place with a thick layer of sod. On either side of the entrance stood the great jawbones of a whale.

As they peered at this strange entrance, wondering what to do, a dwarf man pushed aside the sealskin curtain that served as a door for the house and waved them inside. He had powerful arms and shoulders and a twisted back, and his hair was long and knotted in the ancient style. He smiled at them in a shy and kindly way when they entered.

It was dark inside the little stone house, and Kungo crouched in the entrance passage, waiting for his eyes to become accustomed to the light. He saw the old woman first as she sat tending her stone lamp that was shaped like a half-moon. It burned with an even white flame, reflecting across the pool of rich seal fat that was its fuel. The old woman nodded and smiled and beckoned at them to come and sit beside her on the sleeping platform.

Kungo observed her carefully. Her warm brown face was flat and wide, with powerful jaw muscles that drew the flesh tight over her high cheekbones. Her eyes were jet black, and as she looked at Kungo again, they shone warmly, revealing all the hidden power of life within her. Her eyelids had been drawn narrow by a whole lifetime in the wind and snow and sun. Around her eyes and mouth and spreading up across her forehead, there appeared countless tiny wrinkles like the fine grain in an ancient piece of driftwood. When she smiled, her strong white teeth clamped together, worn evenly from chewing and softening numberless sealskins. Her hair, black and much thinner now than when she had been a girl, was caught in two tight braids that coiled neatly around her ears. Not one gray hair showed.

Bending forward, the old woman made a seat for Kungo, and he noticed that her short body, like her eyes, gave him the feeling of someone with quickness and hidden strength. Her round brown wrists had delicate blue tattooing on them, which had been done for her when she was a child. Her hands were strong and square. The right thumb and forefinger were bent and powerful from forcing bone needles through thick animal skins.

Kungo was startled when he sat down. He had not noticed beside her the old man kneeling on the sleeping platform. This ancient Eskimo was as motionless as though he were carved of stone. The light from the lamp did not seem to touch him, and he remained wrapped in shadows.

"My husband has been away in the storm," said the old woman. "Now he is back and resting. He will wake soon. You two have had a long trip and must be hungry."

She waved to the dwarf, who placed horn bowls of melted ice water, a dark red saddle of young walrus meat, and sun-dried strips of trout before them, and the hunter and Kungo ate quickly. Then the old woman cleverly drew the flame along the lamp's wick until it made the whole house glow with a soft, even light.

30

When Kungo was filled, he wiped his hands and mouth with a soft bird skin. He stole another glance at the old man, who remained motionless in the same position. But now the ancient wrinkled face and hands seemed to glow like ivory, and there was light around the old man's long white hair and the thin traces of his beard. His eyelids fluttered and opened, he slowly turned his head, and he looked at Kungo with eyes that were dark green and shadowy like pools of water on the sea ice.

"You have arrived," he said in a deep voice that made Kungo know he must be a great singer.

"Yes, we have arrived," answered Kungo in the most formal manner, for he felt both fear and respect for this old man.

"You have had a long journey, and now it is time for you both to sleep," said the old man. "I shall think a while and decide what will be best for you now that you are here. Sleep," he said again, "sleep."

The seal hunter and Kungo lay back on the soft caribou furs, glad to be safe in the warmth of this old stone house. Kungo looked up and wondered at the mighty ribs that curved across the low ceiling, and as he drifted off to sleep, he imagined himself inside the living body of a whale as it plunged into the depths of the sea.

When he awoke the next morning, light streamed down through the thin, transparent window above the door. The window was made of stretched seal intestine carefully sewn together by the old woman and was the only source of daylight in the house. Kungo sat up quickly when he realized that the seal hunter had already gone.

"He left very early," said the old woman, nodding above her

32

lamp. "He wished to cross the ice bridge while the weather remained fair and the wind gentle. He asked me to say farewell to you. My husband, Ittok, has gone out, too, for he has always loved to watch the dawning of each new day."

Kungo bent low at the small entrance, and once outside, he breathed deeply in the clear, sharp air. No one was in sight. He looked up at the pale light of day brightening the eastern sky, and then he noticed a movement in one of the entrances in the rock wall. The old man walked slowly out into the daylight. He leaned heavily on the powerful dwarf, one arm draped across the little man's hunched shoulders. As they made their way toward him, Kungo noticed in the old man's free hand a great thick bow.

"You have come to learn, and I am here to teach," said the old man, in his deep rich voice. "This," he added, holding up the bow, "this is Kigavik, the dark falcon, swiftest hunter of them all."

He placed one end of the bow against the frozen ground, and with a swift, powerful downward motion, he bent it and slipped the bowstring over the end notch. This bow was of a size and strength that Kungo had never known. It was made of musk-ox horn from the Eskimo place they call the Land Behind the Sun. It was polished smooth and bound in many places with the finest braided caribou sinew. Best of all, it was beautifully shaped, swept back like the outstretched wings of a plunging falcon. Never had there been such a bow.

Ittok offered it to Kungo, who held it in his hands like a precious treasure. He placed his hand on the string, and the touch made it sing like the east wind.

"Now, draw the bow," said the old man.

Kungo drew back hard, but the braided sinew did not move.

"Draw the bow," said Ittok once again.

It would not move.

"Draw the bow," Ittok commanded.

Taking a deep breath and using all his strength, Kungo managed to draw it back until it reached its full curve.

"Look! See that! See!" the old man called out in excitement to the dwarf. "You who can crack stones with your teeth and break the back of a white bear with your strong arms cannot draw that bow. But this boy, he can draw the bow. He can make the falcon sing. Look. He will be an archer. Perhaps he will be a great archer. Tomorrow our long task will begin."

Together, Kungo and the dwarf helped Ittok back into the house, where they carefully unstrung Kigavik and wrapped it safely in soft skins. Kungo's hands trembled as he looked at the great bow and thought of the fate of his family. "Revenge! Revenge! With a bow such as this I could have revenge!" The thought cut through him like a cruel wind.

That evening they picked rich marrow from the soft centers of caribou bones and ate the sweet flesh of young sea birds that had been preserved in seal oil. When the feast was over, the old man lay back among the thick caribou skins and went to sleep, and the dwarf left the small house for the freezing caves where he slept.

Kungo watched the old woman sew a new pair of sealskin boots. Her stitches were so small that he could not see them. She asked him about his mother, and slowly he told her the story of his life, which until now he had told no one. He spoke of his love for his parents and his sister, Shulu, and of that terrible night when the Indians had come, the night when his whole life had changed. Though he had never before revealed his innermost feelings, he told the old woman every hidden thought within him, every hate and joy, fear and longing. To Kungo she did not seem like other people. She was somehow like the earth itself. Speaking with her, he had the same feeling he had when he lay on soft tundra, warmed by the summer sun, and looked up at the wide blue sky. Then he felt he could understand every word of the wind's song. She was that kind of person.

When he had told her everything, he felt a great relief and went to sleep immediately. The old woman rose stiffly from her place on the sleeping platform and gently spread a warm caribou skin over her old husband and the young sleeping boy. Then she returned to her sewing.

During the late winter moon, the dwarf, whose name Telik-juak means big arms, told Kungo many things about their island home. He showed him the way through the numerous passages inside the granite cliffs that surrounded the little house, and the place where he, Telikjuak, slept. It was a small stone room, icy cold, with nothing in it save the skin of a huge white bear that lay neatly folded on a rock ledge that served as his bed. He showed Kungo the two rear entrances to the caves. One led to the small deep lake where they got fresh water, the other opened at the place where the dogs were kept. Beyond the high rock, the island of Tugjak stretched north, and there they often walked along the cliffs, scanning the frozen sea, looking for walrus or whales in the big open pools of water.

From the time of his arrival, Kungo helped Telikjuak to feed and care for the ten strong sled dogs. The dwarf taught him how to rule the big dogs without fear and to respect the white female lead dog named Lao. It was she who led the strong team and responded quickly to the driver's orders. She was not the strongest fighter, but she was always protected by the biggest male dog in the team. Lao soon began to rub her thick white coat against Kungo's leg and to lick his hands when he came to feed her.

One winter night when the air was still and cold and the moon rose up bone-white and calm as a sleeper's face, Kungo heard the long, lonely howl of a white wolf far away on the other end of the island, where rocky crags plunged straight down to the frozen sea. The eerie sound came to him again and again, and he heard Lao answer the white wolf with a high moaning that he had never known before.

Kungo hurried to the sheltered place where the dog team slept, but Lao was already gone. She was running fast across the hard-packed snow toward the far end of the island. When he turned to enter the passage again, he found Telikjuak standing beside him.

"That big white wolf will kill your little Lao," said Telikjuak.

But he was wrong.

The next day Kungo found Lao back with the team. She seemed tired from her long run but contented. Later, in the spring, Lao grew big, and Kungo built a small snowhouse for her.

One morning he heard her snarling viciously at the other dogs, and looking into her small house, he found that she had eight newborn pups. All of them were white as snow. She let Kungo pick one up to examine it. It had a longer muzzle and larger ears than a husky. Its legs were long and thin, and its feet splayed wide, which would be good for running swiftly on the snow. This was no ordinary pup that Kungo held. It was half wolf and half dog.

Kungo hurried back to the house to tell the news to Ittok and the old woman.

Laughing with delight, the old man said, "If you can raise those children of the white wolf, they will be yours. Wolves are not as strong as dogs, but they are fast and tireless and need little food."

Soon after, the dwarf appeared and spread a large scraped sealskin on the edge of the sleeping platform. On this he placed some long caribou rib bones and a pile of strong sinews that had been drawn from a caribou's back. Beside these he laid several short knives, a sharpening stone, and two special pieces of bone, one for straightening arrows and the other for bending the bow.

Then the old man and the boy began their long task. Slowly they shaped and matched the strong springy rib bones and cut them so they fitted together perfectly into one piece to make a delicate curving bow.

While they worked, the old woman sat silently by her lamp, and with skilled hands she spread the sinews apart with a little horn comb. Then she spun and knotted them between her nimble fingers until they became long strands of strong brown thread.

These she braided together into thin cords. They were each as fine as a single blade of grass, and yet they could easily carry the whole weight of a man. She dampened these cords with snow water and handed them to the old man, who slowly bound each piece of bone in place with the sinew cords. He then ran the cords up and down along the whole length of the bow many times until the strands lay evenly together. These strands he bound tightly to the bow. When the cords dried, they gripped the bow like a falcon's claw and gave springing power to it.

Now the old woman handed them the strongest double-braided strand of all, the bowstring itself, made from the center sinew of a bull caribou's back. When the bone bow was flexed and the bowstring gripped the notch, it drew all the long sinews tight and gave added strength. The bow was much smaller than the great Kigavik and felt lighter in Kungo's hand. It was white like a young falcon. It was made for him, and he wished more than anything to become skilled with it quickly.

A few days later when the bow was finished, they began to make the arrows. The old man took long pieces of caribou bone, split them, shaped them, and bound them together. At the end of each shaft he made a slit, and into this he forced a slim stone arrowhead made of hardest slate. The old man had shown Kungo how to shape and sharpen each head. At the other end of each arrow, after it was notched, they bound the dark wing feathers of a raven to the shaft to guide the arrow in its flight.

When their work was finished, the old woman handed Kungo a trim quiver made of sealskin with two compartments, one for the new bow and the other for the arrows.

40

The long white Arctic spring faded as the sun of summer wheeled above the island. Everywhere the soft gray tundra moss appeared through the snow, and the tiny Arctic flowers unfolded like colored stars. Small birds returned from warm lands in the south and sang their songs as they hopped about gathering dried moss for their nests. The weather softened, and warm mists rose in the early mornings. It was a joy to hear the faint bird sounds after the long silence of winter, for it was as though the whole world were being born again. The sun never left the sky.

"Set up a target, boy," said the old man early one morning. "It is time you learned to use the new bow."

In great excitement Kungo ran out and hurriedly built up two targets with the last soft snow that remained against the north wall hidden from the sun. One target was a model of a bear, the other the likeness of a man.

When Kungo returned to the little house, the old man and the dwarf were waiting for him.

"Are you an enemy of all white bears?" asked the old man.

Kungo thought about this question for a moment.

"No," he answered, "but I hope that one day a white bear will offer himself to me."

"Then do not drive arrows into his image or all white bears will be offended. And men, Kungo, would you do harm to all men?"

"No," said Kungo quickly. "I seek eleven bowmen. Those will I harm. Those I will kill."

"Hear me well, Kungo," Ittok said. "Do not give men cause to fear you, for one who does that is no better than a dog gone mad, wishing only to bite and kill."

Ittok waved his hand, and the dwarf hobbled across and cut out two large square blocks of snow, placed one upon the other, and in the center of the upper block stuck a dark piece of tundra moss about the size of a man's hand.

The old man stepped forward. He took Kungo's new bow and stood for a moment as though he were in deep thought. Then scarcely looking at the target, he aimed, drew back the bowstring, and released it. Although he had not placed an arrow in the bow, he said to Telikjuak that he was out of practice and had missed the mark.

Again the old man seemed lost in thought, and again he drew the bow without an arrow. He released the bowstring and said that this time he had struck the mark.

"Now, Kungo, it is your turn."

Kungo raised the bow, aimed, quickly drew back the empty bowstring, and released it.

The old man stepped forward beside him and said, "You must learn to shoot the bow and guide the arrows with your mind, for it is only with the power of your thoughts that you will become a great archer. Imagine that you have a true arrow. Draw and release it, and guide it quickly with your eye and mind straight to the mark."

Kungo concentrated, drawing the bow again and again without using an arrow.

"Now practice each day," commanded Ittok. "Practice until your mind is tired and your fingers bleed on the bowstring, and at the end of summer I shall let you use one of your arrows."

42

Kungo's mind flashed backward to the dreaded scene that haunted him, waking or sleeping—the scene of his father's broken snowhouse and his sister being taken away. He gripped his throat to keep from screaming out in anger. He must do as the old one commanded.

During the short summer Kungo practiced long and hard. Sometimes he saw the old man and the dwarf watching him from the entrance of the dark caves, but they said not a word.

One morning when he awoke there was a light fall of snow on the ground, almost covering the autumn red of the tundra, and the little ponds were covered with a thin sheet of ice.

When he went outside with his bow, the old man and Telikjuak were waiting for him. Ittok handed him a single arrow. Black feathered it was and long, with a sharp tip. Kungo felt a surge of wild excitement as he placed the arrow in his bow. He aimed at the small target of woven hide and released the arrow. It flew wide of the mark and struck harmlessly in the tundra.

"Bring it back quickly," cried the old man, and Kungo ran across the wide space and returned with the arrow.

"Now, think," said Ittok. "Think what you are trying to do. Guide the arrow with your eye. Force it with your mind to go straight to the mark."

Kungo drew the bow again and held it until it seemed to him that the feathered shaft reached in and touched the very center of his being. Then he released the arrow, and it flew straight down the course, following his line of vision until it struck the center of the target.

"Good!" shouted the old man, and Telikjuak smiled and

nodded his head at Kungo. "You have it now. Practice with that black arrow until the midwinter moon and I, an old man, shall take you hunting."

After they had gone, Kungo stood alone surrounded by the great stone walls and thought again, fiercely, of why he wanted to be a great bowman. Only he could avenge the wrong done to his family. Concentrating once more, he raised the bow and with an easy rhythm drove the arrow straight through the heavy target.

Slowly winter came to them, and it was dark until noon each day. Savage winds blew in from the frozen sea and seemed to hold the land in an icy grasp. A new bridge of ice formed solidly between the mainland and their island home. The old woman had completed her work on their winter clothes, and Telikjuak had prepared the long sled and harnesses for the big dogs. They were ready for the journey.

They planned to leave Lao on the island to fend for her growing family of young white wolf dogs, knowing she would teach them to dig beneath the snow for lemming and to catch hare and ptarmigan to feed themselves.

On a clear day Telikjuak loaded the sled down on the sea ice. Kungo and the old woman helped Ittok down the high snowy passage from their home. Once they were on the sled, Kungo was surprised at Ittok's agility. He sat beside his wife, and although his eyes and legs were weak, his arms were strong, and he rode the sled cleverly, balancing and shifting his weight as they crossed the rough ice. Ittok called commands to the new lead dog in his deep songlike voice, and the dog obeyed instantly.

Kungo and the powerful dwarf sat on the long sled or ran beside it, guiding it across the snow.

That night they slept near the end of the ice bridge, close to the land, where snow had drifted. The dwarf and Kungo built a new igloo, and when it was completed, the old woman hurried inside to spread the sleeping skins neatly over the snow bench. She took a live spark from a small stone tinder box that she carried when traveling, blew it into a flame, and lighted the wick in her little seal-oil lamp.

When the dogs were fed and the men entered the igloo, they placed the thick snow door neatly over the entrance and ate some tasty strips of seal meat. The old woman pulled off their boots and placed them carefully on the drying rack over the lamp. She looked around her new house and saw the white walls glistening like diamonds. She laughed out loud with pleasure, for she loved to travel.

The next day they journeyed beyond the ice of the sea and moved inland, following a flat river course through the coastal hills. The wind blew violently, and that night they built a strong igloo in the protection of the riverbank. Snow whipped into the air until they could not see each other or the dogs, and they were forced to remain in this snowhouse for three days until the storm died.

When they went out once more into the fresh white world, their dogs were buried deeply in the snow, sleeping comfortably in the warmth of their heavy fur coats with their tails curled above their noses so they could breathe.

Now they traveled for five long days across the white flatness

of the inland plain, where land and sky were joined together in a long unbroken line. Sometimes on a wind-swept place the old man told Kungo to set up one stone upon another to mark their trail so that they could trace their way back out of the flat land in case they ever came this way again. On the fourth day they crossed a few caribou tracks, and on the fifth day there were a great many fresh tracks.

They stopped early in the afternoon and built a snowhouse larger than the others of the trip, and on its front they built a small meat porch. This igloo had a clear ice window over the door and a long tunnel entrance to keep out the wind, as they expected to stay here for some time.

The old woman started fixing the inside of the new house, beating the snow out of the sleeping skins to make them dry and comfortable. Kungo heard her singing to herself an ancient song as she lighted the flame of her lamp:

> "Ayii, Ayii,
> Even as a spirit
> Joyfully I'll roam
> Down every river valley
> That leads toward the sea.
> Ayii, Ayii."

That night as they lay among the furs on the sleeping bench, they began to talk. This was the time Kungo liked best, for it was a time to speak, to listen, and to learn. The old man said to Kungo, "Being a hunter is many things. To be a clever bowman is not enough. First you must know where to find the animals, and then when you have found them, you must know how to stalk them on this flat plain or out on the open ice of the sea. A man does not just kill because he is a clever hunter. He succeeds in the hunt only if he is a good man, a wise man, who obeys the rules of life. If the animals or birds or fish see that a man is cruel and stupid, they will not give themselves to him.

"Tomorrow, if the weather is good," continued Ittok, "you will hunt with Telikjuak. He is slow with his legs, but he has become wise with his mind. Do not take a bow or spear with you. Telikjuak does not need such weapons, for he was born among the caribou people and he knows many ways to stalk the animals on the plain."

In the morning, the dwarf and Kungo dressed in their warmest caribou skin clothing, for a light wind was blowing out of the west and it was bitter cold. Kungo shyly handed a pair of wooden snow goggles to Telikjuak, for he had carved two pairs of narrow-slitted goggles during the long blizzard. Telikjuak thanked him and said that now they would not go blind in the glaring whiteness. Telikjuak rolled two skins tightly and tied them across his back, and he showed Kungo how to place a long knife inside his skin boot.

After walking some distance, they came to a slight rise in the ground. The dwarf quickly led Kungo up it, hobbling very fast with his short broken way of hop-walking. When they were on the highest ground, the dwarf showed Kungo how to hold his mittened hands together. Telikjuak then hopped up lightly into Kungo's hands and stepped onto his shoulders. From this height he searched the country with his hawklike eyes and then quickly hopped down.

Kungo looked around carefully and said, "I see nothing."

"Come with me," said Telikjuak. "Just beyond the river there are as many caribou as I have fingers and toes. They are difficult to see when they are lying down, for their backs are almost white with frost from their breathing."

The dwarf then led Kungo on a long walk across the plain.

"Are we near them now?" whispered Kungo while searching hard with his eyes.

"No. We are farther from them," said Telikjuak. "But we are downwind of them, and they will not smell us here. Sit down and rest."

Telikjuak quickly spread one caribou skin over his shoulders and sat down on the lowest part. Kungo did the same with the other skin.

"Look," the dwarf whispered. "They're up and moving, feeding at that place where the wind has blown the tundra clear of snow."

For the first time, Kungo saw the caribou, twenty of them, pale as silver ghosts, blending with the snow and sky.

Telikjuak rose slowly, and bending over, he blew his breath across the dark hairs of the skin so that frost formed and made the skin silvery and difficult to see. It looked exactly like the caribou before them. Then he drew the soft hide around his shoulders until the front legs hung over his arms and the back legs hung down by his feet. The head poked out stiffly in front of him, the big ears spread wide.

"Like this," he said, and started off, bent over and moving slowly upwind like a feeding caribou.

Kungo mimicked the movements of the dwarf and was soon astonished to find himself within a dog team's length of the nearest animal. Then the dwarf slowly led Kungo into the very center of the herd, and none of the animals seemed to notice them.

Kungo saw that caribou were all around. They were so close that he could almost touch them. A bull caribou with a huge rack of antlers suddenly raised his head and snorted loudly, having smelled something. Kungo stiffened in his tracks. But the dwarf moved on, imitating a feeding caribou, and the big bull soon settled down to feed again right beside Kungo. The dwarf under the hide glanced slyly at Kungo and smiled. Kungo knew that he must decide what to do next.

Slowly, very slowly, he reached down and drew the long knife from its sheath in his boot top, and with a short, powerful movement, he drove it into the bull caribou's chest. The animal gave a great leap that tore the knife from Kungo's hand, stumbled a few paces, and then with a sigh sank to its knees. The spirit rushed out of it, and it was dead. The other caribou looked at it for a moment, but believing that it was resting, they continued to graze.

The dwarf walked on among the animals, imitating their

movements perfectly. He seemed not to notice that Kungo had killed a caribou. Kungo watched him carefully, wondering what Telikjuak would do next, wondering also what he himself should do.

Suddenly the dwarf threw off his caribou-skin cover and stood upright, a man among the animals. Their antlers flashed upwards as they saw him for the first time. They snorted with alarm and bounded away, scattering in different directions. Their great splayed hoofs carried them swiftly across the snow, but soon they banded together, once more drawn by their instincts as a herd. In a few moments they were almost out of sight, leaving behind them a whirling cloud of snow crystals. All, that is, save Kungo's dead caribou and two others who stood motionless.

"Start walking behind that one," called the dwarf to Kungo. "Move toward our camp. Keep it before you. We can come back for your dead caribou tomorrow with the dogs and sled to haul it in."

The two caribou moved slowly in front of them as though dazed, and Kungo realized that the dwarf had stabbed them both so quickly that he had not seen the motion. Telikjuak had stabbed them lightly in a special place behind the chest so that they could still walk. In this way the two hunters easily guided the caribou back to the snowhouse. One fell within a dog team's length of the igloo; the other dropped over right at the entrance.

"That is how to stalk and kill an animal," cried the old man, who stood beside the snowhouse watching them drive the caribou home. He held himself stiffly upright, supported by the big bow, and his old eyes glowed with pride as he thought of the boy becoming a man. With excitement he called to the old woman, asking her to come and help them with the skinning. He warned the dogs away from the caribou with a harsh command.

The next day Kungo went out with the sled to bring in his caribou, but a starving wolf had found it in the night, and he brought back less than half the meat.

Slowly as the days passed, the air became warmer, and in the early mornings they heard the short, shrill mating call of the white-feathered ptarmigan. Bare patches of tundra started to show through the snow. The old man was slowly carving a piece of antler into the likeness of a caribou. This carving he rubbed and polished carefully, for he believed that such a friendly act would cause the caribou to wish to give themselves to the hunters.

Because the spirit of the hunt was still strong in him, the old man sometimes took Kigavik and, using it like a staff, wandered slowly up the river hoping to find game. One evening, Kungo met Ittok, and they rested together before making their way back to the camp. The old man told Kungo of a great journey northward to the Land Behind the Sun he had taken when he had been young and strong and his eyes could see great distances. Throwing back his head, Ittok drew in a deep breath and in a rich voice sang a song about the musk ox and about the joy he had had in that far-off place:

"Ayii, Ayii, Ayii, Ayii,
Wondering I saw them,
Great black beasts,
Running, standing,
Eating flowers on the high plain.
On my belly I crept to them
With my bow and arrows in my mouth.
The big one reared up in surprise
As my arrow quivered in his chest.
The herd scattered
Running on the high plain,
And small I sat singing
By the big bull's side.
Ayii, Ayii."

The old woman was always busy and full of singing as she mended their clothes, dried their boots, and scraped the new skins.

One day she told Kungo that she had placed some round black stones on the ice of a lake half a day's journey from their camp. Now she wanted to go and see if the sun had heated them enough to drop them through the thick lake ice and make holes for fishing.

Together they walked out across the land, and with every step they responded to the wonder of the quick Arctic spring as it burst around them. They could hear the water running in streams beneath the snow. So well did Kungo and the old woman understand each other that they did not often feel the need to speak.

Reaching the lake, they both stopped, sensing something strange. Then Kungo saw it. It was a pure black kasigiak, a rare freshwater seal, lying out on the ice near the opposite shore.

"A beautiful skin," said the old woman softly. "That skin could make the best pair of boots in the land. Hurry, boy, before it sees you and dives down into its hole in the ice. Kasigiaks are very easily disturbed."

Scarcely moving, Kungo drew his bow from its case and carefully fitted an arrow to the bowstring. He paused, looking at the ground, thinking only of the black seal. Then with a smooth, even swing, he raised the bow and sent the deadly arrow winging along its course, straight into the animal's heart. The seal scarcely moved as its soul rushed out of its body.

"It was a long way to that seal. I see now that you will become a great archer," said the old woman with joy in her voice as they started out across the ice. Swiftly and cleverly she removed the richly spotted skin from the seal with her sharp moon-faced woman's knife. Cutting away the thick layer of white fat, she exposed the dark red meat underneath.

"When I was very young," she said, "and it was spring, I once came walking here with my grandmother to fish. Six days we stayed, yet she carried no food, no tent, no snow knife, only a little bone hook and fishing line hidden in her hood. When evening came, we lay down near a stone for protection and slept out under the open sky. My grandmother was a strong woman, full of ancient songs. She would put me on her back when I was a child and walk all day to catch one fish. Come now, we must eat meat, for meat in a man is like oil in a lamp. It gives one strength and heat from within."

After they had eaten their fill, Kungo lay down on a high piece of dry tundra with the snow around him and watched the stars come out and grow bright as the sky darkened, and he thought again, as he often did, that there would be no real peace or joy for him till he had avenged the death of his parents.

The next morning he awoke and saw the sun was high, shedding its warmth over the land. There were bird sounds all around him. The old woman was already down at the new fishing holes made in the ice by the stones. She was fishing diligently with her small hook and hand line. Three fat red trout lay beside her.

Later, when they returned to the camp, the old woman scraped the remaining fat from the sealskin very carefully with her moon-shaped knife and soaked it in urine to remove all grease and to bleach the skin. Then she washed it many times in snow water and stretched it on a frame. The sharp night cold and the long sunlight glaring off the snow soon turned the skin sparkling white. Then the old woman cut the beautiful hide into careful patterns. She drew the finest bone needle from her little ivory case, and using the thinnest, strongest sinew, she soaked and shaped and sewed a pure white pair of knee-length boots. She did not give these boots to Kungo but hid them in her loonskin bag.

When the roof of the snowhouse collapsed on them from the heat of the spring sun, they all laughed with pleasure, for it was a sign that the geese would soon return and the fish would run once more in the open rivers. The old woman took many caribou skins and sewed them into a tent. Telikjuak cut the heavy sealskin thongs that held the long sled together, and using the runners to serve as tent poles, he covered them with the skins. This became their new summer home.

For two brief moons before the cold returned, millions of tiny insects swarmed in the clear, still air. The geese arrived in vast numbers to build their nests and to lay their eggs in the safety of the still marshlands where no man's foot had ever trod. Kungo and Telikjuak hunted and fished throughout the short summer.

But soon the tundra turned red with the coming of early autumn. Each morning new ice formed on every pond, and the winds carried within them the hidden whips of winter. The caribou were on the move again, trekking southward toward the Land of Little Sticks, their big antlers shining, their light autumn coats sleek and perfect for making warm clothing.

Early one morning when the air was sharp and the sky filled with heavy clouds, Kungo looked out of the tent and saw the old woman crouching alert and motionless on the far bank of the stream. Taking his bow and arrows, he hurried cautiously to the place where she waited for him. She nodded her head, and looking in that direction, he saw hundreds of caribou pouring along the bank of the river in single file, pawing the ground with their sharp hoofs and feeding. The young males threatened each other, raising their heads, shaking their great antlers, stepping stiffly sideways like graceful dancers.

Kungo strung his bow slowly so he would not frighten the animals and notched an arrow against the string. He aimed carefully at a plump bull caribou, its sides bulging from the rich summer feeding.

"Wait," whispered the old woman. "Look at that beautiful

one. Take that one," she urged.

He moved his bow until his line of sight seemed to reach out and touch the caribou with the light gray back and fine snow-white flanks. He released the arrow, and it silently flew straight to its mark. The animal reared up, ran out of the herd, and fell.

As he raised his bow again, the old woman called to him, "Quickly now, the one with the tan back and white belly."

Seeing it, he drove the arrow from his eye straight into its heart.

Three more she selected because of their whiteness, and three more he killed. Then the herd grew nervous, sensing danger, though they could not see or smell or hear it, and plunging through the shallow river, the caribou ran across the open plain. Swiftly they went, and so well did they blend with the autumn tundra that in a few moments they disappeared from view.

As they approached the place where the dead caribou lay, the old woman cried out with delight at the sight of such beautiful skins. Kungo helped her as they skillfully cut and stripped the soft hides from the animals.

"Telikjuak will bring the dogs to pack home the meat," she said, and rolling up the precious hides, she tied them and flung them onto her back. In her mind she was already planning the scraping, stretching, drying, pattern-cutting, and sewing of the new skins. She hummed a song as they returned to the tent. In each hand, Kungo carried a steaming red caribou liver as gifts for Telikjuak and the old man.

Later that autumn, after a blizzard, when the wind had packed great drifts in the river valley, they built a new snowhouse, the

first one of that winter. Taking down the tent poles, they lashed them together with crosspieces and remade their sled. Both the men and dogs felt the joy and excitement of the new winter with its sharp, invigorating cold. The open space of land and frozen sea became theirs once more to travel upon freely wherever they wished, and during the midwinter moon they decided to leave this inland hunting ground and return to the island.

They broke in the side of their snowhouse, fearing that evil spirits might lurk there and harm some other traveler. Then, like true nomads, they harnessed their dogs and drifted across the white expanse like leaves blown on the autumn wind.

When they reached the coast again, it was deadly cold, as the wind whipped in from the freezing sea, chilling a man until his bones trembled. In the second moon of winter, the long ice bridge formed and grew thick, and one early morning in the inky darkness they started to cross it. Before long, a storm blew in and the wind howled. The ice bridge heaved and cracked like a giant dog whip, but it held together, and by noon the next day they were safe in the shelter of the island's southern shore. Exhausted, they climbed up the steep passage, helping the old man, who could scarcely walk after their long, cold journey. When they entered the little stone house, the old woman lighted her lamp once more. It soon warmed the room and cast a soft glow among the bone rafters.

"It is good to travel far and to see each new day dawn over strange lands, for without moving we would not know the joy of returning home," she said, and the old man and Kungo nodded their heads in agreement. For the first time Kungo realized that

he now thought of this island, Tugjak, as his home, even thoug
the painful dreams of his first home and lost family disturbed h
sleep and caused his face sometimes to burn with anger.

On the following day, when Kungo first saw Lao and h
family of dogs running together, he was afraid. Nine of the
there were now, big and white and swift as young falcons. Whe
he climbed the island's eastern slope, the wolf dogs raced straig
at him. Then Kungo recognized Lao, who leaped and bounde
around him, licking his hands. Two of her children snarled
him, but Lao warned them off with a growl. Although they we
almost as large and strong as she, they obeyed her.

After the excitement of meeting again, Kungo looked at t
half wolves, half dogs, all of which he had last seen as pups. Th
all had thick pure white coats, long heads, and the pale, frighte
ing eyes of a wolf. Their legs were longer than their mother'
and the pads of their feet were wider, perfect for running on so
snow. Although no man had fed them during the year, they we
strong and healthy, for they had learned to hunt for themselve
During the summer when game on the island was scarce, he kne
they would have learned to stand belly-deep beyond the shore t
snatch small fish from the water.

Kungo noticed one of them, lean and handsome, more wolf-like than the others, who lay like a white prince beside Lao. Its strange eyes were more piercing than the rest.

"Amahok," called Kungo, and the animal, answering to the name of wolf, leaped up and came quickly to the place where Kungo stood.

"You shall be the leader," said Kungo. But he did not touch the animal, for as it stood silently before him, he sensed the quick strength and wild fierceness that lay hidden in the white wolf dog.

All through the next spring, Kungo hunted seals and walrus that basked in the sunshine far out on the frozen sea. While hunting, he carefully trained the wolf dogs to work as a team, to obey his every command until they moved swiftly and quietly together during the hunt.

One day Telikjuak said to Kungo, "They are not wide-chested and strong like the best sled dogs that can pull great loads of meat, but they have long legs and can run like the wind. They do not fight much with each other, and they hunt for themselves. I have never seen such a team."

When Kungo fed them rich walrus meat, the wolf dogs grew

stronger and heavier, their chests widened, and their legs grew strong from pulling. All summer Kungo hunted food for the island camp. He practiced shooting from every angle with his bow. Telikjuak helped him make a long knife with a curved antler handle that he shaped and bound until it fitted his hand exactly. This he sharpened, stone blade against stone, until its edge was as sharp as a snow owl's claw.

One day they found a bleached driftwood log that had been washed up on the island shore by the tide. Telikjuak and Kungo split it by carefully driving sharp stone wedges along its center until it fell in two. Then they chipped these with short axes until the two pieces were shaped like long sled runners. These they left in the sun until they bleached bone-white. They made holes with a bow drill along the top of the wooden runners, and with seal thongs they lashed on other narrow slabs of driftwood for cross-pieces in order to hold the sled together.

The autumn came again, and Kungo knew that he was growing up. He was much stronger now, with great muscles in his arms and back from drawing the bow. He could heave his sled through the rough ice with ease. He often helped the powerful dwarf pull huge sides of walrus meat up from the sea to the place where they covered it with heavy stones to protect it from their dogs and wild animals. He felt glad to be alive and safe on their island home, and he thought of the old man and woman and the dwarf Telikjuak as his family. But deep inside him the restless hatred and the terrible desire to avenge his real family remained like a core of hard ice.

Kungo was determined to tell the old man of the anger that

64

burned within him, twisting his thoughts in the light of day and haunting his dreams at night.

One day Kungo saw the old man alone on the rust-colored moss some distance from the little house and thought that now was the time to speak with him. He noticed how bent with age the old man had become as he stood blinking blindly in the autumn sunlight. He seemed to be listening—listening to something far away.

"Telikjuak, Telikjuak," the old man called to the dwarf. "Bring me my bow. Bring Kigavik quickly."

Out of the cave came the dwarf, hobbling past Kungo as he unwrapped the soft caribou skin that protected Kigavik. One black arrow he carried, clenched between his teeth.

The old man took the great bow in his right hand like a staff, and thrusting it strongly downward, he snapped the bowstring into the upper notch. The dwarf handed him the arrow and moved away a few paces and crouched down. The old man dropped slowly, painfully, onto his knees, lifting his old face upward to the sky. His long white hair shifted about his shoulders in the light breeze, and his old eyes seemed weak and pale as mist.

Then Kungo heard the first sounds high and far away. It was the calling of the geese. Snow geese they were, sending their wild music down to the earth as they winged southwards from their summer nesting grounds. The very sound of them sent shivers up and down his spine.

Kungo could now see them flying in a high white wedge against the blue sky.

"Kungo! Kungo! Kungo!" called the geese, for the name the Eskimos had given them was the sound of their call and their name also. Kungo himself had been named for them.

The white geese were soon almost overhead, flying so high that they looked like drifting flakes of snow.

Kungo watched the old man kneeling motionless, lost in thought. Then Ittok slowly placed the dark arrow across Kigavik and carefully notched it in the sinew bowstring. With one powerful movement he raised Kigavik upward, drawing the great bow back as far as it would go. Smoothly he released the sinew, and with a mighty twang the arrow screamed into the sky.

Peering upward, Kungo shaded his eyes and waited. Then, high in the blue he saw the great white goose, the leader, at the very point of the wedge, stagger in its flight and start to fall. At first it turned over several times as its great white wings, out of control, were caught by the currents of air. Then it plunged straight downward, falling, falling. It struck the ground before them with a tremendous thud, its dead weight snapping the black arrow in half.

The dwarf crossed the opening and picked up the big bird. He brought it to the old man, who remained kneeling on the ground, holding the great bow, Kigavik, curved in his hands like the swift dark wings of a falcon.

"These are feathers for a white archer. It is right that you should have them. But you must never kill this bird nor eat its flesh, for you bear its name. You came to us from the wild geese, and when you die, your spirit will fly free and live with the snow geese once more. They are a part of you."

Kungo took the wild goose gently in his hands. It was soft and warm and heavy, and the beautiful head on the slender neck curved back until it almost touched the ground. The powerful wing feathers lay open in death, white as wave tops, curved one against the other like wind-carved drifts of snow.

Kungo wished to speak with the old man, but the right time never seemed to come. Ittok was now almost completely blind, and much of the time he sat nodding back and forth lost in thought. It was as though his body remained with them and his mind went away, traveling in the distant lands of his youth.

One night when the old man was asleep, Kungo quietly told the old woman of his troubled thoughts and that he must go and search the inland for the Indians who had destroyed his family. The memory of that terrible night burned within him like fire and would not let him rest.

The old woman stopped sewing and nodded sadly.

"Yes," she said, looking at her sleeping husband. "He told me four years ago that you would remain until the ice bridge formed this winter and that you would then go forth, driven by your desire to avenge your family. That time has now come, but I must say to you that hatred and revenge follow each other like two strong men piling heavy stones one upon the other until the stones fall, killing both men and perhaps many others."

Kungo heard her words but did not try to understand their meaning, so crowded was his mind with the wild spirit of vengeance. Over and over again he planned the journey in his mind, for he knew that he must go. He must be ready when the ice bridge formed during the midwinter moon.

Silently the dwarf helped him make new arrows, long and straight, with points as sharply ground as a weasel's tooth. To these arrows they carefully bound the feathers freshly plucked from the wings of the wild snow goose. Sadly the old woman made eight strong white sealskin harnesses for the team.

Kungo ran the white wolf dogs every day and heaved the long sled until he, the driver, and his team grew wise and strong as they worked together. When he called to the leader, Amahok, to stop or go, lead right or left, the wolf dog obeyed instantly and the team followed willingly.

One biting cold morning at the end of the first winter moon, Kungo climbed the high stone cliff that surrounded their little house. From Tugjak's highest peak he looked toward the distant mainland and saw that the long ice bridge had formed. He hurried down and told the old couple that if the weather remained good, he would leave the following day.

When he awoke the next morning, a new fur parka with a full hood and new knee-length fur pants lay beside him on the bed. They were cut and finely sewn from the flanks of the caribou he had hunted on the inland plain. He had never seen anything so beautiful. He pulled these over his light inner parka and pants and found that they fitted perfectly. The outer parka and pants were white as snow, and the wolf-trimmed hood rested warmly around his neck. He then put on two pairs of thick, warm fur stockings, knee high, and over these he drew the snug-fitting white sealskin boots.

The old woman, who had made the pure white clothing for him, was still sitting by her lamp. She smiled at him in a sad way and handed him the last three items, a tight hat made of white weasel skins, a pair of white fur mitts with leather palms, and a small white bag of grease and ashes.

There were no words that Kungo could find to say to the old woman, and as he thought of all her songs and the joys they had shared during their long walks over the summer tundra, he felt a great sadness rise up in him. Picking up his white bag, he turned and hurried out of the house, for he could not bring himself to look at her.

The old man stood beside the entrance. The dog Lao was close beside him. His old eyes seemed not to see Kungo, but with fumbling hands he reached down and grasped the great bow, Kigavik. He held it out before him.

"With this bow I give you all my strength and power, my gift to see and understand. Take it. Use it wisely. Take it quickly," he said as the tears ran out of his blind eyes.

Kungo looked at the old man and at Kigavik quivering like the wings of a dark falcon in the old man's hands. He laid his own white bow at the old man's feet and took the big bow gently. He tried to but could not speak. Slowly he turned and walked away down the long snow-filled path that led to the sea ice.

Telikjuak had harnessed the team of white wolf dogs down below the cliffs on the frozen sea. The dwarf did not look at Kungo as he tightened the leather lashings on the sled. Spread over the sled was the dwarf's sleeping skin made from the great white bear he had killed.

"You need that bearskin for sleeping in the cave," said Kungo, starting to take the huge skin off the sled.

"Leave it on," the dwarf commanded in a harsh, rough voice that Kungo had not heard before. "It is yours, white archer. Now, go with strength. Fly with Kigavik," he said, and gave a sharp warning command to the wolf dogs, who howled and strained in their harnesses, eager to start the journey.

"Ush! Ush!" Kungo called to the lead dog, and as the sled headed forward, he jumped onto it.

When the team had settled into a steady running pace across the snow-covered ice, Kungo turned to look back. He saw the little dwarf figure standing alone before the jagged rocks of the island, peering after the team with his sharp eyes. But Kungo knew that the whiteness of his clothing and the white sled and team had caused him to disappear like magic into the great whiteness of the ice bridge.

The wolf team traveled so fast that Kungo dared not run beside the sled to keep warm for fear he might fall behind. He grew cold and would have frozen on the wind-whipped sled had it not been for his new and perfect-fitting clothing. The deep fur-trimmed hood protected his face from the stinging cold, and almost before he knew it, the team had carried him safely across the ice bridge. They reached the coast of the mainland before the winter moon had risen.

Kungo halted the team with one sharp command and, walking forward, unharnessed the wolf dogs, calling each one by its name. From a rough skin bag on the sled, he shook out rich chunks of frozen seal meat that the hungry team devoured in an instant. Sitting quietly on the sled in the still cold, he watched the evening star rise above the coastal hills, while with his knife he shaved and ate thin delicious pieces of the frozen seal meat, the same food he had given to the team.

Kungo then quickly built a small igloo, using his long ivory-bladed snow knife to cut and shape the blocks of wind-packed snow. He cut the blocks in a circle from below his feet and built the walls of the house around himself. Crawling out of the entrance after the blocks were in place, he filled the cracks with snow. Then he gently pushed Kigavik and the skin of the great white bear into the igloo and crawled inside before fitting the snow-block door in place. He carefully pulled off his white outer parka and pants and rolled himself in his new sleeping skin that Telikjuak had given him.

Now he was truly alone, with a terrible task to perform. Lying there in the small igloo, he thought again of the dark night of the Indians and of his parents, lost to him forever, of his sister, Shulu, stolen from his sight. Terrible anger ran within him, and he lay shaking in the warm bearskin as though he were chilled to the bone. When the shaking passed, he drifted off to sleep and dreamed of Indians, lean, gaunt men with faces painted in wild designs.

The next morning he arose long before the light came into the eastern sky. He cut the igloo open with his knife and stepped out. In an instant the team was up, and he harnessed each dog. He placed Kigavik carefully in its long protective quiver beside the separate pouch that held the arrows. He tucked it carefully between the soft folds of the white bearskin. This, along with the meat bag, he lashed to the long sled.

With a call to Amahok, the lead dog, he set the dogs in

73

motion. The whole team leaped forward and rushed southward, following the coast. He called commands to Amahok, who led the team with a long, loping stride.

Two snowhouses he built and three days they traveled on the sea ice until they came to the barrier ice heaved up at the mouth of a great frozen river. Turning, they followed inland the broad path of snow-covered ice. Kungo searched the snowy banks on either side, for it reminded him of his homeland as a child. But he could see no igloos, no sign of life in this lonely place, and the team carried him swiftly forward, following the river as it curved between the coastal hills.

The second night he stopped, fed the team, built his snow-house, and, sitting on the sled, ate his only meal of the day. Kungo watched the moon rise up like a giant's eye and cast its long light in a narrow shining path across the hills. He heard the river ice crack and groan in the still cold as though some monster lay hidden and strained to be released. Although Kungo had never seen the little people, he knew that it was at a time like this a man could hear the river spirits laughing and the answering whistle of the shore spirits. He watched along the river carefully, for it had always been said that the little people of the spirit world loved to crawl out of a crack and lie upon their backs on the ice, kicking up their legs and chuckling in the very path of the moonlight. He thought perhaps he heard a small laughing sound, but in the pale light he saw nothing.

Then all was silent. The wolf dogs lay quietly around the snowhouse, and Kungo curled up in the warmth of his sleeping skin and slept until morning.

74

The third and fourth days' journey carried him far across the inland plain, and on the fifth day a great blizzard swept over the land. At first the air grew warm and huge flakes of snow whirled down, the wind whipped itself into a fury, and Kungo could not see the dogs before him.

He stopped and built an igloo, though the wind was so violent that it tore some of the snow blocks from his hands. He fed the dogs the last scraps of seal meat and crawled into his igloo, where he slept and dreamed and waked and thought and slept again. For five days the winds thundered against his little house and tried to tear it from the land, but he had built it well and it stood firmly until the wind went moaning off across the plain, leaving only a vast white silence.

When at last Kungo cut away the snow door and stepped outside, it was like a white magic place. The giants hidden in the wind had carved the snow into wild shapes, piling great drifts against the riverbanks. They had swept the lake ice clear of snow. Everything had changed, and the leaden-colored storm clouds hid the sun and stars and would not tell him east from west.

Kungo bent down and with his bare hands felt beneath the snow, for under this new snow he knew that the old drifts ran north and south. When he moved his hands along the old hard ridges, he learned the direction that he must travel. Harnessing the team, he set out more slowly now. The dogs, like himself, were hungry from the five days' fasting.

They camped that evening on the edge of a low ridge that ran south as far as he could see. This ridge was what Kungo

had been looking for. From its height he could see any movement of men or animals crossing the plain.

On the following day they journeyed straight south along the ridge. Kungo searched east and west but saw nothing until almost evening when, with a short command, he stopped the team. Far out beyond his right hand on the flat plain, he was aware of some movement. He watched and waited carefully. Then in the distance he made out a long line of caribou, looking like spots of silver on the horizon, slowly moving north. Kungo was very hungry, the wolf team could not continue much longer without food, and he knew he might not see game again in this desolate country. But the flame of anger in him said, "Go on. *Go forward now.*"

He called a command to Amahok, and the team pulled on until the waning moon rose again. Then Kungo built another snowhouse and slept fitfully, for he was now weak with hunger.

When he stepped from his igloo in the morning, he saw a welcome sight. The wolf dogs lay before the entrance, their white coats stained with blood, and he knew in an instant that they had run silently as a free hunting pack in the night and had pulled down a caribou, fed themselves, and returned to him. There was a look of triumph in the green eyes of Amahok and the others as they lay with full bellies licking their white coats clean.

For two days they traveled south, seeing nothing in the land save one snowy owl searching like themselves across the white expanse.

Late the following afternoon Kungo saw in the distance the

Land of Little Sticks. He had never seen it before. The small trees stood like gray ghosts silently listening on the plain. Beyond these first dwarfed trees, he could see there were larger ones and many more of them.

He camped early because he did not wish to sleep among the little sticks and because he feared that the dogs would tangle their long lines in the trees. Before he entered his new snow-house, he looked around him in the twilight and listened carefully, and he knew fear inside himself. He was starving. He cut a piece of leather dog line and chewed it, hoping this would give him strength.

That night strange dreams whirled through his mind. When one of the wolf dogs gave a long, sad howl at the moon, he leaped up almost before he was awake and found himself crouched and ready, facing the entrance, his knife clutched in his hand.

He was out of the little house the next morning and had the wolf dogs harnessed before the moon grew pale. Before he had gone far, he saw the three stone men. These images must be the ones mentioned by the lean man from the River of Two Tongues. This surely was the place. Then he saw the sight that he had dreamed about for four long years, the frozen river that led into the Land of Little Sticks, and far away, almost on the southern horizon, thin columns of smoke rising in the still morning air. There were not ten fires, as the three men had seen long ago, but more than twenty.

He sat down on the sled, starving and alone. He remembered the terrible vision of his childhood, of the strong, lean men with bows and knives and clubs, of the big man lying with the arrows in his back.

But Kungo started off again, driving the team cautiously toward the camp, following the river between the little sticks, and peering fearfully into every shadow. It was growing milder now, and the air was soft.

He halted the wolf dogs, and they lay down in the snow. He drew Kigavik with its arrow quiver from beneath the lashings and turned the sled over to act as an anchor to hold the team. Then, slinging the bow and quiver across his back and checking that his long knife was safe in his boot, he started carefully forward. The soft snow, once he had left the banks of the river, was almost knee-deep.

He walked through the little sticks, guided by the thin columns of smoke rising before him, until he came to the top of a small hill. There spread before him was the Indian camp where he guessed at least twenty families must live. Never, in his whole life, had he seen a place with so many people crowded together.

The shape of their tents was utterly strange to him. They were cones built of many long sticks with skins stretched tightly around them. White acid-smelling smoke rose from the opening at the top of every tent. Men he saw, and women and children, and many thin dogs. The men looked tall and dangerous, and there were many of them. He thought of himself, so young and yet planning to go alone against a huge camp of Indian warriors. Again he felt the terrible pangs of hunger and fear, but deep inside himself he knew that he must act—and quickly before his strength failed him.

When it was dark, he slowly returned through the deep, heavy snow to the river and his team. He could not build an igloo, for the snow was too soft among the trees. Instead he rolled himself in the white bearskin and lay among his wolf dogs, hoping they would give him protection.

When he awoke, the land was covered with a light silver fog and big snowflakes drifted lazily down through the small trees. He rose and staggered off, dizzy from hunger as he once more left the dogs and made his way toward the dreaded Indian camp. He remembered his father telling him that a starving man could live without food for a whole moon as long as he had snow to eat or water.

A sound behind made him whirl quickly and snatch at his knife before he saw that it was Amahok who had worked free of the harness. The white lead dog stared at him with wise green eyes, and when Kungo moved forward again, the animal followed silently in his footsteps.

Kungo chose a different route this time because he wanted to go to a small frozen lake that he had seen near the Indian camp. He stumbled occasionally in the strange foggy light that made all shadows disappear and distances difficult to judge.

Now Kungo stood beside the snow-covered lake and looked across at the Indian fires. He drew the white weasel cap from his parka hood and placed it on his head so that it covered his black hair. He pulled the small leather pouch from inside his parka and rubbed the mixture of white grease and ashes on his face and hands. Amahok remained beside Kungo, sniffing the strong smoky scent of the camp.

For a long time Kungo stood stock-still out on the lake, looking up through the mists, searching for courage, while fearful visions of Indians raced through his mind. Suddenly he shouted in a terrible voice, *"Dog people. Women killers. Kayak rippers. Igloo breakers. Come to me. Come to me now in the dear morning."*

He then howled like a wolf, and Amahok joined him in a frightening chorus. Next he cried out like a loon laughing across a lonely lake. And last he roared like a bear fighting against many dogs.

There was a moment of silence in the Indian camp, followed by excited voices in a strange language that Kungo could not understand. Among the trees he could see men running, bent forward like hunters fitting arrows into their bows as they rushed toward him. He screamed once more, like an angry falcon, and they all stopped and raised their bows.

Slowly he reached behind him and drew Kigavik from his back. With his right hand he selected six white arrows from the quiver and stood them in the snow before him. A flight of Indian arrows struck around him. Some were very close.

He notched a seventh arrow in the bowstring and lowered his head in thought. Then he raised Kigavik and aimed the sharp point straight into the heart of the nearest crouching warrior. But at that moment something strange happened to him.

A whirlwind of doubts rushed into his mind. If he harmed these people now, would they not wait and seek revenge again among his people? Would they not come yet again into the Eskimo land, raiding and killing, carrying the old hatred forward from father to son to grandson? Was he not helping to pile hatred upon hatred like stones that might fall and kill everyone? Was he indeed any better in his quest for revenge than a mad dog that seeks only to bite and kill? Had the three starving men of his own kind not caused all this trouble long ago by raiding the Indian camp and stealing meat?

A vision of the old woman's face seemed to drift before his eyes. Kungo remembered all her gentleness and the wise things she had said to him. He moved the point of his arrow away from the Indian's heart. But his anger was not entirely spent. His eyes narrowed, and he clenched his teeth as he sent the arrow whistling into the heavy collar of the warrior's skin coat. It pierced through the fur collar and cut into his strange hat, pinning them together. The arrow then pressed so tightly across the Indian's throat that he screamed in terror.

Kungo sent arrow after arrow whistling in among the warriors, ripping their clothing, terrifying them, but never killing them. The Indians took aim but held back their second flight of arrows, for they could not see Kungo disguised and hidden in his whiteness. He moved like a silver shadow disappearing in the mists and snow, and they cried out in fear.

They saw clearly the great bow Kigavik, curved like a black falcon's wings, that rose and fell menacingly. Its bowstring sang. Its arrows flew against them, guided by the wild-goose feathers. The Indians were sure this was some winter spirit with a magic bow.

When Kungo's arrows were almost spent, he heard a soft woman's voice among the rough strange shouting of the Indians.

83

It called to him. It called to him in Eskimo. It called his name.

"Kungo. Kungo. Brother of mine, I know your voice. I beg you, put down your bow. I am Shulu, your sister."

The Indians watched in terror. They did not know whether to stand or run as the Eskimo girl, Shulu, walked out alone across the snowy lake to the place where the black bow hung poised in the air.

When Shulu stood before her brother, she rubbed her hand over her eyes, for she could scarcely see him.

"Brother of mine," she said, "are you a ghost? Or have you come to me after all these years when I have thought you dead."

She reached out timidly and put her hand against his cheek to feel if he were real. Then she took his hand gently and began to lead him across the lake.

The warriors stood back as she led Kungo through them into the very center of the Indian camp. A hundred dark eyes stared out at them from the tents and snowy cover of the trees, watching the falcon bow, the great white wolf dog, and this faint ghostlike shadow of a man.

Amahok stalked close beside Kungo, his muscles tensed, ready to spring. A low growl rumbled steadily in his throat, and his green wolf eyes stared suspiciously around him, for he did not trust this place or these strange people.

Kungo, like the wolf dog, was tense and uneasy. None of this was right. None of it was as he had planned it all these years. He had not taken revenge upon these people because of the vision of the old woman, and now helpless and outnumbered among these warriors, he felt that they would surely kill him.

84

He eyed his sister walking beside him; her clothing was completely strange to him. It was made of caribou skin with all the hair scraped away, and it had no hood. It hung evenly to her knees, where it ended in a long, dangling fringe. Her costume was painted with strange red and black border designs of a kind he had never seen. Below the skirt long caribou skin leggings, fringed on the side, hung down to her moccasined feet. On her head she wore a round decorated cap, and her long hair was braided in an unfamiliar way. Strings of bright beads hung around her neck.

Kungo tightened his grip on the long knife that was now concealed in the sleeve of his parka when a dark shadowy figure moved quickly from the shelter of the trees. It was an Indian who went and waited near the entrance of the tent that stood in their path. He was tall and lean, scarcely older than Kungo, dressed in a costume not unlike Shulu's. Over his knee-length coat he wore a wide beaded belt and across his shoulder a wonderfully decorated game bag. His hat was shaped and pointed in a strange and handsome fashion. He stood still, full of dignity, like a hawk, alert and ready to strike. Kungo noticed that he had removed the mitten from his right hand, and it hung tense and ready beside his long iron knife. His face was dark and handsome, but it seemed carved of stone and told Kungo nothing.

Shulu spoke to the young man rapidly in a strange high-singing sound.

She then turned to Kungo and said, "This is Natawa. He knows now that you are my brother." Then she went quickly into the tent.

The tall young Indian held back the skin flap that served as a cover for the entrance. Kungo stepped over a long log and found himself inside the dark interior. Amahok lay down on guard outside.

Once inside, Kungo waited until his eyes became accustomed to the dark. The tent was round inside, with the caribou-skin walls sloping upward to the blackened smoke hole in the center of the roof. Many caribou skins and some brightly colored blankets were piled against the sides of the tent for sleeping. A round flat drum made of stretched caribou skin hung by a long leather thong from the tent poles. In the very center, within a small circle of stones, Kungo could see some glowing embers and the long log he had crossed at the entrance that was the main fuel for the fire. The log was never cut but merely pushed further and further into the flames. A large iron pot simmered over the fire.

Shulu led her brother to a special place by the fire and arranged the thickest skins for him to sit upon. The lean young Indian stepped inside the tent and squatted down across the fire from Kungo. Much of his face was caught by the firelight, but his eyes were lost in shadow, and Kungo could not read his face or guess what he was thinking. Kungo saw the place where his arrow had torn open the skin of the Indian's garment at the throat.

"This man, Natawa, is my husband," said Shulu. "We have been married together since the first moon of summer."

Kungo felt the cords of his neck thicken, for he could scarcely believe the words he heard.

Seeing the look on her brother's face, Shulu added quickly, "You must be hungry, brother of mine," and bent forward to stir the rich yellow broth that covered soft chunks of caribou meat.

Kungo refused the meat and remained silent, watching the Indian carefully, ready for any sudden movement. He knew by the sound of Amahok's low growl that the tent must now be surrounded by bowmen.

"For all these years," said Shulu, "I have feared that you and all my relatives were dead. When they first brought me here, I was always afraid. The children laughed at me and threw stones at me, and I was only used to carry water and skin out birds. But later I was adopted and had a mother and father. I learned to speak the language of these people, and all the children became my friends, and my new mother and father were always kind to me and taught me many things. Now I speak slowly and badly to you in our own tongue, brother of mine, because I have almost forgotten my own language.

"Sometimes in spring my soul cries out as I look across the barrens and remember how it used to be. I think again of times long ago when you and I made the long trek inland with our family. I remember the snow geese that laid their eggs on the soft tundra and the fat red and silver trout that drifted under the holes in the melting lake ice. I will never forget the night skies of the far north in summer when the sun walked on the hilltops and it never grew dark.

"But that is long passed now, like a dream. I am here among the little sticks with these people, and I think of them as my people. I wish that you could know Natawa as I know him and that he could know you as I know you. You and Natawa might have killed each other out there on the ice of the lake, and even now across the fire I see you each watching the knife hand of the other. I am only a foolish girl, but now I understand how wrong that is. I have love for both of you, and I have seen each of you dancing, singing, laughing, crying, and I know that, though you speak strange languages, you are truly brothers."

Then turning her gaze toward Natawa, Shulu said many words that Kungo could not understand. Looking at her, Natawa's face softened, and he knelt forward and drew his iron knife from his belt. He drove it into the big pot and caught a great chunk of meat on its point. Turning the handle toward Kungo, he offered him the knife and then lay back on the pile of soft skins.

Kungo shook the long knife from his sleeve and pushed it aside. Then he placed the big bow, Kigavik, behind him. His hunger returned to him in a rush, and as he smelled the rich meat, he remembered that he was starving. Not wishing to show his hunger, he ate slowly, savoring every bite until he was full.

Natawa stepped outside and spoke to the people who had waited there, and after he had spoken, the bowmen returned to their tents and Amahok ceased to growl.

Almost all that night, Kungo told them of his life after he had last seen his sister, and Shulu interpreted this to her husband.

When Kungo had finished speaking, Natawa then told him of the time he had first seen Shulu when they were young, of their marriage and of the long adventure they had shared that autumn. They had paddled south in a canoe on a wide river with many white rapids whose banks were covered with tall trees. Natawa's white teeth flashed as he smiled and spoke of a country that seemed filled with wild animals of a kind that Kungo had never seen. He spoke of black bears, of big red-headed birds that hammered the high branches like drummers, and great furry animals that climbed in the trees. He said these creatures had spotted coats, yellow eyes, and the long sharp claws of an eagle.

Toward morning they lay down on the soft furs, covered themselves with colored blankets, and slept together. When they awoke, Kungo gave a start, for he could not remember at first where he was.

Shulu rose first and pushed the long log further into the embers of the fire so that it started to blaze briskly, and she placed the meat pot closer to the flames.

Natawa spoke to her for a long time, and when he was finished, she turned and said to Kungo, "He asks you to stay with us, to stay among his people. He asks you to join him in forgiving old wrongs, to hunt together with him, to fish with us when we travel to the high falls on the Singing River when it is springtime again, and to live together like brothers. Oh, will you, Kungo? Will you do as he asks?"

"Tell him that I understand the things that you have said for him, that I would like to hunt with him and learn to speak with him, and that I am sorry about the arrow that came so close to his throat. I am horrified by the thought that yesterday I had it in my mind to kill him.

"I must return to the island, for the old people have become my family and I must help them. When I have seen that they are well and have food enough, I shall return to meet you at the high falls in the spring."

Together they left the tent and walked out through the Indian camp. Big flakes of soft snow drifted down through the dark trees, catching on and clinging to the branches and to the sides of the smoke-stained tents. Before each of these dwellings hung rich beaver and otter pelts stretched on sapling frames to dry. Shulu had told Kungo the night before that the Indians prized these furs as trimming for their clothing. It was also their custom, she had said, to trade fur with strangers further south for iron knives, pots, beads, and blankets.

As Kungo walked, small Indian children, as motionless as frightened rabbits, peered out at him from the tents. They watched carefully, for he was almost invisible in his white fur clothing against the snowy background. Behind Kungo strode the yellow-eyed wolf dog.

When they came to a grove of trees, Natawa pulled delicately laced snowshoes from his back, slipped his moccasined feet into their bindings, and stepped off the trodden path. He traveled easily, with a swinging gait, over the top of the soft new snow until he arrived at the place where heavy haunches of caribou hung from the trees. Reaching up, he pulled four of these down and loaded them onto a toboggan that stood nearby. Throwing the line over his shoulders, he hauled the toboggan to the path, and with Shulu's help he followed Kungo across the lake and through the little sticks until they came to the place where Kungo's team waited patiently.

After the white wolf dogs were fed, Kungo gave a short command, and they leaped into position, ready to go, waiting for the second command.

Kungo looked into his sister's face and then at Natawa. The

Indian stared back at him, his dark eyes narrowed as if in pain. He said one short sentence to Shulu and was silent.

Shulu said, "He asks me if I wish to go with you. He says that he will hide his eyes if I wish to go with you."

One word she replied to Natawa.

Then to Kungo she said, "I will always stay with him. But come as he asks in spring and fish with us at the high falls between the two lands."

Kungo turned and faced Natawa, and in the ancient way of his people, he dropped his mitts on the snow and pushed back the sleeves of his parka to the elbow, showing that he concealed no weapons against the man before him. Natawa, understanding this gesture, drew back his own sleeves and stepped forward. Their fingers touched briefly, and without any spoken words they understood each other.

Kungo called out to the dogs. They lunged forward and rushed out of the Land of Little Sticks toward the open wind-swept tundra. He looked back once and saw his sister, Shulu, standing silently beside her husband. A warm feeling spread through his body as he thought of her, alive and happy. All his anger was gone from him, gone, he hoped, forever.

Then the sharp sting of cold struck him, and he laughed aloud with pleasure. He was returning to his own land. He would travel to the island of Tugjak and talk with the old man again. Ittok was a great teacher and had taught him many things about archery and about life. The old woman had tempered his feelings for revenge and had helped him to understand himself. They were his people.

Kungo shouted with joy. Soon he would see the dwarf once more and hear the songs of the old woman. Shulu was safe. His wolf dogs ran fast. The great falcon bow, Kigavik, was lashed safely to his sled. But, best of all, when the spring sun came and released the river at the high falls, he knew he would see his sister and Natawa.

A great happiness rose up in him, and suddenly the words of a song rushed into him from the sky, and knowing them, feeling them inside himself, he sang them boldly into the very teeth of the north wind. His ears, once hearing the words, would remember them forever:

> "Ayii, Ayii, Ayii, Ayii,
> I walked on the ice of the sea
> And wondering I heard
> The song of the sea,
> The great sighing of new-formed ice.
> Go then, go, strength of soul,
> Bring health to the place of feasting.
> Ayii, Ayii."